ENGLISH MONSTERS

ALSO BY JAMES SCUDAMORE

The Amnesia Clinic
Heliopolis
Wreaking

ENGLISH MONSTERS

James Scudamore

JONATHAN CAPE
LONDON

1 3 5 7 9 10 8 6 4 2

Jonathan Cape, an imprint of Vintage,
20 Vauxhall Bridge Road,
London SW1V 2SA

Jonathan Cape is part of the Penguin Random House group of companies whose addresses can be found at global.penguinrandomhouse.com

First published by Jonathan Cape in 2020

penguin.co.uk/vintage

A CIP catalogue record for this book is available from the British Library

ISBN 9781787331860

Typeset in 11.5/14.6 pt Bembo
by Integra Software Services Pvt. Ltd, Pondicherry

Printed and bound in Great Britain by Clays Ltd, Elcograf S.p.A.

Penguin Random House is committed to a sustainable future for our business, our readers and our planet. This book is made from Forest Stewardship Council® certified paper.

I M
W. R. Skelton
1921–2005

To Rose, John, Clem and Sylvia

And to CFM

For ill or good, let the wheel turn.
For who knows the end of good or evil?

T. S. Eliot, *Murder in the Cathedral*

Energy cannot be created or destroyed; it can only be changed from one form to another.

The Law of Conservation of Energy

Two boys have been found rubbing linseed oil into the school cormorant.

Monty Python's The Meaning of Life

ONE

Mongrel

1

My grandfather liked to be in bed before the nine o'clock news, so he started drinking early and worked fast. The first cork was drawn around five, and another would soon follow. By the time the headlines came on he'd have eaten his bedtime cereal and left his teeth grinning in the washing-up bowl to soak until morning.

With each finished bottle, the call for the next would go up with more alacrity, and he'd make a point of including me in the moment – especially if, as on this occasion, we had company.

'Max!' he said. 'Be a good lad. Shin up that counter and fetch us the Frenchman.'

The tingle of hearing my name on his voice: adrenalised excitement, well short of fear, but enlivening still. He knew just how to pitch it. I had been eating my bread and butter, happily submerged, adult chatter breaking over me like sunlit surf. But he would never leave you alone down there for long.

Up I sprang, eager to keep them at the table. Buttery light on the yellow butter, always on the turn because it never went in the fridge. The corkscrew, a French one with arms and vertebrae, had its own nail on the wall, and what with the soft loaf, the two cold roast chickens, the ripe tomatoes and several cheeses on the go, it was time to open another. This was in 1986. The usual Sunday-night quartet of me, my grandparents and my Great-Aunt Dee. I was ten.

He might easily have left the corkscrew on the table between bottles, but then there'd have been no role for me. No chance for the sound of my name on his voice.

'And when he's older, he'll say, *My old grandad used to make me climb the kitchen units to get the corkscrew down when he wanted another bottle opening.* What will he think of us?'

He had a way of banking memories for me like that. Much of the time I didn't notice him doing it, but this evening I clocked him instructing me to remember. Consequently, the instant is bookmarked. The striped T-shirt I was wearing. The scrape of my leg on the Formica as I climbed. Window blinds teased by the breeze. Their lined faces lit golden. One moment like many others that flares on demand because he told me to keep it.

One of the birds on the board had now been picked clean by him. He raised it in his palm, slick skin ribboning beneath, and whistled for his collie.

'Bob. Not at the table,' said my grandmother. But Jack only had ears for him and gently took the carcass from his hand. 'By goodness I shall make you jump if any of that gets on my floor.'

His voice dropped to an urgent whisper, his special canine frequency. '*Goo'n'see.*'

The dog surged outside, nails skittering on the quarry tiles, despoiling them only with spots of saliva.

Jack was the latest in a long line of collies with scrambled parentage and unpredictable tempers. He was a known biter, but I had a sense of what lines not to cross and he'd never gone for me.

'I thought you weren't to give them chicken bones,' said Dee.

A familiar look of disgust fell over my grandfather's face. 'That only mattered when we ate brittle old broiler hens! These birds you get now are so young, they bend. I wouldn't even need my teeth in.'

As he spoke, his strong, dark-wrinkled hands swept the table for crumbs, wetting them to a paste with a dribble of wine and packing it into the knothole near the top of his plate. He did this at every meal, tamping down the fudge of food with his thumb then smoothing it over. He'd made the table himself from a diseased elm and it was as if he were always trying to finish the job. My grandmother thought it a disgusting habit, and would ream out the knothole when he was elsewhere, but it was always replenished again by the end of the next meal.

When he reached the cheese and was a bottle or two down, the pace would slow, because this was the best bit. He'd run his hands up and down his forearms, then back to the tabletop. He did this with my limbs too sometimes, appraising my grain as he might that of a piece of wood. Then he would sit back from the table, which affected the mood, since he was a big man, and home in on a story.

He'd circle for a while, refining his angle of attack. No account could begin without dissent. Only when he and my grandmother had haggled out an opening could we proceed.

It must have been that wet spring when the lambs all got daggy.

Yes, good Lord, do you remember, you had to shear the lot in two days.

I went to Cambridge that winter to buy a thresher.

You never did. You've dreamt that.

The misfires were essential to the engine's ignition. It was as much an exercise in digesting their lives as an act of storytelling. They were moving into their late sixties. Many of their cherished people were gone, and there were few photos. So they sat around these Sunday evenings going over the dead. Rendering memories like stock. Addressing the bewilderment of having lived.

Poor old Ev. She'd love to be here now with a glass of wine and a fag.

She would.

She'd be ninety next year.

Would she really?

This was the late mother of my grandmother and my great-aunt. But it might just as easily have been his best friend Jim who died at Arnhem, or his Uncle Harry who shot off his own arm while vaulting a gate.

War stories might ensue. How my grandmother cycled into Coventry to work the morning after it was razed and fell into a bomb crater. How he stayed to farm and joined the Home Guard and watched his mates disappear. My attention would wax and wane with my understanding, but he always hauled me back if he sensed I had been alone for too long.

I had dipped out again, fallen away somewhere. He'd noticed.

'Pay attention, boy,' he said, with mock severity. 'We haven't always lived like this. We worked bloody hard. You need to work bloody hard as well, you hear?' I nodded, trying to smile. 'He's not listening to a word. Never mind. Maybe some of it will sink in. I remember my grandad, and how hard he worked, so it must keep somehow. He was a marvel, my dad's dad. He rented one farm from Lord Binley but he ran two more on top of that. He worked a thousand acres. By the time he retired he had two sets of threshing tackle, two steam engines, the lot. He went like hell. *You've got to go like hell, you hear?*'

His big hand ferreting into my abdomen.

'I will,' I said, hoping to acknowledge the moment and get it over with.

'What about your father?' said Dee. 'It didn't go so well for him, did it?'

'It was harder for him. The twenties were rough for farming. Then again, he and his brothers were useless. It skips a generation, I reckon.' He shot me a look I didn't understand.

Dee pulled a Rothmans from her packet and it dangled from her arthritic fingers, shaming their root-like gnarliness. My grandfather leaned over, eyes widened in my direction, and with a quick pull upwards from beneath his trousers produced a lit match. The old routine delighted me still. He held the flame for her then popped it in his mouth, chewing and swallowing with contentment. I'd yet to catch him removing the spent matchstick. Dee pulled in the smoke then exhaled a blue line that smelled acrid and delicious and tapered into marbled layers above us.

'Then of course the younger Lord Binley took over,' he said. 'And his daughter turned out to be a bit of a goer. We found her knickers in a field once after she'd had a tumble with one of the local lads.' Always the stray possibility here that the lad in question had been him, if you sought the glint in his eye.

'You never did.'

'His Lordship was no better. He was a tup. He had a wooden prick.'

'Yes, he was up half the night, wasn't he?' said Dee.

'Famous for it. He had a special Rolls-Royce, with a trapdoor in the back.'

'For goodness' sake, Bob,' said my grandmother.

'What?' I said, sensing mischief. 'Why did it need a trapdoor?'

'Can't you guess?'

'Bob, do you have to? The boy's ten years old. What'll I tell his mother when she asks me where he's got these stories from?'

'His mother knows the story too. He had the trapdoor so he could stand up when he had a friend in the back with him.'

'He never did,' said Dee.

'He did. So he could park somewhere and have a proper bit of leg-over room.'

'You've got a filthy imagination.'

'And one day he was up one of the lanes giving some girl a seeing-to when the car got shunted by a tractor. Broke both his legs. Nearly took them off.'

Dee was a good accomplice. She was shorter than my grandmother, and wickeder, and had the dirtier laugh. She had had *quite a life*. She was never not in poor health. After the war she'd married a Pole called Joe who had since died, and she was fond of saying she was *going on top of Joe* when her time came. She called me *genius*, and I could ask her anything so long as I didn't ask her how she was.

Eventually I might summon the courage for an intervention of my own, always mindful of the danger of accidentally going too far. You could say anything to him and Dee, but my grandmother was more shockable, or pretended to be. Earlier that evening my grandfather had told the one about the man from Devizes, so it seemed only natural for me to recite now the next one I knew, even if I wasn't sure why it was funny.

There was a young fella from Ghent
Whose prick was so long that it bent
To save him the trouble
He kept it bent double
And instead of coming, he went.

'Good Lord,' said my grandmother.

But he was off. He was beyond speaking. Keeping eye contact with me, then shifting it to Dee as the laughter played out in waves.

It wasn't the limerick itself, which he had almost certainly told me in the first place. It was the words on my lips. Ten-year-old Max with the smart mouth, what a precocious fellow.

'To think he knows something like that,' said my grandmother. 'Isn't it awful?'

And instead of coming, he went. I just thought it meant he was facing the wrong way.

Always a suspended moment after the first gale of laughter had blown through. Always the chance it might settle into a silence that bordered on discomfort, in which I realised later they were questioning their status *in loco parentis* and wondering if they had exposed me to too much. But this time I got lucky. Just as the hilarity was fading it got a boost from Jack the collie, who sidled in, opened his jaws and brought up the chicken carcass in a grey heap on the floor. By the time my grandmother had banished the dog, mopped up the sick and disinfected the site, she was laughing as much as the rest of us.

He would send me to the piano in the next room to clatter through a few simplified Scott Joplin rags while they did the dishes, then we'd take in the last of the daylight outside. Tonight we were throwing a heavy oak ball he'd turned on his lathe for the dogs. He hurled it with big, underarm sweeps down the track that led to the park. The lump of wood hung aloft, unspooling slobber lending it a tail like a tossed hammer, then came to earth, kicking up clouds of late-summer light. Jack and the pup competed to bring it back until the ball was splintering and the dogs' gums foamed with a pink emulsion of blood and saliva.

'There's nowhere better than this,' he said, savouring the day's final grassy exhalations. 'This is as good as it gets.'

Then the sun slipped off and the air cooled and I went round with him as he saw to the animals. The dogs slept in a stable near his workshop in a packing crate filled with straw and sawdust and the heavy reek of dog meat dog breath dog hair dog. Their food was in unlabelled wholesale cans shrink-wrapped and stacked on a pallet. He pulled two tins from the tray, turned them in the wall-mounted opener, then shook the contents of each into a bowl, the cans sucking at the cylinders of meat as he jerked them out. He dumped the cans and lids in another packing crate and stood back to watch them eat over the stable's half-door.

'Twenty pence each I pay for these tins. I tried to get them down to one between them last year. Then I thought *Well, I suppose it's Christmas*, and started giving them one each again. Now they're fat as pigs.'

He'd drop off in front of the television before bed. My grandmother was too deaf to hear what was on, preferring to sit in what she experienced as a companiable silence, puzzling over her poets. She had her favourites – Auden, Blake, Eliot – and she absorbed them in a constant cycle, waiting patiently for them to reveal themselves. For all that she did it in plain view, it was a private activity, and the extent of her musing only became clear to me after her death when I was old enough to decipher the questions in the marginalia of her *Songs of Innocence and Experience* and her *Four Quartets*. Like him, she hadn't had a lesson since leaving school at fourteen.

Her recurrent fear was that he might have died without us noticing. She couldn't hear his snoring unless it was very loud, so she assessed whether or not he was alive based on movement, and if he had been still for too long, her voice would pierce the air.

'Bob? Are you with us?'

I had thought about telling her that I would listen so she didn't have to worry about it, but I couldn't think how to phrase the suggestion. Besides, the responsibility would have consumed me, and there was no changing their habits now. It took no more than two of her interventions to provoke the reassurance she required: a sudden inhalation like a punctured vacuum, with follow-up snorts and an uncanny rearrangement of his teeth. She'd have returned to her verses before the sequence had fully played out.

Whether this woke him or not, he would slope off soon for his nightcap of Coco Pops, then I'd hear his heavy treads on the stairs. Later, when I went to the kitchen sink to draw a glass of water, the teeth would be there waiting, somehow always a surprise, laced with tendrils of chocolatey milk.

He'd be up in the night, sitting for an hour with a pint of tea and the *Farmers Weekly*, but teeth were not required for that, and the dentures wouldn't go back in until he got up for real at six, when he'd shuffle outside to unkennel the dogs and begin again.

This is how it went.

Fanciful perhaps to imagine some blood-wisdom transfused to me round that table, setting me up for the future. But his code for life did far more than amuse. It hard-wired compassion. Stoked outrage at cruelty. The credo was simple. Work hard. Live well. Be kind. Speak up. But especially speak up.

2

He was born in 1921 and grew up on his father's tenanted farm, often missing school to do milk rounds as a boy, then leaving at fourteen to work for his dad full-time. After he married he was offered tenancy of his own ruined little place, and did well enough to buy it for himself. He knocked down the old farmhouse and built a new one. To lay his driveway he bought a bulldozer and a steamroller and did the job himself, then sold both machines for a profit. The version of him my mother grew up with was relentless.

Then came the motorways: first the M1, then a junction of the M6, cutting the farm into pieces and forcing him into retirement at fifty-one. It was too early to give up, and too late to rededicate himself to farming, but he wanted to keep his money in land. He heard of a ruined country house for sale nearby, bought its parkland and outbuildings, and made the former coach house his home. Its carriage doors became their downstairs windows, the grooms' quarters above their bedrooms. He made a walled garden of the old stable yard, its blue cobbles broken up with lines of pebbles and strewn with tin baths planted with flowers. He grew rhubarb here in rusty wheelbarrows and stacked pot plants in the bellies of rotting upright pianos.

The Hall had been stripped of its assets after the war by a succession of unscrupulous owners. When the roof lead was sold it became derelict fast. It might have been torn down and replaced with an optimistic housing estate. Instead the hulk and its gardens were acquired by a London stockbroker who used the ruin as a backdrop for one garden party a year, and paid my grandfather and an old man called Tom Slingsby, who'd worked there as a stablehand in the 1920s, to maintain the grounds. For several years the two of them kept the garden immaculate while the house decayed sweetly behind them. Then the stockbroker grew tired of his toy. A developer made him an offer and converted it into luxury flats. The Hall was sanitised and subdivided, but standing.

So there was Grandad, having made enough of himself to buy his own land, only to be looked down on by a bunch of weekend squires who thought of the countryside as a plaything. They pretended to like him, and let him fix their lawnmowers, but even at ten I knew what they were saying behind his back. It particularly enraged them that my grandfather still owned the park, which he refused to prettify and rejected all inducements to sell. They wanted estate fencing and a herd of ornamental deer. Instead they got mud and bullocks, and him capering around in his Renault 4 van, Louis Armstrong or Fats Waller jumping within. Bits of farm machinery were dotted around in varying states of disrepair. In summer, thistles grew in outrageous clumps, which he decapitated as he drove, taking aim at the clouds of down that clung to the tops to propagate them far and wide. In winter, he fed his beasts on waste matter from the McCain oven chip factory, a pungent slop of fermenting potato peelings he called *splodge*. I still like to picture the aroma drifting up to the Hall and offending its occupants as they sipped their sherry and lamented the squalor.

In photos taken before retirement he is a different person. Whip-thin, pipe on the go, and a mouthful of his own teeth. He'd always loved sweets. At some point, which probably coincided with the acquisition of extra weight, he got bored of all the dentistry and had the lot removed. The man in the pictures looked wrong. The teeth seemed overemphasised. He looked like a boxer with his gum shield in. By the time I knew him his build had settled into something comfortably Churchillian, with a bullish neck and a full head of greying blond hair. His wisdom had nothing to do with education and everything to do with experience. Idleness infuriated him, but nothing disgusted him more than those who lived meanly, or with a deficit of grace. Such people, he would say, *wanted shooting out of a cannon.*

Modernity had pursued him all his life, but he'd seen it coming and evaded capture every time. The farm he'd run with his father was by this time an industrial estate in the Coventry suburbs, the house to which it had been attached a wedding-venue hotel. But that didn't matter to him any more than that the Hall had become a condo for stately-home fantasists. He was from this mid-land and knew it far too well to let a bit of change affect him. In other words, he was as from one place as it is possible to be, which is not something I have ever been able to say for myself. I had none of the security of a tether. But no tether either.

You've got to go like hell.

I would hear the refrain for years, especially in my twenties, when he worried I was pissing away my life. However many drunken nights there were (and in time I would be participating myself), I was always made aware of how hard he and my grandmother had worked for them. He never even drank that much before, he claimed, though his best stories always involved booze and you don't acquire a facility like his without practice.

'Drinking and driving never used to matter,' he told me once when she was out of the room. 'I remember sitting in the back of a Ford Eight with Jim and a girl called Minnie and a bottle of port wine. He'd have a snog and I'd have the bottle, then I'd have a snog and he'd have the bottle. Marvellous.'

Another summer evening and more animals to feed. At the chalk pond behind his workshop I held the bucket of grain while he flicked scoops of it in ribboning arcs that brought ducks batting across the water. When the last of it had drummed into the grass we settled ourselves at a table by the water's edge. Beside him was one of the bin bags of unsold stock he got for nothing from a local baker. He reached inside, took out a loaf, and began breaking it into pieces. The first dropped crust idled in the water before a gaping orange mouth rose to suck at it. The black backs of other carp arrowed in as more baked goods hit the surface. I opened the bag wider, inhaling a bouquet of éclairs, doughnuts and Chelsea buns.

'A lot of this stuff isn't stale at all,' I said, licking my fingers between throws.

'I know. They're spoilt rotten, these fish. And you can't even eat them. They're bottom-feeders. They'd taste horrible. But my God they can breed.'

We stopped flinging a while and sat back to watch the surface churn. He poured himself a glass of wine, then cracked a Coke and slid it in my direction. There were two earthenware pots on the tray, one of chicken pâté and one of tapenade, both made by him.

'Early night tonight,' he said. 'Market day tomorrow.'

'Can I come with you?'

'Your grandma says you can't cos she's got to take you up for this interview at lunchtime.'

This I had forgotten.

'What time's the interview?'

'Twelve. You'd be back in time easy, only she thinks you'll be tired.'

'I'll be okay.'

'Right you are. I'll get you up. And if you don't leap out of bed I shall put a dog up your sheets.'

As if on cue, a ruckus of barks kicked off by the house, alerting us to the arrival of Tom Slingsby, who had puttered up in his grey Fiesta. He climbed out slowly, reaching for his stick and planting it before standing up. He saw my grandfather's raised arm, lifted his own leathery hand and started advancing.

'Jump up, boy. Give him a steer.'

I ran to Tom and fell into step so he could hold my shoulder.

'Good lad, Maxy,' he breathed. He had white hair and a round, wrinkled face that combined with his stoop to make me think of a kindly ape.

My grandfather called out 'How do', then angled out the chair I had been sitting on to offer it to Tom. 'Fetch the old bugger a glass,' he said to me.

'I don't want to hinder you, Bob.'

'Shut up and sit down.'

When Tom was settled we got on with tossing the rest of the bakery into the water.

'Miss Bandy's in a right state about that spaniel of hers,' said Tom. 'Says she's no idea how it happened.'

'I bet she is,' said my grandfather. 'Hell of a thing to be dealing with a litter at her age. I told her: that bitch is in pup. She's bagging up. Only she didn't believe me.' A carp was struggling to suck a chunk of bread off a patch of blanket weed, so I knelt down to knock it off. 'Course, I had a fair shout knowing in advance.'

'Bob,' said Tom in a low voice, 'what do you mean?'

Now his giggle was uncontrollable. 'Jack gave that bitch a damn good fucking. I watched it happen while I was deadheading Miss Bandy's roses.'

Tom had gone. The laughter had claimed him.

'Who was I to get between them?' said my grandfather. 'I wasn't going to stop him having a good time.' Then he remembered me and corrected the conversation. 'This one's got a big day tomorrow. It's his interview up at the place on the hill.'

'What have you got to do?' said Tom, wiping his eyes.

'We've no idea,' said my grandfather. 'Can't be much. Especially given how much his dad's company is paying them to take him. He reckons he's going to market with me all the same.'

'You know what time he gets up, don't you?' said Tom. 'You'll get a fright when he comes in.'

The old man and the older man carried on laughing as carp slopped in the milky water, apparently insatiable.

Ripped from a dream of hot beaches and jellyfish by the feeling of claws on my ankles and breath on my skin as he sent the terrier scrambling up my bedclothes.

'Get out of it, you rubbishing bugger!' His staged anger, full of joy. 'It's quarter to five.'

'I'll be down in a minute,' I groaned.

'You'd better be else I'm going without you.'

He was off, whistling the opening bars of 'Hello, Dolly'. Muffled movement downstairs. The kettle's reedy whistle. Total darkness at the windows.

When I made it to the kitchen I found him standing at the stone urn which contained his home-made cider vinegar.

He plunged a tin mug inside, drank a shot, refilled the mug and passed it to me.

'Do it in one or you'll never do it.' Too tired to disregard the instruction. Electric jolt. Scalp ripple. Stomach fire. 'Good health. That'll get you going, boy.'

Dawn leached up the sky as the van reached the outskirts of Leicester, where street lights were flickering off one by one. Near a nightclub we passed a young couple arguing in the street.

'Bloody hell, look at these two, they haven't been to bed.' As we slowed, the boy must have said something that crossed the line, because the girl dropped her kebab-van chips and clocked him on the cheek. 'Look out! That's it, girl. Give him another.' He almost ground to a halt to watch the scene play out in his rear-view mirror, loving the life of it. 'Dear oh dear. She didn't half set about him.' He was still enjoying it when we reached the market. It was a momentary respite from life not living up to his standards. Whatever else might disappoint him today, he'd have this to fall back on.

We entered the strip-lit cavern of earthy smells and beeping forklifts and he started loading his sack barrow with fruit and vegetables. He bought so much stock that many traders assumed he was a grocer. Those who knew him better understood his predilection for wholesale, and for supplying to family and friends. Their ongoing joke was that it was all for my grandmother.

How is she then, Bob? She needs another sack of shallots, does she? Righto.

We returned to the van with laden barrow several times before he'd bought enough to stop for breakfast. I grappled with the nausea of tiredness while he ordered *sausage and chips twice and two mugs of tea* at the on-site greasy spoon.

'Summer's on the wane,' he said, looking at the clock on the wall and noting the time of the sunrise. He was prone to melancholy about things like this, to a Falstaffian sadness at the ending of the revels. But it was offset against his farmer's understanding of the wheel turning, of there always being something to appreciate if you knew where to look. 'I bet that poor bugger's still rubbing the side of his head somewhere,' he added, smiling. He set down his fork and drained his tea. 'Right. Better get you home and present you for inspection.'

Before the interview my grandmother dunked me in a shallow bath, handed me a clean shirt and brushed my hair in the reflection of the oven door. She wound her own waist-length grey hair up into a bun and we set off in their Citroën estate. He had unloaded his produce and gone to work, and as we drove down the lane that skirted the edge of the park we passed him cutting hedges in a tractor. When we slowed, he wished me luck and dropped a ripe peach through the sunroof, which she said I wasn't to eat until later in case I got juice down my shirt.

We crossed the humpback bridge in the base of the valley then climbed the opposite side through unfamiliar ironstone villages. The road steepened sharply then proceeded through a pair of pillars topped with stone bulls' heads. We passed a thatched lodge on the left-hand side then swept down a long avenue of ashes and oaks. A groundsman chugged round the outfield of a cricket pitch on his sit-on mower.

I saw it first at its most seductive. Battlements against a fierce blue sky. Honeyed stone in full summer light. The church with its crippled, leaning steeple. The resplendent, clock-towered stable block. A balustrade of urns bursting with flowers. The fragrance of cut grass. A Border terrier and a black Labrador lazing on the lawn. There was a surreal sense of ascension, of having risen from arches and market grime to this plateau of ancient walls and scented gardens. It felt like a different life.

We got out of the car, footsteps sinking into deep, grey gravel. While my grandmother looked for the way in, I stared into the roses that grew over the porch, lost in their folds and creases. Above the front door was a carved stone crest in which another bull's head glowered sideways under a jagged crown. My grandmother opened the door and we entered what I would come to know as the Great Hall. Swords and shields mounted in velvet pads. A walk-in fireplace with blackened walls. Tapestries, panelling and silence. I picked up on my grandmother's unease.

A woman in a waxed jacket with raked-back blonde hair and a slash of red lipstick came out to greet us. In the years that followed I rarely saw her looking any other way, or experienced any warming in her manner. She was one of those Englishwomen whose pride is indexed to their acidity.

'Fiona Sutton. Or Mrs Headmaster,' she added to me.

She seemed disappointed in my grandmother from the off. Too earthy. Too real. The country lilt to her voice, the deafness, the corduroy skirt. She took my grandmother's arm and led her away as if she were an unwanted animal, leaving me standing by the door with a tall, stammering man who, after a few false starts of speech that made his leg jiggle, said enough for me to understand that he was her husband. So, I would only later realise, began the interview.

We sat outside together on a stone bench. He told me about the school, using the first-person plural as if he and it were one and the same thing. He said how proud they were of the house's seven-hundred-year history. Finally he asked me with great solemnity and further stuttering if I could spell the word *Leicestershire*. I don't know whether or not I got it right.

He gave me a tour. Floorboards shiny with polish. Shadows of the great cedar on the North Lawn. Ranks of iron beds labelled with surnames. Then he took me over to the stable block and showed me a few classrooms, and we re-emerged outside by a rectangular concrete pond.

'This is what we rather grandly call the b-boating lake,' said Tony Sutton. 'And this,' he said, pointing at a boy who was crouched down at the water's edge, 'is one of your future contemporaries. His m-mother works as my secretary, so he has the run of the p-place during the holidays. M-Max Denyer, meet Simon Drake.'

He was tall for his ten years of age, with a peppering of freckles on either side of his nose, and hanks of light brown hair that got in his eyes. He stood up, extended an aerial on the radio controller in his hand and directed a small but powerful boat across the water.

'It's fast,' I said, aware that Sutton had left us alone.

'I've changed the gearing of the servos. They never give them enough power because they worry about motors burning out. Are you coming to school here?'

'Maybe. What's it like?'

He shrugged. 'I guess it depends on how much you enjoy being at home.'

'My home's a long way from here.'

'Not really up to you, anyway, is it?' He gestured abruptly towards the balustrade. 'See that urn there? The one on the end? Do you see how all the other urns have flowers in but that one has a top on it? It's got the ashes in it of the boy the old urn fell on. They buried him in a copy of the thing that killed him.'

I tried to think of a reply, but my grandmother was calling me back to the car to say goodbye to the Suttons. I can't remember what else was said or done. Only that as we drove away and the battlements fell out of sight behind us, I sank my teeth into the peach, leaning back in the seat to catch every drop of falling juice with my shirt.

3

THE CHURCH WAS at the end of a long footpath behind a door in the wall which skirted the coach-house lane. The door's paintwork was scored with the claw marks of my grandfather's dogs, whose scrabbling and whining would threaten to turn violent if you didn't throw it open in time. As soon as the handle was turned and the door kicked away the dogs pelted off, leaning into the bend like greyhounds. He trudged alongside me bearing his heavy churchwarden's key.

'What are we doing?' I said.

'Clock's broken,' he replied, the steady gravel crunch broken up by the panting of the dogs, who had already circled the church and returned. 'That, and we've got to see about smartening the place up for the Domesday Book people.' It was the nine hundredth anniversary, and notable buildings from the register were being refurbished in celebration.

My grandfather pulled open the porch's chicken-wire gates then unlocked the main door. The dogs sharked in ahead of us. He took a double palmful of holy water and leaned down to hold it for the pup, then gave the lip of the font a quick tap. Jack was up straight away, loudly lapping, then dropped with a sated crumple to the floor.

He walked to the tower and called me over. 'When I tell you to, grab hold of this,' he said, taking a bell-rope. 'And don't let go.' He gave the rope a downward jerk, let it fly upwards, then pulled it smartly down again. On the third pull he put his weight behind it, then released the rope and stepped away. 'Now.' A single bright clang sounded above. I clutched the rope and shot into the air, too scared to give vent to the joy. 'I'll get you to heaven in a flash, boy,' he said when I was down. 'Do you want a go on the organ?'

'Not today.' I looked at the altar. 'Why do you never go up for communion?'

'Because I think it's a load of rubbish. When you're dead, you're finished. And I wouldn't drink with that lot, anyway. The number of folks you see queuing up there of a Sunday to soss at the wine with streaming colds and I don't know what else. You could be poorly all winter.'

'You don't believe any of it?'

'It's made up, isn't it? By men. And what do they know?'

'What about the sermons?'

'I don't need some bloke in a frock to tell me what's right and wrong. Their shit smells the same as everybody else's. Which I know for a fact, cos I unblock all the drains.'

'Why are you churchwarden then, if you don't believe it?'

'Someone's got to keep the lights on. Let's have a look at this clock.'

I wasn't just there to keep him company. When I'd reached the top of the winding stone staircase that led to the belfry, and he had wheezed his way up behind me, he stood in the doorway giving instructions as I set off across the rafters. The problem was obvious: a dark, textured mass hung from the tower beams, giving off an odour of must and carrion.

'Jackdaws?' I said.

He nodded. 'They've probably been building it three years, poor buggers. Fetch it out then. Keep to the joists and you'll be right.'

I looked down the length of the bell-ropes at the tiled floor below.

'Why do I have to sleep there?' I said. 'Why can't I just go for the day and come back here at night? I could get a bus if you don't want to drive me.'

His voice cracked. 'It's not like that. We're too old, mate. And it's not up to us. It's all paid for by the company. Watch your step.'

It was an awkward angle but I leaned across and pulled at the base of the nest with both hands. Feathers, moss and sheepswool fell to the floor.

'You can ask them about it later, can't you?' he said. 'Phoning day today. And we'll only be down the road. We shan't be far away.'

Embarrassed now by my own trepidation, I gave the centre of the nest a big yank. It collapsed, smothering me in sticks and nearly pitching me through the rafters. He'd started laughing long before it was clear to me that I was all right.

'Let's put on the wireless and see if anything awful's happened,' said my grandmother, snapping the knob of the green Roberts beside me and turning up the dark voice of the Establishment to an ear-splitting volume.

She went on assembling lunch, shuttling pans from hob to hostess trolley to keep warm, augmenting her never-ending jug of gravy with fresh liquid. I sat at the table, waiting for the call. When the phone came to shrill, metallic life, I turned off the radio and uncradled the receiver. The static broke into a background hiss, and there, behind it, was my dad.

For years afterwards, comparable sonic textures would bring these conversations to mind: the white noise of television; clicks in the murmur of a shortwave radio; the hash of blips and fuzz that characterised the dial-up era. The line popped and snapped. There was a disorientating delay. You couldn't be in a hurry to exchange information. You had to dance to its tune.

'There he is! How's my boy today?'

'Fine.'

'What's the weather like? You wouldn't believe how hot it is here this morning.'

'What time is it with you?'

'Honestly, I doubt you'd be able to move if you were here, much less run about. We've been sleeping with the air con on full. It's beautiful, though. I can see a little flock of parakeets out … what?'

'Is Mum okay?'

'It's 10 a.m. I'm flying out this morning so I can't chat for long.'

'Where are you going?'

'She's fine. Are you keeping well? You're not tiring out your grandparents?'

'Can I talk to her?'

He put on an exaggerated Spanish accent. '*Yucatán, señor!*'

I pictured him standing in our echoing hallway with its tiled floor and dark-wood furniture. Polo shirt and chinos for the journey. Case full of business suits nearby. Chauffeured car outside, shaded by the coconut palms of the communal driveway.

'You must remember that they're older than us, so it's important to … Mum? She had to go to some fundraising thing. She'll give you a ring later.'

My grandmother was standing over me wiping her hands with a tea towel.

'Grandma wants a word,' I said.

'Nick?' she said. 'Everything okay? Yes, we're all right. Soldiering on. Eh? Well, it's a peculiar sort of place, but they seemed to like him well enough.'

This, my third solo summer. The first having come about through necessity, and gone so well that I had begged for it every year since. The parental warnings about not being a burden had got increasingly dire, but in truth the arrangement suited everybody. My grandparents could dote. My parents could stop worrying about how I would entertain myself over the long weeks of the holiday. And I got to keep a channel open to country and kin. Out in their world my environment changed so often that nothing stuck. Here was continuity: the pitted lane; the workshop; the rusting pump in the paddock.

But here now was the interview, folded between the pages of the summer, and every bit as ominous as the PROTECT AND SURVIVE leaflet I'd found bookmarking one of my grandmother's volumes of poetry. (I had read it through once then tried not to think about it again, even as its radioactive sentences glowed in my head. *If nuclear weapons are used on a large scale, those of us living in the country areas might be exposed to as great a risk as those in the towns ... When there is danger from fallout you will hear three loud bangs or three whistles in quick succession ...*)

The interview hinted at an end to the smug thrill of being from two places. Of playing the veteran unaccompanied minor, the changeling, the third-culture kid accustomed to solitude and the string around his neck. Seasoned stewardesses would see me coming and clock a fellow pro. The younger ones tried a maternal approach at first, all fragrant tactility and warm smiles. They soon learned. I would tolerate their efforts before requesting my Coke and nuts and assuring them I was happy alone. I yawned in the face of turbulence. Lowered the shade against silver cloudscapes and pink moonrises to focus on my reading or my sleep. I was a citizen of the world.

This was learned behaviour.

My father was *going like hell*, in a way that his father-in-law didn't comprehend but could only respect. After university (first in his family to go) he'd answered a job ad promising opportunities for foreign travel, and had been taking in the world ever since as he worked his way up the ranks of a multinational consumer goods company. Over the ten years of my life thus far, his work had taken us for extended periods to Rotterdam, Singapore and, for the last three years, Mexico City. The more we travelled, the better he did, and the further they deviated from the narrow range of destinies suggested by their points of origin: the Midlands farm, the Liverpudlian suburb. He had outgrown the small world of his youth with a near-desperate ferocity. He could read a menu in Chinese. Bribe a policeman in Spanish. I was his eager apprentice, ready to be dazzled from a young age by his latest revelation of what the world had to offer. *This is Chinese New Year. This is surfing. This is tiramisù.* I would experience this all over again from the other side with my own son when he arrived. Renewed astonishment at all the handed-down human habits we take for granted. Swimming pools. Christmas. Steak and chips. But for now I was still on the receiving end.

Mexico had been treating me well. Pool parties, white jeans, Hawaiian shirts, girls who wanted to kiss me and knew how to do it. Weekends at the beach, sleeping jumbled alongside the kids of my father's work colleagues. Smells of lime juice and grilled meat and sun cream. Chickens pecking at chicken bones under the awnings.

All of which does rather beg the question.

*

All right then, if we must.

The company was a cover. In actual fact my father was a spy. He had been advised by his true employers at the Foreign Office that given the hazards of his employment, it would be safer for everybody if he were to operate from now on without the encumbrance of a child.

Or:

Being moved around so much had taken its toll. I had been dissociating. I had no friends. I was losing sight of myself. There were moments when I seemed to be on standby and they didn't think I was going to come back. Getting me to some sort of stability was urgently important.

Or:

I had begun to integrate too much. To speak more Spanish than English. My parents had seen the state of the kids a few years older than me, smelled the weed on their breath, heard of their sexual escapades and decided it was time to correct my course. Then came the tipping point: I ran away from school with a friend. We disappeared for several days, eventually turning up at a beach resort miles away, where my companion had been involved in a horrible accident.

Or:

The kidnappings were getting worse and worse. A girl in my class had been snatched and it had taken two Jiffy-bagged fingers through the post before her parents had seen sense and raised the ransom. Then at a conference, my father met a charismatic Brazilian businessman who said that the same thing had happened to his daughter, and if it was him, he wouldn't think twice. *With all those wonderful schools you have at home,* he'd said, *I can't think why you let the boy dice with death out here.*

★

The less colourful truth is simply that it was a matter of company policy. Private health care kicked in early. Even more life-defining perks arrived later. My father had now reached the level at which the option of paid-for education back home for one's offspring came into play. It was well timed, coming just at the point when they might be starting to worry that my culture was being irreparably defined. And the offer would stand, in the interests of stability, for a full three years after you came home. Nevertheless, I'm not sure they would have gone for it. It wasn't where they had come from at all. But then there was the carol concert.

I sensed it had mattered at the time, though I didn't know why. The texture of it had stayed with me. A trip home, two years before, during which we'd attended the service of Nine Lessons and Carols at a local public school. This was in the north-west, where my father's mother still lived. A long sandstone chapel in December: candlelight, overcoats, incense and a very English sense of occasion. The silence of a primed pipe organ and polished shoes standing on ceremony. Then in the deafening quiet, the voice of a thirteen-year-old chorister singing the first verse of 'Once in Royal David's City'. The slow procession. Candle-flame of that solitary blond boy illuminating his round face and round eyes and round O of a mouth. The notes glacial, breakable. I only realised my mother was crying when she sniffed just before the organ kicked in and I saw her shining tear-trails as the mystery and purity of the first verse were engulfed by the groaning mediocrity of the congregation.

That moment, I realised later, when I'd learned more about the labyrinth of class, had planted a seed. She saw me in that surplice. In spite of the fact that in going away they'd become refugees from the class system, or maybe because of that fact, she wanted to feed me into the machine which had produced that boy. To baste me with opportunities and watch me rise. Some time would pass before the chance presented itself, but the idea was born there.

I think about tracking down the choirboy sometimes to find out how he's doing. Whether he sank or swam. But I'm not that sure I'd want to know.

4

'WHAT'S UP WITH you?' he said.

'Nothing.'

'You've hardly said a word this morning.'

I didn't reply.

'Shall we get on and make this box then?' he said.

We were standing in his workshop surrounded by parts from his current restoration project: an old caterpillar tractor, shorn of its cladding, its radiator standing tall at the front like a portico to the world of cranks and pistons behind.

This old machine shed had been the engine room of the big house. It was a place of greened-out windows, of dirt-caked calm, of greasy tools in self-made boxes. The kit enthralled me. The irresistible machine drill with its spoked control wheel. The magical lathe that coaxed block-wood into shapely legs. The compressed air pump that sent the dogs berserk when he directed its jet into their mouths. The blood-red machine saw with its whirling blade of teeth. The apocalyptic brightness of the welding rod, the smoked-glass mask he put on when using it, the alien he became when bathed in its impossible light.

I stood on the pad of the vehicle jack and morosely pumped myself into the air. 'Why do we have to make the box now? I'm not going until after Christmas.'

For some reason it had been decided that I would not go straight there at the start of the next academic year but spend a final term at my old school in Mexico first. For now I was still telling myself that this implied the move might never even happen.

'Doesn't mean you're not going to need it,' he said. He reached for one of the oak sheets he had cut in preparation. 'They gave maximum dimensions in the letter, so I'm going to make it as big as possible. They won't notice if we go over a bit.'

I watched like someone overseeing the assembly of his own coffin. 'What am I supposed to keep in it if I'm not allowed my own food?'

'There's a sweet shop, I expect. Tell you what: why don't we give it a false bottom in case you ever want to sneak something in?'

I smiled. 'Okay.'

'And we should put your name on the lid.' He had the soldering iron ready to go and made the letters quickly. D E N Y E R. The smell of singeing wood rose. Sick of my expression, he smoothed over the cooling marks with his palm and set down the iron. 'We don't have to finish it today. Tell me what you want to do instead.'

I pointed at the toboggan hanging on the wall, which hadn't seen active duty since the winter. 'I want to go sledging.'

'You're a contrary sod, do you know that? It's *August*.' He looked at me, then at the full summer day outside. 'All right. You're on.'

The laughter seemed to come from a place I didn't understand, and got more hysterical the more dangerous it got, the more cow shit sprayed up in my face. He never slowed down, even when he lost sight of me in the van's wing mirrors, even when I feared the rope might snap. Dragging me into a better frame of mind at forty miles an hour, shaming me for my tetchiness in the face of a world such as this.

A party at the Hall, not long after. An event he'd have dreaded anyway, made worse for happening in the week we'd lost Tom Slingsby. He finally agreed to attend, but only after the three of us had spent some time by the chalk pond with one of the plastic drums of wine he'd brought back from France, drinking to 'poor old Tom'.

'How old was he?' I said, staring at the spot where he'd sat a few weeks before, wondering if either of them was using his glass.

'Eighty-six,' said my grandfather. 'Old as the century.'

'He'd been ill for ages,' said my grandmother.

'He's supposed to have been dying since we moved here fourteen years ago.'

'He wasn't expected to live when he was *born*,' said my grandmother.

Eventually he loaded the drum of wine onto a sack barrow and pulled it behind him as we set off for the Hall. She'd put up her hair and he was wearing his best waistcoat, but he wasn't going quietly. 'Why are they having this thing, anyway? And who's doing the catering?'

'Everyone's bringing a contribution.'

'Bloody hell. Listen up, boy, don't eat anything until you've seen someone else try it and live to tell the tale.'

The three of us crossed the stable yard and out of his dominion through the white gates that led onto the Hall gardens, hearing music from the cloisters as we approached. Here were the residents in all their perfume and laughter.

He hollered a greeting and heaved his wine onto a trestle table. I saw them assessing his offering with unease. I was shown to a bottle of Corona lemonade and helped myself, unnoticed by two women setting out food.

'Talking of characters, I must introduce you to *Bob*,' said one. 'The old farmer who owns the park. Pa Larkin had nothing on this one.'

They approached him with dishes outstretched. He took a breadstick and dipped it into something and his eyes widened in alarm as he put it in his mouth. He called me over and made a face.

'What the hell's this pink stuff?' he muttered. 'I thought perhaps it was Angel Delight.'

A suited man with an air of entitlement was making his way through the group.

'May I introduce the Junior Minister for Transport?' said one of the women.

'How do,' said my grandfather.

'The Minister has just moved into the Gatehouse. He'll have a lovely view of all your tractors,' she explained.

'If he's the Junior Minister for Transport that should suit him just fine.'

'Bob is the wonderful man who kept up the gardens all those years that the Hall was in disrepair,' she said.

'Not just me,' he said. 'Tom too, poor old sod.'

'Who's Tom?'

'We'll be burying him on Wednesday if you're interested.'

'And you, young man,' said the hostess, a woman called Mrs Fowler. 'I hear you're destined for the school on the hill.'

'Not until next year,' I said.

'Enjoying his freedom while it lasts!'

He got more flirtatious with the women as the evening progressed, making steady inroads into his own wine while everybody else kept to their own safely bottled stuff. I was vaguely aware of changes in the conversational weather. Then of a souring in his mood. Finally, of a voice striking out for a frankness that had not been invited.

'We do wish you'd just get on and let us buy it. It would be a wonderful price, and then you'd never have to worry about it again.'

He let the silence thicken before speaking. 'You mind your own worries and leave me to mine.'

Then we were walking back, my grandmother wheeling the empty sack barrow while he used his shooting stick to keep his balance.

'*Tarrismalata!*' he boomed to the stars. 'Now I've seen it all.'

'Very cosmopolitan, you are,' she said.

'None of them touched my wine. And those bacon sandwiches tasted like the pig had pissed on them.'

'Keep your voice down.' She laughed and quickened her stride.

'This stick's not taking my weight. Give us your shoulder, boy.' There was a scattering of gravel and a soft exhalation and he wasn't beside me any more but somewhere on the ground. 'Now I've wet my bloody arse,' he said, lost in giggles and darkness.

I was outside with him the next day when Mrs Fowler appeared, looking awkward as she lifted his drum from the boot of her car. It had been emptied and scrubbed clean.

He watched her without rising from his bench by the back door. 'Lovely spread last night.'

'Well! Thank you for your delicious wine.'

'You finished the lot, then! It was quite a job to bring all that back from France in my trailer. I'm glad it went to a good home.'

'It was generous of you to bring so much.'

'Some interesting grub, too,' he said.

I spoke without thinking, parroting the line, remembering only the laughter. 'Grandad said that the bacon tasted like the pig had pissed on it.'

Not only did he not tell me off, he laughed just as much as he would have done if she hadn't been there, and made no effort to disguise it.

'You keep on speaking up, boy,' he said, when she'd gone. 'Tell them all what's what.'

It was always going to end badly. As the days counted down and my return to Mexico loomed, I became more uncomfortably aware that the next time I was here, it would be under very different circumstances.

He was working on the van. Its exhaust kept getting knocked off on the park's undulating terrain, so he'd decided to reconfigure it with a snorkel-style pipe rising up at the front. The narrowed eyes of the Renault 4 looked on anxiously as he removed its bonnet, fixed it in several vices and cut a hole in it. I moped in the driver's seat idly playing with the gear shift that slipped in and out of the dashboard like a trombone slide. On the stereo, Louis Armstrong was blowing the melancholy phrases of 'A Kiss to Build a Dream On'.

I'd said it twice before he heard me. He turned off the angle grinder, lifted his visor and put his head in at the window. 'You what?'

'I don't want to go.'

'Eh?'

'You always tell me to speak up. I don't want to go.'

He sighed. 'You know what it's like, where they are, don't you? Tearing about all over the place. Dangerous. And it won't be forever. He's doing well, your dad. He only wants what's best for you.'

'Why can't I just stay with you?'

He lost patience: something to do with feeling ambushed in the middle of a dangerous job, not having answers to questions it wasn't his responsibility to answer. 'It's not up to me. All I know is you've got to do what you're told.'

My grandmother called us in for lunch. He downed tools and tramped down to the house, cursing at the pain in his arthritic fingers. Inside, he pumped Swarfega from the dispenser by the sink and scoured his hands with the gritty, scented gunk. Wordlessly he leaned to one side to offer me the customary squirt of my own. I shook my head. It was a deliberate rejection of our usual intimacy.

The petulance infuriated him. He raised his dripping hand in threat as he would have done to an animal. 'You need to get on and do what you're supposed to do. The chances you have. I was out delivering milk for my dad by the time I was your age.'

'At least you were with your dad.'

'Shut it now, will you?'

I should have understood that he was as frustrated as I was. Instead, I lashed out.

'*Que no quiero hacerlo, cabrón!*'

That I scratched him was not the worst thing. The worst thing was the bark of Spanish, intended to sound as foreign as possible. He smiled in bafflement, rubbing his forearm. I wanted to correct the mistake, to reassure him that I was still me, but it was too late because I had done it on purpose and it had worked. Then I stepped backwards onto Jack, who, already wound up by the shouting, snarled and bit me on the calf.

I ran outside and didn't stop until I had reached the icehouse in the park. I stepped under its stone lintel and peered within, steadying myself with a hand on the wall since I well knew how steep the drop was into the pit. The white shape of a long-dead sheep was visible in the gloom. I dropped down inside and found the old footholds cut into the wall. The heat of the day was shut off as if by a door. I stared up at the skewed square of light above. Lifted the leg of my jeans and felt for blood, knowing there'd be bruises at least.

I hated myself for having pretended to be alien to him; more worldly, even. But what really made me convulse was that he might have seen through that pretence, giving him a clear view of the malice behind it. The bad feeling had been real and there was no way to take it back.

On the day before they took me to the airport, a storm swept up the park, thrashing the kitchen windows. He spent the day in his workshop, smoke scurrying from the chimney, and I didn't see him until the evening when the rain had finally stopped.

'Fancy a drive?' he said, going out to the van without waiting for my reply. When I got there he was sitting in the passenger seat.

His instructions were issued quietly as we lurched down the track. When I struggled to reach the clutch fully he held the wheel while I stretched, and made the gear changes for me. Periodically came the thunk of wet thistle harvested by the bumper. The newly installed bonnet exhaust swayed metronomically with the dips of the land. When I'd got the hang of it he started to sing.

'A life on the ocean wave, ta da da da da da tee dum. There never used to be fences in the countryside, you know,' he said.

'How did they know where one field ended and another began?'

'They didn't. People were free to graze their animals wherever they wanted. Nobody owned a square foot of ground. *And birds and trees and flowers without a name, All sighed when lawless law's enclosure came.*'

'Is that a song? I've never heard that one.'

'Poem, I think. Your grandma says it sometimes. Gear down for this bit, it's steep.' We were approaching an area of scalloped depressions outside a wood known as Sandpits. 'Stop.' He snapped off the ignition and pulled on the handbrake.

'What's the matter?' I said.

'Don't move,' he said. 'Look over there.'

A vixen and three cubs were playing in the area of kicked-over dirt at the front of their den. We watched the young tussling and gnawing at their mother's neck before stopping abruptly as if their brains had been wiped. Plush bib of white at the presiding vixen's throat. Sleek promise of danger in her narrowed eyes. We didn't move or speak until one by one they'd gone to earth.

'That was special,' he said. 'You don't get to see that sort of thing very often.'

That night he sat in his armchair for an hour listening patiently to me stumble up and down the piano. He said he needed the music to *keep him going* over the coming months.

The next day I was gone.

5

Later, after they were both dead and the contents of the house had been dispersed, I inherited the old upright on which I used to bash out the blues and ragtime tunes which made him so proud. I lift the top sometimes, put my head inside and use the instrument as a time machine. The smell of dust and velvet. The ferrous shimmer of the strings. Those obedient hammers ready to nod forward and change the air. Close your eyes, inhale, listen for the tremors of all the music that has travelled through it, and you might drop out of the here and now and visit any moment in the instrument's history.

Christmas! Church bells, frosty mornings, the Hall and its stately bearings making more sense at this time of year than ever. Cards strung up like bunting. His tabletop production line of sausage meat, which must have stuffed the turkeys of half the village. Carols. Me on the piano, him on his battered old saxophone.

We were back, all of us this time. I'd spent one last term in my old life, almost allowing myself to forget what was coming. Now here it was.

Always the feeling of apprehension when I first saw him after a break, as if some of the affection might have withered.

Always the joyous obliteration of that feeling as soon as he said something that kindled the nervous thrill of being alive in his company.

The big sitting room. Only time it was ever really used. Here is my mother. She relaxes, curls up on the sofa like a girl. She is after all with her parents. She misses them when she is away. Here is my father. See how he can't settle. He is after all with his in-laws. His mind on the wider world even as he lovingly tries to fit into this environment.

He goes out for a walk, then returns after mooching around in the gloom.

'You've not stopped out long,' says my grandfather. Ribbing him for not being comfortable with the outdoors, just as he does whenever my father takes on anything practical.

His attempts to speak my grandfather's language backfire. He refers to the 'crows' outside and is gently rebuffed. 'Jacks.'

Is he ever hurt by how close his son is to his father-in-law? Does it bother him that I can finish most of my grandfather's sentences but sometimes don't understand what he says at all? If I wasn't so distracted with hero worship of my grandfather I might do well to take note of how good my father is at adapting to his surroundings. What does it matter that he doesn't know the difference between a crow and a jackdaw when he knows how to read the mood of a meeting in Japanese, or cut a deal on a fishing trip to the Gulf of Mexico? This is his skill: he takes his colours from his surroundings. As I will soon have occasion to do.

On Christmas Eve my grandfather and I went out to fetch the turkey from an outbuilding near his workshop. Footsteps crunching in frost. Evensong bells tumbling. His terrier followed us out and decided to bag a duck from an area of water which the flock had kept melted in the centre of the chalk pond. We only knew the dog had fallen in when we heard a washing of paws and he turned his torch over the frozen water, the beam's reach finding the green dots of pathetic canine retinas.

'We'll drag the boat over,' I said. 'I'll chuck it onto the ice and when it breaks, I'll be floating.'

'There isn't time,' he said. 'And if the ice doesn't break, you'll be stuck. Fetch the ladder from the workshop and walk out on it. It should spread out your weight.'

'What if it doesn't?'

'You'll get chilly,' he said.

I ran to the workshop, collected the ladder and returned. I slid it out over the ice, looked back at him then set out, tentatively finding each rung, speeding up as I got the hang of it.

That shimmer you hear in railway lines when a train is coming. That high tremble. Cracking ice has a tone.

As the hole opened up beneath me and the ladder upended itself, diving irresistibly down, the last voice I heard was his.

'Kick off your wellies.'

Oh, I thought. *I'm under.* The horrid intimacy of freezing water entering my clothes. Ladder gone. Hole lost. Fearsome downward tug as my boots filled.

But because his words were there with me, rather than panic, I did as I was told and kicked the boots off, which freed me to tread water and search the flat expanse of ice above me with the palms of my hands, keeping my eyes closed to concentrate on the only thing that mattered, until I found the hole. Every time I tried to haul myself out, the ice broke, so I made a channel back towards the bank with the dog paddling behind, swearing as colourfully as my ten-year-old vocabulary would allow.

As I sat in a hot bath afterwards, trying to banish the chill, my parents and grandparents crowded in to go over the incident and make sure I was all right. Already the story was finding its humorous rendition – the sight of me dropping through the ice, my bad language when I surfaced. There was something hysterical about their relief. I felt suddenly ashamed of my nakedness and asked them all to go.

It was the second time that pond had brought me close to death. The first had been when I was seven and he was dredging it with his dragline excavator. I'd been playing in the newly dug shallows on a sloping bank of mud when I felt a blast of wind as the drag cable broke, sending the four-tonne bucket swinging like a wrecking ball from its hoist rope and missing my head by inches. On both occasions we laughed. On both occasions I only knew how much danger I had been in when he allowed his genuine reaction to emerge later, after a drink.

Keeping me out of trouble was never his thing. It was far more his style to leave me in harm's way and hope I was properly armed.

We'd celebrated the previous New Year's Eve at a famously boisterous party held every year by one of our Mexican neighbours. The kids had been lined up on one side of the pool and issued with hand-held fireworks. One of the fathers had walked the line lighting each one in turn while the rest of the adults counted down from ten. Sparks shot down our forearms as they went off. When midnight struck we'd all jumped into the water. I remembered a kiss sometime after that with a girl called Carolina.

This year my evening was spent watching television by the electric fire with my grandmother as she sewed my name into a mound of grey clothes, my grandfather's snores rumbling upstairs. My parents had left by then – called away, I was told, by work. I was convinced that they'd returned to go to the party, and told myself I couldn't blame them if they had.

*

The snow started falling on the day before term started, and did not stop. As we sat at the kitchen table in the dark afternoon, my grandfather reached behind my ear and conjured a large, old coin. Its face was so smooth that it was almost flat in places, but you could still make out the features of the young woman it depicted.

'This is a Victoria crown,' he said. 'Minted in 1844, only a few years after the coronation. It dropped out of my Uncle Laurie's pocket when I was ten, same as you are now. He came home drunk one night and fell backwards down the stairs. The sole of his boot made this great big crescent mark on the wall. My auntie was that cross with him, she gave it to me, and said that if he couldn't look after it I might as well have it myself. I've kept it ever since.'

'Why are you showing it to me now?'

'I'm giving it to you. Keep it with you while you're up there. I've got another one somewhere. I'll dig that one out and carry it with me. That way they'll talk to each other, and I shall know you're all right.'

'Does that happen?' I said.

'Course it does. Try it if you need to. You'll see.' He slapped his palms onto the table. 'Right. We better get on and feed those ducks. They'll be worrying we've left them to it.'

There's a photo of me in my duffel coat by the car, hands in pockets, cheekily grimacing into the blizzard. The trunk has already been loaded into the boot. My grandfather is visible on his knees in the background, cursing as he fits the snow chains. I expect there was a last-minute brush of my hair in the oven door's reflection. Max '87, newly minted, going off into the world.

The all-out Narnian winter was so fantastical that there was nothing else to be talked about on the way. The buried valley. Shackled tyres rumbling through the unploughed lanes. Hedgerows become white humps, spangle-skirted with icicles.

We careened up through the villages I would get into the habit of counting off one by one to measure the approach, culminating in the hamlet where many of the teachers lived in a terrace of thatched cottages. Then we were into the final approach of the avenue, pitches and boot hut flickering in monochrome behind the trees like a silent film. We crossed the threshold and pulled level with the balustrade. I thought of the dead boy in the urn.

Ragged flakes of snow darkened the sky as we alighted. I saw two trunks stacked by the front door but there was a pronounced absence of other people. We began wondering openly if we'd got the day wrong. Then a tractor arrived pulling a covered trailer from which two ruddy-faced boys, who would turn out to be the sons of a farmer called West, leapt down to haul off their possessions. It was the right day, but not everybody had snow chains.

'I reckon we might just go home, don't you?' said my grandfather. The joy was explosive.

But even as he said it a bearded man in a blue parka appeared round the side of the main building. He squinted at us through his glasses, raised a hand and approached. A slobbery Irish setter batted around him kicking up powder.

'Well done you!' he said. His hair stuck up in random places, as if he'd just got out of bed. The squint and the hair made him look confused, though the voice was warm and full of authority. 'How are we all?'

'Surviving. How are you?' said my grandmother.

He stopped and stared at the ground as if noticing something for the first time. 'Do you know,' he said, 'I really am most extraordinarily well. Ian Crighton,' he added. 'Deputy head. But this lot all call me Crimble, so I suppose you should too. And you are Max Denyer.'

'Yes,' I admitted.

'We didn't meet when you came for interview.'

'No.'

'But I'm well briefed about you, don't worry. Is this Grandmother?'

I nodded.

'And Grandfather too. Well done to all of you. Not a lot of snowstorms back in Mexico, I suppose! As you can see, most people haven't made it up here, so we're sort of on holiday until they do. All rather fun.'

I would learn that his eccentricity was variable. The undiluted version was available exclusively to pupils. With parents, especially new ones, there was a danger that the scattiness might seem inappropriate, so he dialled it down. Warm but firm. Exciting but properly tuned.

'Where's he meant to put his things?' said my grandfather.

'Quite right,' said Crimble. 'David West! Help this boy with his trunk and show him where he's sleeping.'

The kid he'd shouted at fled the snowball fight which had broken out near the stable block. Nearby a few coated figures slid across the ice of the boating lake. Sounds were bright and flat against the cold.

As they left, I felt in my pocket for the Victoria crown. I had failed to anticipate the eventuality that they would drive away and I would not. It was out of my imaginative range. Yet drive off they did, skidding softly down the avenue as I nibbled the tog of my coat and waved. After which there was nothing to do but turn and go inside.

6

A WORN RED rug sprawled across the stone floor of the Great Hall. High on the wall clung a shaky-looking minstrels' gallery. Above it I could see dots of grey afternoon light among the dark rafters of the roof. Boys sat reading comics on a pair of crippled sofas by the fire. It was a parody of the adult world, Bugsy Malone does gentlemen's club. Gazing over your *Tintin* or your *2000 AD* to see if tea is on the horizon.

Introductions were made. Nonchalance was key, with a dash of entitlement. *You're new, that's cool. Yeah, I'm new, and that's cool.* I was conscious of displays being put on, and realised that some time would pass before anything happened that I could trust.

Where's your accent from? A frequent question in the coming days, which I had never before been asked. Somehow I had been cast as from elsewhere. A compound of woodsmoke, floor wax and radiator dust began to attach itself forever to one room and one moment.

Brisk shuffle of shoe soles on the rug and sudden awareness that a finger was uncomfortably close to my face. Just time to register that the finger in question was dirty and not fragrant, then a feeling like the quick dart of a needle on my cheek.

'Zap! Welcome.' The dirty kid approached his next victim, charging himself anew with static on the carpet.

'Are we starting that already?' said one wearily. But others were up, the hearthside now a giggling arena of boys with digits outstretched. Some recoiled as the finger approached, others pointed their own pre-emptive retaliation. Others still offered up their faces voluntarily to take a hit for the delectation of the crowd.

This agitator, instigator, dispenser of shocks, was Luke Price.

'Do you need to be shown around?' he said. 'Or did you see it all when you came for interview?'

'That was in August.' A world ago. 'I haven't been here since then.'

'You're here now. Bad luck.' He led me down a corridor of worn stone slabs to a room furnished with battered wooden cupboards. 'Lockers,' he announced. 'Which you can't lock. This is also where you put your tuck box, which isn't allowed to contain any *tuck*. Have you got a hamster?'

'Do I need one?'

'You're allowed food if you do. For the hamster. Changing rooms,' he continued, descending into a long, low chamber lined with pegs and benches. 'Which, weirdly, *are* used for changing. Some of the time.'

The room was warm and close. Scalding pipework snaked round the walls. I saw handwritten surname labels in alphabetical order, one per peg: *Adams, Adebayo, Beech, Butler-Wilson* . . .

'Let's find you,' he said. 'Denyer with a D?'

'Yes.' I reasoned the time had not yet come for sarcasm. I hooked my bag over the peg, and taking a cue from Luke, sat down.

I heard footsteps as someone else arrived: a tall boy with long brown hair, hugging a bulging drawstring bag. I knew him already.

'Simon Draaake.' Luke drew out the name in a mocking fashion, relieved at the arrival of someone to share the chore of settling me in.

'Here you are then,' said Simon, regarding me through the awkward curtains of his hair. 'Unlike most of the school. What are we doing, coming when nobody else is here?'

'I suppose you've got no excuse,' said Luke. 'Simon's mum works for the enemy.'

'He knows,' said Simon. He went through to the wash-basins with a plastic tumbler, then we heard a cry of exasperation. 'There's no water!'

'The pipes have burst,' called Luke. 'You've got to clean your teeth with snow. And poo in it,' he added to me, grinning. 'You think I'm joking? We did it yesterday. My top tip is, don't lose your balance. The ground's already nasty.'

'Why were you here yesterday?'

'Me and my brother have been here three days. Our parents had to go to their house in Italy. They always get us in early if they can, and Sutton's a family friend.'

When I needed to go, I asked the least threatening boy I could find, who directed me to the walled garden at the top of the North Lawn. I was already changed for bed so I went out in my new dressing gown, slipping on the flagstones of the cloisters then enjoying the bite and pack of fresh powder beneath my slippered feet on the lawn. I met Simon coming back, carrying a bucket, snow flurries chasing around his head.

'Not. Fun.' He handed me a roll of paper. 'There's a stack of buckets up there. You've got to bring one back full of snow every time you come, for people to wash and clean their teeth with. Don't get it from too near the crapping place.' He strode off shaking his head. For all that it was an act, he was good at disgust and it made me smile.

The walled garden was a grid of desolate vegetable beds and scraggy roses. The cold settled on my skin. I smelled woodsmoke on the air. As I lowered my pyjama bottoms and squatted, I noticed the illuminated roof of a phone box poking up from beyond the wall, capped with a fresh dome of snow. I thought how much my grandfather would love this story. Only we weren't allowed money and I already knew that phone calls were strictly forbidden.

As I made my way back bearing my bucket of snow, I noticed for the first time a tatty static home against the back wall of the garden. In front of it stood an old man in a black coat. He wasn't looking at me but at the bird table in front of him. He held a bag of seed in mid-scatter and some balls of fat on strings.

'The trouble is,' he said, 'one never knows how much to give them. Conditions are awful for them at the moment, of course. But one doesn't want them becoming dependent. It would blunt their skills of survival.' His gaze met mine lazily, like a rising bubble. 'Are you new?' I nodded. 'Well, I'm sure my son will look after you.' He released another pinch of seed onto the table. 'Get inside before you catch your death.'

He died later that year, so this would be my one and only encounter with Mr Sutton Senior.

My dormitory was called Agincourt, and it was one of the smaller ones: five beds, three on one side, two on the other. Mine was the middle bed of the three, under a window looking out onto the North Lawn. The room was panelled in polished, dark wood. The sections and their uniformity reminded me of Roman shields in tortoise formation. Alone in the room, I browsed the names of my future companions which were taped to the beds around me, then got into my own, wondering if I should turn off the light.

'Knock knock,' said Crimble from the door. 'Well! Private quarters. The luxury. Have you got something to read?' I held out the Spanish-language horror comic I'd brought up with me. The cover showed a werewolf sinking its teeth into the throat of a woman in a nightdress. 'Very improving. Word to the wise: I think some of the others might be congregating up in Hastings. Although they aren't telling me about it, of course. You can probably find your way up there after I've gone.'

He winked.

I winked back, confused.

'Here he is,' they said, as I pushed open the door. They were gathered round an electric hot ring toasting bread on a bent coat hanger. 'Come to join the campfire. You made it past Crimble, then?'

'He was the one who sent me here,' I replied.

Nobody responded, as if I'd said something embarrassing.

They had stolen the loaf from the kitchen. They were rolling the slices into cylinders and eating them at speed, hot butter squirting from the ends. They told me more about what to expect. I didn't believe them.

More snow fell that night and even fewer parents attempted the journey the next day, so lessons were called off. I thought how stupid we'd been to rush up here. It was the first time I had ever resented my grandfather's capabilities.

Then again, there was sledging. It was announced over breakfast to the twenty or so of us present. Several had brought their own equipment, which it would never have occurred to me to do. That afternoon Simon and I stood at the top of a steep hill overlooking a pond, watching them cannon down.

'Step aside,' said David West. He wore a fitted purple snowsuit and mirrored goggles. He stepped into his skis and poled himself into a slalom, narrowly avoiding two kids on sledges.

As we stood clenching and unclenching our hands against the cold, Luke appeared at our side carrying a slashed-open plastic fertiliser bag.

'Do this.' He held his arms straight at his sides with the hands at right angles to his body, and moved his shoulders up and down. 'Pumps blood into your hands.' We did as he suggested.

David West was back, skis over his shoulder. 'You three look like penguins,' he said. 'What you need is one of these.' He took from his pocket something in black leather that looked like a cigarette case. He handed it to me, and I felt its uncanny heat. 'Pocket warmer,' he explained, clicking the side and opening the case to reveal a glowing stick of charcoal.

'Do you want to try mine?' said Simon. 'Take a glove off and stick your hand in here.'

'Very funny. I'm going to find your dick in there, aren't I?'

'In my duffel-coat pocket?' said Simon. 'I've always said this place should teach more biology.'

David West took the bait, then recoiled. 'Is that a rat, you sick bastard?'

'Stoat, I think. And I'm keeping him warm, not the other way round. He's been dead three days.'

West pulled his glove back on in disgust. 'I see Simon Drake hasn't got any less weird over Christmas. Lovely sledge, too,' he added, pointing at Luke's bag.

He skiied off again, sending up a wave of powder at the lip of the frozen pond.

'That guy's a pillock,' said Luke.

As West began walking up again, Luke threw down his bag, gripped it by its corners and chucked himself down the slope. He judged it well. West didn't move fast enough and Luke took him out in a clatter of skis and poles. Simon and I could hear West cursing, just as we heard his laughter when Luke carried on past him and onto the surface of the ice, which immediately opened up beneath him. Luke staggered up, mud-caked, soaking and triumphant.

'Well,' said Simon, 'this is a good start to the year.'

On the third day the thaw began. Estate cars streamed down the avenue and swept between the balustrades. Crimble had scrubbed up, and now wore a tie and a tweed jacket. Simon and I watched from an upstairs window as the population swelled. The change in the weather lent the previous few days a dreamlike quality. Inside, the atmosphere was charged. Every particle awoken. Boys rushed. Girls congregated in their ghettos. There were girls.

As I watched the new arrivals, the tearful farewells, Simon worked on his current project – expanding the memory of a BBC Micro – feeling around in a bag full of screwdrivers and wire.

'What happens now?' I said.

'Assembly. And it will be Weapons Davis on duty.'

'What does that mean?'

'It means wash your hands.'

'I did them this morning.'

'Do them again. Scrub them till the skin comes off.'

'Are you serious?'

He set his screwdriver aside and looked me in the eye. 'Deadly.'

*

Unbroken voices pealing, shattering in the air like glass.

In the Lower Gallery the mass seethed and swarmed. Changes to hair got the mocking they deserved, as did anything notable about your person that hadn't changed. Dead arms were administered. Old jokes dusted off to see if they still stood up. The fresh gizmos of Christmas produced for inspection. Laundered jumpers, creased trousers, clean shoes: this was as hygienic as it was going to get.

'Price! Get in line!'

For a moment I thought Luke had gone mad, because the person screaming the word 'Price' *was* Luke Price, or would have been if you smartened up my new friend. Then I noticed the differences: Hitlerian parting of the hair, finer bone structure, taller. Then I looked where he was looking, and saw the real Luke. I hadn't known his brother so resembled him, or that the brother was head boy. Did the brother – his name was Ali – call him 'Price' at home too, or was it only when they had assumed their school-time personalities? Where had the brother been for the last few days?

Luke smirked at the rebuke and took his place. Then the sound was sucked out of the room as Eric 'Weapons' Weathers-Davis entered, followed by Miss Fletcher the matron, with her Bambi eyes and her gravity-defying wall of hair.

He savoured the charged quiet, as if it were a pleasure he had been denied over the festive period. He tested his silence, setting one foot then the other on the stone flags to see how reverent it was. His gaze drifted down the line through the yellow lenses of his hunter's sunglasses, a smile tweaking the corner of his mouth. His beige jacket was replete with loops and button-down pouches.

'A New Year,' he declared. 'And everything to play for. I have a good feeling about 1987, and I hope you all do too. Are you pleased to be home, Webb minor?'

'Yes, sir.'

'Miss Fletcher and I are delighted to be here, aren't we, Miss Fletcher?'

'Thrilled, Mr Weathers-Davis.'

'We're bursting with energy, aren't we?'

'We are.'

'And we're going to start as we mean to go on. Hold out your hands for inspection. I know that dear Mama will have got you all scrubbed up for the start of term, so this shouldn't be too painful.'

Silence but for the sound of his rubber soles wincing on the floor.

'Good grief, Wallace. Is that what passes for a haircut in London? Don't think for a moment that that's going to see out the week. We shall get Miss Fletcher on to you with her clippers before you know it.'

Laughter.

'Price minor.' He closed his eyes as if some wearying memory had resurfaced. 'Is it too much to ask that even on the first day of term your fingernails might not contain enough mulch to breed award-winning roses?'

'I've been here three days, sir.'

'And yet, look at your brother's hands. He's been here for three days too. But he hasn't regressed to the state of a bog-creature the moment his parents gleefully boarded the plane back to Tuscany. Does it keep you up at night, Price minor, to know already how much better-equipped for life your brother is than you? How you've lost the battle before it's even begun?'

Nervous laughter.

'Go and scrub them. Use a nailbrush, for Christ's sake. And take this as your first shot across the bow. Next time you'll be looking at a direct hit. I'm going to sink your dreadnought. Capeesh?' Luke left, and Weapons Davis's voice lurched into an abrupt boom. 'We are not getting this year off on the wrong foot. Tight. Ship.' He brushed a caterpillar of dust from the panelling and rid himself of it with a grimace. Now he stood before me. Insectile flickering of eyes behind the lenses as new information registered. He hooked his forefingers into his trousers.

'Name?'

'Denyer.'

'Denyer, what?'

'Max Denyer.'

'Max Denyer, what?'

'Sir, sir.'

'Where did you spring from, *Denyer*? We're not used to fresh meat in midwinter.'

'Mexico, sir.'

'God save us.' His head shot to the left, lips wisecracking apart. Then he spotted something over my shoulder and the expression snapped back to hostility. 'Nobody move. If that's a catapult, Overton, you'd better surrender it right now if you want to see out the day.'

And so on.

We filed through to eat, past the toilet block and shoe-cleaning area, whose distinctive aroma of urine and boot polish was already becoming associated with the imminent consumption of food. The door was wedged open and I saw Luke scrubbing his nails at the sink, apparently singing.

Here was the dining room at full capacity, a ballet of milky tea chugging from huge steel urns, of Spam, of Stork on sliced white. The walls were covered in pea-green panelling topped by a frieze which listed the names of those who'd attained scholarships to senior schools.

The conversation came off a rolling boil and settled into something calmer. Luke rejoined us in a cheerful mood which soured as soon as he saw his plate.

'I don't believe this,' he said. 'They're not doing this to me again.'

'What?' I said.

'He's got a history with sweetcorn,' said Simon.

'I've told them this. They know about it. I bet he made sure I got extra after that hands thing.'

'Can't you just leave what you don't want?' I said.

'Yeah, why not try that, Luke?' said a boy called Ishaq Jafari. '*Please, sir, I want some less*. See how that works out for you.'

'This is masses,' he moaned. 'Look, I've got twice as much as Ish. Or you, Simon. They know.'

'He's got his eye on you,' said Simon. 'Eat it.'

'Yeah?' said Luke. He'd taken an envelope out of his pocket, and keeping his eyes on Weapons Davis, filled it with every yellow kernel on his plate.

'Nice one,' I said. 'You can stick it in the bin later.'

'That's of course what he should do,' said Simon.

'But it would be a waste of perfectly good stationery.' Luke brought the distinctive, red-tinged envelope to his mouth, sealed it and put it back in his pocket. As we left, Weapons Davis was occupied at the other end of the room. Simon nudged me to watch as Luke slipped the envelope into the briefcase he'd left on the masters' table, and fled.

The pipes hadn't yet been fixed, so we cleaned our teeth with meltwater and went straight to Prayers, a glorified bedtime story where everyone gathered in their dressing gowns around the table in the Lower Gallery to hear a pupil read a Bible passage or *Reader's Digest* excerpt which the duty teacher would use as a springboard for moral instruction.

My new dressing gown had been found by my grandmother in an ancient school outfitters while on holiday in

Wales. It was made of thick wool and had a long, golden cord like a stolen bell-rope. Putting it on for the first time that evening I had felt self-conscious, but with the heating still off it was keeping me warm.

'What have we learned from tonight's reading, boys and girls?' said Weapons Davis. 'Whatever it is, you can all go to bed and think about it in silence. I do like Master Denyer's dressing gown,' he added as I passed. 'As luxurious a garment as I have ever seen. And a positively monastic length of cord keeping him trussed.'

They often spoke like that, as if playing the part of a commentator for some conjectured fellow adult, as if to remind themselves that other adults still existed, that these little people they oversaw were not the world's only other sentient beings.

After dark that night I heard a sigh followed by a splatter on the carpet and understood from the smell that the boy in the bed next to mine had been sick. He was a slight kid named Neil Lynch, who went around with a hunted look, tripping over his shoes. He never hid the fact that he was in trouble, though all I ever saw him receive from other pupils was sympathy, partly because his twin sister was very popular. The lights were put on and Neil's face angled up pathetically from his bedside.

'Sorry,' he said.

'Shall I get someone?' I asked.

'I'd leave it till the morning if I was you,' said the boy in charge.

'It will smell,' I said. 'Someone should tell Miss Fletcher.'

'Rather you than me.'

What could they be afraid of? There was sick on the floor. Someone should be told. I pulled on my dressing gown and was grateful for it again as I navigated the dark corridors past Somme and Passchendale and arrived at the landing that led onto the matron's pantry. I'd seen boys queuing here before bed to receive doled-out spoonfuls of extract of malt.

The door was closed but I could hear voices within. I knocked, then pushed it open. The surgery was in darkness but light shone from Miss Fletcher's quarters beyond. I assumed there was no need to announce myself further so crossed the surgery and opened the next door.

Weapons Davis and Miss Fletcher sat on opposing sides of a folding table in front of the electric fire set into her green-tiled hearth. His shoes were off. She wore a pink dressing gown over a blue nightie. Her piled-up do had been dramatically swaddled for the night in a menacing hairnet. A sweet stink of booze filled the room – not the old wine smell you got in the stables after one of my grandfather's parties, but familiar all the same. It felt only natural to offer one of his favourite toasts.

'Up yours,' I said.

'I beg your pardon?' said Weapons Davis.

'That's what you say when people are drinking.'

'You'll shut up right now, you cheeky little sod.'

'I was just—'

On his breath the wine was like rotting apples. 'Do you hear this, Miss Fletcher? I really don't hold with any of this *give them a few weeks to settle in*.'

'I think Denyer was trying to be polite, Mr Weathers-Davis. What is it, Max? Why are you here?'

'Neil's been sick in Agincourt, Miss.'

'And so it begins. Come on then, Max.'

She opened a drawer in the surgery and took out an empty Stork margarine tub and a long-handled jam spoon. When we reached the dormitory she knelt and spooned the vomit into the tub with efficient scrapes. She sealed the lid, offered a word of sympathy to Neil and prepared to leave.

'Don't you need Dettol?' I said, thinking of my grandmother.

'Jesus but this one's got a mouth on him,' she muttered. 'I'll disinfect it in the morning, Your Lordship, okay? Lynch, try and make it to the toilet if it happens again. I don't need to be disturbed more than once.'

When the lights went out I stared upwards, trying to make out the ceiling and failing to ignore the smell.

There must have been a day when the pipes were fixed, but I have no memory of it, so here incident begins to merge with habit. There would, for example, have been a first experience of bathtime, but the bathtimes of years exist in one ever-present moment.

The stew of steam and bodies. The cracked pink soap struggling against hard water to lather. The white-tiled communal trench for the brash, the comparative seclusion of uncurtained shower stalls for the remainder, but these are arguably less private since you're standing up, and they are not reserved for one. Nothing is not extreme: the air freezes, the water scalds. Combine them too quickly when in from games and chilblains ignite on your skin.

Different masters, different styles. Wagstaff, a florid force of nature and Good Man, booms away, chivvying, challenging boys to press-up contests. Crimble hunches in the doorway, squinting into the middle distance. Weapons Davis brings in a chair from the Lower Gallery and enthrones himself, watching, daring you to transgress.

The constant is the boys, who whoop and splash and cavort, or cower and dash and cover, depending on their personality and how well integrated they are. There is a paradoxical stigma attached to puberty: those who have launched early are sometimes derided for their pubic hair and pendulous penises. Those on the cusp of change – those who haven't yet sprouted but are about to, whose voices still squeal but have the first crack of substance behind them – are the most assertive. The brash one in my year is of course Luke Price, who does tricks with his dick at the slightest provocation, manipulating it alarmingly, or slapping it upwards with hand-over-hand motions in a compulsive, peacocking gesture that achieves little, but demonstrates intent.

How did I behave, that first bathtime? What was my strategy? I probably leapt in and out of one of the shared stalls before dashing for my towel, which at that point would still have smelled comfortingly of home.

I do remember assuming that washbasins were to be shared as well, but there was a different rule for that. Mainly I remember the gratitude I felt when Simon, whose basin I had hopped onto while I did my teeth, glanced up from the brushing of his own, spat a red smear of Signal towards the plughole, and quietly set me straight.

'Separate,' he said, with a brief smile.

Different masters, different styles. The blitzkrieg of Eric Weathers-Davis had shocked the term into life, opening the way for a more relaxed approach from others. Prayers with Crimble was spiritual by comparison. Magic and incantation. Where shall we go? The parent-facing version of him was gone and we hung off his words. He knew how to thrill without terrifying. He didn't talk to himself. He listened.

'I'll tell you a few things you may not know about sleeping,' he said one night. 'One is that it's virtually impossible to go to sleep with your legs crossed. Just try it if you don't believe me. You'll be awake all night. I mean, think. Have you ever seen anybody sleeping cross-legged? You haven't. Another is that you must never go to sleep with your hand resting on your throat. When you sleep with anything in the palm of your hand, there are powerful involuntary contractions. The tightening impulse is irresistible after a while, and if you don't wake up you'll be unable to stop yourself.'

You mean—

'Yes. There's a good chance you could strangle yourself in your sleep.'

His words were a self-fulfilling prophecy. Of course you can't go to sleep if you're concentrating that hard on trying to make it happen. But in bed that night, for the first time I wasn't thinking of home. Instead I lay with my fingers splayed across my throat, daring myself to allow sleep to approach. Then I was conscious of a new smell and realised that this time Neil Lynch had wet the bed.

Miss Fletcher wasn't entertaining tonight so the transaction was more businesslike. She turned on the lights and stripped his sheets and pyjamas in full view. He stood naked and cold.

'Are we going to have more problems like this, Lynch?' she said, fitting the shameful cover. 'Are we going to be sleeping on plastic like a baby?'

There was a history here, about which I knew nothing. It was like plunging into traffic on a multi-lane highway.

Not long after, when the room was quiet again, I was aware of torchlight on the wall. I kept my eyes closed to the whispered voices, and when I looked over after the door had closed, Neil Lynch was gone. Then the morning bell was ringing and he was back, asleep in his bed beside me.

7

No visitors were allowed for the first few weeks. The bedding-in period lasted just long enough to allow local anxieties to replace any lingering thoughts of home. Our weekends were full of time to fill.

If you were lucky you might get permission to go on a Free Walk. The very name a taunt. What, after all, could one do? The village had a pub and a phone box, and if you went anywhere near either, you were dead. But off we went, excited anyway. Blue tracksuits and striped scarves. Four of us: me, Luke, Simon and Ish.

The magical winter weather had been replaced by something more attritional, but at least the mud was frozen. I thought of the deep blue of the mosaic tiles at the communal pool in Mexico, of its deserted loungers accumulating leaf litter and seed pods from the tropical trees around it.

We walked the long field below the school checking the ground for clay pigeons. A gun club shot there on Saturday mornings (we'd hear the clatter during lessons) and you could get tuck-shop credit for bringing them up to school intact.

'What do we do when we get there?' I asked.

'That's where Ish comes in,' said Simon. 'There's a barmaid at the Graven Image who's soft on him. She's usually good for crisps and a Coke.'

'Soft on you?' I said.

'She's just a family friend. Her dad runs one of my dad's shops. But she may not be working today,' said Ish, collecting his clays.

'Are you lot planning to walk round all afternoon with stacks of clay pigeons in your hands?' said Simon, who was hardly travelling light himself, having brought a fishing rod and tackle, just in case.

I let my eyes travel the length of the field, belatedly aware that its topography made the cruel line of sight across the valley fully available.

'What are you staring at?' said Luke.

'That's where my grandparents live.'

'Where are your parents?' said Ish.

I was about to offer one of several answers I had already given to others who'd asked the same question. Then, as if sensing their apprehension as to what the worst answer might be, I said: 'They're dead.'

'Oh. Sorry,' said Luke.

Simon's expression was unchanged. He knew I was lying but was happy to accept it. 'How?'

'I don't like talking about it.'

'My father's dead too,' he said.

'I'm sorry,' I said. I meant, for the lie. He nodded.

'This is a fun walk,' said Luke.

The village was at its drowsiest and most inconsequential. We strutted in like gunfighters nonetheless, crossed the green and entered the Graven Image, a coaching inn built of the same old stone as the school. Inside, we stood adult-struck by the Saturday-afternoon crowd. Cigarettes smouldered in tin ashtrays. Conversations hung in beery breath. The rest of us waited by the door while Ish went to the bar and asked for his friend.

'She's off today,' said the landlord. 'Now get out of it, you lot. You know you're not allowed in here.'

'Bastard,' Luke fumed as we left. 'Can't he take pity on us just once? Fine. On to the phone box.'

When we got there he yanked open the door and stepped inside.

'Don't you get in trouble?' I said.

'Not if nobody sees you,' said Ish. 'You can always … call the grandparents I suppose?'

The fierceness of sympathy this carried was shaming. I realised I was going to have to come clean about my lie but couldn't face doing so now. The others had moved away to give Luke space so I did the same, but his call was mumbling and brief.

'Me next,' said Ish.

'What do you say?' I asked Luke.

'Whatever you want. You might want to get the oldies to bring you stuff when they come to chapel. Some gloves, for starters.'

From inside the box I heard Ish addressing the operator, then the conversation switched into a language I didn't understand. When he came out I raised an eyebrow at Simon, who shook his head. 'I see my mum every day, don't I?'

'What about you?' said Luke.

'No,' I said.

We returned to the stream on the village green, where Simon took out his rod and began putting it together.

'You're not going to catch anything here,' said Luke.

'Doesn't mean it isn't worth fishing,' said Simon.

I'd been glancing at the phone box throughout. As they bickered I walked back, entered, unhooked the receiver, dialled 100 and gave the operator my grandparents' number. I watched the others messing about on the bridge as the phone rang.

'Two double seven?' said my grandmother's quavering voice.

'Will you accept a reverse charge call?'

'Eh?'

'Grandma, it's me.'

'Will you accept the charges, madam?'

'What?'

The operator took pity. 'Go ahead, please.'

'Hello?' shrieked my grandmother.

'It's Max,' I shouted.

'Max? Are you all right? What's happened?'

'Nothing. I'm just in the village so I thought I'd ring.'

'How you getting on?'

'The water's back on now. We had to clean our teeth in the snow for a bit.'

'Good Lord. I expect that was a bit chilly. Grandad's up the workshop. Do you want me to get him?'

I pictured the amount of time it would take, and while I wanted to hear the sound of her crossing to the back door, then carolling the word *Bob* at ear-splitting pitch, and then relish imagining his slow descent of the hill, there wasn't time.

'Just tell him I'm fine. I haven't had to use his coin yet.'

'Eh?'

'Nothing.'

'Your mother's ringing tonight. She'll be pleased to hear you're all right.'

As we said goodbye I became aware of a wash of blue light in my peripheral vision. Two fire engines had swept into the village and pulled up at the pub. Luke, Simon and Ish had disappeared. I stepped out of the phone box to watch as heavy-jacketed firemen filed round the building, scanning its roof and windows before going inside. The regulars stood grumbling by the door.

When they began conferring with the firemen and pointing in my direction, I turned to walk away, aware of a male voice saying *excuse me* with increasing urgency. No way was I stopping now. *Hey!* shouted the voice. But by then I had broken into a run.

I knocked at the open door and entered. Floorboards with heavy rugs. Huge, dark-wood cabinet laden with glassware, which simmered with every step I took. It was my first visit private-side since the day of the interview. Wagstaff had collared me as soon as I'd got back, asked me straight out if I'd used the phone box, then told me to report to the headmaster before tea.

I could hear Mrs Sutton's heels in the next room. I cleared my throat. The clicking stopped, then restarted in my direction.

'Denyer, is it?' she said, half visible in oak-panelled shadow. Perfume.

'Yes.'

'He's in his study.' She gestured to an archway to my right, in which I saw the foot of a stone spiral staircase. 'Get on with it. We've got dinner guests.'

I pulled myself up with the thick rope handrail. He sat hunched at his desk behind a circle of lamplight.

'C-couldn't wait to get at the phone, eh?'

'I'm sorry, sir. I just wanted to call my grandparents and tell them I was all right.'

'Is that so?'

'Yes, sir. Sorry, sir.'

'And you made no other c-calls?'

'What?'

'Do you know how b-busy the fire brigade is? How dealing with p-prank calls actually p-puts lives at risk?'

'The fire brigade? I didn't—'

'Oh shut up, I don't want to hear it. They saw you running away.' I would come to learn that he never stuttered when he was angry. 'I do hope we aren't going to have a problem with you.'

He reached behind a filing cabinet, sighing with the effort, and brought out a stick. Not a whippy, swishy cane but a gnarly, wizarding cudgel. It would not leave whippy swishy marks. It would bruise. It would break skin.

'You get one p-pass. Next time it's a proper b-belting. For now, fingers did the dialling, fingers m-meet the stick. Hold out your hand.'

'Sir, I—'

'Not another word. Hand out.' I held it out. He closed his eyes to the stupidity. 'Because you're new to this, I will be k-kind. Are you sure you want to offer me your right hand? Be p-practical.'

I held out the left, palm upwards, and he turned it over, still patiently instructive. He shifted his grip to my wrist, then struck, three times, as if dispatching a wounded animal.

The first blow was numbing. The second brought the world and the hand into sharp focus. The third blasted the hand far away, to a place below this carpeted floor, or the foot of the tower itself. Then I was somewhere else, watching jellyfish suspended in the dark wall of a breaking wave, its imminent crash like white noise which drowned out the pain and was the pain at the same time. It was only the feeling of sprung sweat on the back of my neck that returned me to the there and then. I looked round as if appealing to an unseen audience.

'Eyes front,' he said, giving my wrist an oddly tender squeeze before striking the hand another three times.

The thing had taken no time to happen but would exist forever. Nothing stays with you quite like injustice.

'I suppose that was as good a way as any for you to find out,' said Simon, appraising the damage. 'If in doubt: lie.'

'But I didn't need to lie,' I said. 'We weren't the ones who made the call.'

'Who did you think Luke was phoning?' said Simon. 'His parents are in Italy. He couldn't call them even if he wanted to. And there isn't much he won't do if he thinks something's unfair.'

8

Echo of the door's creak and slam as I braved the toilet block. Always colder in here, regardless of weather. Eight cubicles painted dark blue. Weak winter light further hindered by cobweb-choked skylights. After dark, sketchy reflections of any occupants were visible in these panes, should you care to look. Two adjacent stalls engaged this Saturday evening. I entered one quietly, threw the bolt, unzipped and sat. Slender gooseflesh thighs. The cold like a cough trapped in your chest. The conversation proceeded.

'What are you doing?' Confident, older voices.

'Putting paper down. Don't you ever do that? To stop the water splashing up. *Deaden the fall.*'

'Why are you scared of a bit of water?'

'It's what's in the water I'm afraid of.'

Tee hee.

There'd been a folded wad of paper already in the pan when I came in, which I hadn't bothered flushing away. The 'deadening' clearly standard practice.

The conversation moved on to Dungeons and Dragons and I waited for them to leave before I could relax. Precious silence. Stark light. Cold drips. *NOW WASH YOUR HANDS.*

Today's strangeness: a visit from the hunt. I'd been in the group who were instructed to take them sherry as they sat in their scarlet jackets astride enormous horses. Schooners sliding on polished silver trays as we dodged hooves which ruptured the turf we would normally be beaten for setting foot on. Nothing was a surprise any more.

I inspected my left hand. The swelling had gone down but the bruises had split over the last week into a spectrum of bilious yellows and blackening blues. The pain was still sharp but the healing process had introduced a maddening itching too.

Few items of clothing still carried the fragrance of my grandmother's detergent. Most by now had been assimilated into the system and impregnated with alien odours. But today my jumper still had a ghost of home about it. I held a sleeve to my face and inhaled, squandering the smell, believing it finite. For the first time I thought I might cry, and was grateful that the lapse had happened here. I let it happen. Took a couple of handfuls of paper to dry my face and blow my nose and stuck them between my legs into the pan.

Too quiet. Must be late for something. I stood and yanked the chain. Water chugged into the pan but the paper only balled and did not shift. I waited for the cistern to refill and tried again. The water level rose more, pooling at the lip of the bowl, fragments dancing. Time to leave.

Whether because I was panicking or something to do with the cold, when I tried to unlock the door, it wouldn't move. Anxiety sped things up. I dropped to the floor, rolled under the partition into the next-door cubicle and got to my feet.

NOW WASH YOUR HANDS.

Horror. A brisk flush from a far stall I had not believed occupied, and appearing in the mirror behind me was the face of Ali Price.

He would question my activities. Report them. On top of everything else.

But his features were chilled. It was the face of someone elsewhere entirely. He didn't wash his own hands, or acknowledge my presence. If I didn't know better I'd have thought he was in pain.

The next day was Sunday, which meant letters. Telling the truth was a waste of time. Your envelope was handed over unsealed and if you'd written anything they didn't like you'd have to start again. More practical to produce what they wanted and get on with the day. We sat in silence at rows of desks in one of the big rooms on the ground floor, dashing off different variations of the same fraudulently bland communication. The air smelled of ink and pencil shavings, with a backdrop of meat and vegetables as lunch massed behind the scenes.

My left hand shook as I rested it across the top of my pad and tried to strike the right tone of response to the flimsy blue aerogramme I had received from my mother. She had asked me to tell her all about my new life and reassured me that I was missing nothing back there in the old one, in a place which I now knew myself without question to have imagined.

Weapons Davis stopped by my desk and smiled. 'How's the hand, Denyer? I must say, it's wonderful to see someone new throwing himself into the life of the school. I heard all about your disgusting antics with the fire brigade, and I see Mr Sutton has responded in kind. He never lets me down.'

The encounter might have gone on further had it not been for the surprise entrance of Clive Whittle the caretaker, who appeared in the doorway carrying a plunger and said, 'Word with you, Eric, if you please.'

Weapons Davis performed a camp turn on his heels. 'It goes without saying that there will be nothing but the scribble of platitudes to Mummy until I return.'

When he'd gone, two older boys half-heartedly chucked the paper balls of their abandoned early drafts, but by and large peace was sustained, so we mostly had our heads down when he reappeared, and it took time to work out what was going on, because what we were seeing was nonsense.

'Right.' Triumphant. Incandescent. He carried in both hands a waterlogged lump of paper flecked with something dark. It dripped on the floorboards and was the shape of a rugby ball but bigger. He took up a position behind the supervising desk and planted the offending object on its surface. Water pooled on the wood and ran forward.

'Mr Whittle informs me that someone has seen fit not only to block the toilet but also to abscond beneath the cubicle partitions, leaving the door locked while the bowl continued to fill and causing a major flood. It is of course hilarious, and the boy responsible will now take the credit.'

I wondered who would do such a thing, suspecting the hand of Luke Price. Then I felt blood prickling the skin of my face and heard a rushing in my ears.

'I've got all day,' he said. 'I'm going nowhere.'

He craved something like this. Something he could really get his teeth into. The situation would only deteriorate, and surely if I just explained then it would be obvious I hadn't done anything wrong, so just after he'd passed my desk I raised my left hand, hoping perhaps that the sight of it would help my cause, closing my eyes in anticipation of the reaction when he took it in.

He never saw it. Simon Drake sprang from the adjacent desk, grabbed my hand and threw it back at me with a stare of such intensity that the urge to confess was quashed. Meanwhile, Weapons Davis had stopped at Luke's desk with an ominous leer.

'Why are you looking at me?' said Luke. 'I had nothing to do with this.' Always the direct approach with him, the fearlessness.

'I was just,' said Weapons sweetly, 'admiring that smart red stationery of yours.' He reached into his jacket pocket, withdrew the weeks-old envelope and threw it on the desk.

'That proves nothing! Anyone could have put their sweetcorn in there.'

'Idiot.' He grabbed Luke by the front, propelled him out of his chair and pinned him to the wall with a forearm across his neck. The inequality was stark. 'You're going to actually tell me what was in the envelope? Idiot.'

The next few sentences came out mumbled as they were punctuated by slams of Luke's body against the wall. There was a stack of canvas chairs in the way, and rather than move his activities elsewhere he incorporated these into his routine, driving Luke repeatedly against their edges, letting them list and topple, using the hindrance to sustain his rage. Clear windows of opportunity like this didn't come along often.

... had enough of you thinking you can get away with showing no respect in here ...

Silence from the rest of us, thick with nausea. You'd think the question in my head would have expired by now but it hadn't. Not quite yet.

Can they do this?

I closed my eyes, so I could only hear the impotent connections. Even so newly arrived, I understood that we were bonded in our determination to keep quiet. Years later I would look back with pride at the implication that we had decided to stay silent because it was more shaming for the teacher. Which it was. But it wasn't the reason we said nothing. We said nothing because we were terrified children.

Which was what made Luke so unusual.

His head was down as he was pushed one last time against the panelling, so when he spoke, Weapons Davis couldn't hear him at first. 'Speak up. What are you saying?'

He sniffed up bloody snot. The words came out with calm contempt. 'I'm saying: you just carried a ball of shitty toilet paper in here. You should probably wash your hands.'

The helplessness of the laughter that erupted took it out of him. He tried finishing with a cuff to the head but it glanced off and Luke's flushed face glared up, daring him to do more. Luke even waved the ripped sleeve of his jumper like a trophy.

To know something's wrong is one thing. To be ten or eleven years old and call it out is entirely another.

'We'll see what Mr Sutton has to say about this,' said Weapons Davis. 'The rest of you, finish in silence and leave your letters on the desk. Cheer up, everyone!' he hollered from the door, holding Luke by the scruff. 'It's Chicken à la King for lunch!'

All this, on the day I had longed for. The day that would temporarily return to me something so taken for granted before. But the morning had jumped in front of the day, and now the day was gone.

You had to hand it to them: the systems were tried and tested and devil-clever. Only a week earlier I might have been close enough to the other life to tell him more. Now he would come and go and new life would thunder on. Which is not to say that my pulse didn't skip with pleasure when I came out of chapel and saw his van parked alongside all the parental saloons and hatchbacks.

So began the first of many precious half-hours spent in passenger seats cursing the inevitability of Sunday lunch. I got inside to the smell of dogs and the cannoning forward of Jack from the back and never had the lick of a collie been more welcome.

'How do,' he said.

I pulled my coat sleeve forward over my left hand and dropped it to the side of the car. He passed me an open box of pre-hammered Thornton's toffee. He didn't ask questions. He waited for me to decide what I wanted to tell him.

'We had to take sherry out to the hunt,' I said.

'Bloody hell.'

'I had to carry it on a silver tray.'

'Bunch of prats. I'd like to send them off into the woods with a lot of dogs chasing them and see how they get on.'

Weapons Davis was making his way down the chapel path, passing dangerously close. Tinted glasses. Mustard sports jacket. Tie tucked in trousers. These entities should never meet. It was against the laws of physics.

My grandfather laughed full in his face. 'Who's that rum bugger?'

'History teacher,' I muttered. To name him might show we were talking about him, and then what would happen? As he passed, he stared at the spray of muck up the van's sides, at its butchered bonnet and bolted-on vertical exhaust. He'd heard us. There was no doubt. 'He's strict.'

'How do you mean?'

'He gets cross when people don't wash their hands.'

'Shouting at them?'

'Belting them too, sometimes. I think.'

'Well then, we better not laugh at him too much. Have another toffee.'

I shook my head. I was already feeling sick from the first. 'Can you get me signed up for extract of malt?'

'What?'

'People have it before bed. You have to give permission.'

'What do you want that for?'

I shrugged. 'It's food.'

'All right. I'll get your grandma to tell them. Here. Brought you something.' He reached behind my seat and pulled up a big unmarked plastic bag. 'Cash-and-carry special. Nuts, raisins and chocolate pips. Don't eat all the chocolate first, else you'll never want the rest.'

The very idea. 'I can't take that.'

'Course you can. Take it in your jacket and stick it under your false bottom. Then you shan't need any bloody extract of malt to keep you going.'

There was no way of telling him how far apart our worlds had become. Already I foresaw Weapons Davis waiting for me behind the door, swatting the package from my coat onto the flagstones and sending me in to Sutton for a pre-lunch beating. 'Can you bring my gloves next time? And a torch for reading.'

'Righto.'

'Better go. Lunchtime.' I had noticed a boy sprinting across the car park and now he grabbed the bell-pull on the side of the building and tugged it into life.

Halfway from the van to the door I slowed down, fighting an impulse to run back and say *Drive. Drive away now.* I knew he'd have done it without question.

It was an acutely puzzling moment. Why hadn't I said more? I felt dumbstruck by the terms of a contract I had no memory of signing. The system had imposed its own logic so completely that it already felt absurd to ask the person I most trusted in the world whether or not this was how things were supposed to be.

He didn't like to drive off having dropped me somewhere until I was out of sight. This habit would destroy me later in life, watching him sit patiently behind the wheel outside railway stations as I waited for my train. But my contraband wasn't going to hide itself, so I ran inside, trying to tell myself that he wasn't about to go, that I was only popping back in to fetch something.

I rushed through the Great Hall to get to my box before going in for lunch, rehearsing the lock's combination in my head, when a voice from behind a gaping *Sunday Telegraph* near the fire shocked me into paralysis.

'Was that your grandfather in that plausibly agricultural vehicle?'

'Yes, sir.'

'Most parents find the energy to greet the masters when they come and visit. And struggle into chapel.'

'I think he was more interested in seeing me,' I said.

'Ha!'

I tried not to break my stride, thinking *rum bugger rum bugger*, like an incantation, hoping to retain my grandfather's outlook even as I knew it was vanishing down the avenue in the whistle of a Louis Armstrong tune. I shot straight past my box, slipped into the toilet block and hurled the food to the bottom of the paper towel bin before going into lunch.

'The rumours are true,' said Simon, studying the type-written menu as I slid onto the bench beside him. 'It's Chicken à la King.'

At the end of the meal Tony Sutton rose to his feet and prepared to speak. Always a torturous process, this. We fell silent, and those of us who worried we might laugh during the agonising silences of his word-hurdles began preparing our straight-face strategies. It wasn't that we laughed at the stutter, but that there was a long-standing competition in place to make others laugh as he stood there, jiggling his leg against the obstructions of his stubborn mouth. It was the Holy Grail of sabotage. If you could get someone to lose it while it was actually happening, we could only imagine what kind of punishment would ensue.

He opened with some housekeeping notices, then said, 'It won't have escaped anyone's attention that we had a hunt m-m-', heel tapping, eyes closed, savour the earnest looks of interest on the faces of the other teachers, as if they're *competing* to empathise, 'meet-up here yesterday m-morning. And tradition dictates that the day after, weather p-permitting, we p-play ...?'

Silence as everyone assumed he was grappling again, then he turned an expectant face on the room.

The chant started quietly so that I didn't get what they were saying until it had risen to a shout and been joined by the thunder of feet stamping on floorboards.

Hare and Hounds. Hare and Hounds. Hare and Hounds.

We lined up in our games kit outside. Golden winter light splashed through the trees, picking out the dark masses of crows' nests in their branches. Everyone wore hats and gloves, even those who were usually proud of toughing it out unaccessorised.

Wagstaff was master of ceremonies. 'Well then, you lucky people. The excuses are in, and everyone who wants to wimp out has made their case to Miss Fletcher, so by my calculations we have fifty-three able-bodied players. Here's the bucket of joy. Take one and only one. Take it quickly. No feeling around. Chop-chop.'

The bucket contained fifty-three balls of screwed-up paper. Soon everyone held one in his or her hands.

'On the count of three ... open.'

I had assumed we were playing some variant of orienteering, so I unballed mine expecting to find written instructions. What I found instead was a curled-up length of red ribbon. All around me people were whooping with relief at not having found a curled-up length of red ribbon.

'Denyer! Denyer's a hare, sir.'

'Wags.' I was surprised to see Simon holding up his hand. 'I don't think it's fair on him. He's new.'

Wagstaff exhaled grandly. 'Well! What do you propose, Mr Drake? Are you going to do it instead of him?'

'If you like.'

'The nobility! But think of how your gesture will deprive poor Denners here. Think of the shame he will feel.'

'I can do it,' I said. Whatever *it* is.

'Good man,' said Wags.

Simon spoke so quickly I had to process it later as I ran. 'Listen carefully. They always pile off the main hill. So your best bet is to head down the back lane, not where we walked the other day. If you hear anyone coming, hide. Even if it's me and only me. Nobody's allowed to behave normally while this is going on. If they see you, run. If you hear them getting close and you can't decide where to run, climb. The most important thing is—'

'Enough jabbering! Form a line. Ribbons round your arms. Nice and high, so everyone can see them.'

The head start was two minutes. A whistle was blown and the four hares ran off down the hill. One of the others was someone I knew called Ross Hawkins. We jogged alongside one another until he got frustrated and told me to go in a different direction. Then I must have wasted time deciding where to go because before long I heard the cold honk of a hunting horn and high-pitched, approaching voices.

I stumbled into a shallow depression riddled with fox holes. The earth was overturned from the day before. I found a tiny scrap of fur, picked it up and rubbed it on my cheek, in scrambled hope that it might bring me better luck than it had its owner. Then I heard crunching bracken and a lanky kid called Chris Webster was looking down into the clearing.

He gestured frantically. 'Get out of here. Go.'

'Isn't that the end of the game? You've found me.'

'That's not how it works.'

'Why can't we hide together?'

'Because if they find me hiding you, I get it worse. Go.'

I looked at him, unable to understand. His eyes changed and he ran at me and kicked me hard in the thigh. 'Fucking run. One minute, then I'm joining in.'

I bolted, slipping in the mud, caking my tracksuit bottoms. I found a tree and climbed it, higher than anybody could think to look.

The horn. Voices below. My deafening breathing. Two-dimensional figures. Heads and arms.

'He was right here,' said Chris Webster, saving face. 'I saw him. He's nearby somewhere.' I held my breath, trying to achieve the impossibility of hiding behind leafless branches.

A figure in a baggy blue tracksuit who hung back from the rest looked up, and Simon's face was locked on mine. His head snapped away. He pointed. 'There.'

'Where?'

'That holly bush. Go.'

The crowd surrounded it. Sticks were grabbed and used to poke inside. Ross Hawkins broke free and got some distance before they took him down.

After a while, the pack moved on, Jack West waving the red ribbon above his head, leaving the beaten hare lying in the bracken.

Hawkins fled the scene, sniffing softly. I waited until I could hear no human sound, allowing myself to step back from the situation as I had in Sutton's study. Then I climbed down and moved off.

The temperature was dropping, the light failing, the ground laid with traps. I had somehow cut my right knee through my tracksuit bottoms. I pulled them up to see a thin delta of blood trickling down my ankle. I circled the grounds until the tea bell rang out, then took a circuitous route through the undergrowth that brought me out onto the North Lawn. From there I could see the steamed-up windows as the meal proceeded within, and inside along with tales of the chase it would be all *swap your ham for my fish paste* and the milky tea would be gushing from the urn and maybe a few of them would be wondering where I was. It was tempting to sidle in but I knew that appearing in the middle of the meal might bring unwelcome attention.

That did leave the possibility of a solitary shower. I entered via the cloister and plunged into the heat and silence of the changing rooms. My clothes fell stiffly to the floor. I took a towel to the cubicle with the big shower head and stood with my eyes closed feeling the chilblain fire spread.

How was I no longer charming in this place? I would work on it. I would win these people or lose myself trying.

'Hare!'

The shout echoed from the doorway then passed down the line of kids who had finished eating and come looking.

'You didn't get me,' I said. 'Doesn't that mean I won?'

They piled into the shower stall. The first kicks came in. I balled myself up, watching water spiral into the plughole.

Hare. Hare. Hare.

'Enough.' Weapons Davis barged his way through to the front of the group and looked down at me. 'Well, Denyer, in trouble again. Why weren't you at tea? We've been worried sick.'

'I was the hare, sir, and they didn't catch me so I—'

'We don't miss meals. Report to the headmaster when you're dressed.'

9

I SPENT MORE time alone. I was capable of being alone without feeling lonely. It was not my first time in a new school. But my brushes with the law had not gone unnoticed.

The girls were an afterthought, incorporated comparatively recently in a bid to drum up more cash by bringing in the sisters. There were twenty at most. You could tell some of the teachers would have preferred it if they weren't here. Yet here they were.

The heat of scrutiny as I walked out from the shop one Sunday with my sweets. The kiosk under the cloisters was open only once a week, and like everyone else, I had developed habits when it came to the little white bag. I liked to hold mine for a bit, anticipating what was within. Beer bottles. Fizzy cola. Jazzles. I had perhaps lashed out on a Caramac, though they made a big dent in the weekly 30p allowance which would be tacked onto your bill at the end of term.

Becky Lynch and two of her friends stood in a posse by the swing on the North Lawn. She was in my year, but looked older. She was talked about. Poor Neil Lynch was her twin brother but in their levels of ease and integration they couldn't have been more different. I remember once hearing Weapons Davis joke that she must have preyed on him in the womb.

'Don't you eat your sweets?' said Becky, pointing at my neatly folded bag.

I approached, sensing permission. 'I will soon.'

'You can't save them. It's not allowed because of the rats.'

'I'm not going to save them.'

'You're friends with Simon Drake.'

'Yes.'

'He's weird. Why do you like him?'

'He's kind to me.'

'Let's have a turn then, if we're not eating.' She stepped onto the seat of the swing. 'Are you coming?'

'What do you want me to do?'

'Stand here, of course.'

The other two girls, one Moroccan, one English, exchanged words and laughed. I pocketed my sweets and took a chain of the swing, pulling myself up as confidently as I could manage. Becky's feet shot apart, forcing me to place mine between hers. I had seen her doing this with others but now it was my turn.

'What now?' I said.

'What do you think?'

I could smell aniseed on her breath and sweat through her Aertex shirt. I felt pressure at our centres as we occupied each other's space.

She applied herself with a forceful plunge, digging into the motion and sending me back and upwards. Her eyes communicated that I must do the same. I did not. We fell back to the position we had started in.

'This one's good for nothing,' she shouted for the gallery. 'It only works if we both do it.'

This time I was ready. As we reached the apex of the backswing I took as much of my own weight as I could in the grip the chains, then threw it into my feet.

The energy of her centre of gravity. The surprising control she exerted. Her hair whipping at my face. Eyes meeting, her smiling, then biting on her lower lip to apply herself and shock me into going higher. Uncomfortable at first, then not. Working against each other, then working towards a common goal.

Later that week I married Becky Lynch in the sunlit chapel doorway. Her friends from the swing officiated. We used ring-pulls from cans of Tango that were left over from a sailing trip to the reservoir.

Such unions did not last long but they were binding for as long as they did. You wouldn't call them crushes. Associations would be a better word. You might sit together during Prep. Leave notes in each other's lockers. Meet somewhere in secret like the boot hut or the cricket pavilion. Rumours abounded of the stuff people had done during such assignations. The attention boosted vanity. A sort of priggish, proprietorial air came over the participants. Let nobody say we weren't in training for adulthood.

The transition from one lesson into another, different classes merging in the stable-block corridors. The rising chatter of voices unbridled after class.

I wasn't looking out for Becky Lynch. I only noticed her because a loud, blond kid in the top year called Joel Evans had sneaked up and begun humping her from behind like a randy goblin. Without consciously deciding to and even though he was two years above me I grabbed a handful of his hair and yanked his head backwards. Miraculously he lost his balance and the rest of Joel Evans came too. The crowd laughed. Becky Lynch turned.

'What's wrong with you, Denyer?' he said from the floor, his face bright red.

'She couldn't see you,' I said.

I had broken so many rules you couldn't even list them.

The following day Joel Evans and I fought under the arch of the stable block surrounded by a circle of baying spectators, who doubled as cover in case we were found. We had appointed seconds. Simon took my coat with a resigned expression on his face, keen to return to his servos and switches.

I wanted it to be over and wanted to let them know I was serious and these two objectives seemed to align. I hit him near the mouth, grazing a knuckle on his tooth. The lip bled. Shocked faces stared. The thing was pageantry and I had failed to understand.

When the crying began in earnest I watched it from some cool, internal room. It might as well have been happening to somebody else.

I had been dreading the moment when it happened in front of other people. But when it inevitably did, nobody took the slightest bit of notice. It was as if some prime directive had come into force, overriding all empathy. Pupil and teacher alike looked away as if it simply wasn't happening.

So I did it more. I embarked on a grand public project of crying. The question of shame was redundant. Since nobody was taking any notice, there was no reason to hide it. I cried in chapel. On the games pitch. During meals. At bedtime. When asked a question in class I could answer it without breaking my flow.

Still, nothing. It was if they all believed that the supply of tears, however voluminous, must surely be finite, and the best option was just to get on with other things while it exhausted itself.

I began to doubt my own existence. To wonder whether there was anything I could not do, if they were seeing this happening and failing to act on it. I could strip naked. Light a fire. Look up girls' skirts. Follow them into the shower. Cut someone. Cut myself.

In the evenings I gave up reading and stared at the ceiling instead. I perfected the trick of dropping out of myself, of contemplating a piece of dried-out Sellotape from some long-past year's Christmas decorations until it, and I, had ceased to mean anything. I thought about death, and imagined I was preparing myself for it. I imagined that this nothingness might be what it was like.

I discovered the awesome cleansing power of a good dream – the ones I had at this time were more powerful than any others I can remember, perhaps because I needed them so badly. Tropical environments of flowers and hummingbirds. Burger bars and guardhouses. Yellow, infinite cities.

I wondered if what was happening was my fault. If I had been made permanently alien by living abroad. To those who had always been here it was logical that you could get beaten for breaking a rule you didn't fully understand. That unscrubbed fingernails could lead to caning of the buttocks. That the wrong pair of shoes or the right pair of shoes improperly cleaned could cause you to be chucked around a room by someone impossibly powerful and angry. That speaking to your family or possessing food could get you attacked.

I missed my grandfather and his words for things. *Jacks. Strawbs. Goosegogs.* I missed feeling at home in his world. In any world. He was able to find any world charming for the humanity he divined therein. Might he be able to help me here if I learned to think like him?

I lay in bed gripping his Victoria crown and hearing his voice. I let it chunter on, telling me all the old stories. Uncle Harry who shot off his own arm. Uncle Laurie who fell down the stairs. And then, abruptly, I understood that it was pointless. He couldn't help me, no matter how tightly I held his magic coin. I was alone. The moment was very calming.

In bed one night not long after that, I had turned onto my side to cry, screwing up my eyes to facilitate the release in my now customarily pragmatic way. So I missed the torchlight playing on the panelling as Crimble came in.

Here was a curious oceanographer descended to explore the gloom, his beam igniting my tear-trails like bioluminescence. The torchlight reflected off his glasses. His face lacked definition because of the beard. He spoke at a level that was audible to me but didn't wake anyone else.

Up you get.

He unhooked my dressing gown and held it while I slipped my arms inside. To have been found crying felt embarrassing now it had been acknowledged. I concentrated on slowing my breathing as I followed him out of the room. Final shudders. Get it out.

The carpet slipped under my feet where the stair rods were loose. From the stairwell I heard the squeaking of hamsters in their wheels. The smell of rodents and sawdust rose.

His room was off a long corridor opposite the two largest dormitories, Waterloo and Trafalgar. It contained a desk, a sideboard and a bed. I could smell his dog, but the dog wasn't here. He told me to sit on the bed, poured milk into a pan and put it on a hot ring on the sideboard.

'You've had a rocky start,' he said. 'Many do. It's perfectly normal. Do you understand that?'

'I guess.'

'So there's no need to feel ashamed for feeling the way that you do. Every one of these tough boys around you felt like this when they started. Okay?'

'Okay.'

'What is it in particular that's getting you down tonight?' I shrugged. 'You're missing home.' I nodded. 'So – tell me about it. What would you be doing if you were at home today?'

I could have told him about life back in Mexico. About the driver who used to take me to school. About the club where I played water polo on Saturday mornings. But it seemed easier to talk about life down the hill with my grandparents. He listened, and laughed, and asked questions. Before I knew it I was telling longer stories, working my audience. As I talked, he spooned chocolate powder into a mug and poured milk on top. When he handed me the mug it was so hot I could barely hold it. I thought this a very good thing since it would take ages to cool and that way I could stay here for longer.

'The thing you have to remember is,' he said, 'none of what you're describing has gone anywhere. It will all be there when you go back. And wouldn't they be happier, knowing you were happy up here? Do you want them to feel miserable? Don't you owe it to them to make the best of this?'

I was working out my reply when I heard a blurted sound from something in the room I hadn't taken in: a large, cube-shaped object under a paisley throw. My first thought was that he must have a parrot in a cage. He pulled away the fabric to reveal a machine with dials and backlit gauges and a wire connected to a handheld mic.

'Ham radio set,' he said. 'It lets you to talk to people anywhere in the world. Even people you've never met before.'

'Why do you want to talk to people you haven't met before?' My guard was down. I was speaking without thinking. Allowing myself to be happy.

'Why *wouldn't* you? You can find all sorts of people on here. Talk to them about anything. We could probably find someone in Mexico if you like. You could talk to them in Spanish. Only we can't at the moment, because it's broken.'

'What's wrong with it?'

'Not my forte, I'm afraid. I have no idea how these things work. It's probably just a loose connection. But at the moment everything is garbled, and I just don't trust Mr Whittle enough to send him poking around in there to fix it. Anyway – when I get it working, you should come up here again and we'll go round the world. Would you like that?'

'Yes.'

'It's a deal.'

'My grandfather could probably fix it,' I said.

He smiled. 'Good old Grandad. I can tell the two of you are close. But I wouldn't dream of imposing my problems on him. Where do they live again?'

'About six miles away.' I gave the name of the village. 'I could have been a day boy only my parents didn't want me to stay with them because they're too old and tired.'

He laughed. 'You don't hold back, do you?'

'Grandad says it's important to say what you're thinking, even if other people don't like it.'

'Well, he sounds like a very wise man.'

Given how close his mother lived and that she was there most days, it seemed odd that Simon didn't sleep at home – painfully so to me. But I could see that his dual-citizenship brought advantages. Because there was always somewhere else he could have been, and because his mother was, while not a teacher, employed by the school, it was uniquely possible for him to be in charge of his own affairs. When the need arose he could slip down the hill with his fishing rod or pop the hood of a computer and be gone. I had been learning to open my inner escape hatches, but he had real ones. And this advantage, this competitive edge, was most evident of all during our lessons in what was still called Information Technology.

His expertise was so far ahead of anybody else's that during IT he was given a desk to himself where he could pursue his projects uninterrupted, breaking only when he was needed to assist others, teacher included.

The lessons were taught by a retired Cornish airman resplendent in the name of Austin Spinks. He was red-faced and red-haired and his face was so angular it looked like it had been designed with a set square. In the usual run of things, Spinks was not to be trifled with – he was known to be free with a wooden metre-rule in Maths classes when his temper took him – but in this context he was positively deferential.

'Drake, I wonder if you could give me a hand over here please,' he said, scratching at his head as he gazed at the screen.

His bewilderment was a picture. It was too good.

'On my way, sir,' said Simon, trying to keep a straight face.

Such moments provided a fine opportunity for me to visit Simon's workstation and sabotage whatever he was doing for fun. Flickering on the monitor of his Commodore 64 was a pixelated image in purple and blue, with text beneath it.

You are outside a rocky cave.
Command > W
Inside, the cave is cool, damp and rock-strewn.
Command >

The game was called *Mindshadow*, and he was obsessed with it. You woke up on a beach with no memory and had to navigate your way around a desert island until you found a way to get rescued. After that there were levels on a pirate ship, then in London and Luxembourg, where finally, having entered the right prompts, you arrived at the hotel room where you would discover the truth about who had betrayed you and left you for dead. Simon would spend hours in this world. He considered it to be training for the composition of his own labyrinthine game based on the topography of the school.

I exited the game, rebooted the computer, and typed the only lines of BASIC I knew before returning to my ZX Spectrum on the other side of the room.

10 PRINT "MAX DENYER RULES"
20 GOTO 10

The infinite message ribboned across the screen as Simon returned to his desk.

'Hilarious, Max Denyer,' he called, without looking up.

'I've got a job for you,' I said after the lesson, and described the problem of Crimble's broken radio. I had assumed Simon would relish the challenge. But there was something spiky about his reaction.

'Why would I want to fix his radio?' he said.

'Because you like fixing things.'

He looked away. 'I'll think about it.'

An inkling of something. 'What's the matter? Don't you like him?'

'How could I not like him? Everybody likes old Crimble, don't they?'

'I don't get it.'

'Why does everyone suck up to him so much? Why do *you* want to fix his radio?'

'He was kind to me.'

'Oh, yeah. Crimble's brilliant. He's a saint.' He stopped walking and made a real effort to speak without hostility. 'I know you're trying to help me by pretending you don't know, but you don't need to, okay?'

'Don't know what?'

'You really haven't heard? Nobody's told you?'

'No.'

He sighed. 'He's having a … thing with my mum.'

'Oh.'

'At least, that's what everybody says. You haven't heard that?'

'No.'

'You're not just saying that to make me feel better? I thought everybody was talking about it.'

'Not to me. Does he stay at her house and stuff then?'

'I don't want to know. You seriously haven't heard anything?'

'No.'

It made sense that this should be something he would dread. Even before you got into the weirdness of a teacher getting together with your mother, the survival strategy Simon had evolved was about never interacting with staff unless he couldn't help it. It was how he had kept on the right side of Sutton, Weapons Davis and the rest.

After this conversation, I did start to hear things. Snarky remarks. Mutterings about special treatment. It was common knowledge soon enough. But people were never as mean about it as he had feared, and eventually it was declared to be off-limits. I think the majority felt sympathy. No matter how much any of us wanted to be nearer to home, we didn't want home to be here either, and we certainly didn't want our mum mixed up in the life of the school like that.

Simon's mother never features in my account of the strangeness of the beginning, because she wasn't strange. Her company was respite. She was a tall, dark woman, with an inherently serious resting expression, which everyone took at face value: her husband had died, so she was assumed to be sad. This made her waspish asides feel all the more subversive and joyous, should you be lucky enough to hear one. She went along with the school's weird ways but let those of us who were listening know that she thought them ridiculous. Which led naturally to the conclusion that her home life with Simon was equally open and uncomplicated. I see her now, standing in some unfrequented corner on a break from typing Tony Sutton's letters to parents, screwing a heel onto the butt of one of the many cigarettes she thought nobody noticed her smoking. I see her, seeing it all, or so it seemed, for what it was.

Simon stood nervously as we waited for Crimble to answer the knock. I thought he was going to bottle it and walk away. Crimble hadn't been expecting us and his hair was stuck up as if he'd been sleeping. We went in and he unscrewed the back of the radio set. While Simon was peering in and unpacking his kit, Crimble produced two Mars bars and set them down.

'Fuel for the workers,' he said.

Simon set about identifying the faulty wire and soldering it back together. It wasn't long before the radio crackled into life.

'You're a miracle worker,' said Crimble. 'You're wasted here. You should get out into the world and start changing it.'

Simon smiled in spite of himself. 'You could have done it yourself.'

'But I didn't,' said Crimble. 'Because I didn't have to. And now I can talk to all my friends again. You've made me very happy indeed. Now both of you better get off to your ablutions. It's Mr Weathers-Davis on duty tonight, so whatever you may have done for me I fear you are in his hands.'

10

I COULD SAY that everything felt different after that, and it would be true, but even though Crimble was the main reason why, he wasn't the only reason. The strange can only be strange for so long. Look what happened after that plane crash in the Andes with the Uruguayan rugby players. At first they were just stripping off bits of thigh meat from bodies buried by avalanches. By the time they were found there was a production line in progress: strips of flesh drying up and down the plane's fuselage; favourite bowls fashioned from the skulls of dead friends. You can get used to anything at all.

So the place was fitted onto me as it had been onto everyone else. And whether it rubbed you sore or gave you special powers, it was on you all the same. Friendships waxed and waned. We played wizard games with many-sided dice, gravitating to these as we did to role-playing books because they provided an element of self-determination which was entirely lacking in our real lives. Witches and warlocks were one thing but they were nowhere near as fantastical as the concept of choice. We extrapolated from these and devised new games of our own. Developed our own eccentric customs and habits. We became less knowable to our parents by the day, and our own strangeness went entirely unchecked so long as we observed the strangenesses imposed on us by the school.

I am struck by the recollection of how much everyday life was characterised by violence. An unofficial contest was under way at all times to see who could fashion the most devastating weapon: multi-pronged shanks of compass points and art-room razor blades; slingshots of rubber bands lashed to protractors; set squares glued together and sharpened into throwing stars; balls of Blu-Tack studded with drawing pins or sharpened pencils. They were devices with terrible wounding potential, and no mere ornaments. They were put to use, either to settle scores or to launch unprovoked lightning attacks on the usual grounds: anything as long as it's funny. Just try unsheathing your new SHATTERPROOF ruler if you dare. As soon as one of the right people had laid eyes on it, it would be mangled, twisted, chipped. The very word a provocation.

Our scabs told drawn-out stories. We played with our wounds, cherished them. It was quite normal to biro doodles around a pair of skin-punctures from the points of a set of dividers, or sit idly evaluating whether a stray flap of skin was worth trying to reattach or good only for chewing off. Ordinary pastimes were gingered up with pain. A game of cards was incomplete without the penalty of the loser having his or her knuckles skinned with the deck by the winner. The packs we carried were edged brown with the blood of the vanquished. We fetishised catalogues of air rifles and slingshots, having subscribed to them for the excitement of receiving post as much as anything else. Weapons Davis would browse the range approvingly over our shoulders, lip curling in fascination, advising on what the most effective hypothetical purchases might be.

'That's a very good one,' he'd say. 'Splendid.'

It was a dispassionate kind of violence, born less of anger than of boredom and the examples we'd been set. Ultimately, we all knew it was us against them. However long it took, everybody came round to the realisation that a lot of them were furious with us, and it was pointless to try to understand why.

Small wonder that we cleaved to Crimble. He was respite from all that. From the horrible ways we treated each other when none of them were looking. From the corrosive anxiety we felt around so many of his colleagues.

There was an ensemble cast, of course. Plenty of benign characters and some perfectly nice ones in addition to the demented martinets. Women in floral dresses with hair in their eyes. Haggard, elbow-patched men smelling of tobacco and sweat. An elderly, bald Canadian who taught Science in a pandemonium of escaped locusts and dicey experiments. A succession of hearty northerners who did stints teaching Games. A man with a long beard who taught Art and Scripture, and was said to be so biblical in outlook that he used the word 'yonder' in everyday conversation.

I realise now that many of them were racked with boredom too. The lifers depended on their hobbies to address this. Spinks and his computers. Crimble and his ham radio. Weathers-Davis and his weapons. The younger staff were freer to see the place as it was, and frequently, when they thought no one was looking, appeared as bewildered as we were to find themselves there.

When holidays came round we returned to the compartments of our other lives, and didn't look back. Because children don't analyse, they only experience. Far easier to relegate the other world to the status of a dream, and hope it didn't recur.

After that first term, things gather pace and the memories of years coexist like jumble in an attic. Incident, habit and legend are indistinguishable from one another. Once the everyday strange has been accepted, events stay with me for less obvious reasons, or for reasons that only come into focus much later.

The watery-green dining room on a winter morning. Tea urns steaming furiously. Steam so thick it seems granular, shot through with sunlight from the North Lawn. Panes running with condensation, gathered grime silting in the curly stone frames. It might be an agreeable scene if we were permitted to talk above a whisper, but since Weapons Davis is of the opinion that conversation steams the windows up more, a clenched silence characterises the meal.

Sitting beside me, the man himself, who often prefers not to use the masters' table but to place himself instead in the pit of the children, the better to curb all babble. He broods over his *Telegraph*, a plate of fried bread and egg in progress. Periodically he snorts when something amuses him, then lays down his paper to prepare another mouthful, mashing yolk and white into a glistening square of bread before placing it inside his mouth and reopening the paper. You'd think he was in the breakfast room of a hotel.

On the next table a dispute has arisen over command of the Marmite. Someone wants it down one end. Someone else is refusing to pass it. But since it's Weapons Davis on duty, the whole thing has to play out in silence. As I watch, Ali Price, at one end of the table, holds up the jar, eyebrows raised. At the other end a boy called Guy Robertson raises a casual arm to receive it. It's madness. There are ten pupils on each side, and a minefield of plates and cups in between should the throw go awry.

But the dare has been set. Glancing to make sure Weapons Davis is distracted, Ali brings back his hand and releases the big black jar, which flies in a perfect trajectory, finding Guy's at the other end, although the throw is so powerful that Robertson has to sit up in his chair to reach for the catch, nearly falling backwards. There's a submerged gasp of triumph, one hundred boys and twenty girls in one glorious, secret moment.

'Ha!' says Weapons Davis.

Cardiac plummet. He reaches to his belt and unsheathes his Bowie knife. He brings it up and cuts into the newspaper, filleting it of the article which has tickled him. He removes the jagged rectangle, sets it down, then stabs it into place on the table. Behind him, Robertson throws the jar skywards in triumph and catches it again, and Ali Price's face is lit with joy.

Weapons Davis shoots me a tetchy glance, sweeps the room and returns to his paper. 'Denyer,' he says, 'if you want anyone to take you seriously in life, you're going to have to learn not to gape in fear at the slightest surprising thing. People will think you're touched.'

Sunday morning, sometime that year. Summer? Who knows. I'm walking past the classroom in which, as head boy, Ali Price is allowed to do his prep by himself, with his own music. I greet him through the open door. He says nothing, stands and shuts the door in my face. Inside he presses play on his ghetto blaster and the introduction to 'Money For Nothing' fades in. Moodiness has its place in this world. It is tolerated and even encouraged one pupil to another in a way that baffles me now. Later I will think I understand that it has something to do with trying to be grown up. To march around demonstrably having problems you don't want to discuss. But Ali Price's behaviour on this day is puzzling. As the rest of us get on with our Sunday he stays bunkered in that classroom, listening to the introduction over and over again, rewinding the tape every time it gets to the point when the song properly kicks in. The high voice of Sting's backing vocals. *I want my MTV.* The metallic burps of Mark

Knopfler's guitar. Rising anguish. The beating of drums. The same excruciating crescendo, never resolved.

Just one more anchor to that first year, because I can date it. June. Election night. Unaware of what I'm seeing, I watch boys sprinting up the stairs to spread the news. *She's done it! She's back in!* This is before it is even formally announced by Wagstaff the next morning that *This remarkable Conservative victory* will mean that there will be *no afternoon lessons* and *no Prep* by way of celebration. *Four more years!* They shoal up the stairs, dressing gowns flying behind them, elated at they know not what.

TWO

Mayday

11

MAY DAY. LITTLE Venice. The canalway cavalcade. Festooned narrowboats on display in the marina. Bunting. Neckerchiefed mongrels. Strings of light.

And the way this particular May Day is talked about, you'd think it must have felt like a nationwide version of that moment in late spring when you enter the bus or the train carriage and want to get it on with about half the people in your immediate vicinity. Blossom and pheromones. Sun blazing fittingly on the polling stations. The evil empire overthrown. Only that's not how I remember it at all.

I sat up waiting for Holly on the roof of the boat. We didn't have a television so I assessed the mood of the country from a deckchair as revellers wandered down the towpath, each group more abuzz than the last with news of the latest electoral stronghold to fall.

I stayed there all evening, still hopeful that she might turn up, smoking the last of the tobacco to stave off hunger. I drank four tins of lager, then one half, then the other of the bottle of wine I'd kept aside for us. The last thing I heard before turning in was one passer-by saying to another that they would *remember this night for the rest of our lives*, unwittingly lodging herself in my memory for good.

This was in 1997, not long before my twenty-first birthday.

It was after four when Holly got back. I'd dropped off in spite of the interruptions but I was alert enough to flip onto my front as I heard her heels scuffing on the towpath. It was the best strategic position in case I already had an erection by the time she got into bed, which might appear needy, or presumptuous, or both. I was always hopeful that she might launch a speculative fumble, but there was the element of theatre to consider.

She crashed and cursed and I heard the zip at the back of her dress and she was beside me. A sour cut to the air hinted that she'd been sick. Strong fumes in the foreground told me she'd drunk again since. She launched without delay into a set of snores that sounded as if a vacuum hose had strayed into standing water, and I assumed the moment had passed. Then the snoring stopped, and some time after that I felt an appraising palm on the seat of my boxers. I pretended to stir in my sleep.

I didn't mind being her comfort food. Or even that I was occasionally her second partner of the day. I had accepted that I was what she came home to: the dependable cheese on toast after the fussy gourmet meal. It had to happen at night, and only when she wanted it to, and was never spoken of in the morning. I used to imagine myself interestingly damaged for tolerating this arrangement. Now I think I was able to do so precisely because I wasn't.

She wasn't the first person I'd slept with but she was the first person I'd slept with more than once. She knew how she liked to get herself off and saw it as no problem but her own. Her ability to do this no matter what might be going on in her head seemed admirable to me at the time. It was like being in the company of a seasoned traveller, shuttling herself through customs with the minimum of fuss.

'Don't worry,' she said that night. 'Your secret's safe with me.'

Then she was asleep, and I was more awake than ever, staring at canal-water swirls cast on the ceiling by the reflected light of the rising sun.

The boat belonged to an aunt of Holly's, an academic who'd taken a year's posting at a university in Germany. When she returned in a few months, this life would be over. There was something relaxing about knowing it was only ever going to be an interlude. My life had been made of interludes, but I hadn't always known in advance.

We'd met one November afternoon in my second year when I had fled the student bars in search of a quieter drink and noticed a head of red hair and a pale hand reaching to pin up a flyer with a scissored skirt of phone number slips.

KEYS WANTED BILLIE DINAH ELLA NINA.

I still see the long, stripy scarf she was wearing whenever I think of her. In my memory she is all autumn like a film poster.

'Why no Sarah?' I called, and her shoulders relaxed and she replied without turning round that it was the first useful thing anyone had said to her all day.

She tried me out that afternoon when we found a pub with a playable instrument. From the moment she opened her mouth I knew it was touch and go whether or not I'd be good enough, but by then we were drunk and she knew she liked me. It helped that we weren't studying at the same place, and that we had in common the tendency to use music as a way out of being alone.

By the end of the following summer the gigs were regular enough to be earning us proper money. She made it clear that my plan to accept a teaching assistantship in Madrid for the third year of my degree was less than convenient. She asked me whether I was really about to *give it all up* to peddle English to a load of Spanish kids. Then she revealed her carrot in the form of lodgings on the boat. While we were viewing it she remarked that since there was only one bed, we might as well get the sex out of the way now. She was joking, but it happened before long.

Like most twenty-year-olds I thought myself fully grown, but when I look at photos from that time I see the frame of a boy. I liked a black overcoat and a Doc Marten boot. I had stupidly long hair, which I never washed. My friendship with Holly was the best thing I had to show for myself. Friendship was nominally all it was. Our sleeping arrangements had been devised to ensure we wouldn't forget this: we shared the bed top to toe, with extra pillows to keep us from one another's feet. This aspect of our otherwise overturned space was strictly regimented. We slept chastely, except when we didn't.

We fed ourselves using a strategy passed on to me by my grandfather: buy a chicken at the weekend. Ration the meat over as many weekdays as you can for sandwiches and casseroles, supplementing it with vegetables as it dwindles. When there's absolutely nothing left, boil up the bones for soup. This usually kept us going until Wednesday or Thursday, but Fridays tended to be lean.

Nevertheless when I got up the next morning I left her blasted in the bedclothes and went out for coffee and bacon sandwiches. Our drinking fund would take a hit, but I knew she'd be struggling. Where had she been this time? I wondered. Evidently with someone who'd paid the tab.

I walked out into the bright light of the new world and made for the sooted back of Paddington Station. Nurses were ducking out for cigarette breaks, their scrubs sharp against the bricks of St Mary's Hospital. The commuters looked as harried as ever. As I queued at a food stand on the station concourse, a twig landed on my head and I looked up to see a pair of magpies trashing a nest in the girders. No way of knowing if it was theirs or if they were just vandals, high on the moment.

On the way back I stopped at a phone box to place a call to my academic supervisor, assuring him that my year in Madrid was winding up nicely. I had learned so much, I said. The cultural immersion had been as enriching as he'd promised. I felt sure that this would be reflected in the extended essay on Cervantes that I owed him, to which I was putting the finishing touches. I'd been checking in with him like this for the past nine months, never more than two miles away.

'Morning,' I called, stepping on board. She had taken command of the bed with a lavish diagonal sprawl, and held a pillow clenched to her face. The smell of sweated booze hung heavy. 'Momentous day.'

She flung the pillow away. 'What do you care?'

'I thought that was what I was supposed to say.' I handed her a coffee. Her breath was powerful.

She sat up and reached for the spiral-bound *Real Book of Jazz Standards* that was her favoured rolling surface. 'I suppose you're going to tell me you didn't get tobacco.'

I shook my head. 'Coffee and pig cleaned me out.'

'So be it.' She reached for the ashtray and began sifting through it for ends with usable threads. 'How much charcoal can you take this morning?'

I watched her unpicking the ends, teasing the good tobacco, building a little pile on her book. The baggie of eked-out green waiting.

'Good night, then?' I said.

'I fell in with a group of jubilant researchers. Very free with their drinks. All of them apparently critical to the victory. Ditched them later on. The conversation got … monotonous.'

'So where did you end up?'

She reached testily for the Rizla and thumbed one free.

'Was it the Russian?' I said.

'Oh for fuck's sake.'

'You don't have to tell me.'

'Yes, it was the Russian.'

'How is he?'

'He's fine, cheers for asking.' She brought a miraculously passable joint to her mouth and licked it shut. She set it down again, relaxing with anticipation. She took the lid off her coffee and sat with it near her mouth, taking a moment to reassemble herself. 'Put something on, then.'

I selected a 1976 recording of Nina Simone at Montreux, and we surrendered to the piano introduction to 'Little Girl Blue'. There was an ongoing contest between us to find the perfect song for the moment, the cardinal rule being that you couldn't be obvious. My hope was that the soft opening phrase that borrowed the tune of 'Good King Wenceslas' might somehow not clash with a Friday morning in May but place it somewhere melancholy and beautiful.

'Yes, boy,' she murmured.

'Glad you approve.'

'We should play this tomorrow,' she said, when we had both been mellowed by the smoky voice, the smoke in the air. Holly dropped irresistibly into the song's conclusion. '*All you can count on is yourself … Little lady … Miss Sadie …* And you play this so damn well.'

'What is it this weekend?' I said, aglow at the compliment.

'It's the gig at the place whose name we agreed contained the three most offputting words in the English language.'

'How could I have forgotten,' I said. 'What kind of person has a party at the Imperial War Museum, anyway?'

'I think you know *exactly* what kind of person.'

We told our stories. Drew maps of the versions of ourselves we wanted the other to learn. Sketched out the peaks and troughs.

Hers were higher and deeper than mine. She'd had an older sister who'd died in infancy before she was born, a catastrophe which she said had defined her relationship with her parents. She'd spent her adolescence feeling simultaneously smothered by them and deficient in their eyes for not being someone she'd never known. She attributed to this the run of what she called 'impulsive behaviour' which had characterised her late teens.

A rebel prodigy, then. But a clear-sighted one: she knew music would save her and had never rejected it, though it had dominated her life. Public performance at a precocious age. Scholarship to an expensive Cheshire school her parents would not otherwise have been able to afford. She'd breezed into the Royal College of Music, not to sing, but to play the cello. The singing, she said, was for herself. When I asked her why she hadn't just advertised for a pianist at the college she said, 'They're all too accomplished. Too fearful of interesting accidents.'

Her dedication to the music of black women wasn't without complication: she fretted endlessly about whether or not it belonged to her, which it would never have occurred to me to do. One of many ways in which she prised open my eyes and made me look at myself. But then she was better than me at everything I wanted to be good at. Independence (she hadn't spoken to her parents in six months when we met). Music. Sex.

Here, I trod carefully. I knew I wasn't being invited to ask about it but from the start she put out enough signals for me to understand that there lurked somewhere in her past a bad experience with men. That was why when it came to us she was always the initiator, and (I told myself later) why she always went on top: to ensure that there was never a hint of coercion on my part. Though it was also because I liked it.

We were on different trajectories. The music would only ever be a distraction for me. I was out of her league. But that didn't matter when we were performing, because Holly drew all the attention. All I had to do was keep time and not mess up too obtrusively.

The sight of her undid me even when she had a cold. At the time, that seemed to clinch it.

One of the pastimes we'd developed was to randomly select a cassette from the other's collection and play it through in its entirety. If it was deemed unworthy it would be jettisoned from our cramped quarters. One lazy afternoon in the spring of that year when the stove was lit and rain was beating on the roof, she'd taken a tape of mine and put it into the machine without telling me. The sound that emerged had made us both look up.

'What the fuck's this?' I said.

'According to your sleeve notes, it's *Tango in the Night*,' she said. 'But I have a feeling that isn't what we're listening to.'

A click. Shallow breathing, close to the microphone. Two sniffs. Distress. Then a whisper, urgent, desperate.

Help me. Help me. Help me.

Then another click and Fleetwood Mac came flooding in.

The moment was entirely alien.

As the music played on she looked at me with an eyebrow raised.

'Interesting,' I said.

'Is that you?'

The memory surged back. Returning to the dormitory, panting, hair still wet with chlorinated water, back aflame. Grabbing the machine and pressing record, desperate to give some vent to the feeling before I sealed it away again.

'Yes,' I said. 'I think it is.'

'When?' she said.

I am woken by water being poured onto my face. I sit up abruptly, confused as to whether what's happening is hostile or benign, to find Simon holding the tumbler I left on my chair, concentrating on the dribble he is releasing onto my eyes.

'What are you doing?'

'Get up. Quietly.'

The nuclear glow of my father's old wristwatch tells me it is after 11 p.m. We creep out of the dormitory and down the stairs. In the Lower Gallery he plants a foot on the radiator, pulls himself through an open window and drops outside.

'Where are we going?' I whisper.

Gravel crunch. Something glinting near his smile in the moonlight. 'Crimble left the pool key on his desk.'

He closes the door and locks it behind us. In the changing room, the contorted shapes of dried trunks hang from pegs. The orange dots of the electric showers gleam in their stalls. We change.

We enter the pool area and stand at the water's edge. Our arms are close. Warm air between us, subtly displaced. The green light of the emergency exits finds tiny peaks of barely shifting water. Chlorinated air rises off the surface. Do we dare?

I am wondering what to say to help us along when Simon is gone. Flash of his soles as he plunges. Slap of water on the sides. For a moment I wonder if I have sleepwalked here, dreamt the presence of Simon, woken up alone. Then he breaches the surface halfway down the pool and I feel the impact of the wet tennis ball he lobs at my chest.

We swim in near-darkness, bodies free of the disappointing tug of gravity. The water is warm, which enables us to stay in for some time before deciding enough is enough. When we have finished we each put our trunks through the ACME mangle, observing protocol even as we break the rules. The escapade lacks joy. It's as if we are only doing this because someone has told us to.

But the thrill of having got away with it lifts our spirits on the short walk back, and when we reach the window we are daring to speak, though it is the most dangerous time to be doing so. It's only when Simon turns back to me with panic on his face that I realise the window has been closed from within.

The moonlit scene behind us turns like an illustration on the page of a book as the window is reopened. A torch beam plays on our faces.

'Gentlemen,' says Weapons Davis. 'Do come in.'

We climb inside.

'Stand there, both of you.'

Instead of closing the window, he opens it wider. We stand with wet hair plastering our faces.

'Dressing gowns, please.'

We take them off and hand them over.

'Pyjamas.'

We hesitate.

'I'm sure you didn't remain fully clothed on your little jaunt to the pool. So it should be the work of a moment to slip out of those things again.'

We say nothing.

'Now.'

He keeps us naked in the draught. He turns two chairs around and tells us each to grab the back of one of them with both hands. He pulls up a chair for himself beside us.

He takes his time. Discipline, rules, responsibility. He draws it out. By the time the lecture is over, we're shivering. I notice that he has removed the cord from my dressing gown, tied knots in it at one end and wound the other end round his hand.

'Denyer's monastic rope,' he mutters. 'Been dying to get my hands on this for years. Don't either of you dare let go of those chairs.'

Deftly I step back from the beating. My breathing slows and my own bare shoulders come into view. I watch as Weapons Davis puts in his best effort, and feel nothing. He alternates between us, striking anywhere from the tops of our legs to our arses and backs. The knots do their work, but we're damned if we're going to let him know it hurts. Frustration messes with his accuracy. I keep my eyes closed just in case he strays too high, so I don't know Wagstaff has entered the room until he speaks.

'I think that's enough now, Eric.' Wags looks calm but his breathing gives him away. 'You two, bed.'

Weapons Davis slowly unwinds the cord from his hand. Simon gives me a whack between the shoulder blades and I understand that the less time we spend on this, the more it can be said never to have happened.

We gather our things and shoot back to our dormitories in silence, hearing the receding noise of the mounting argument.

'Does that cover it?' I asked.

'No,' said Holly. 'That does not begin to cover it.'

In telling her about myself before then, I had favoured other things. The country-hopping childhood. The prelapsarian life with my grandfather. The various twists and turns of my education. And when it came to the school on the hill, an account which played up its eccentric side but skipped over the brutality and fear. She had dug up a lead on something far more compelling.

So off we went. The frozen arrival. Cleaning my teeth in the snow. Learning the violence. The little ways we'd coped and triumphed. Mainly she couldn't believe the sheer anachronism of it all going on so recently. The sense of being the last generation to experience a certain brand of Englishness. She interrogated me about the school so exhaustively that I began to wonder whether she'd found me at all interesting before. We hadn't talked about it much since, but it was there. I could feel it informing her assessment of me at every moment.

12

WE ENTERED THE museum forecourt and faced down the barrels of the two monstrous naval guns mounted in front of the entrance. Powerful spotlights lit up the green cupola of the old Bethlehem Royal Hospital, shorn of its wings and filled with old weapons. We would be playing in the main atrium, once Bedlam's courtyard, now a gallery of war machines.

The location was saying something about the event, but what? Perhaps there was an intent to make guests mindful of the fierce currents of history. Perhaps it was simply that tonight's clients were the kind of people who liked drinking champagne among simulacra of Fat Man and Little Boy, with a Spitfire hanging from the ceiling. Then I saw the banner hung across the columns which announced the name of the exhibition whose opening tonight's party was celebrating: *Legacy of Empire*.

We stopped near the graffitied section of Berlin Wall to the left of the entrance (*CHANGE YOUR LIFE*). Close by a few kids in black tie of about our own age were sucking on Marlboro Lights.

'I'm getting the measure of it,' said Holly, observing their confidence, their floppy, public-school haircuts. 'I'm beginning to see what we're up against. Why is there *always* one cunt in tartan trousers?' She sat on a bench and unzipped the holdall containing her heels. 'They promised me they'd have our kit set up in good time, so hopefully there won't be anything to do.'

The atrium was booming with guests, some in black tie, some in military uniform. Two young men in wheelchairs I took to be Gulf War veterans were receiving lots of attention.

'Are we late?' I said.

'No, they're coming down from the exhibition space upstairs. Get us a drink?'

Waiters held trays of champagne flutes on either side of the staircase down which the audience now streamed. I took two and returned through the swelling crowd until I found her inspecting our piano and microphone, which had been set up against the backdrop of a First World War tank.

'Looks all right,' I said.

'Can you believe what the cheeky fucker who booked me just asked?' she said, dropping into her idea of a posh accent as she took the drink. '*We thought this was a good spot because you could, you know, sprawl on the tank tracks when you're singing.*'

'Sprawl?' I said.

'That's what I said. *Sprawl?* I said. And he goes, *Yeah. Michelle Pfeiffer style. D'you know what I mean?*'

'Hmm.'

But she was already smiling. 'Actually, it's not such a bad plan.'

Perhaps it was going to be a good one after all. As I sat at the keyboard my hands felt loose and confident. With the champagne on top of what we'd had before setting out, I'd drunk enough to free myself up without making mistakes, and I could tell from her mood that Holly was going to knock them dead.

We had something specially prepared for the party. We'd taken the soundtrack of the winning election campaign and slowed it down from hectic pop confection to dark Nina-style lament. Holly had decided it would be funny to do it using her most soul-crippled voice, to mock the lyrics and rupture their optimism.

Things ... can only get better. Can only get better ... now I've found you.

In her mouth the song was laden with portent. Its addressee could only possibly be bad news, some seductive, dangerous force, leading the poor victim to darkness. She was especially excited to sing it now she'd had a taste of the party's demographic, expecting this to be a gathering for whom the election result was a disaster. Then a cheer went up as we began to play, and I realised that this was a crowd primarily motivated by a sense of heroic detachment from the serious.

As the atmosphere ripened I became aware of a middle-aged man staring at me. When he was joined by the woman who must have been his wife, he asked her a question and she said something to him. I could tell it was my name.

All this was distracting enough. Then as the space filled up and more alcohol entered the system, people started to crowd round the piano, which always makes me claustrophobic. When a hand fell on my shoulder I felt anxiety at the encroachment, followed by hostility. I shot a stern glance backwards so the fool would get the message and withdraw. The hand did retreat, but then returned a moment later and moved further down my body, towards the breast pocket of my jacket. It slipped something inside and I looked down to see the pinks and reds of a folded fifty.

'Just let us get to the end of this song then I'll take your request,' I said.

'You got it, maestro.'

Something about the voice.

When we'd finished, I turned to see what he wanted and found myself looking into a face that was both new and familiar.

'It *is* you,' he said. 'Holy shit.'

His features tumbled into place. 'Luke.'

'My mother said she'd seen you but I didn't believe her at first. How the fuck have you been?'

Eight years had passed, and all the changes of puberty. His jaw had grown out and his hair was blonder, possibly dyed. But the pale blue eyes and the air of mischievous possibility were the same. Here he was. Comfortable in black tie. Free with a fifty to get what he wanted.

'The boy who dropped off the face of the earth,' he said. 'I don't believe it.'

I stood up to shake his hand and he threw his arms around me, clapping a hand on my back and giving it a lot of *how the fuck ARE you, man* and *long TIME*. I reciprocated as best I could, though I was still in the flush of surprise.

Holly was watching the encounter with interest. 'Don't worry,' she called, giving him a smile that worried me immediately. 'I'm working up to that *sprawl* for you. Maybe in the second half.'

I was rescued from having to plunge further into conversation with him by the sound of cutlery against glassware and the crowd's attention settling on the man I now recognised as his father.

'Welcome, ladies and gentlemen, to what has been referred to as *the most magnificent boys' bedroom in London*,' began Roger Price. 'And thank you for coming to support our exhibition.'

He gave a speech in which he asserted that the purpose of a good curator is to ask questions, and that the one he'd been asking himself in this instance was whether or not one could allow pride to enter any discussion of an imperial past.

Then he declared that he was no longer of the belief that history was doomed to repeat itself because of the *great wave of liberal democracy* that had crashed over the world in the previous ten years, which was allowing us to *bow out gracefully* from places like Hong Kong, which would be handed back to the Chinese in precisely two months' time. As he spoke, I was aware of a young serviceman walking in my direction. Something about his dress uniform and the purpose with which he moved made me want to get out of his way, but when he reached me, he stopped.

'Good to see you again,' mouthed Ali Price. His hand held mine with a sincerity I found oddly moving, perhaps because of a hangover of the hierarchical terms which had defined our association in the past.

'How are you?' I said, when his father had stopped speaking.

'Working too hard. You know.'

'I really don't. What have you been up to?'

'Well, I got stoned in West Belfast last week.'

'That doesn't sound like work to me.'

He laughed. 'Real stones. Anyway, many thanks for your help tonight. It's much appreciated.'

There seemed little point in telling him it was a coincidence.

Holly's head snapped up from a nearby plate of canapés. 'We are getting paid, though. There wasn't any doubt about that, was there?'

Ali laughed again and made his excuses.

During the second set Luke insisted on drawing the party's focus towards us until a large crowd was gathered round the piano joining in at the choruses. After a few more numbers he and Holly were duetting on Fats Waller's 'All That Meat and No Potatoes'. In the final verse he launched into a surprisingly tuneful if tastefully dubious Satchmo growl. As a cheer went up at the end he kissed her on both cheeks. The confidence was breathtaking.

'Where have you been hiding this guy?' he asked Holly. 'He disappears completely then pops up at the piano keyboard as if he's been there all along.'

'It's where he's happiest,' she said, beguiled into honesty.

The party diminished until, as waiters tidied the atrium, the gathering consisted only of me, Holly and the Price family. I met Katharine, the younger sister of Ali and Luke, who I vaguely remembered once seeing at Sports Day when she was a toddler. She was now a tiny, serious-looking girl of eleven who had got special dispensation from the school on the hill to attend the party during term time. She spoke of the place with disarming familiarity. I almost couldn't believe it still existed.

'And what are you up to now, Max?' said Selina Price.

'I'm in my third year of a degree in Modern Languages.'

'Very good,' she said. 'So you might not end up being a cocktail pianist all your life?'

Before we left, the family crowded round to give thanks for our performance and delight in the coincidence. Then one of them, I forget which, said that we must of course come and perform at the reunion.

'Sure,' I said. 'Where?'

'Where do you think?' said Luke.

I knew Holly would want to play down the extent to which she'd been charmed. Somehow it was okay for her to talk about private education as if it was only something that happened to other people. On the Tube home she looked through the envelope Roger had given us to make sure the cash was right. When a man came into the carriage asking for money, she took out a twenty and folded it into his foam cup.

'It's dirty money,' she said. 'Take it before I change my mind.'

But even as we walked along the towpath under the carnival lighting of the canalway cavalcade, she was asking me to tell her more about Luke, as I had known she would.

'Your secret's safe with me,' she repeated that night, bolstered away by my side.

'What secret?' I said this time.

'I know you're a closet posho.'

'*Today we have naming of parts,*' reads Crimble. '*Yesterday, / We had daily cleaning. And tomorrow morning, / We shall have what to do after firing. But today, / Today we have naming of parts.*'

The children yawn in sequence at all of the neighbouring desks, and today we have naming of parts.

He stands up to inhabit more fully the role he has assumed, of sergeant major drilling his young recruits. The aggression is laughable on him.

'*This is the lower sling swivel. And this / Is the upper sling swivel, whose use you will see, / When you are given your slings. And this is the piling swivel, / Which in your case you have not got.*'

The branches hold in the gardens their silent, eloquent gestures, which in our case we have not got.

When the poem ends he takes us round it as usual, coaxing us towards an understanding. It is, he says, about the way systems co-opt people into doing the unthinkable, dulling them with routine, repeating the same strange terminology and beliefs until what becomes unthinkable is that the systems of man could ever be any other way. Thus war and its machinery become normalised. And nature, vibrantly available if you only cared to look out of the window, is deformed into something alien.

Or words to that effect.

But typically he doesn't care as much about whether we understand it as he does about lodging it in our memories through repetition alongside the key lines of all his other pet poems – *What passing-bells for these who die as cattle? / Gas! Gas! Quick, boys! An ecstasy of fumbling* – which is probably for the best, given that if we weren't thirteen years old and looking the other way, we might actually take heed of what the poem is saying.

The boy who dropped off the face of the earth.

Only his earth. But it was true that I hadn't maintained contact with any of them. There was the odd letter to begin with, but who *keeps in touch* at the age of thirteen? Either someone is there or they aren't. At least until the day when their swollen adult face heaves into view on some social media site years later.

Then of course there was The Conversation.

By the time I left the school on the hill, my parents had returned to England, and this time they were staying put. My father had reached a level of seniority at which there were fewer overseas placements, so they settled in the south-east, near the company office where he would spend the rest of his working life. They bought a house in the stockbroker belt with laurel hedges and a remote-controlled double garage. He drank more, put on weight and became another person sitting round a table talking about the things he'd seen.

True to its word, the company was signed up to fund my continuing advancement at a boarding school nearby. We'd visited the place. It had seemed as big as a town. The pupils in their tweed jackets and ankle-length skirts looked like grown men and women. Had I gone there it's possible I might have run into the likes of Luke and Ali at away fixtures and other inter-school activities, because I would have remained in their world. But I didn't.

We were on holiday near Toulouse. My parents and grandparents had jointly rented the kind of place they loved, a cottage surrounded by fields of nodding sunflowers. It must have been only weeks since I'd left the school on the hill. Preparations were under way back home for the new destination. Uniform acquired and labelled. Trunk ready to be stuffed anew. But for now it was trips to market and lunches that devolved into afternoons of wine and cheese while I read or swam.

An evening meal. Stories. My grandfather and my father in competition: bawdy farmers' tales on the one hand, glamorous international ones on the other. The location probably helped. I doubt I'd have spoken as candidly as I did even had we been in my grandparents' kitchen. But we were under a vine-draped pergola in the sunshine, and it felt free of consequence.

I was dropping out again. Falling away somewhere. Keen to include me, my grandmother mentioned the forthcoming change of school. 'At least you shan't have to sneak down to the village to make a reverse charge call when you want a chat.'

'Or get beaten up for doing it,' I replied, almost without thinking.

Four faces were regarding me with a different kind of attention.

'What do you mean, beaten up?'

But especially speak up.

'Well.' I cleared my throat. 'They hit us. Quite a lot. I thought you knew that.'

'Good Lord,' said my grandmother.

'How could we have known?' my mother asked.

'I thought you must have signed up to it or something.'

'Hit you for what?' said my mother.

'Anything. Making that reverse charge call. Not shining your shoes. Dirty fingernails.'

'How badly? With what?'

'Gym shoes. Canes. Rulers. Some of them had special things they used, with names. Hairbrushes and stuff.'

They'd been drinking and the atmosphere was convivial. Consequently their first reaction was laughter. After all, here I was, laughing about it myself. Enjoying my captive audience, I kept talking. For the first time, I left nothing out. I told them about not being able to make a fist for weeks after the phone box incident. About how Weapons Davis had liked to throw boys down stairs and pin them against walls. How Sutton had even been known to use a riding crop. Then I went beyond my own experience and described the more serious beatings that Luke and others had received. It was only when I had got onto the subject of poor Neil Lynch that I saw I'd gone too far. The laughter had stopped. When my grandmother handed a tissue to my mother, I realised she was crying.

I was not the only one who'd been keeping secrets. They had withheld from me the fact that my mother had essentially had a breakdown when I started at the school. I'd always understood that there was something in Mexico they had to get back for at the beginning, but heard now that she'd been so distressed it was feared her presence would make my departure much more traumatic.

Until that point my father's attitude towards the school had been one of benign amusement. The ideas he had of boarding were formed not from any experience but from the books he'd read when he was younger: Jennings and Molesworth and Billy Bunter. What I said now had overturned all that. It didn't matter that the place I had been destined for was entirely different, and only a few miles from where they were now living. I would not be going.

That one conversation diverted me from the trajectory of the boy in the surplice, and poisoned for them all the company's promises. An irony being that I doubt I would have had the skills to damn the place as eloquently as I did had I not been educated there.

13

Any sensitivity I might have felt to be attending my own school reunion as an employee was annulled by relief that this meant Holly could come too. I didn't trust myself to see it clearly alone. And now she'd get to meet my grandparents.

'This is where it is for me,' I said, as our station taxi pulled onto the coach-house lane.

'Home?' she said.

'I guess.'

'That's the way to the church?'

She had remembered. Absorbed all my self-centred anecdotes. I wished I was bringing her as more than a friend. And knew that no matter how much I had stressed that a friend was all she was, my grandfather would pretend otherwise.

I nodded. 'Good job we're early. They can't do lunch later than twelve.'

Dogs pawed at the taxi door. The pup was now very old and Jack was long dead. This collie was some nephew or son, comparatively unknown to me. My grandfather sat on his bench by the back door peeling potatoes over a washing-up bowl with a tumbler of red wine at his side, its glass muddied with pale starch. I held out the bottle I'd brought.

'How do,' he said.

He had foreseen the decline of his mobility, staying ahead of it with canny solutions: wall-mounted handrails, strategically placed stools. He was determined to reject the joylessness of old age. Not for him the segmented plastic pill dispenser or the mobility-centre walking aid: his medication travelled in a polished cedar box, and the stick he leaned on was a magnificent Victorian item with a pornographic ivory grip.

But things were slipping. With every visit, he seemed diminished. He'd had one hip replaced and the other would have to go soon. Meanwhile my grandmother's vacant episodes were becoming more frequent and prolonged. There had been troubling incidents with her at the wheel of the car, and a war of words raged over whether she should be allowed to keep on driving. His body and her mind were breaking down at the same pace. Neither was reconciled to the adjustment, but they were merging into one person.

He teetered in the doorway, unable to propel his own bulk over the threshold.

'Hang on, I'll be back in a minute,' he said, laughing.

Holly wouldn't have seen it, but I could tell that an effort was being made. They were raising their game to entertain us. He let me take over the vegetables and sat drinking with her while the meal was finished.

'Keep an eye on that one,' he said, gesturing in my grandmother's direction. 'She poured a jug of custard over my roast beef the other day.'

'I bet you ate it anyway,' I said.

His voice dropped so she couldn't hear. 'It's no joke. She went missing in the Tesco car park last week and it took me and the trolley kid an hour to find her.'

'What's he saying about me?' she muttered, more to herself than to us.

The tone of their reminiscences felt less celebratory than before. Now they just sat in quiet, occasionally naming the dead, my Great-Aunt Dee having finally passed on the previous year. But there was still joy to be taken in the follies of the living.

'I've been reading about all this lottery money,' he said that lunchtime, when we'd devoured a heap of lamb chops and were on to the cheese. 'Something about it being put to use to make *shagging places* for the gays. Is that what they need?'

He was genuinely interested. Holly was happy to explain the practice of cottaging to him without implying that he might have got his wires crossed about it being a publicly funded enterprise. Which led him, as more wine was poured, to decide she was a trustworthy source.

'What about lesbians?' he asked. 'I always wonder how it works. Do they have to use one of these double-ended things?'

'I haven't got enough experience of that,' she said. 'Unless you count the unwholesome attentions of my school gym teacher.'

'Unwholesome attentions,' he said, laughing. 'Course, there's going to be a *register* for that now. They're going to be on a list.'

'Who are?' said Holly.

'You know. People who interfere. Like your man,' he said to me.

'Which man?'

'You haven't seen it? Your mother said she was going to send it you.'

'Seen what?'

He made to get up but it was a slow process.

'What do you need?' I said. 'I'll fetch it.'

'You won't know where to look.'

My grandmother followed him into the next room and we heard the conversation escalate.

'What are you looking for?'

'What the bloody hell do you think I'm looking for? The *article*.'

What eventually appeared was a cutting from the local paper. It was only a tiny piece, but the news it contained was that a formerly local schoolteacher named Eric Weathers-Davis had been arrested and charged with *offences against minors*. The allegations were historical, and related to his time at the school on the hill between 1975 and 1982.

Just reading the name again was enough.

The personalities of all of them had come in and out of my head over the years. The apoplexy of Wagstaff on a touchline. Spinks whacking boys round the head with his metre ruler. All the million things we'd learned and delighted in thanks to Crimble. But over and above any of this, the anger of Eric Weathers-Davis.

He'd come when I was dropping off to sleep, or about to wake up. Kick my door down and get stuck in. Any adult, male shout in the vicinity and there he'd be, Weapons Davis on the rave, feasting on his own words, stoking his outrage. Furnishing replies, then shooting them down. All of it an exercise in getting his blood up as much as possible.

... didn't come here to watch you all just MESS ABOUT like babies ...

... and I'm supposed to stand here and let THIS happen? No, sir. Not on MY watch ...

I read the article again, as if it might have more to tell me.

My grandmother's voice surged to a high pitch as the thought occurred. 'Nobody ever interfered with you, did they?' She didn't wait for an answer. 'Good Lord. To think.'

'Creep,' said my grandfather. He shifted in his chair. 'Right. I shall be asleep in ten minutes. Are you two going to play me some music or not?'

We settled on 'Ain't She Sweet'. He sang beached on the furniture, terrier on his belly, half tucked for comedy effect into his unbuttoned trousers. His voice had a heartbreaking crack of frailty. Holly tapped out the rhythm and did lovely, smoky harmonies.

Oh me oh my. Ain't that perfection.

When we'd finished Holly commented on the view of the stable yard outside.

'I remember you tearing about here on your bike,' he said to me. 'You did it for hours, going round and round in a circle. We used to watch you sometimes from this window and wonder if you were all right.'

'I was fine,' I said, slightly puzzled.

'You should have seen him when we dropped him off up at that place,' said my grandmother. 'Standing in the doorway in his duffel coat. I've never felt so awful.'

'And what about the weather?' he said.

'Ooh, yes. That terrible hurricane. Trees down all over the place.'

'It was snowing,' he shouted. 'The storm was later in the year. It was *snowing* when we took him up the first time.'

'Was it?'

'It was. And we left him there without even talking to anybody. Terrible, really. We should have thought about it more.' He was misting up, emotional with wine.

'But you didn't just leave me there,' I said. 'There was a teacher. Crimble.'

'Who?'

'Mr Crighton. You spoke to him.'

'I just remember driving away thinking we'd done something awful,' he said.

'It was a funny old place, wasn't it?' said my grandmother. 'But you were all right in the end.'

He leaned over to Holly and pointed towards my grandmother's near-destroyed paperback of the second volume of *Remembrance of Things Past*. 'Have you seen what she's reading? She's been at it six years, I reckon. Just gets to the end and starts again. Cos she can't fucking remember it.'

Later in the afternoon, while Holly was getting ready, I realised he'd finished his nap and went up to see him in the workshop. A half-finished cupboard lay in pieces on the table.

'What do you think of this thing?' I said.

He sniffed. 'Horrible. But I had my eye on you. I'd have known if anything was up.'

There was unease in his voice. I wondered if this was his subtler way of asking the same question as my grandmother.

'I know,' I said.

'I did think of going up there to speak to him.'

'Who?'

'This one who's been arrested. Weathers-Davis.'

'What would you have said?'

'I don't know. Told him I'd heard he knocked the boys about. And that if I ever found out he'd laid a finger on you, I'd come up there with a lump hammer and set about him. Only I didn't. Who was I to do something like that? The place was always so … sure of itself.'

I felt awkward at the scale of the love. 'I was fine. You know that.'

'I should have done more.'

I hugged him, the usual half-hug of his bulk now tipped in my favour due to my height and his frailty. 'You did enough,' I said. 'You did everything you needed to do.'

The familiar approach. The lurching stomach. Our driver refreshed and jovial after his afternoon kip. I was trying to play it cool but he saw to that.

'You should have seen the moods he got into on this journey,' he said to Holly as we dipped into the valley. 'He'd have stopped talking by now. The eyes would be staring into space. You'd have thought we were taking him off to a war.'

'You were,' I said.

'Listen to the soft bugger, will you? You lot don't know you're born.'

There was something infantilising about being driven up there again, and I found myself enjoying that. I felt a stupid burst of affection towards Holly for being by my side. Twice in one day. I would need to watch that.

'Before you start, you're not coming back to fetch us,' I said as we drew through the bulls' head gateposts and onto the avenue. 'I know you'll want to be in bed. We'll call a taxi.'

'Don't be daft.'

'You're not,' I said. 'Okay?'

And then everybody in the car fell silent as people always did when the corners started rearing over the trees.

They hobnobbed on the North Lawn, throwing down shadow in the strong summer light. A balding man who must have been a pupil about twenty years before me appeared to be in charge. He showed us to an upright piano and a microphone in the cloisters. Playing at the beginning provided a welcome opportunity to scope things out without having to interact. And since nobody knew Holly, those who passed didn't bother looking at me, imagining us to be a randomly hired act. As we played, my eyes scanned the crowd on the lawn. I saw Ali Price in deep conversation with someone from his year, which meant Luke would be here somewhere too. Other faces emerged from the crowd, lengthened and augmented.

We finished to a brief spatter of applause then began drinking wine at catch-up speed as we skirted the crowd. Holly was still taking in the beauty of the building, the light tumbling through the canopy of the cedar tree, the blindsiding first impression of sanctuary and privilege.

'So this is where you went to school,' she said. 'It explains so much.'

'I went to a lot of schools.'

'Yeah, but this is the one that mattered, isn't it?'

Dinner was announced and the crowd began funnelling into the cloisters to go inside. I took Holly round to the front entrance to give her a quick tour. I showed her the Great Hall, then we walked up to see a couple of dormitories, the iron beds in their serried ranks. It was half-term, so the beds were all made up and labelled. It felt simultaneously more dilapidated and more comfortable than I remembered. There were cosier touches throughout, such as artwork by the kids that had been put up in many of the rooms. I saw Katharine Price's name at the foot of a nice sketch of the stable block. The most striking change was a payphone bolted to the wall of one of the downstairs corridors. I stared at it, wondering how to convey how unthinkable a sight it was, when a familiar voice boomed behind me.

'Huzzah for the Children's Act! You'd have probably appreciated having access to one of these, eh, Max?'

Wagstaff wore a white dinner jacket and a red-and-gold-striped bow tie. His hair was greyer and his laughter lines had cut deeper into his face, lending him more Toby-jug amiability than ever. He asked if Holly was my wife, which communicated how fluid his perception of time was. Most of them had been there for decades. However adult we might be now was irrelevant.

'I was so looking forward to this evening,' said Wags. 'It happens so rarely that we get people back here to let us know what the rest of their lives had in store. My only worry is that this business with Eric will end up tainting the whole thing. We hadn't heard from him at all. He's been living somewhere out east, I think – could it be Great Yarmouth? – and now here he is, back to bring us all this unpleasantness. Ghastly.' He sighed. 'I used to argue with him all the time. I told him, you can't beat them as much as this, it's not on. And he would back down eventually. It was a struggle, though.'

'But ... this is about more than beating though, isn't it?'

'Ugh,' said Wagstaff. 'Awful. Let's not spend the whole night going on about it. It upsets me so much. What a mess.' He took a heavy glug of his wine. 'Now, Max. Tell me what *you're* up to. I see you're still doing your music.'

'You heard us, then?'

'Beautiful,' he said. 'Especially you, my dear, no offence, Max. I'm not surprised. We couldn't keep you off the piano. I still remember that time the antique harpsichord was installed in the chapel and you went up there bold as brass in front of everyone and played "Maple Leaf Rag". The look on Tony's face. He thought you'd mince out a Mozart partita, but you didn't do what was expected of you. Always respected you for that. Well, better get in for the nosebag. Chop-chop.'

'Lordy. The plot thickens,' said Holly as we walked through the Lower Gallery towards the dining room.

'Wags was one of the good guys,' I explained. 'He used to tell boys who'd done something wrong to pretend they'd been beaten so he didn't have to do it to them.'

'Well, that's nice.'

'Yeah ... on threat of a proper belting if you didn't pretend well enough.'

'Ah.'

They'd put out candles and hired wine glasses, but the water was served in the school's familiar plastic jugs and tumblers. The adult voices, the smell of booze: being back was already tinkering with my memories, making the past harder to see.

There was a note of defiance in the way people behaved, especially those who had left most recently (they hadn't invited anyone under eighteen). A desire, perhaps, to show the place up now they were big enough to defend themselves. I sensed competing undercurrents of declaration. Some seemed to want to make it clear that they despised the school for its grand pretensions (yet here they were). Others strutted in a different way, broadcasting that this was only a staging post in a journey they were now proudly completing.

Luke had set up an enclave of our generation at one end of the table nearest the window. I recognised the West brothers, Chris Webster, Becky Lynch and a few of the other girls. He called me and Holly over and made a show of seating her beside himself.

'So, what do you think?' he said.

'I think you all look very well for people who went to school in the fifties,' said Holly.

'What about old Weapons Davis, eh?'

'Someone finally caught up with the bastard.'

'What do you think he's actually been arrested for?'

'Come on,' said David West. 'We all know what it is. Don't you remember the way we used to have to line up for him? So he could look inside our games shorts to make sure we weren't wearing underwear, because it was supposedly against regulations? Least surprising news of all time.'

'It's all the older lot were talking about outside,' said his brother. 'There are three accusers, apparently. All saying he fiddled with them in the late seventies and early eighties.'

'Well, well,' said Luke. 'How about that?'

'Any sweetcorn for you tonight, Luke?' said Chris Webster.

'Don't,' he said.

'He was quite a handful, this one,' Chris said to Holly. 'Wasn't it you who stood in front of that junior matron with a massive hard-on?'

'Couldn't possibly comment,' said Luke.

'It was you, wasn't it? And she goes, *It's all right, no need to be embarrassed, just put it between your legs.* And Luke says, *I'd rather put it between yours.*'

Out came all the old tales. The legend of the boy who'd sliced open his fried egg one morning to find a chicken embryo inside, and been made to eat it, gelatinous beak and all. The ghost stories about the Grey Lady and the Dangling Man. The story of the day Weapons Davis drove his car onto the cricket pitch during a match with the *A-Team* theme playing at full volume, pretending to machine-gun the players with a walking stick. All the other fables we'd exchanged and embellished over time. There followed the obligatory rundown of all the foods we'd been tortured with in this room. Spam. Fish Paste. Liver. Cheese Pudding. Spotted Dick. Rhubarb Fool. Pineapple Charlotte. Tapioca. All typed out on the menus with their ominous red-lettered heading of *MANNERS MAKETH MAN.*

My eye kept returning to Becky Lynch, who had grown into a destabilising beauty, and knew it. She was with the same old cabal of friends. It hadn't occurred to me to think that there would be groups that had remained physically close and therefore stayed together. There was no sign of Neil, which was hardly a surprise. In the hope of capitalising on the spirit of reminiscence, I called over to her, something like *how about a go on the swings after dinner*, but I misjudged the moment and she was already looking somewhere else as I said it. It was only because of this minor embarrassment that I came to be looking out of the window at the right time. Papering over a misfired joke by pretending to have my attention focused on the middle distance. If it had been half an hour later the outside light would have faded and I would only have been gazing at my own reflection in those familiar old windows.

Silhouetted against the last of the sun, a tall figure with shoulder-length hair was walking along the wall at the end of the lawn. He dropped into a flower bed and approached the building. Baggy black cardigan. Torn jeans. A canvas backpack. Almost as soon as I'd seen him he had vanished round the side of the building.

I tuned back into the conversation around me. Emboldened by wine, people had started telling more disrespectful anecdotes. Jack West was doing a brazenly exaggerated imitation of Tony Sutton's stutter which nobody would have dared attempt before. Fresh from the reception he received, he called over to Holly. 'Lovely singing, by the way. You were a couple of years below us, weren't you? Always thought you were beautiful.'

'When I was, what, ten? There's something a bit creepy about that, isn't there?'

I noticed Luke watching her closely. She was doing what she did best among new people – taming the brashest of them without passing judgement for or against. Letting her probable distaste twitch alluringly like a fishing fly.

'What's so interesting out that window, boy?' she said.

'I'll be back in a minute. Will you be all right on your own?'

'Are you joking? I'll make mincemeat of this lot.'

As I slipped out of the room, the sight of the toilet-block door and the changing rooms beyond brought a memory rocketing back.

Weapons Davis in his chair, watching bathtime, presiding over his cavern of squealing cubs.

'What do you reckon?' I say to Simon, nodding in the direction of the toilet block.

'You wouldn't dare.'

'No?'

'With him right here? You wouldn't dare.'

Challenge accepted.

Kick open the door, checkerboard floor. Tacky underfoot. Sweet smell of urinal cakes. The beast is distracted, but this is playing with fire. I grab two fistfuls of paper towels, fling them into the sink, spin the taps on full. I pump liquid soap from the dispenser, flick it onto the soaked wads, make three balls of soapy wet tissue. I hold one, weigh it in my hand, then hurl it upwards as hard as I can. It hits the ceiling with a wet thunk and stays deliciously in place. Get it right and they dry into carbuncles that remain until whenever poor old Whittle is sent to knock them down. It has become my signature move. The public threats are ever more dire. If the perpetrator were found, the consequences would be unimaginable. But they won't be catching me any time soon. I am a creature of the system now. I know its ways.

I am ready with my second wad, preparing a throw of theatrical excess for Simon's amusement. His nervous laugh becomes a terrified start as the door is kicked in behind him.

'Well, ALL RIGHT.'

'Bastard.'

The laughter becomes hysterical with relief as Luke stamps in doing his best Weapons Davis strut, freshly washed and grinning. 'I knew you shady characters were up to something in here.'

'Bastard.'

Jacked up on subversion and not to be outdone, Luke stands at the trench and releases a stream of urine which he directs up the wall until it departs from the porcelain. He tugs back his foreskin and bears down and the jet acquires staggering velocity, hitting the ceiling as he attempts to shoot down one of my carbuncles.

Simon and I flee, leaving Luke cackling on the other side of the door, ready to take the bullet for all of it should the need arise, almost willing it, because he's that perverse.

The noise of the meal dwindled and died behind closed doors. I stood at the foot of the gloomy stairwell. No hamster cages here during half-term, only a scent of hutch. Vision of some kid taking out another's pride and joy and parading it in front of others in his clammy little fist. *Squeeze them hard enough and their eyes pop out.*

The carpet slipped under its stair rods in all the usual places. Memory of trooping after Crimble the night he found me crying. Him receding down the corridor, me following, craving anything over that dark room of beds.

I glanced now towards the closed door of his room, then took the other branch of the staircase. The low door in the wall was ajar. I pushed it open and hoisted myself upwards on the frayed bannister rope. The attic room was empty. I crossed the bare boards towards the window that led out onto the roof.

Simon stood with his back to me, searching his rucksack, sunset splashing over the fields behind him. 'Now who can this be, I wonder?' he said before turning round.

He'd filled out his height. Sinewy and strong. Sparkle of the eyes, pepper of the freckles. Beneath the black cardigan he wore a baggy white T-shirt, punkily slashed open in several places down its front. The skin of his arms looked messy, littered with abrasions.

'How've you been, old chum?' he said, putting a palm on my shoulder. He smelled of smoke and sweat. His broken voice had changed in other ways too. The vowels had rounded. The endings were dropping off. He'd gone less clipped since we were all being trained up here as little lords. We'd last exchanged letters at fifteen, two years after we'd left this place. I wondered if we could be said to know each other at all.

'I thought this might be where you were headed,' I said.

He grinned. 'What are they all doing, coming back like this? It's ridiculous. I liked your playing. From what I could hear of it up on the wall.'

'What's going on?'

'It's good to see you,' he said. 'But this isn't the best time to catch up. Where are you living?'

'London. Paddington. You?'

'Acton. Though I'm staying with my mum tonight.'

'Is she here?'

He shook his head. 'She hasn't had anything to do with this place for years. She isn't far away though. Listen, I'll be back in town next week. Let's do it properly then, okay? We're practically neighbours!'

He pushed up the sleeve of my jacket and unbuttoned my shirt cuff. He took a marker pen from his bag and wrote a phone number up the inside of my arm.

'That won't come off in a hurry,' he said. 'Just in case you forget this ever happened. Which might not be such a bad idea.'

For one mad moment I wondered if he meant to plant a bomb.

'Aren't you going to come down?' I said. 'Luke's here.'

He smiled. 'I saw him. Tell the old bastard I send my love, okay?'

'Why don't you just come and see him?'

'Call me on that number next week. We'll meet up for a proper chinwag. All right?'

I tried not to look too impressed that he had a mobile phone. Or to be too distracted by the fact that he was now apparently the sort of person who said 'chum' and 'chinwag'.

'Go well,' he said, turning away. 'Hope the food's better than it used to be.'

The whole thing had taken less than fifteen minutes. I was back before they'd finished their starters. After dinner – slices of a smoked salmon roulade followed by a purgatorial venison dish – Wags got to his feet to speak. 'Welcome, everybody. This year our reunion has a slightly different dimension.'

'You bet it does,' said David West. Sniggers. Was it only in our little corner, or was the atmosphere turning volatile throughout?

'As you know,' said Wags, 'Mr Sutton is finally retiring. It's no exaggeration to say that he's given his life to this school. Twenty-five years as headmaster, and nearly a decade under his father before that.'

I took in Mr and Mrs Sutton for the first time. They looked old, and slightly bewildered, as if they had taken a step back from life. It hadn't occurred to me until then to wonder why so few teachers were present.

'Many of you have contributed generously to his retirement gift and I'm delighted to announce that tonight will see its unveiling. But you'll need to come outside.'

On the lawn they'd lit braziers and were serving coffee from a trestle table. Groups of younger guests broke away to sit on the lawn and smoke. Holly settled down with Luke and a few others and began efficiently rolling joints. She'd light one, pull on it once or twice, send it off into the group, then begin another.

Wags resumed his speech, but now there was an open air of disregard, and he had to shout to make himself heard. 'As you might remember, it gets pretty dark out here at night. So we're going to shine a bit of light on the old place. Ladies and gentlemen, I present to you the Tony Sutton Memorial Floodlights.'

There was a dutiful, almost sarcastic gasp as the switch was thrown and the facade of the building came into radiant relief, but almost immediately it was overtaken by a genuine ripple of laughter as the crowd saw the banner.

Fabric fluttering over the ramparts. Stark, painted capitals. Old bed sheet. Black on white.

HOW MUCH
DID THEY
KNOW?

Tony and Fiona Sutton were like a dictator and his wife unaware that the mood of the crowd had turned against them. They carried on chatting to those around them as if they'd seen nothing, and who knows, maybe nothing was all they had seen.

My memories of the end of the evening are sketchy. Wags setting off to the roof to haul down the banner, furiously denouncing whoever had put it there. Holly with her face locked to that of Luke Price on a bench made for children. Ali going berserk, goose-stepping up and down the balustrades trying to kick off the flower urns. Then all of it made irrelevant by the wave of guilt I felt when I found my grandfather sitting in his car in the same old spot by the chapel and realised he'd been waiting patiently there for some time, long past his usual bedtime.

14

THE HOT BREATH of the Tube pushed me up the station steps. West London. Acton. Summer city air, jacked up with fumes, tacky with pollen. I followed Simon's directions to a tall concrete block, pushed a button on the entryphone and waited for it to crackle.

'Enter.' Portentously posh. 'Seventh floor. Lift might be screwed. And it stinks. But by all means take your chances.'

The lift ascended, shuddering in its shaft. I emerged on a landing with functional brown carpet and blue walls scuffed with bike marks. Halfway down the corridor a door was ajar. As I approached, the burble of kids' TV from an adjacent apartment shaded into the nervy synths of the Prodigy.

Simon stood with his back to me in a narrow galley kitchen, mashing the bags into two mugs of tea. He was barefoot and wore a white T-shirt and a tie-dyed sarong. I took in the cloak of habitual weed on the air, the towers of Wembley Stadium through old net curtains.

'Tea okay for you?' he said.

'Sure.'

'I couldn't touch it for years after leaving. Post-traumatic stress. Dishwater and UHT milk in those little white cups. The smallest whiff of a cuppa was all it took to take me back to Spam and rhubarb and all the rest.' He took out the tea bags and dropped them in a bin. 'But now I make it strong and banish the memories by doing things right.' He set down his spoon and turned as if I were a treat he'd saved himself up for. 'Hello, old friend. I'm going to hug you now.'

When we'd embraced he kept hold of me with one arm and stared at my face, for so long that eventually I said, 'Everything all right?'

'I'm just trying to connect the two yous.'

'How do you know there's only two?'

He grinned. 'Ha. There he is.'

The sunset-yellow living room was mostly occupied by two huge red sofas littered with wires. His school trunk served as a coffee table between them. Towers of defunct hardware rose from the floor. There was a traffic cone with a hole in the top, which served as a giant ashtray, and to which remote controls were attached with string so he could hoist them out from under stuff. The walls were piled high with shoeboxes, arranged in stacks of ten, short end facing out, with different years or letters written on each in marker pen.

'Turns out I'm not very good at throwing things out,' he said, swiping away two Nintendo gaming controllers so I could sit down. 'Have a look at this.'

He pulled out a shoebox marked *1989* and set it down like a curator handling an artefact. He removed the lid and laid out some of the contents. Exercise books. Wizened conkers. String. Then he pulled out a faded Post-it note which had something written on it in the shaky capitals of my own thirteen-year-old handwriting.

IF YOU CHOOSE TO FACE THE OGRE, GO TO THE LETTER 'O' IN THE LIBRARY. IF YOU CHOOSE TO FLEE, GO TO THE LETTER 'F' IN THE BOOT HUT.

'Do you remember what this is?' he said.

'Ha. Of course. It's a clue. From the game. *English Monsters.*'

He smiled and put the note back in the box. 'All that time we wasted just keeping busy.'

'The Agincourt stuff is very stirring, of course,' says Crimble. 'But my favourite scene in *Henry V* is the one before the battle, when he punishes the *traitors in his midst.* They've been trying to curry favour with Henry by saying no mercy should be granted to those who conspire against him, not knowing that he knows they've been doing exactly that. He busts them good and proper:

> *The mercy that was quick in us but late*
> *By your own counsel is suppressed and killed.*
> *You must not dare, for shame, to talk of mercy,*
> *For your own reasons turn into your bosoms,*
> *As dogs upon their masters, worrying you.*
> *– See you, my princes and my noble peers,*
> *These English monsters.*

'Loyalty, boys. It's everything. You've got to stick by your people.'

Simon and I begin devising the game that same afternoon. It's like a treasure hunt with a Dungeons and Dragons storyline. It quickly gets complicated. Notes are left all over the school: in library books, under desks, behind toilets. Unused plotlines are picked up by new stories. Places become overlaid with their unreal equivalents. Our monsters are far too fantastical and outlandish to be frightening. I like to imagine any stray notes we leave behind being discovered by the pupils who come after us, perhaps entering their own unique mythologies.

★

Here was his life in all its paper and string. And here he was in his box of boxes, this person I'd known so well. We had lived by Crimble's advice, shown fierce loyalty to each other, taken one another's bullets whenever we could. Opening the shoebox was his way of bringing that back. I had never before visited this room in the sky, but now he was showing me that I was already here.

As before, much went unsaid. But there was also an element of display. Of serving up the new personalities we wanted the other to find. He'd seen me for shifty, which I liked. He meanwhile was fidgety and damaged but I saw no evasion. His weaknesses were out there. The honesty made him seem invulnerable.

He lit a joint, ashing into the traffic cone as we passed it back and forth. When we'd finished it he dropped the butt inside. I heard a quenching sound and realised that the cone was half full of water. I told him about my existence on the boat with Holly. About my parents and grandparents and what they were up to.

'I'm still in touch with a few of them,' he said. 'Zahra Nasri. Becky Lynch. Didn't you have a thing for her at one point?'

'We got married,' I said.

'Of course you did.'

His continued ease with names I'd long forgotten fascinated me. He'd stayed tethered to the area, gone on seeing the same people. Unlike mine, his life hadn't been periodically wiped, the stage cleared and recast. He'd gone on to another local boarding school, which sounded comparatively benign. But it hadn't ended well and he'd had to go and live with his mother when completing his A levels on threat of expulsion. Now he'd sidestepped university and been hired by a software company as a game developer.

'Here, I'll show you.' He reached behind the television, unplugged the N64 leads and connected a powerful-looking PC. 'The gameplay needs work. And I'm still getting to grips with C++. But you'll get the idea.'

He pulled up a keyboard off the floor and typed something in. A prompt window appeared on the screen followed by an intricately pixelated rendering of a building. There was no mistaking the teeth of the battlements, the leaning spire of the chapel.

'The number of times they made us paint it in Art,' he said. 'I didn't even need a photo.'

'It's a good likeness,' I said.

Green letters oozed down overhead:

ENGLISH MONSTERS

A set of arms came up holding a gun. From a queasily accurate first-person perspective, the figure advanced.

'The sound gets recorded later,' he said. There'll be some breathing and footsteps at this point. Where do you want to go? Great Hall? North Lawn?'

'Straight in, I guess.'

It wasn't the realism of the demo that was making me anxious, or even that I was stoned. It was the sheer wish fulfilment of stepping over that threshold with a loaded weapon.

His hands moved quickly over the keyboard. 'I've done it as a haunted house instead of a school, of course. The trouble is, it doesn't know whether it wants to be a first-person shooter or an RPG. A lot of developers think you have to choose between violence and role play, but I don't see why you can't have both.' When his character reached the front door, Simon opened a dialogue box and typed in a command. 'Imagine a booming knocking sound here.' The door swung open and inside lurked a bulbous creature in a butler's uniform, wearing a loosely knotted gold-and-orange tie. The face was covered with scars and grossly inflated, but I recognised it.

'Wags!'

'I thought he'd make the best gatekeeper. It's not really him – or if it is, it's him meets Fungus the Bogeyman.'

'What about the others?'

'I haven't done them all yet. Weapons Davis is a kind of zombie sergeant major. Lots of guns. Spinks is a mummy.'

Wags was now swinging from the beams hurling cricket balls that exploded on impact. Simon typed in a command and left the Great Hall. The corridors crawled with snarling, bug-eyed rodents.

'Is Crimble in it?' I said.

'Of course. He's my Jekyll and Hyde.' He paused the game and jumped to a different level. A thin, bearded man with kindly eyes wearing a grey frock coat stood before us. Then his mouth opened in a howl and a set of extra arms broke free from the coat. Talons sprouted from all four hands as they advanced.

Simon laughed at his own work. 'I might have to tone that down a bit,' he said. 'It even gives me the heebie-jeebies. Still, I reckon he'll find it funny.'

'You're still in touch with him?'

'Not so much these days.'

'How is he?'

'The same.' He tossed the keyboard aside. 'Shall I skin up again, or are you ready for a beer, or both?'

We'd drunk a few cans. Smoked. Laughed. The smaller barriers had fallen away. Eventually I realised he wasn't going to mention it until I did.

'So. The reunion. Did you stick around to see the aftermath?'

'Of what?'

'Your sign.'

He smiled. 'No. How was it?'

'It certainly made a splash.'

'I guess it wasn't very subtle. But I knew they'd all get away with pretending it wasn't happening otherwise. And I thought that wasn't on.'

'Fucking Weapons Davis,' I said. 'I still can't believe it. I guess we were lucky he was only throwing us down stairs.'

'Yeah. Lucky us.'

'Do you think he was still at it while we were there?'

'Yes,' he said. 'I do. There are people we were there with who I'm sure he did it to.'

'Like who?'

'Ali Price, for one.'

'Really?'

'Look back. Read between the lines.'

'Come on. You can't be sure of that. Where's your proof?'

'Where's your brain?'

'What?'

He rubbed a hand over his face as if to scrub away the hostility. 'Sorry. Can I ask you something?'

'Sure.'

'You seem genuinely surprised by all this. Are you really?'

'I had no idea.'

'Really? Because if it's okay for me to say this—' He seemed to think better of it.

'Say what?' I said. 'Go on.'

'I always assumed it had happened to you.'

I stared at him. 'Me?'

'Yes.' He held my gaze. 'You can tell me if it did. I won't judge. Or tell anyone.'

'It didn't. No.'

'Okay.' He stood up and went to the kitchen. 'Another beer?'

He returned with two fresh cans and started flicking through his CDs. 'Where shall we go now? Ah. *Leftism*. That will do nicely.'

'Why did you think that?' I said. 'About me.'

He put the disc on and sat down. 'It wasn't a fair question. But I've wondered about it over the years, so I had to ask. And now I have.'

'But what made you think it?'

'I guess ... because he used to take you off to his room in the night.'

There was a silence as we both weighed this up.

'Crimble?' I said.

'Yeah.'

'What are we talking about here? Are we talking about the same thing?'

'It happened at my other school as well, but we were older then, so we knew who to steer clear of. And you can work as a team when you're older. Keep each other informed.'

'What do you mean, it happened?'

'You want me to spell it out?'

My skin itched. The room felt airless. His words were filling it, defining the shape of something huge by omission.

'I mean,' he said, 'the way he had that group of us. Favourites. He kind of tailored it, don't you think?'

'You can't be serious.'

'Fine,' he said. 'We don't have to talk about it if you don't want to.'

'Crimble?' I asked again. Simon sat back and shrugged. 'Do you think they'll come after him as well, then?'

'I don't know. But I'll have something for them if they do.'

My senses swept the room for clues: dead insects, paint specks, dust motes. He returned to his wall of shoeboxes and moved one out of the stack, revealing another behind it, labelled *Crim*. He tossed the box casually onto the sofa beside me. 'Something for a rainy day.'

I lifted the lid to find a neat stack of envelopes tied together with ribbon. I recognised the handwriting instantly. It had been scrawled on my play scripts, my English homework, inside the Bible he'd given me when I left.

As you journey through life, remember that Christ is the Way, the Truth and the Light.

'Handwriting,' said Simon witheringly. 'In a few years' time we'll wonder how we ever relied on it so much. Anyway, have a look. Read as many as you like.'

I unknotted the ribbon and the pack of letters relaxed in my lap. I selected one at random and unfolded it. Held in the letter's folds was the slick red tongue of a fifty-pound note.

I took in some of the paragraphs. Names. Dates. Allusions to meetings.

The *tone* of them, though.

'It would sometimes be a twenty when we met in person,' he said. 'But always fifties in the letters. Quite a chunk of change on his salary. They were originally the old Christopher Wren ones, of course, but they stopped being legal tender last year, so I switched them for the reds. In case I ever need them.'

I looked through more of the letters. Some were handwritten, others were in the bubble-jet print of early word processors, graduating to crisper type as he had switched to a computer. What they had in common was that inside every one of them lurked a crisp fifty. There were postcards, too. Scotland. Peak District.

Simon was back in the kitchen.

'There must be over a grand in here,' I called. 'Why haven't you spent it?'

'Like I say, it's my rainy day fund.'

'Why did he give you so much? I mean, you said he stopped seeing your mum years ago.'

He put his head through the door and smiled sympathetically, as if he'd done something unpleasant to me. 'I am fucking ravenous. I'm going to go out and get us some takeaway.'

'I'll come with you.'

'Nah. Stay here. Lap it all up. I won't be long.'

'Do you need cash?' I said, smiling and holding up the box.

'They stay in there. I've got my own money. Back in a bit.'

Before I could object he'd left me alone with the letters by my side. They gave off a glow that rendered the setting sun irrelevant.

I opened the first one and started to read.

'I went for a box of chicken – hope that's okay.' He lingered in the doorway, as if my privacy were under infringement instead of his own.

Over an hour had passed. I was sitting on the sofa where he'd left me. When I'd finished reading the letters – there were twenty-two in total – I had put them back in chronological order, trussed them together and replaced them in their shoebox. It had felt important to do this before he returned, as a corpse is stitched up after an autopsy. Then I had sat, resisting the urge to get up in case I accidentally pry further into his life, listening to the roar of the renewed past.

He put a plastic bag on the table, humid and fragrant. He slumped down beside me, as if leaving me with the letters had brought him close to something like relaxation. I could tell from his gait and the smell on his breath that he'd been in a pub.

'I've got some questions,' I said.

'Oh, I bet you have.'

The trust we had banked in each other years before was maturing. We both wanted the impending conversation to have happened, but neither of us wanted to begin it.

'Let's start with a simple one,' I said. 'What's *posting*?'

'Ah.' Gratified smile. A professor applauding the perceptive question of a student. He tugged down the sides of the bag and opened the box of chicken. 'It was a game we played. It's how he would give me money. I'd open my trousers and he'd post the envelope into my underpants. Sometimes it would take a lot longer than others.' He chucked a paper napkin at my lap and gestured for me to dig in before pulling out a drumstick and plunging his teeth into it.

'When? Where?'

He wiped his mouth. 'All sorts of places. He'd come to my school and take me out for tea. Sometimes we'd go for picnics. At home as well, during the holidays. I stayed local, don't forget.'

'Simon. What about your mother?'

'She was busy enough trying to work him out for herself. Then later, when she'd given up on the idea of being with him, he'd been established as a sort of replacement father figure, so it made sense for us to keep seeing each other.'

I was asking the wrong questions. The obvious ones wouldn't come. They were too shouty, too prurient. And the tone of the letters had given me the answers to them anyway.

'I don't know what to ask next,' I said. 'Where do you start?'

He discarded his bone and tilted the box of chicken in my favour. 'Let me talk for a bit.'

He stayed active throughout, roaming the room, eating, guzzling booze: anything to deflect attention from the candour of his revelations. He lurched between directness and flippancy but never said anything without checking to see what effect it was having on me.

'Can you remember learning how to wank?' he said.

'Sure.'

'Did anyone show you?'

'It wasn't as if people weren't talking about it.'

'So it was there? At school?'

'Yeah.'

'Well, me too. Only I was shown how to do it. By Crimble.'

'No.'

'It's not so weird when you think about it.'

'I think it is, Simon.'

'Actually that's not even how it started. It started with the interviews.'

'Interviews?'

'On tape. You remember that big camcorder of his? You must. I could draw you a picture of it right now, I know it so well. He used to interview me with it every six months. A sort of video diary. To chart my progress. How I was changing. Then the questions started to get weird.'

'Where was this?'

'In his room. Sitting on that bed. Once or twice at his house.'

'And he taught you to ... really?'

'It was useful in a way. Gotta learn somehow.' The blitheness was disarming, but it was the mode he had chosen. 'You have to understand – he was like a friend.'

If I didn't ask it now, I never would. 'So how far did it go?'

He hooked a finger in the aperture of the traffic cone and dragged it roughly across the floor to where he was sitting. 'If we're doing this, I need more ammunition. Oh fuck, what am I doing? Speed up. This is only happening once. If you don't get on with it I'm going to lose my nerve.'

'Sorry.'

'Before you start, don't forget, this all happened over years. And if I'm completely honest, none of it ever felt that bad. You read about the shock when stuff like this happens to people for the first time. How they walk around afterwards unable to understand what's been done to them. Strangers in their own bodies all of a sudden. But I never really had that, because everything happened so slowly. Each step. Then you look back one day and think, *Where am I? What have I got used to?*'

'And?'

'And what?'

'What *did* you get used to?'

'You have to ask me.'

'Kissing?'

'Sure.'

'With tongues?'

'Of course.'

'That beard.'

'Scratchy. Come on!' he said, pacing around. He grabbed a cricket ball from one of his shoeboxes and chucked it from hand to hand. 'Get serious. I'll tell you anything, but you have to ask.'

It was dark. I took a breath. 'Did he make you touch his dick?'

'Make me?' He grinned. *Get a load of this. Get a load of what you fucking missed.* 'Yup.'

'Shit.'

'But not to start with. For a long time it was the other way round. Touched mine. Touched his own. There were stages. Years, don't forget. Keep going.'

I closed my eyes. 'Did he come?'

'Sure. With this weird, surprised noise, like he was hearing a bit of gossip, or finding a mouse in his biscuit tin.' He knew that was going to get me. 'Come on! We're only doing this once.'

'I'm only laughing because you are.'

'It's the only way to do it. I'm fucked if I'm doing it the other way.' More manic energy. Jumping around on his toes.

'Oral stuff?'

'Stages again. But yes. Both ways round.'

'I'm beginning to understand the money.'

'The money is to keep me friendly. Not that it's ever been phrased that way. Although it's not as if I would do anything.'

'Why not?'

'I don't want to. Keep going.'

'Did he ...?'

'Did he what?'

'You know.'

'Attempts were made.'

'So not—'

'Only one attempt, really. It was a write-off. He was drunk, I think. Said *this might hurt*. And it did. Didn't last long. And he was in bits afterwards. He cried, actually.'

'Fucking hell.'

'Come to think of it, you'll know exactly when it was. It was just before I came out to your grandparents' house for the extra exeat. Do you remember that? He was furious with me for going. I think he thought I was going to tell you. Or maybe your grandfather. Things de-escalated again after that. But it wasn't over until much later.'

The table was littered with grey bones and scraps of battered skin. We'd finished the beer and moved on to cheap red. Simon was sweating. I was drinking fast to dull an animal urge to flee the room.

With the hard revelations out of the way it was possible to step back from it, so we talked about other things for a while. But it had become the base layer of the conversation. Eventually we arrived at a more mundane level of questioning. Housekeeping. Current affairs.

'When did you last hear from him?'

'I stopped responding to his letters when I got kicked out of school. There was one more after that, on my eighteenth birthday. Arrived at home. You saw it. The one where he talks about me reaching my "majority". I never replied.' We were stinking drunk now. He raised an eyebrow. 'That's it? That's all you want to ask? No *was I scarred*?' He eyeballed me in a salacious way. 'No *did I enjoy it*?'

Not questions I'd have had the maturity to put into words. And I doubt he'd have been able to answer them. I probably didn't want him to.

'Do you think Crimble might have done it to other people?' I said instead.

'I don't know. I seriously doubt it. But having the Weapons Davis thing confirmed made me think. If it wasn't just one teacher, that opens up all sorts of nasty possibilities, don't you reckon? For collusion. Collaboration. Cover-ups. Did the Suttons know, for example?'

'How could they have known?'

'How could they not? Loads of us did. I mean, not you, apparently – but those of us who were remotely switched on knew that something was up. Don't get me wrong: it makes sense now that I know how cut off from it all you were.

You were always … a bit younger, somehow. It was one of the things I liked about you.'

What about him? I wanted to say. *That caring, magical person he pretended to be. The sheer fucking lie of it.* But clearly as far as Simon was concerned, that person had never stopped existing.

'So there it is,' he said. 'Nobody knows but me and you. And him, of course. I doubt he's ever told anyone. Poor fucker must be shitting himself now wondering if I'm going to come after him. Which I'm not going to do. But *somebody* might. We shall see.'

We should get round there, I thought. *There should be a torchlit mob outside his house.*

'You've got to go to the police. I'll do it with you.'

He shook his head. 'No way. And even if I wanted to, I can't.'

'Why not? You can't say there isn't evidence. Look at this stuff.'

Now he was angry with me. 'Because. Of. The. Tapes.'

'You think he'd—'

'He only said it a couple of times. But I got the message. Loud and clear. *Don't worry about the tapes. They're in a very safe place.*'

'I can't believe there's nothing you can do.'

'What would I do? Send him to prison? I don't want to do that.'

'If you just—'

Firm now. 'Stop. Okay? I didn't tell you so you could *do* something about it. You've helped me by listening, but that's as far as it goes. I mainly wanted to find out if it had happened to you too. And it didn't. So that's good. Lucky you.'

'You know,' I said, 'I thought of telling you it *had* happened to me, just now. To make you feel better.'

'Why do you think that would make me feel better? It might make me feel worse to know I wasn't the only one. Anyway, I'd have known if you were lying. You can see it on people a mile away. They wear it. Then again, I hadn't seen you in all this time, so ...'

So.

All my smug stories, honed over years. And all along there had been a dimension to the experience of others that had passed me by completely. What I had billed as the defining trauma of my young life had turned out to be absurdly, pathetically uncomplicated.

A dormant fairground ride was easing back into life. Music groaning up to speed. Gaudy images starting to flicker. The memories were my Zapruder film, my Ripper letter. *Back and to the left. Catch me when you can, Mishter Lusk.* And now, a terrible realisation was looming.

'It's my fault,' I said.

'What? What are you talking about?'

'I led you to him. I persuaded you. It's my fault.'

He threw down his cricket ball in frustration and got to his feet.

'Yeah. That's right. Because in the two years I was there before you, he'd never come near me until you alerted him to my existence. Nothing happened before you. Fuck's sake. Come on, Max. Did you think this story only started when you entered the frame?'

I stared at him, defeated. 'I don't know what to say.'

'Then don't say anything. Be happy. Pass me the bottle.'

When I left the following morning, sheer relief at what I had avoided made the world run lush and vivid. Then the anger returned. I sat alone on the boat, lit up with its energy, eyeballing the coots and moorhens outside.

The more I thought about it, the more I realised I could only remember Crimble taking me out of my bed. I had no memories at all of him putting me back. I remembered the relief as I sat on the edge of his bed in my dressing gown. Imagined I could smell the scalded milk as he poured it over the chocolate powder in the mug. Was it so hard to picture where things might have gone from there? To step in and populate that darkness?

How do you do it, though? How do you go from not doing it, to doing it? Do you go for the mouth, like an adult lover? Beardy-lipped pecks up the neck? Unwelcome intimacy. The smell of someone else's fridge. A school friend's grotty family car. Accidentally using your father's toothbrush. The lowering of those blue tracksuit bottoms. Dark reek of mature male. No. He'd have been clean, wouldn't he? Quite the stickler for that. Always on about hygiene. Sensitive too, no doubt. Clear from the letters that for him it was love. He'd given it airs. But airs are all very well until you get down to solids. Crimble's chicken-skin scrotum, the seeking bulb of his cock.

All that before you even got to good old Eric. How sharp was the pain of cloven skin? How did it feel to be so occupied? Was there a numb moment in the aftermath when you thought you had cleaned yourself up, sat on the edge of the bath and planted a crimson kiss on the enamel? Did a scab form within you like a stone at your core? Was there a compound aroma of blood and shit and come?

One thing I could name but never hope to imagine was the shame. Because empathy only goes so far before inexperience abolishes it. You can feel yourself right out of a thought but you can't think yourself into a feeling.

It had so nearly been me. But I had given the impression that I wasn't a safe bet. That I would have talked. Though I almost certainly wouldn't have. Because who on earth does?

Over the coming days I developed a new method of dissociation to manage the blaze of memories ignited and reconfigured by Simon's revelations. I would picture my hand working an ancient metal crank inside a giant carousel of slides. As I turned it, all the possible images I could alight on would flicker around me until the machine came to rest and a memory selected itself, and I would walk into it. It was a way of giving the whirligig some sense of order. There was no stopping it. However much I might try to think of other things, my mind was set on casting backwards, imposing new logic on my memories in light of what I now knew. Whatever it threw up, the present could only feel plodding and predictable. The past was where it was at.

15

Time to go, if we're going.

His soft voice folding into my dreams.

He's good at waking people up. He does it quietly. He isn't one to defibrillate you into consciousness with a dog up your sheets.

He harvests his chosen ones before sunrise, the group swelling dorm by dorm like Zorro's posse riding out from behind the rocks. We struggle into our shorts and stumble through dewy fields to his hollered encouragement. His dog orbits us. Our legs go fiery numb. He wears a tracksuit and it is okay to joke about that.

'What's the matter, Mr Crighton? Afraid of a little cold air?' we say, parroting him. We know how far we can go without ceasing to charm.

'I'm a million years older than you lot,' he says. 'And you don't want to see the state of my legs.'

As we struggle up the hill he trots backwards at the head of the group, beard wet, glasses fogged, shouting louder, gunning our engines. At the top he breaks up a Kendal Mint Cake and bestows generous pieces. The mentholated sugar detonates in our systems, an early-morning high. We return in time to shower before breakfast, which never tastes as good as it does after these early starts.

The excluded heap their scorn.

'It's the Crimble-gang,' drawls Luke, eyes clotted with sleep, nursing his eggy bread and tomatoes. 'You lot must be insane.'

But we are still in the afterglow. 'Do you good to get out a little more,' we say. 'Look at that complexion.' Crimble's words in our mouths again.

Before Crimble's intervention in my life here, the only pastime I could reliably use to escape was the piano. I'd sneak off to one of the music rooms in those early days and address myself to whichever knackered upright was available. Pick one of my grandfather's favourite songs and play it until I could do so with my eyes closed, which would enable me to inhabit the tune so fully that I could almost hear my grandfather's breathing nearby as he listened. It was my first inkling of an understanding that music is the best weapon we have against time.

Two years on, I do this still. But now, thanks to Crimble, there are other ways of getting out of myself. One is his exhausting activities. The other is books. Not just the horror fiction I would choose myself but the novels prescribed by him. Their sentences blaze in my head. I write them down.

Mr Holmes, they were the footprints of a gigantic hound.

O my poor old Harry Jekyll, if ever I read Satan's signature upon a face, it is on that of your new friend.

The only way to get rid of temptation is to yield to it.

No one would have believed that this world was being watched keenly and closely by intelligences greater than man's and yet as mortal as his own.

Does he choose them deliberately, these stories of transformation? They feel entirely realistic to me. Of course a painting can come to life. Of course a man can turn into a monster when he drinks a potion. Of course a person can be invisible. Of course Martians exist. Just look at this lot.

He has spent the last two years feeding me up on distraction. When I reach one plateau, a new slope is introduced. Running. Acting. Climbing. He has me in his web of responsibility and reward.

My responsibility has a title. I am Captain of Gallipoli, the younger boys' dormitory. It is thought that my *rocky start* puts me in an ideal position to watch over these new arrivals, some as young as eight. Their fragility and confusion are evident to all. They are as soft as the stuffed toys they still clutch. Fertilised eggs themselves, cracked open too soon. Their dorm is on the East Wing, alongside the girls, whose own quarters, having only recently been established, are called Goose Green.

When my charges have stopped crying and fallen asleep, I read before bed in the corridor armchair. The girls flit out in twos or threes.

'Max Denyer. What weird book are you reading tonight?'

'It's about the Nazis getting hold of the spear that pierced Christ's side and using it to gain a supernatural advantage and win World War II.'

'What was the last one about again?'

'Mutant rats eating people all over London.'

I can see into their pyjamas. Smell their smell. I feel an intoxicating sense of vulnerability at being the only male in their company.

'Was that the one with the cut-off arm on the front cover?'

'That one was about radioactive killer crabs.'

'What's the difference?'

'The crab one mainly happens by the sea.'

'Any good bits in this one?' says Becky Lynch. Colour flushes my cheeks. The others don't know what she means, but I do. The rats or crabs or whatever they are tend to favour striking after their victims have enjoyed about a page and a half of vividly described intercourse. Sex which is interrupted by the first tingle of a bite or a pincer on the unsuspecting limb of (typically) the woman. I have shown such pages to Becky, who affects disgust then asks to look again, sitting close.

Thundering feet and breathlessness.

'Quick, Zahra's having another vision.'

Oh God.

Let me handle this.

Don't crowd her out.

Zahra claims to be especially sensitive to the spirits that are said to haunt this place: at carefully selected moments, she trades in hysterical sightings of malevolent eyes at the window, of the Grey Lady, of the Dangling Man. I will understand later that like other foreign pupils she is weaponising her exoticism. Turning it from weakness to strength. And getting confused into the bargain. It's a perfectly natural response to a place where myth and fact are interchangeable as a matter of course.

She can sure pick her moment. Everyone energised. An audience in search of a performance. By the time I reach her corner of the dormitory the show is in full swing. She glances back at the window and screams again. 'It was a face a FACE and it wanted to tell me something.'

'Calm down, Zahra. You've got to calm down.'

She assumes a more catatonic posture, broadcasting her sensitivity on full. 'He looked so sad,' she says.

Miss Fletcher flames in the doorway. 'Back to your beds at once, girls.' I stand impassively, assuming the anger will be reserved for the females. Then she turns. 'As for you, young man.'

'As for me, what?'

'Watch your tone. You're only allowed to read outside if your boys are sleeping. And you're certainly never allowed in here. Those little buggers are running riot next door while you're in here messing about with these girls. Mr Crighton will have something to say about this, I'm sure.'

The reckoning takes place in his room the next day. There is no hot chocolate. The ham radio is not hissing comfortingly in the background. He does not invite me to sit on the bed.

'Did we do the wrong thing, putting you in charge of Gallipoli?' he says. 'You don't seem to be coping at all. If you are up to it, why are you mucking about on the girls' side? And you can spare me the ghost stories. It's hopeless. After all we've done for you. It's taken you longer to settle in than anyone I've known, and this is how you repay us. I've half a mind to give you a dose of Jemima.'

Jemima. His punishment tool. A large, flat brush.

Don't do it. You're not that weak. But here the treacherous tears come. Try to keep your eyes wide open so they stay up in there. Always a fool's errand. The liquid dams, then breaks, and the droplets tumble under their own weight.

'You're crying,' he says. 'And that's good. It means you're taking this seriously.'

'Can I go now?'

'There's one more thing I wanted to ask you before you do: are you coming to Music Club this Saturday?'

'Yes.'

'Make yourself useful and see if you can get Simon along too. I just can't get him interested in any of my stuff at the moment.'

'Okay,' I say. 'I'll try.'

★

We reach the end of the avenue as night is beginning to fall.

'I can't believe I'm doing this,' says Simon.

'Rather be sat watching *Doctor Who* in your dressing gown with the others?' I say.

'Fiddling with your circuit boards?' says Ish.

'*Not joining in?*' says Becky.

'It's great,' I say. 'You just listen to records and he brings you food.'

Simon grumbles all the way down the hill, and says nothing as Crimble welcomes us in. But his mood changes when the burgers come out and we gather round the hi-fi in his cramped, dog-scented front room.

'So,' says Crimble, 'what have we been listening to?'

'Louis Armstrong,' I say.

'Good old Satch,' he says. 'Extraordinary man.' Bloom of pathetic pleasure. 'But his music sounds a little unsophisticated after a while, don't you think? If jazz is what you're after, how about this?' He pulls down a record, puts it on the turntable and drops the needle. Live recording. A tentative piano phrase. Repeated a few times before a tenor sax mournfully swoops in above it. 'Ellington and Coltrane. "In a Sentimental Mood". Two schools of jazz meeting for the first time. The older man is being deferential to the younger man. Letting him show off. And in response, the younger man plays with the most beautiful restraint. Can you hear that?'

Simon looks bored. We eat our burgers. He brings out cake.

'I want you to say nothing for the next sixteen minutes,' says Crimble. 'We're going on a journey.' The sound of a thin snare drum beating a tattoo strikes faintly up. Crimble's voice rises with the music as the plucked strings fall in and the melody starts. 'I want you to put all thoughts of ice skaters out of your mind. This piece is far too important. Ravel describes it as *one very long, gradual crescendo.* But it's more than that. The orchestra adds layer after layer, trying to overcome the mechanisation of the drum with melody. But it fails. It must fall into step with the machine of the beat. This, boys and girls, is the effect of *modernity*.'

We move on to Flanders and Swann, his idea of light relief. Then there is some Brahms. Afterwards he asks if anyone has brought anything they want to play to the group. We get out our tapes. Bon Jovi. Paul Simon. Soul II Soul. He listens attentively to each submission.

At the end he makes an announcement. 'It's time to start casting the school play. And I want you all involved. Including our new arrivals.' As if he's heard Simon's objection in advance, he adds, 'There will be important technical work to do as well as the acting. And anyone who moans will be given a bigger role. So, let the show begin!'

Before we leave, the conversation turns back to ghosts, as it has often of late. To the Grey Lady who is said to walk the corridors. To the Dangling Man in the Upper Gallery.

'Aha!' says Crimble, seizing on Simon's smirk. 'You think it's nonsense! Of course. We all know you're a man of science.'

'I've never seen one,' says Simon.

'Well, I have a sensible head on my shoulders too,' says Crimble. 'But I've seen things walking around up there after dark that I can't explain.'

'Like what?'

'I'll come and fetch you one of these nights and we'll have a wander.'

As we walk up the hill I am already looking forward to descending it again for the next music evening. The world feels augmented, as if reality has been connected to a massive power source that makes everything bolder and more precarious at once.

'This play,' says Simon, from within a reverie of his own. 'What *technical work* do you think he's talking about?'

'Don't know,' I say.

'Well, nice try. But I'm not going anywhere near it.'

Wake up.

That voice again. Transmitting only to me. My charges asleep. The torchlit lenses of his glasses as welcome a sight in this dark as the windows of a well-loved house. But he is not alone.

'Spook-hunting time,' says an unbroken voice at his side, and there in the side-glow bobs Simon's animated face.

I collect the strange litter of my thoughts, new information jostling with scraps of dream.

'What about this lot?' I say to Crimble.

'They'll live,' he says.

So off the three of us go, following in the wake of his torch beam to the Upper Gallery. Canvas chairs stacked against the wall, the television on its high shelf, the struck stage silent.

'I notice you're both looking up,' says Crimble. Because he has said this, we both look up. 'And I know what you're looking for.'

'Have you ever seen him?' I say.

'The Dangling Man? It's funny. He's quite famous. You can read about him in several books on England's haunted houses. But I always thought it was rubbish. Then one night something happened in here that changed my mind.'

He spins his yarn. Doing the rounds one foggy night he glimpses a pale shape in the rafters. Hears a creaking rope. The curtains sway. He moves to shut the windows and finds them already closed. Then he hears a noise from under the floorboards. A whining, like that of a trapped animal.

'Did you know that there's a tunnel under this room?' he says. 'You can get to it from the trapdoor on the stage. Very handy for plays. But I think it's been there a lot longer than our little theatre.'

Simon goes down first. Crimble uses his torch to show him the extent of the passage but does not offer him the torch itself. 'If you want anything to show itself, you're better off in complete darkness,' he says.

We hear Simon's movements beneath, getting quicker as he crawls away. I drop down after him. Torchlight plays behind me. I can see Simon's slippered feet, his pyjamas furring with dust.

'Good luck,' says Crimble. The hatch slams shut overhead.

Nervous laughter. We move forwards. He hears the breathing first, but I hear it too. Then Simon screams.

Later, after much questioning, I finally manage to get out of him what happened. He swears, no joke, that down there in the dark, something licked his face.

Crimble advises us to keep the story to ourselves, knowing full well what the chances of that are. When I arrive at the first play meeting two days later, Simon is sitting in the front row as if it had been his intention all along.

'The most important thing is that you get the lines down before rehearsals start,' says Crimble. 'They need to come off your tongue like the best lie you've ever told.'

We sit in a circle of canvas chairs in the Upper Gallery. Those of us in the know glance at the stage trapdoor, wondering if it will feature.

Crimble's mind-reading powers are as sharp as ever. 'By the way, we won't be performing any of it in here. Part One by firelight in the Great Hall. That's where we shall see the Tempters at work, and watch poor Thomas walking wilfully towards his destiny. Stop that, Price, or your part will be downgraded to Third Attendant. Then, during the interval, the audience will move to the chapel, where the graceful archbishop will give his sermon, and the grisly business of Part Two will play out. And where the knights will address the audience directly to justify their actions as his broken body lies on the floor.

'*The last temptation is the greatest treason: / To do the right deed for the wrong reason.*

'What do these lines mean? They are the crux of the play. While Thomas knows that to martyr himself is the right thing to do, he must be certain that he is not doing it out of vanity. Because he knows that his death will make him famous. Immortal, in fact. You, Drake, will need to think about this more than anyone.'

Simon sits up in his chair. 'Why?'

'Because I have decided that you must be our Thomas.'

It is a masterly move. The challenge laid down in public, when Simon's confidence is high. Even so Crimble has to talk him round afterwards. I hear later that he's promised Simon plenty of private rehearsals to help him get the part right. That he, Crimble, will make sure everything goes well. And that I, Max, will be tasked to help him get his lines down perfectly in the meantime.

Luke is seething. The only concession he ever makes to the Crimble-cult is to put himself forward for the play when it comes around. He has a proper talent for acting, and until now has always been given a prominent role. He obviously thought the part of Thomas was a done deal.

'Why has he given it to Simon?' he says. 'He doesn't even want it.'

'I think he thinks it would be good for him,' I say.

'Jesus, the stuff you get away with if Crimble's bonking your mum.'

★

The thin hiss of my walkie-talkie in the darkness. Coughs from adjacent beds.

'A misshapen hag with foul hair stands before you. Will you confront her or flee? Over.'

'Is it Miss Fletcher?' I say. 'Over.'

'Enough stalling,' says Simon's voice through the static. 'Choose. Make the wrong choice and the consequences will be dire. You will only have yourself to blame. Over.'

'Why can't I just go back down the mountain? Over.'

'Because the mountain's on fire, you idiot. You've got to get inside it or you'll never get past the Dangling Man to face the Prime Monster. Over.'

'Hang on a minute. Back in bed! Why is it always you, Miller?' I stare down the room to make sure the rest aren't moving. 'Enough games. Back to the script. He's worried you aren't going to learn this in time.'

'Is he now?' says Simon. 'Come on then.'

'Have you put your book down? There's no point in doing it if you've got it in your hand.'

'It's down.'

'Right. Go from *Mirth matches melancholy*. Over.'

'Okay. *We do not know very much of the future, / Except that from generation to generation, / The same things happen again and again …*'

On the day of the dress rehearsal Simon and I are on our way to collect our costumes when we see a police car parked outside the main entrance. Crimble stands flanked by two officers. He raises an arm to call us over.

'These, I think, are the two you're looking for,' we hear him say.

'Afternoon, boys,' says a friendly, young policeman. 'We wanted to have a word about your walkie-talkies.'

'Our what?'

'It's fine, you're not in trouble,' says Crimble. 'You've been using them to learn your lines for the play, correct?'

'Would I be right in thinking you didn't get them in this country?' asks the policeman.

'My dad bought them in Japan,' I say.

'Thought so. We need to take them off your hands, I'm afraid.'

'Why?'

'Because you've been broadcasting every last word on the police waveband, that's why. It's taken us a while to locate the source, but after we heard a few telltale signs in what you were saying we realised it could only have been coming from up here. Don't worry, we won't tell Mr Crighton what you've been saying about him.'

The policemen think this is a very good joke.

I produce the offending items and they assess that they are mere toys.

'Hang on to them,' says the policeman. 'But no more using them round here, okay?'

When they've gone, Crimble holds out his hand. 'Radios.'

'But he said—'

'Do as you're bloody well told.'

Crimble is so distracted during the rehearsal that he makes no comment on how it's going, and sits clutching the walkie-talkies as if they were something deadly. His mood only lightens towards the end, when there is a mishap during Becket's murder. Crimble has concocted a mixture of boiled beetroot, rhubarb and dog food that is meant to be the archbishop's brains. I keep it in my pocket in a freezer bag. After Luke, Ish and I have smashed Simon's head in with our swords I am supposed to lean down to check his injuries, dropping the bag behind him before standing again to deliver a stamp to his skull which will spill the 'brains' all over the altar steps. It is the highlight of the performance. But my foot slips on the bag and instead of delivering his *coup de grâce,* the knight Reginald Fitz Urse skids across the floor in a spray of vegetable and dog meat, then falls into a choir stall.

'Don't worry, boys,' calls Crimble from his pew. 'It'll be all right on the night. Dear me. History repeats itself, first as tragedy, then as farce.'

We watch the arriving cars from the window of Trafalgar, made up and affixed with facial hair. Crimble sets up his Super-8 camera on a tripod to video the performance. This is off-putting enough even before I realise that my grandparents are sitting in the front row. He sits with an amused expression on his face whenever I'm on, and looks on the verge of sleep the rest of the time. She fiddles with her hearing aid and follows the text of the play in her lap.

Crimble's calculation pays off. Simon's calm precision with the lines, his bloodlessness, translate plausibly into the holy calm of St Thomas. And the acting is ... who knows how the acting is? We're thirteen years old.

It does get to me, though, at one point. This much I know. There is a feeling out of time as I bang on the church door with the other three knights. I *am* that warrior in the cold, here to murder a man.

On the night, the brains scatter beautifully.

16

THAT WE SHOULD actually volunteer to spend a week of the Easter holiday in the Peak District with him shows how far things have come. As the minibus heads north I can't believe I've agreed to it myself. But this is a handpicked squad, eight of his closest pals, and there's no resisting its allure.

We stay in a youth hostel beside racing water. We abseil off cliffs. We slide face first down grassy slopes, sheep shit caking our sweatshirts. We eat chocolate and crisps and pies. During evening meals we endure the forced conviviality of the youth hostel dining table, thigh-to-thigh with men who smell of damp and mud. Before retiring to our bunk room we sit outside supplementing our dinner with Pot Noodles. Forever after, the rush of fresh water over stones, the bleating of sheep, the sight of a fizzing cloud of midges, will recall for me the delight of vinegary, salty strands drenched in MSG, the chemical rush when you down the final shot of spicy sludge.

Crimble brings a length of rope to the picnic table to teach us knots, and pours cans of bitter with ceremony into his pint mug. The conversation is wide-ranging, the mood ecstatic. A bold spring sunset illuminates the pasture.

'Why do we like green fields?' he says. 'Those without faith say it's because we've evolved to like them. That the fields were there by accident, and over the millennia we progressed from being swamp slime to sophisticated Bach-loving ale drinkers. That this is why we find beauty in our surroundings. Now. Does that *really* seem more believable to you than that someone designed the fields to look beautiful in the first place?'

The atmosphere is so freeing. The inhibitions are down. Why wouldn't I speak up?

'If that's the deal then leave me out of it,' I say.

He puts down his rope. 'Where did you get that from?'

'It's something my grandfather says. Sorry.'

I fear I've offended him, and realise I've never understood the expression anyway.

'Well, I say Grandpa's wrong. It doesn't work like that. There is no *out of it*.'

The final term begins. There will be exams. For now it's cut grass and evening light and late games on the lawn.

A morning run with Crimble. I am later than the rest, dressing at speed, hungry for breakfast. I hear soft cursing from the next changing room. When I investigate I find Neil Lynch leaning on the bench at a strange angle.

He is no longer the slight boy he was when I arrived, but life has continued to have at him. Only last term he was beaten in front of the whole school by Weapons Davis for wearing brown shoes instead of black ones to assembly.

'You all right?' I say.

'I can't get them down.'

'What?'

'They're stuck.' He lifts up the back of his dressing gown so I can see the rusty dots which have dried the fabric of his pyjama bottoms to his buttocks. 'Blood blisters. They burst in the night if you don't remember to sleep on your front. Which I promised myself I was going to do.'

Don't cry, I think. *That will only make you feel worse.* 'Do you want me to help you?'

'I thought if I got in the shower with the bottoms on I could get them off without it hurting.'

'Come on, then,' I say.

He follows me dumbly to the stall, removes his top and steps in. 'You better not tell anyone about this.'

'You know I wouldn't.' Voices outside as everyone piles in to breakfast. 'Hurry up.'

I turn the water on slowly, just enough to let it flow down his back and into his pyjamas. The wet patch spreads down the striped fabric. The dots darken. The fabric separates itself from the skin. I am not prepared for the blues and yellows, the scored, broken tissue.

'Neil,' I say, 'what happened?'

'Okay,' he says. 'You can go now.'

He runs soon after that.

They try to keep it from us, but we are their best bet at resolving the situation before the police, and therefore the parents, find out, so they can't keep us out of it for long. Our first indication that something is up is the unusual concentration of teachers on the premises at one time. Normally they leave whoever is on evening duty to exercise his unique style in private, but not tonight.

'All right, where's Lynch? Has anyone seen Neil Lynch?' Wagstaff pounds down the ranks at Assembly. It's a bright summer evening and we are keen to get back outside. There has been talk of British Bulldogs.

The game is cancelled. Wagstaff, Spinks and Crimble all drive off in different directions. A police car arrives and parks outside the Great Hall. We become urbane, knowing commentators.

It's been clear for ages that he shouldn't be here.

Does Becky know?

Do you think he's dead?

Neil is picked up trying to hitchhike on a dual carriageway nearly four miles away. When I eventually get to ask him what happened when he was brought back, he says that Tony Sutton took him into his private-side and offered him a double ration at the tuck shop for the rest of term if he didn't tell his parents.

'Did you take it?' I say.

'I told him I'd think about it,' he says. It's the first time I've ever really seen him smile.

But perhaps he does talk to them. And perhaps they do something. Because it is announced not long after that, like so many of us, Mr Weathers-Davis will be 'moving on' at the end of term, no doubt in possession of a glowing reference.

By now, so far as I know, most of us have got there. Some are rumoured to have shown others the way, and in fabled instances whole dormitories are said to have rushed there together. I was not one of the early ones, in spite of a better than average awareness of the broader subject matter thanks to my grandfather and his stories.

For a long time my body simply doesn't do what I have heard it is supposed to do. I can bring about a pulsing pleasure which feels as if it's to do with blood flow more than anything else, but nothing more. Then, quite unexpectedly one night (torchlight, charges asleep), there is for the first time a little gem of liquid, its quantity and viscosity increasing with each of my eager throbs. A few goes later, the issue has become a messy inevitability. I will remember only relief. The conversations of others on the topic have worried me for some time. The legend of the biscuit game, apocryphal or not, is at least no longer incomprehensible.

The description of *milk boiling over* in one of the books Becky and I read together now makes sense.

Simon is far too secretive to have released any details of his own journey, but true to form he has risen to the mechanical challenge. Last year he fashioned a device using seven toy tractor tyres glued into a tube, attached to a piece of wood with a hole in it. He then attached the tube to the drive shaft of a motor colonised from a Scalextric car-racing set. His wanking machine, which was passed around for a while before it was acknowledged to add no value to the experience, became known as the Stale-sex-trick. Luke's coinage. He was proud of that.

The aftermath of a summer storm. The looming exams have prompted a relaxation of normal protocols as we are given time to revise, which brings new opportunities.

'They won't be here,' says Simon.

'They will.'

We reach the outfield of the cricket pitch, step over the boundary rope and head for the cover that is wheeled out to protect the square from rainfall. I drop to the ground, roll under the frame and enter the domed world inside. The short grass perfectly dry. Cracked earth, warmed plastic.

Simon's feet linger impatiently outside. 'Well? I'm not coming in if it's just you in there.'

'You should come in,' I say, eyes locked already with those of Becky Lynch, who lies in wait at one end wearing an impish expression. Beyond her, in a separate compartment of the cover, lies a bored-looking Zahra Nasri.

Simon's face appears at the other end. He is told to get in quickly to avoid detection. My mind is no longer concerned with him or how he might be feeling.

There is giggling, then a concentrated silence. I don't know what's happening at Simon's end but at my own,

Becky's thin lips and mine have indeed met, and our bodies are touching in more places than they ever have before. It is exquisite awkwardness. I could exist forever in this limited, limitless space.

The experience ends abruptly, with a sharp shout from the other end. *I don't want to.* Then he's gone. He must have bolted, because when I stick my head out to look, he's nowhere to be seen.

'What did you *do* to him?' asks Becky with admiration.

'Nothing at all,' says Zahra, who then grumpily announces she isn't about to lie there waiting.

It's more than enough to talk about.

The morning of the extra exeat is as traumatic as ever. Kids who haven't made the cut weep at windows as the getaway vehicles arrive for those who have accrued the requisite number of Good Marks, each car a capsule world bearing the smells and comforts of loving environments.

Today the specific drama involves the Turner brothers, only one of whom has qualified for release. Simon and I sit like elder statesmen watching the separation play out. Mrs Turner weeps. The boy going home weeps. The boy left behind sobs, clenched in the long arm of Tony Sutton, his wails getting louder as the car pulls away through the balustrade.

'I don't think he thought they were going to go through with it,' I say.

'Well, he knows now,' says Simon.

Then all other thoughts are vaporised by the solar flare of joy as my grandfather's van sweeps onto the gravel.

Lunch is a feast of his home-made meatballs, followed by my grandmother's jam tarts with whipped cream. I watch Simon throughout, on the lookout for any hint of indifference. But there's wonder in his reaction, a stunned silence, particularly at the kind of thing it's okay to say here across the border. He sits awkwardly at the table, unfamiliar with its protocols. I, by contrast, am keen to showboat the available freedoms and pleasures, prompting my grandfather's most colourful anecdotes.

'Tell him about Stumpy Witney,' I say.

'Not now, Max.'

'Grandad used to know this guy called Stumpy Witney. His dick was so long that when he put it on the bar in the pub it hung down the other side. Tell him.'

Embarrassment, bordering on irritation. 'Shut up and eat your bloody lunch,' he says. It frustrates me. I can't work out why the parameters have been set the way they have.

Simon's legs are curled around the legs of his chair as if he were in danger of falling to the floor. His hair covers his face as he addresses his food. When he's offered more lemonade, he nods and grips the glass but does not drink.

My grandfather changes tack. 'What are we going to do with your afternoon, then? Bit of boating on the pond? Summer sledging?'

'Simon's brought his computer with him,' I say.

We get as far as plugging the Commodore 64 into an old black-and-white television and showing my grandparents the first screen of *Mindshadow*.

'So what do you do?' says my grandfather.

'You wake up on a beach with no memory and you have to travel around and find out who you are.'

My grandfather loses patience quickly. 'Turn that thing off and let's go outside. I'll show you who you are.'

He tells us to wait by his van and disappears to the workshop. We stand under the shade of the barn hearing him whistle in the distance. He reappears carrying spray cans with different coloured tops and a packet of disposable face masks.

'Thought you might like to give the old girl a fresh lick of paint,' he says, pointing at the van, which has been so shaken up by its many trips round the park that it is nearing the end of its life.

'What colour do you want it?' I say.

'Paint what you like. You can write "balls" all over it for all I care. Though it better not be too rude if I'm going to take you back in it later.' This last remark comes with a provocative raising of the eyebrows. Simon smiles for the first time that day and we reach for the cans.

We're tentative at first. But before long we are firing great sweeps of paint up and down the van's sides. I write *CRAPMOBILE* and *SKILL* and decorate the words with stars and crosses. When I go round to Simon's side I see that he's sprayed a series of immaculate swirls and concentric circles, in the middle of which he's written the title of his current favourite song, *BACK TO LIFE*. We collaborate on the writing of the word *BALLS* in massive block letters on the back. At the last minute, when we're running out of energy, Simon sprays underneath it: *TO THIS PLACE*.

By teatime he is a different person, delivering the kind of quip that he'd say to me in private, animated by the thought of us pulling into the school in the gaudily decorated vehicle, and the message he hopes someone in power will notice as it pulls away.

My grandfather opens a bottle, and finally we get the one about Stumpy Witney. Then he asks me what kind of cake I want bringing up for my birthday next week.

'There's no point, really,' says Simon. 'They cut them up so small to make them go round that nobody ever gets a proper-sized piece.'

'Well,' says my grandfather, 'we shall have to see what we can do about that.'

*

The cake passes into legend from the moment it arrives. It takes four boys just to carry it inside. Nine double sponges filled with jam and cream, iced together into one square on a specially made board. It takes up the entire boot space of their Citroën estate. The singing of 'Happy Birthday' nearly takes the roof off.

Weapons Davis wears a contemptuous smile throughout, and takes pleasure in cutting the same mean little squares as usual. We watch in disbelief as the majority of the cake is carried away. It will reappear so often over the coming days and weeks, increasingly desiccated and tired, that the cake, and the cocky boy responsible for it, will become a positive source of resentment.

But there is a night, two days after my birthday, when Luke gets me, Simon and Ish out of our various beds and leads us to the larder. Fired by injustice, making no effort to lower our voices, we stand together on the moonlit flags of the kitchen eating a slab of night-cake each, cramming our mouths with rightfully owned jam and cream.

And then the final assembly is upon us. It goes like any other, but for the standing ovation given to Eric Weathers-Davis, who is presented, with great ceremony, the leaving gift of a pair of binoculars. When the cars file in for chapel, that will be the end of it. 'Jerusalem' will be sung. The trunks will be loaded up. Home addresses will be exchanged on scraps of paper, to be lost soon after.

On the roof, Simon unfolds a penknife and scratches his initials into the lead, then invites me to do the same. The meticulous lawn-stripes; the bees zoning in and out, the riot of flowers: all of it is the same as it was when I came here for interview three years earlier. I might look down on myself and my grandmother getting out of the car and wonder whether any of it had happened at all.

Ish and Luke spot us from the ground and quicken their pace, eager to come and join in with whatever we are up to.

Simon speaks quickly. 'Let's make an agreement. If we haven't seen each other before, we'll meet on this roof in exactly ten years' time.'

'What – in the year 1999?' I say. 'We'll be *twenty-three*. We'll probably be married with kids and stuff.'

'Is it a deal?'

'Okay, it's a deal.'

He's still holding the penknife but we just shake hands instead of going for anything more dramatic.

'I've never got that hymn,' he says as we wait for our friends to arrive. 'Why would anybody want to build Jerusalem here?'

17

8 October 1989

My dear Simon,

Nearly there! It will be half-term before you know it and I am writing to see how you've been getting on these last few weeks. It seems a long time ago now but I much enjoyed our 'day out', and I hope you did too. If you want to do it again I'm sure I could get clearance from Shuttleworth, who seems to me to be a decent sort (I've met plenty of housemasters over the years and believe me you could do a lot worse). But I suppose I had better not push my luck, so it will probably have to wait until next year.

That does leave us half-term, though. Shall I come and take you out one day? We could go for another drive. Or have you got plans with Mum? It might be better to set a date now so that you don't get too caught up in the excitement of being at home. If we said the Monday, would that work? Tell your mother as soon as she picks you up so you don't forget.

Have you managed to spend more time in the computer room? The equipment you described sounded exciting. Do try to get outside as well. It saddened me that you hadn't done any fishing since you started. You don't need me to tell you my views on the benefits of fresh air! Anyway, you look very well in the photos I took. It's been weeks now so your hair is probably growing out. I noticed you'd had it cut shorter before starting school, but not as drastically as I had feared. Thank you.

And I was very sorry to hear you say that you hadn't made many friends. Two things: (1) it's very early days, and (2) you must remember that you are so clever and so grown up in your outlook that you probably seem a bit threatening to others. In time I'm sure they will come to realise how much stronger you are than them and start looking up to you instead of finding you intimidating, and then you will find some kindred spirits.

Life continues at this end. I'm soldiering on with Music Club and starting to think about what play to put on next term. I think it's going to be a farce called Charley's Aunt *– hardly the highbrow fare of last year! – but I just don't have anyone now with whom I would want to put on anything as ambitious as* Murder in the Cathedral. *In general I've found it impossible to settle into the new school year. I think I've been trying to pretend for as long as I could that the world hasn't moved on. What (or who) could have made last year so very special, I wonder . . .?*

The wheel must keep turning, of course (you remember that line?), but I am finding it harder than usual this time round. I don't know how I shall put together another climbing trip next Easter knowing that so many of my old friends will be absent (I think you know which one in particular). I shall always think of my friend most at the high hostel by the river, and in particular of our afternoon above the scree slope.

I was so pleased to have so much of your time when we met. It's true, isn't it, that time spent with your closest friends is the most intense kind of time there is? That, at any rate, is how I feel.

I hope you've noticed that when I write to you, I do my best to talk about my feelings as much as what I've been up to. Do you think you might do the same when you write to me?

I felt terribly twisty inside after we said goodbye.

(I think you know what I mean.)
With much love from,
Crimble

16 March 1992

My dear Simon,

The week of the big trip! You must be buzzing with excitement. I know we went over all the kit in some detail but just in case: there should be three fully juiced-up batteries in the bag as well as the charger, and that plug will fit European sockets. I don't know why I'm presuming to tell you anything about electronics, you could probably rewire the whole thing in about five minutes, but I know I'd feel sick if I'd somehow forgotten something and you weren't able to make a record. PLEASE make sure you don't accidentally wipe the stuff that's already on the cassette – it's the one we began at Christmas and I adore what's on there, I just haven't had a moment yet to put it on one of your 'master tapes'.

I can't seem to lay my hands on the tape we were using last year. It's not 'Simon's Travels', which is full, or 'Further Adventures of SD', which was the one from that day on the boat. It might just be called 'Simon Drake' and it's important because it has your third Big Q&A on it, which I have not yet transferred. You're growing up fast and we need to be good custodians of our archive! If this doesn't make sense, call me at school after 9 p.m. on Wednesday. (Hopefully they will be in bed by then, but you know how it is.)

I was delighted by your last note, and there's absolutely no need to apologise for your handwriting: it's splendid. I would far rather you wrote to me naturally instead of getting into a fluster over it as if the letter were a bit of Prep to be marked. My tummy flipped when I read that you missed me: you can't possibly know (do you?) how much I've been missing you, and how much I too wished that we could 'be together', to quote your words.

It was lovely that we managed to steal that extra hour on our last day out – I was dreading having to rush you back too quickly. Posting the note was a hoot, and I felt rather tingly when you asked me to retrieve it. It was probably a bit tingly for you too, but you liked it as far as I could tell! Did you? I hope the pressie comes in handy. I know the rules are different now but do be careful not to go flashing it around to people at school as they would surely ask you where it came from.

Have a wonderful time. You'll find the atmosphere around the trenches very powerful, I think. Be respectful. If you're wondering what the best use of the camera might be, perhaps you could recite a poem there for me. Can you remember "Naming of Parts", I wonder? Whatever you do, try not to let the shot wobble and don't jump too much from one scene to another. I'll look forward to seeing all of it – and all of you – when you're back. Don't wear anything too tight if we're going to post!

Love,

Crimble

3 April 1994

My dear Simon,

Now what on earth do I say to you here on the cusp of your formal 'majority', when I of course know how grown up you've been for so many years? It's been a privilege to watch you flower over the last decade (most of it at least) and I feel especially blessed to have received the gifts of your companionship and your warm and open personality. I really do treasure them. Never forget that.

Our last meeting was a bit of a disaster, wasn't it? I had hoped that I would be able to provide you with some guidance in light of all you've been going through. I am sympathetic to the difficulties you've been having – you know my feelings about the smoking and the drinking, but I accept your explanation that what happened was a one-off, even if the school doesn't. There's probably a great deal I'm unaware of, but you know you can always tell me anything. God knows my own life at your age wasn't free of complication.

What I wasn't quite prepared for was how uneasy you were with me when we met. I thought that all was well when we said goodbye but I'm not so sure now. Maybe I'm overthinking it. Or maybe we just don't know one another as well as I had imagined. After all, it was a pretty uneventful encounter. As you know, it's been a point of principle for me that I have never forced anything, and have always wanted you to meet me at least in the middle. Some of the messages you've put out on that front over the years have been mixed to say the least!

Perhaps it was the location. I do loathe the proximity of cafe tables to one another, and we should perhaps have travelled a little farther from home to make us both feel more comfortable. Having said that, some of our most memorable moments have taken place in quite public places, since when we are alone and in private together I find it hard to get the right words out and feel myself stiffening up (no, I'm not going to put that another way).

Oh dear, I've probably messed it all up now. Back to my main theme, if you're still reading. I know that things have been difficult in more ways than I understand because of the loss of your dad, and I hope that my friendship has been of some help in dealing with that. The main thing I want to say to you is that you are your own man now. You can make your own choices, and become the person you want to be in life. As I know you will. On that subject – you must do what you think is right, and if you truly don't think that university is for you then that's all there is to it. I know I made a fuss but then I'm only an old fogey who has no idea about the world of gaming and all it has to offer, so don't take any notice of me.

I suppose it's unavoidable that we shall grow apart as more time passes. I very much hope that we stay in touch one way or another. I want to make sure you know that I'll always *be here (with a bit of luck) and that I will always have your back. No matter what happens. Whatever you end up doing with your life – and it might be something amazing – I'm full of pride to have been able to call you my friend, and to have had some involvement in forming you during the years we've had together. God bless.*

With much love from,

Crimble

18

It was my turn to change the music. I hauled myself out from under Simon's bed and picked my way across the room. There was no knowing what might be concealed under one of the tumbleweed balls of cabling on his floor. I once saw him peel a dried Bloody Mary in one piece off the sitting-room carpet. We'd started listening to music under his bed because it was the one place we knew to be relatively clean. Then we'd discovered that with the speakers set up under there, the music sounded incredible. We'd got into the habit of lying side by side, heads together, smoking ourselves like kippers, inhabiting the noise.

His toes curled as he adjusted his position to get comfortable.

'State of your feet,' I said. 'You look like a hobbit mechanic.'

'There aren't any cars in the shire, motherfucker.'

'Do you want anything while I'm up?'

'No thanks. Put something on before I get bored.' I heard the scratch of the lighter as he relit the joint.

Crossing to the window to sneak a bit of air, I ejected the Nightmares on Wax CD he'd chosen and got *In a Silent Way* out of my bag. He only knew *Kind of Blue* and *Sketches of Spain* and I was looking forward to dropping this on him.

I paused at the machine. 'Don't you want me to at least read it to you?'

'No.'

'You're really not interested?'

'I'm really not.'

The conviction of Eric Weathers-Davis had gone national and was now a story in his own favourite newspaper. I had cut it out and carried it in my pocket ever since.

'And you're sure you don't want to come to Oxford with me?'

'I've told you: no.' The legs shifted. 'What is this thing of everybody clubbing together again? Haven't they got lives to be getting on with?'

I knew why I wanted to go, and it had little to do with old friends. Since the reunion I'd hardly seen Holly, and never out of Luke's company. When she'd asked me to come with her to meet him out of his last exam, I'd blustered that it *might be interesting from an anthropological point of view*, thinking she and I would at least get to spend the journey together.

But I realised now that Simon was right: it did feel correct somehow that we should be gathering under one banner as the story played out. Which was precisely the sort of thing he dreaded.

'I could summarise it for you,' I said. 'I don't have to read it out.'

'Enough!' He emerged red-eyed and scruffy-haired, stood up and went to the bathroom. I heard a heavy torrent hitting the water. 'How many times do I have to tell you – we're not talking about it again. Fuck's sake. That was the one condition.'

'Sorry.'

'It's okay,' he said. 'Jesus, I've got a splitting headache.' His voice slipped into an uncanny imitation of Crimble's. '*Right!*

Which one of you revolting creatures has left piddle all over this floor? I have to use these facilities as well. If you can't aim straight, put the damn seat up. Make the target bigger.'

The flush drowned out his laughter. I put the disc in the machine and pressed play, but he didn't return. I left Miles blowing alone under the bed and went to the kitchen, where I found Simon leaning over the counter as blood dripped from his nose into an empty milk bottle.

'It just started,' he said. 'While I was looking at myself in the mirror. Isn't that weird? And I thought: people always try to stop nosebleeds, don't they? And I wondered what would happen if you decided not to.'

'You'll lose a lot of blood.'

'Yeah. Let's see if we can get a whole pint.'

The blood had coated the base of the bottle and now its level began rising. He nodded to quicken the flow.

'Don't you at least want to know what they're saying about him?' I said. 'The stuff he's supposed to have done?'

He closed his eyes. The blood fell in larger gouts, making deeper, more satisfying noises. 'I think I've got some porridge oats somewhere. Isn't that what you need to make black pudding?'

I watched as the clotting blood made a glossy dome of its own crimson surface, fascinated in spite of myself.

The crowd gathered at the barriers, four- or five-deep in places, readying their faces to break out in plausible joy for their friends. Their inoffensive weapons were primed and ready: chilled bottles, confetti, bags of flour. The more hostile items were kept out of sight in ominously weighty bags from fishmongers and butchers. Stewards stood by wearing hi-vis jackets. Permission would soon be granted for a controlled loss of control, at an agreed distance from the gated courtyard and the presiding clock.

Holly and I knew what we were supposed to do. We were here to mark Luke's moment. To heap it with significance, pile it on him physically, because, having walked these cobbles, on which of course the sun was now shining, his moment warranted marking. We were here to make it memorable.

There was still plenty of the old Luke there, the rebel Luke who would always stand up for himself and others. But the environment in which he'd been steeped had ejected him with a new velocity. He was out to take from the world and had seen no evidence suggesting he couldn't.

The idea of him and Holly was no longer a throwaway quip. Something would mess it up before long but for now they were both happy to feign compatibility. It suited him to have a fun-loving girlfriend to spend the summer with after graduating, and while she was still making a display of her ruined principles, the pretence that she didn't really like him was wearing thin. She'd put on make-up over the smattering of acne that broke out on her chin when she'd been drinking too much, and now, as the first examinees began to emerge, she fussed with her hair. Uncharacteristic self-betrayals that only I would have noticed.

Each face found its party of welcome. Tentative expressions at first, crowd-struck until their pocket of support launched into its shrieks and hollers.

'All this just for finishing a few exams,' I said. 'No wonder this lot get big heads.'

Finally there he was, hair swept back, spinning his mortarboard on one finger. A red carnation was pinned to his suit under his scholar's gown, and his trousers were held up by a frayed ethnic belt he'd acquired on some expensive foreign adventure. Holly raised a hand to get his attention. His eyes widened in a mockery of elation. Then, further down the line, an animal roar erupted and his face lit up in a cockier, more defiant way.

Relief made me cruel. 'What?' I said. 'You didn't think we'd be the only ones meeting him, did you?'

The louder group was composed of Luke's Oxford friends, one of whom, I was delighted to see, was Ish. He wore a beautifully cut suit and a silk tie. His face had lost the fat that had rounded him out as a boy, his cheekbones defining a fierce, vulpine beauty.

'Have you had an exam too?' I said.

'That's just how he dresses,' said Luke. 'He's quite the dandy these days.'

Ish watched alongside Holly and me as Luke's other friends went to work on him. They sprayed him with cava, stood him against a wall and pelted him with eggs, confetti and flour. Finally one reached into a bag and took out a rope of raw offal that turned out to be a goose's neck, draping it around Luke's own like a scarf and slotting a cigar in his mouth. Others were coming off worse nearby. One beaming rascal stood grinning for the camera while pig's blood was poured over his head. When the display was over, the support group crowded as one down the narrow alley of a courtyard pub to take things further.

I fingered the cutting in my pocket. My hand kept returning to it as if it were a love letter. The more student pageantry we witnessed, the more it became the only thing I was conscious of, pulsing there, existing, merging with the fabric of my pocket as its lines bled into life.

THE MONSTER ON THE HILL

Luke stood in the yard outside the pub, holding court

has heard how a former preparatory-school teacher,

spliff in mouth, champagne bottle in fist, threads of booze-sodden party popper clinging to his face, quite happy to be the object of *a catalogue of humiliating and depraved abuse lasting nearly eight years.*

Ali Price arrived late and made up for it by buying round after round of drinks for Luke and his friends, dropping shots into his brother's pints in a

brazen violation of the trust placed in him

to get Luke drunk as quickly as possible. The army had made him trim and powerful. He looked every inch the kind of trusty officer

that any right-minded person would consider to be sadistic and evil.

Ali watched benignly as the group got rowdier. When one of Luke's friends knocked a glass off a table, he sprang forward and caught it before it hit the ground, to a lot of guffawing about Jedi reflexes. When a glass was inevitably smashed he thrust cash at the barman,

exploiting the most vulnerable during after-school activities.

'Don't kick them out,' he said. 'I'll keep them under control, I promise

masturbation and oral sex.

I tried to get on Ali's side by distancing myself from the Oxford group and said to him, 'I bet this is nothing compared to what you lot get up to

several times a month over a four-year period.

Ali smiled. 'True. Though my lads are all so fit they get hammered after two pints. They're not in practice like this bunch of layabouts.'

'Guilty as charged,' hollered one of Luke's friends

of fifteen charges of indecent assault and five of attempted rape.

'You shouldn't be paying for everything,' I said. 'Let me get the next round in. I haven't

even drank boys' urine from a bottle while pleasuring himself.

I couldn't afford to buy a whole round, but my plan was at least to get one for Ali, since it seemed so unfair for him to be *haunted by the accused's repeated use of the word 'splendid' during his ordeal and cannot now hear it without crying.*

'Put it away,' said Ali. 'This is on me. God knows Luke would be doing it for me if he

said his client had found religious faith and now understood his actions to be profoundly wrong.

'Besides, we've got all afternoon. This is going to go on

living with the horrific consequences of his actions for the rest of their lives.

I brought my hand out of my pocket to reach for my wallet and the cutting fell to the floor, opening like a butterfly. Ali watched me pick it up.

'I mean it,' he said. 'Put your money away.'

Later, when Luke noticed that his brother and his girlfriend and two old school friends were sitting apart from his Oxford group, he came to join us. He'd ditched the goose's neck and his jacket and gown but the coating of eggs and flour and wine on his shirt gave him a doughy, sour smell.

'Ridiculous place,' he said. 'Ridiculous people.'

'You love it,' I said.

'I expected more, to be honest,' said Holly. 'There's a lot of noise but not much application.'

'The afternoon is young,' said Luke.

'Where now for Luke Price, then?' I said. 'The world is your oyster.'

'That's right, little brother,' said Ali. 'Sky's the limit. What's it to be, banking or law?'

'Fuck off.'

'You must have something lined up,' I said.

'Of course he has,' said Ali. 'He's got internships dancing in front of him, begging to be chosen.'

Luke rubbed at his eyes, smearing the damp flour on his face. 'Actually I do have a plan. Ish and I are going into business together. But please let's not talk about the real world. I definitely never want to sit another exam. Or even pretend to understand how Hegel's concept of individual rights and rational consciousness becomes objectified in the apparatus of the state.'

'Listen to his fancy chat, will you?' muttered Ali. He gulped at his pint and met my eye. 'Go on, then.'

'Go on, what?'

'Show him what you've got in your pocket. I bet he still hasn't seen it because he's been up to his eyes in revision. However much he pretends he doesn't work, we all know he's been gunning for glory.' Ali saw my discomfort. 'Max, don't let my freakish powers of observation unnerve you. It's part of my job to notice things.'

'I wasn't going to bring it up,' I said, handing the cutting to Luke.

'What else is today about,' said Ali, 'but the benefits of a proper English education?'

'Christ,' said Luke, scanning the text.

'He sounds like a cartoon character,' said Holly. 'How could anyone be that sadistic?'

'There's a story that supposedly answers that question,' I said.

'I remember,' said Luke. 'Wasn't he supposed to have been a prisoner of war in North Africa? Tortured by a German soldier. Made to dig his own grave in the desert. Everyone always said that was why he was such a mess.'

'That would do it,' said Holly.

'Never mind that in 1989 he wasn't a day over forty-five,' said Ali. 'Which would have made him, at the most generous estimate, about one year old when the war ended.'

'All this has got me thinking whether I experienced a bit of institutionalised racism there,' said Ish.

Luke frowned at him. 'What?'

'I mean, look around this table. Look at what he had to choose from. Luke was a total pain in the arse, who never, ever shut up. Max famously cried for about a month when he arrived, so he wasn't a safe bet. And nobody in their right mind would try it on with Alistair Price if they didn't want to get the shit kicked out of them. What about me? I was willing. I had a cute smile. I probably wouldn't have told anyone. What's more, it's turned out I fancy men rather more than I do women. So I reckon the only reason he never tried it on with me is because I was brown.'

'To be fair, pal,' said Luke, 'it's probably more to do with the fact that you were carrying a little extra timber back then.'

'Well, fuck *you*,' said Ish.

I watched Luke shocking the conversation into less uncomfortable terrain, and remembered him being slammed against the stack of chairs aged eleven. His laughter at the anger. His quip about washing your hands.

'I wonder what old magic-man thinks of all this,' he said to me.

'Who?'

'Crighton. He must be going spare thinking about all this happening on his watch. Don't you think?'

'I bet he is.' I took a big drink. 'What about your family? They're friends with Sutton, aren't they? What are they saying?'

Luke and Ali looked at each other and laughed simultaneously.

'*I just think it's terrible for poor old Tony, that's all,*' said Ali, his mouth tightening as he took on the voice of his father. '*You may joke, but he's a close friend and I fear for him.*'

Luke joined in. '*It's very unfortunate of course, but these boys need to think of the consequences. Dragging it through the courts. Will that help them? Will it help the school? They could shut the place down.*'

'After all, you lot had a lovely time there, didn't you?'

'Perhaps I'll write Tony a letter.'

'Yes. A good letter is just the ticket.'

'Harm? What do you mean, harm? Never did me any harm.'

'He doesn't actually say that, does he?' I said. 'That's just what people say people say. People don't actually *say* it.'

'He says it,' said Luke.

'I think what we had was a picnic compared to what Dad went through under Sutton Senior,' said Ali. 'It's why he's such good mates with Tony.'

'Dad reckons Sutton Senior was the reason Tony's stutter got so bad,' said Luke. 'He'd mock him for it in front of the whole school. And thrash him worse than anybody else, to make sure he was never accused of giving him special treatment.'

'Anyway.' Ali raised his glass. 'Here's to getting the fuck out of school.' He drained his beer, planted the foam-laced glass on the table, and turned to me. 'I'll take that drink now, Max. I think a large whisky might be in order.'

I went to the bar, having taken orders for the others as well. When I came to pay I realised I didn't have the cash so I handed over my debit card, which was swiftly declined.

A twenty was wafted over my shoulder. 'Here, take this,' said Ali. 'Those two need space, anyway.' Ish had returned to the Oxford group, leaving Luke and Holly kissing in earnest, settling right into it. Ali leaned back against the bar. 'That one just rides on through, doesn't he? Never even notices the bumps.'

'Aren't you the same?' I said, gratefully pocketing my card. 'You seem to know exactly what you want to do with your life.'

He drained his double Jameson's and ordered another. 'I know what I'm supposed to do,' he said. 'Which isn't quite the same.'

'I think,' I said, 'that the people who brought this case are very brave. There's no knowing how many more people he might have done it to if they hadn't come forward.'

'They might live to regret it. I don't think we can know how much you give up to go through with something like that. I don't give a fuck about the school, but I think my dad's probably right in some ways. About the cost to yourself.'

'Yeah, but. If one of these guys had had the balls to speak up before, it might have saved those of us who came after. Likewise, who's to say there wasn't a whole silent generation even earlier who could have spoken out and stopped it? All it takes is one person.'

'You think? Saying something isn't everything. You can say something and not be believed. You can even be told off for it. For spreading malicious lies. Told off for *telling*.'

But especially speak up.

'Did you?' I said. 'Say something?'

His voice dropped and his hand was like iron on my arm and I was eleven again and he was thirteen and terrifying.

'Mate,' he said. 'You need to take a step back.'

A few days later Holly told me that Luke had invited her to spend the summer at his family's house in Italy, and that as a result she would be vacating the boat earlier than planned. Simon said that if I didn't want to go back to my parents for what would be left of the holidays then I could always stay with him. As if thinking ahead to this arrangement, I spent more time at his flat, completing my extended essay there while he was out at work. His shoebox archive surrounded me, and more than once I was tempted to delve into it, but all I did instead was reread Crimble's letters over and over, trying to see between their lines.

In some ways it was like getting to know someone for the first time. But the terms were underwritten by our shared past and its newly shared secrets. I had forgotten how finely calibrated Simon's kindness was – so subtle that you might not even see it for kindness. Whenever he sensed that I was unhappy with some arrangement we'd made, he'd come up with his own reason as to why it wasn't a good idea to save me the trouble of saying anything myself. These low frequencies were where he operated. I understand now, or think I do, that the coercion to which he'd been subjected had left him with a keen sensitivity to emotional manipulation, and a terror of being seen to practise it.

Conversely, if he was feeling vulnerable he would seek confirmation of my allegiance, which is what I now recognise was going on when he would eat nothing for days, then binge on some food he craved and expect me to do the same. It was never explicitly stated that I was under assessment at times like this, but I knew better than to test it.

And then for all his sensitivity he sometimes did things which implied the opposite of kindness. There was an almost deliberate carelessness with things of value. A scorn of the notion of things of value. As if, having earned his intimacy, I must sacrifice those concerns he deemed beneath it. Treasured possessions of mine would go missing, never returning, or returning damaged or broken. Precious CDs irretrievably scratched. A pen of mine which he knew to be of sentimental value which I found down the side of the sofa with its nib trashed and its clip twisted off.

For the first time I began finding out about his home life before. I learned that his father had been dead for over two years when I'd met him standing by the boating lake. That his mother had never intended to work for Tony Sutton, but that they'd persuaded her, creating the job to help her out and all but waiving the fees to enable her to keep Simon there. It was during one such conversation that he allowed himself to stray into talking about what had happened between his mother and Crimble.

'They were never properly together, in spite of what everybody said,' he told me. 'But she liked him. She was very lonely, of course. I used to hear her crying down the phone to friends after being with him, wondering what she was doing wrong, why he wouldn't open up more, be more normal. She started off thinking it was something to do with propriety because she worked there, then concluded in the end that he was one of those people who are basically sexless. But I'll tell you something: I don't think there are nearly as many sexless people around as some seem to think.'

19

In late June I was alone on the boat watching summer rain spatter the deck when my mobile phone rang. This was still a novelty. The phone was a gift from Simon, who'd been ridiculing my pager from the moment we re-established contact, and I hadn't adjusted at all to the way it could suddenly burst into my life.

My mother was calling to tell me that my grandfather had had an accident. He'd been out on his JCB when the bank of the chalk pond had collapsed and the vehicle had slid sideways and landed upside down in the water.

'If he'd been in that Massey Ferguson without the top on it he'd be dead,' she said. 'But the cab broke the fall and he managed to swim out from inside. With a broken ankle.' All I could think in the moment was that I had never in my life seen him swim. 'That's not all,' she went on.

She then explained that something else had happened with what she described as *cruel timing*. After he got back from hospital he'd been in bed and heard the dogs barking from the stables but his ankle made it hard to get up. My grandmother's deafness meant she couldn't hear him calling her from the downstairs room he was sleeping in. He'd concluded they were barking at a fox and gone back to sleep. So it wasn't until the next day that they'd discovered the bodies.

'I've been telling him for years he needed to sort out the wiring in those stables,' she said. 'It's a miracle there was only smoke damage and not a full-on fire. They could have been burned in their beds if it had spread to the house. Those dogs didn't stand a chance. Anyway, they're both shaken up. If you're not busy, you might go and see them sometime.'

She and my father had made their feelings on the way I'd spent my year lying to my tutors very clear. It wasn't the time to claim I had anything more important to do.

I dreaded the doglessness. It was all I could think of as my station taxi pulled up outside the house. There had always been the sense that whatever decrepitude life had in store for him, it wouldn't matter so long as his familiars were going out into the world on his behalf, extending his reach. I tried not to look too closely at the blackened stable door frame as I went inside.

The accident and the fire had taken them several steps forward on a journey they had both been deferring for some time. My grandmother seemed less tethered to the here and now than ever, while he, in addition to the broken ankle, had sustained many cuts and bruises getting himself out of the upturned tractor.

He had his leg up on a bench and was scratching inside his cast with a knitting needle while she tended to a weeping coin-shaped wound on the side of his head. He wore only a pair of white boxer shorts and an open shirt.

'Go on then, put it on,' he said, pointing at a flannel that floated in a steaming bowl on the table. There was a strong smell of disinfectant.

'By God you'll jump if I put this on your head,' she said. 'It's boiling.'

'Stick it on. I can feel the infection. Needs something to draw it out.'

'Sorry about the dogs,' I said.

'Poor buggers,' he said, instantly on the verge of tears. 'They were hollering half the night trying to tell me, and I didn't do a thing.'

'Oh dear, he's off again,' she said.

'*Now* she can hear me,' he said, with more affection than bitterness.

I had brought what was for me at the time an expensive bottle of wine. When I put it on the table, his mood brightened a little and he pointed to the corkscrew on the wall. 'Fetch us the Frenchman, then.'

He stripped off the foil with a practised fist and set about drawing the cork. But his shaking hands wouldn't let him do it.

'Look at these forks,' he said, his hands stilled on the table as I opened the bottle. 'I've been putting these forks in my mouth for fifty years.'

'Where did they come from?' I said.

'They were a wedding present from my Uncle Harry.'

'Do you remember him?' said my grandmother.

Up went the voice. 'Of course he bloody doesn't! Harry had been dead twenty years by the time Max was born.'

'You told me about him,' I said. 'And your Uncle Laurie. You gave me the Victoria crown that fell out of his pocket, remember?'

'Course I did,' he said, his sadness intensified by the memory lapse.

'Shall I play something for you?' I said after lunch.

'Later. Let's get some air.'

He surged round the side of the house on a rented mobility scooter, wearing a big green dressing gown, grinning at the absurdity of his own spectacle. At the pond we assessed the site of the accident. The overturned JCB lay at the bottom of the scoop of fresh earth that had given way under its weight, its buckets clutching desperately at the banks. As we watched, a duck swam out through the window of the half-submerged cab.

'At least the engine's out of the water,' he said. 'I'll get it going again.'

'You were lucky. You should take it easier from now on.'

He closed his eyes in irritation. 'Shut up, will you? Anyway, there's something I need you to do. That one's away with the fairies so she wouldn't even remember it hasn't happened.'

'What?' I said. 'Anything.'

'Someone's got to bury these dogs.'

They were in a sack together in one of the stables unaffected by the fire. Their fur smelled of smoke. The collie's eyes were closed in an almost blissful expression. The terrier's face looked like that of a gargoyle, all snarling teeth and staring eyes. I hefted the sack of stiff bodies onto my shoulder and rejoined him. My grandmother paused at the kitchen window inside, mouth moving, devising some explanation of my behaviour.

He directed me to a spot under the ash tree in which we'd put his old hip when it was replaced a few years before, lodging it high in the crook of a branch. *You can stick the rest of me here too when I'm done*, he'd said. He sat back in the seat of the scooter, taking sympathetic breaths and holding them in as I made each cut of the spade.

'Come on, boy. Put some beef into it. Blimey, you dig about as well as my missus.'

When he declared the hole deep enough I stood back sweating, and asked him if he wanted to say anything. He shook his head. But as I started dropping earth onto the bodies he did mutter some words. 'Bye, then. You're going home. I shall see you before too long.'

*

Before we went back inside he wanted to check the plants in the courtyard. He hummed along in the scooter by my side as we went over his rhubarb crop, whose leaves were so colossal that they threatened to overturn the wheelbarrows in which they grew.

'We'd only just moved in here when your folks got married,' he said. 'We hung the front door on the morning of the wedding. Your dad slept in the laundry the night before.'

This was an old one. We settled into it comfortably.

'You made Mum's hat out of a cornflake packet,' I said.

He smiled. 'I did. We had some material left over from the dress. Funny old world.'

'You were lambing then.'

'Were we?'

'That's what Mum says. She says she was scratching her legs under the table all through the meal because she'd been up feeding orphan lambs in some old shed the night before and got covered in flea bites.'

'Does she? I don't remember that.'

'Why did you stop farming sheep?' I said. 'You've never done it for as long as I've been around.'

He leaned over to pull a weed from the cobbles. 'It got too upsetting. We even went vegetarian one year because we couldn't bear the sight of the lambs playing in the fields.'

'You went vegetarian? I don't believe it.'

'We did. Didn't last long.' He laughed. 'Couldn't help but miss a good chop after a while. But it's not a very nice business, watching things be born and looking after them and then sending them off to their death.'

'I guess I've always thought that if you were a farmer, you accepted it.'

'Yeah, but it's horrible, what farming's become. And there's a right way and a wrong way to do everything. I've known some nasty slaughtermen. Sadists. Knew one once who kept a knife on his belt to blind the animals when they wouldn't get out of the truck, cos if they lie down then legally you're not allowed to kill them, you've got to send them home.'

'Jesus.'

'But my mate Dave Bosworth was a good man. The thing about slaughtering animals is that it should be calm. The animals should be calm. The slaughterman should be calm. And for the most part, they are. There's only one thing that annoys them. They're hopping mad if they're ever sent a pregnant animal. And one day Dave had one, a pregnant ewe, but somehow nobody knew she was in lamb until after she was killed. The lamb was cut out of the carcass and it grew up in the slaughterhouse. It became a pet, and old Dave used it as his Judas. You know what one of those is, don't you? The first one in. The one the others all follow inside. Because they're not afraid. Anyway one day Dave had a new lad working for him, who'd come from some big industrial place, like a factory – and he forgot to tell this kid about the Judas. So of course the kid zapped it without a second thought. Bosworth nearly fucking killed him.'

'Fuck,' I said, realising I was swearing because he had.

'The thing I always found strange about it – or didn't like, when I'd had time to think about it – was, why get so upset about that one lamb? The one he'd trained up for himself to help him kill the others more quietly? If you're going to mind, why not mind about all of them?'

That evening, a bottle down, he got emotional and started worrying about what would happen to the house after they'd gone.

'We shan't be here long, you know.'

'Don't be silly,' I said. 'You've got years in you yet.'

'You can't let this place go. Can't you bring that girl of yours and come and live here?'

'She's not my girl any more,' I said. 'If she ever was.'

'Get her back.' He reached for the wine, energised by the prospect of a problem to solve.

'I'm not sure that's possible.'

'Your father wouldn't take no for an answer from me,' said my grandmother. 'He just came back every week until I said yes.'

'*Grand*father,' he said, his usual frustration muted by fondness.

'Time marches on,' she continued. 'How old are you now, anyway?'

'Twenty.'

'Twenty!'

'For a week or two, at least.'

'Strewth,' he said. 'Eight years since we stayed up baking that bloody great cake. Remember?'

'Good Lord, yes,' she said.

'The big two-one,' he said. 'You shan't have any excuses left then. *You'll be a man, my son.* What are you going to do to celebrate?'

'I'll think of something,' I said. And suddenly I knew what I had to do. A chemical change had taken place in my brain, and the next step had been revealed.

'Before I go tomorrow, can I do anything for you?' I said. 'Some shopping?'

'Don't worry about us, mate. We've got a freezer full of meat and sackfuls of veg. And as you know, I'm not letting certain people anywhere near that car.'

'In that case, can I borrow it?'

'What?' he said.

'The car.'

Another crossing of the river. Another ascent of the hill. I parked away from Crimble's cottage to allow myself time to change my mind. It was exam season, so I made it to the gate by telling myself he would probably be occupied at school. Then the gate was behind me, the doorbell's ring was dying away, and there he was, broken into yellow hexagons by the glass of his front door.

He seemed slighter. The face had contracted with age. The beard was greyer than I remembered. His expression was nearly blank, just on the apprehensive side of neutral.

'Mr Crighton, it's Max Denyer,' I said, letting the name hang in the air. Put the onus on him. Watch him remember.

The familiar squint over the glasses, vague, but practical – as if some unforeseeably large obstacle had come into view, albeit one to which he was more than ready to apply himself. 'God bless my soul.'

'How are you, sir?' The old way of speaking, rocketing back. The controlled cockiness. Safely operating within agreed parameters.

'Do you know,' he said, 'I really am most extraordinarily well.' He put out his hand. It felt both soft and bony. Smaller than mine. I resisted the temptation for a show of strength. 'Max,' he added. 'What a pleasure to see you.'

I was pleased to see him too.

The cottage was darker than I remembered, and the principal smell was of frying onions, but the back notes of sweat and fabric softener were deeply known to me. I greeted the long-standing accumulations of clothing and paper and records as if they were old friends. No sign or smell of dog now. More dead dogs.

Landscape photographs he'd taken lined the hallway walls. Some featured a boy or two with rucksacks. Some were of generations that predated our own, some more recent. One was of Simon. The back of his head as he looked down a long valley strewn with boulders. Most wouldn't have recognised him, but I did.

'You're cooking your lunch,' I said. 'I won't stay.'

'Nonsense!' He unhooked an apron and put it on. Must have removed it to answer the door. Endearing urge to be presentable, not knowing who'd come to call.

I stood in the kitchen doorway as he got out tea bags, washed up one mug and sought another. I noticed a broom propped against the wall with a mound of dust beside it, as if he swept frequently but never picked any of it up.

'What brings you back to these parts?' he said.

'Do you remember that my grandparents live close by?'

'Of course. The dear old man in the van.'

'I was visiting and thought I'd look in. I won't take up too much of your time.' He asked me what I was up to, and I found myself wanting him to be proud. 'I've just got back from a year abroad. Part of my degree. Languages.'

'Wonderful. Where have you been?'

'Paris for some of it. Then a small island off Venezuela.'

'You always were an intrepid boy. Story after story of what you'd seen around the world.' He was frowning down at a frying pan that contained onions and a modest piece of steak. 'I'm pretty certain,' he said, 'that if I were to supplement this with some fried bread, and perhaps a tin of tomatoes, it would make a perfectly feasible meal for two.'

'I won't stay.'

'You will.' He smiled, as if it were just a question of making me understand. 'You'll hurt my feelings if you don't.'

He set the pan of steak and onions on a mat between two mismatched china plates, onto which he'd put the bread and tomatoes, whose smell sent me half a mile up the road and eight years into the past.

'Fancy a beer? I'm having one.' He took out two cans of supermarket bitter and set them on the counter, the idea of tea now apparently forgotten.

'I was sorry not to see you at the reunion last month.'

He was pouring with his back to me. 'You know, there is very little I would change about my life. But it is a sadness to me, the way you all come and go, off into the world. If you want the truth, I didn't think I could stomach it – the gallery of old faces, gone on to new lives, our time together a footnote. It would have upset me too much.'

'You might be surprised at how well we all remember you.'

'Ha! That's good to hear. I think.'

'It was great seeing Simon after so many years. We'd lost touch completely. I don't know how we let that happen.'

'Dear Simon. I had no idea he was coming. His name wasn't on the list. Is his mother well, do you know? There was talk of an illness of some kind.'

Flare of shame. 'I didn't know about that.'

'This was a few years back. Perhaps she's better. I do hope so.' He sat down and raised his glass. 'Absent friends?'

We sat so close that I could feel the currents of air made by his breath. My eye kept returning to a patch of inflamed skin near his beard line.

The fried bread was soggy with fat. The onions sweet. The steak overcooked. The beer was too warm, too bitter, too fizzy. But in this environment, all of it was exceptional. I fell on it like a treated boy.

'This is very kind of you,' I said.

'Bachelor food. I'm afraid I don't know anything else after all these years.'

I cleared my throat. 'Simon and I were talking about all the videos you used to make when we were here. Of plays and things. Do you still have them all?'

'They're lying around somewhere. I may have taped over some of them. The trouble is that so many of you come and go that it all blurs into one.'

'We should get everyone together sometime, and watch them.'

'Tell me,' he said, wiping foam from his beard. 'Do you change colour?'

'What?'

He considered me carefully. 'I think your complexion must be a little like mine. No matter how much time I spend in the sun I never change colour. Unless I'm burning, that is.'

'Sorry?'

'You tell me you're just back from an island in the Caribbean, but you look as if you've been soaking in this wet English June just like me.'

'Yeah, well, I came back a while ago.'

'Tell me which authors you've been studying,' he said, setting down his fork with anticipatory relish.

'Lorca. Neruda. Flaubert. At the moment I'm reading a lot of Gide. We're doing *The Counterfeiters* as a set text.'

'I don't know it. I must fix that.'

I asked him what play he was putting on. What climbing trips he had coming up. After a few more rounds of inconsequential conversation he removed another dish from the oven.

'My signature pudding,' he said. 'You remember?'

Apple Crimble. How could I have forgotten? The apples underdone as usual. The topping more of a mush than a crumble. Thick, gloopy custard, indistinguishable from the stuff they were doubtless still serving up the hill.

He made two instant coffees. I watched him stir the granules into the boiled water, and thought of the hot chocolate in his room.

'Where did you go, Max? After here. I realise I have absolutely no idea.'

'My dad's work took us around the houses for a bit,' I lied.

'*Here no elsewhere underwrites my existence*, as grumpy old Larkin said. Have you found yourself changed from one place to the next? You must have been quite a lot of different people by now.'

'I guess so,' I said. 'But I hope I have a good enough handle on myself by now to carry something with me.' There it was again. The desire to be precocious. The eagerness to please.

'Yes, I remember that about you. Sense of yourself. Sense of right and wrong.'

I'd taken on so much fluid that I needed to use his bathroom. There was only one in the cottage, accessible down the narrow corridor where his socks and underpants aired on radiators. I found myself noticing the nail scissors in the soap dish, the toothpaste stain in the basin, the folded-over tube of haemorrhoid cream on the cistern. Here was his life in all its toiletries and towels. Here too, whether I wanted it or not, was my sympathy.

'You know,' he said when I returned, 'I've got to clock on in an hour or so for the evening shift. Why don't you come with me? You could read a story at Prayers. Wouldn't that be a fun thing?'

'I've borrowed my grandparents' car. I should get it back or they'll be wondering where I am.'

'Well. Next time then.'

'There's something else I wanted to say,' I said at the front door. I couldn't look at him. I found myself staring instead at the opening to his letter box, at the sign above it in his familiar handwriting saying *NO JUNK MAIL*. 'I mean – in case you were worried. Because of all that's been happening with Mr Weathers-Davis.' He stood up straighter. 'Simon isn't going to show anyone the letters you sent him. He told me himself.'

'You know, if I'd had an address for you, Max, we could have stayed in touch as well. But I simply had no idea where to find you.'

'A letter would be nice,' I said. 'The only problem is that I live on a boat.' And here I did lock eyes with him. 'So I don't have anywhere you can post it.'

He blinked. A calm smile dropped down his face. 'It was lovely of you to drop in, Max.' The door didn't move. He waited for me to turn and go of my own accord.

20

FOUR DAYS LATER, Simon called to ask me to come over. Something in the way he spoke – cold, distracted – made me think I ought to go quickly.

I found him on the sofa wearing only a pair of shorts and a necklace made of paper clips. The curtains were closed. A ripe fug of bodies and food hung in the air. On the trunk in front of him burned a thick church candle. A paused scene from his game flickered on the screen.

'What are you working on?' I said.

'The usual. I'm trying to build in more possibilities for surprise. When players mean well, but make *terrible mistakes*.'

'I see,' I said. 'How long have you been drinking?'

'Day or two?' He scratched at his right eyebrow as if it was annoying him.

'I like the jewellery,' I said.

'Do you know what these are?'

'They're paper clips.'

'That's right. They're paper clips. I didn't quite have enough before. The length was always too short. But now I've got a new one.'

I felt like someone sent to talk down a jumper from a ledge. 'You've got a new paper clip?'

'And new paper clipped between it.'

Now I saw the envelope sitting on the trunk beside the candle, and felt the shame zeroing in. 'Is that what I think it is?'

'He's still sending me cash,' he said. 'Isn't that weird? Doesn't he realise I earn quite good money these days?'

The shoebox was open on the floor ready to receive its newest arrival. The letter obscenely crisp and fresh. The writing the same as ever. Its ink committed to the paper – when? – as soon as I'd driven away from the cottage?

'Why would he suddenly write now, after all this time?' said Simon. 'And how did he even find me? Mum must have given him the address.'

'I guess he's feeling vulnerable because of the court case.'

'He doesn't sound very fucking vulnerable.'

'What does he say?'

'A lot of guff about how much time has passed. How he hopes I'm doing well. Asking whether I went to university in the end or not.'

'That sounds all right.'

'And then he talks about the tapes. He comes straight out and mentions them. You know what that really means, don't you?'

'I think so.'

'Why would he turn on me? Why would he suddenly think I was going to go for him now?'

'I'm sorry,' I said.

He'd been absent-mindedly rubbing at his face throughout and now he angled it in my direction with his palm splayed across his own neck. 'Why are you sorry?'

'Only because ... I know how upsetting it must be for him to have contacted you again.'

'Max, I know you want to help me. But there are things about this that you don't understand.'

'I'm sure.'

'One is – there is no solving it. It isn't going away.'

'Okay.'

'The other is even more important. I don't necessarily want it solved. I wanted it to happen at the time. I made it happen, or at least let it happen. He would never have done it otherwise. If I could go back and rub it all out, I'm not so sure that I would. Do you understand?'

He took the bundle from the box and undid the ribbon, selecting one of the letters and opening it. He left the money in the envelope and brought the letter to the candle's wavering flame.

'Wait a minute,' I said, as fire trickled up the paper. 'You don't want to do this.'

'Don't I?' Ash broke and flurried. He positioned the letter over the traffic cone so that its fragments fell inside, hissing as they hit the soup of ash and butts within. He sat down with purpose. 'We keep the fifties in the envelopes. That will be the record.'

'Stop.'

'These are mine to do what I want with. Letters to me. Private letters. You didn't even know about them a few weeks ago.'

'Please stop.'

He looked at me. 'Max, if you were ever my friend, this is what is going to happen.'

I paused, then nodded. I handed him another letter and picked one up for myself. Our eyes met across the candle flame and we burned them together.

What I did next was risky. In spite of all the time that had passed there was no way he'd have forgotten all the cheap misdirectional tricks I'd picked up from my grandfather. But this was more than a game of cards.

'What about that smoke alarm?' I said, flapping the letter I had in my hand so it produced a billowing plume of smoke.

'Shit! The sprinklers. Don't panic. Keep going.' He ran to the kitchen and returned carrying an empty Pot Noodle container. He stepped onto the trunk and planted it neatly over the smoke detector in the ceiling.

'You've done that before,' I said.

He grinned. 'How many of those fuckers did we eat over the years? Some habits die hard.'

'Know what you mean,' I said, shifting in my seat to ensure that the three letters I'd managed to slip from their envelopes were snug against the line of my jacket.

'Right.' He downed his drink. 'This feels good. Let's finish the job.' He turned on me with terrible triumph. 'And the next time you decide to go visiting Crimble in secret, you can tell him yourself that they're gone. Okay?'

July was miserable. I barely left the boat. Simon dropped out of contact completely, and with Holly gone too it was hard not to conclude that I was in for some time alone. I might conceivably revive the few university friendships I'd made, but for now it looked like I needed to write off the year on the boat as another one of life's rabbit holes and hope to kindle something fresh when my final year began in the autumn. I began preparing myself accordingly. Took stock of my supplies and laid the ground for a stint in the bunker. It wouldn't be the first time.

But there were inconvenient emotional loose ends: vestiges of the dependency I had developed on Holly; other feelings brought about by my reconnection with Simon and all that had come with it. Dangerous impulses, crackling like live wires in a puddle. Because of them, I fell prey to something that I hadn't allowed to happen since the early days at the school over a decade before: I felt sorry for myself. And it was in this mood that I called the police to request the name and telephone number of the case officer who'd led the prosecution of Eric Weathers-Davis.

My plan was to use the three letters I'd kept as models for letters of my own from Crimble, which I would forge. Having created my own evidence, I would destroy the originals, as Simon wished. Then it would simply be a case of making my statement. To begin with, I would only need my own experience. Then, when required, I would start using Simon's. But for a few minor details, all of it would be true.

I must have tried placing the call five times. Every time I was put through, I rang off as soon as the phone was picked up. This sent me to an even more wretched, self-hating place than I'd been in before. I'd been telling myself that my grandfather had encoded in me a philosophy that was also a form of vaccination. That thanks to him, I could always be relied on to talk. But here was a situation in which no words would come. My own cowardice stunned me.

One afternoon as I sat there mustering the courage to try again, a voice said, 'Have you just been staring at the wall all this time?' I looked up and there, tanned and dusty, was Holly.

She'd left the Price holiday early. Left Luke too, it seemed. She'd just woken up one morning in their Italian house and decided that it, and he, weren't for her. Luke would never have let such a minor blip spoil his summer, so the thing had ended quite amicably. He'd even offered to buy her a plane ticket home but she'd said she wanted to travel by train. She'd made her way slowly up through Italy and France over the last week, deciding in the process that more travel was what she needed. Her plan now was to find work with a good European orchestra. In the meantime we had to vacate the boat. Her aunt would be back soon and it was now time to scrub it of ourselves and our floating year.

'Was the holiday awful, then?' I said hopefully.

She sighed. 'They're a weird fucking family. But you don't realise it at first because they know how to be charming. After a while, I just wanted to escape. Got bored of heading down into the valley to scream at the river. And what is it with rich people going on about how shabby their lives are? They kept saying how generous it was of me to give them so much of my time, and apologising for the way they liked to "slum it" out there. They own practically a whole village.'

'Were they all there?' I said.

She nodded. 'The whole bunch. Right down to that obscenely precocious sister.'

We slept together. It was more tender and slow and sober than any previous encounter. Afterwards she said, 'And what have *you* been up to?'

'Nothing much,' I said. 'Why?'

'You're different,' she said. 'More generous. Less in your own world.'

'Well, the only person I've been sleeping with is Simon Drake.'

'That must be it then.'

Having decided that we ought to mark our farewell with something special, she used a contact at the Royal College of Music to get us tickets to a Prom on the last Friday in August. Johnny Dankworth and Cleo Laine leading a concert of their own compositions as well as others by George Gershwin, Duke Ellington and Billie Holliday.

The dead of the summer. The election long forgotten. The newspapers full of pictures of a princess and a playboy on a yacht. We got drunk on the sun-frazzled turf of

Kensington Gardens, then carried on inside the Albert Hall. It wasn't the Last Night so there was no need to dress up, but it was our last night, so we did. There was a feeling of breaking into adulthood, or what felt like it to us. Taking up a position we felt we deserved in this world of music, perfume and wine.

She'd gone ahead to our seats while I ran to the bathroom. As I returned through the curved corridor at the rear of the auditorium, I heard a familiar laugh over the two-minute bell, and recognised something in the shape of a hurrying, adult back. Couldn't be. I took my seat beside Holly and let my breathing settle in the cool, grand space as the lights dimmed and the audience clapped on the performers. I felt good. We were coming to an end, and that was okay. The universe was telling me I'd done the right thing by not going through with my plan. That sometimes it was better not to speak up. That it was not, after all, my story to tell.

But as the orchestra launched into 'Strike Up the Band', I kept hearing again the sound of the laugh in the corridor. Holly, who hated the poor-quality rental opera glasses you got in places like this, had brought an expensive pair of binoculars to study the playing up close. As the music continued, I used them to sweep the audience. Holly whispered something to me like *fuck's your problem*, but I said nothing and carried on, because I needed to make sure I wasn't going mad.

I found Crimble as he was usually to be found: by the glint of the spectacles over which he had always squinted so myopically. Of course he was a Prom-goer. I was so busy marvelling at the fact that I had hunted him down purely because of a fleeting gesture in a corridor that it wasn't until the first number was nearly over that I thought to shift the gaze of the binoculars to the adjacent seats and saw that he was sitting with Simon.

THREE

Dying Days

21

HIS LAUGH PRECEDED him, as usual.

Raised eyebrows. A flare of mischief in his expression at the fact of a young woman leading him in. A nurse was always fair game. Reason to be cheerful even in this prison of stained carpets and storage heaters.

'Look out,' he said. 'Here we come.'

'All right, none of your colourful language,' said the nurse. 'He's a piece of work, your grandad.'

She settled him in a chair, directing his bulk, which was still considerable though he'd lost plenty by now. He was wearing his best waistcoat, with red braces beneath clipped onto wide-gauge green cords.

He offered up his big, soft hand. The feel of it containing my own so familiar. The excitement at seeing him, kindled as if I were still a child, outranking any worry at his physical state, because how could he ever not be okay?

This was in 2006. He was eighty-five, and I was twenty-nine.

He'd been given between three and six months to live nearly two years before, and in spite of protestations from his family had agreed to enter the home for palliative care on that basis. He had rejected all other offers of accommodation, adamantly refusing to be a burden, then just gone on not dying.

'How do,' he said, allowing his breathing to settle.

'You look smart.'

His middle finger unfurled like a priapic flower.

When the nurse had left us to it, he leaned in. 'She's got a new boyfriend, that one. Great big black fella. I bet she has the time of her life.'

'And I bet she loves you asking about it. Especially if you talk about him like that.'

'She doesn't mind,' he said. 'She's a lovely girl. She told me off the other day for not being decent in my pyjamas. The trousers have a fly with no button, so there's not a lot you can do. I was stood talking to this old boy in the next room while we were getting ready for bed and she walks past, and prim as a pansy she says, *Excuse me, Bob – the hamster is out of its cage.*' That was him gone. The chest shuttling up and down, the high wheeze, the tears in the eyes. Followed inexorably by the depth charges of phlegm-hindered coughs.

'All right,' I said. 'Don't do yourself an injury before we've got outside.' I put out an arm to steady him for the journey to the car.

'I daren't look forward to getting out until it's happening,' he said. 'It drives you potty, this place. Every breath you take's passed through the lungs of about twenty old buggers by the time it comes to you. Bloody hell, look at that.' I glanced up from the book by the front door where I was signing him out. In the car park a minibus was being loaded with residents for a day trip. He stuck out his tongue at the ashen faces. 'I mean really, what's the point? They all want taking out and shooting.'

'You should go with them sometime. Liven things up.'

'Nah. All they do is sit them in some awful cafe. Bit of dry cake and a swill of tea, then they come back. There's no joy in it. Come on, let's get out while we can.' The receptionist unlocked the door and we were outside. 'That's better,' he said, inhaling deeply. 'Spot of fresh air.' He closed his eyes. 'Spring. Gets you every time. You can't believe it's happening.'

He was right. In less than a week, the season had changed. Bare branches erupting with green. Blossom foaming. The snowdrops and daffodils were nearly over but the bluebells were rampant, vaporous purple haze in the skirts of every wood. And here he was locked up in a geriatric farm, smitten with farmers' lung and MRSA.

'Have you got everything you need?' I said.

'Course.'

'I meant, what about your oxygen?'

'Bugger that. Let's get some lunch. Bloody hell, what are you driving?'

'Present from Katharine's father. It's meant to be practical.'

Roger Price had chosen the used Škoda estate in preparation for the forthcoming *event* – something I don't think either of us had allowed ourselves to believe was going to happen, in spite of mounting evidence to the contrary.

His nostrils flared. 'Very practical, I'm sure.'

'Come on then. Let's lever you in.'

'I can manage, you cheeky sod.'

I knew the restaurants that were and weren't acceptable, the current favourite being an Italian place by a canal. The waiters knew him, and leapt into action with a lot of continental exclamation that delighted him.

'I'll try for a pee before I get settled,' he said. 'You wouldn't believe how often you have to go.'

He lumbered off, pressing heavily on his stick. There was no compromise. Illness had taken centre stage, with all its ruthless refusal to negotiate.

I ordered a double vodka and orange and took it down in a couple of gulps. Relaxing into the first flush of the alcohol, I read through the menu, then realised he was taking too long. I got up so quickly that I almost knocked the chair over.

I found him at the urinal, hand on the window ledge, eyes closed. As I walked in his angle seemed to tip from that of a relaxed person rocking back on his heels to something more irrevocable. I stepped forward to steady him, putting my hands on his shoulders. He started and turned and his face flashed with anger.

'What the hell are you doing?'

My hands shot up. 'Sorry!'

'You didn't think I was going to pop my clogs at a fucking urinal, did you?'

'Sorry. I'll be at the table. Do you want me to order you something?'

'Nothing for me. I can't do it at lunchtime any more.' He moved his left hand to the wall, shaking himself off with his right. My eyes shot skywards. 'Go away, will you?'

By the time he finally came back I was already halfway down the beer I'd ordered. I watched as he negotiated himself into the chair.

'You don't want to get old, mate,' he said. I laughed. But he was serious. His eyes widened, the whites yellow and flecked with red. 'You don't. It's awful. Bugger it, get him to bring me a glass of wine.'

I jumped up to collar a waiter, and when I returned he had relaxed.

'How's the Pocket Rocket?' he said. I'd taught him this expression not long after Katharine and I had got together, and he loved it so much he never called her anything else.

'Grumpy. She says she wants to go to Italy this summer before the baby comes, but I'm worried about her flying that late.'

He pointed a finger. 'If that's what she wants, that's what you'll do. Only thing for it. And just be glad you don't have to squeeze one out yourself. It's a marvel, what they put up with.'

'I can't wait for it to be over.'

'And then it'll only be beginning. But you're right, there's the birth to get through first. She's a little thing. And you've grown into quite a big bugger. I worry about how they're going to *fetch it out*.' He accompanied these last three words with a vivid grasping gesture that made us both laugh, even as I rode out a wave of embarrassment at the reference to my weight.

I knew he'd always wondered why I hadn't ended up with Holly. Typically for him, his way of communicating this was the opposite of cynicism – to remind me of the ways in which Katharine was a force for good, rather than question why I hadn't held on to the glorious redhead with the voice and the sass.

Combines before cabs. All those years he'd harvested in a cloud of dust. Not in itself a bad thing, but any mildew on the barley and his present condition was the result. Funny to think that crops cut in the fifties and sixties could be killing him now. Then things were worsened because the last time he'd come out of hospital he'd been more ill than when he went in. Taken to the brink by the brush of some junior doctor's tie. Meanwhile there was I, with everything before me, unable even to get through lunch with him without a cushion of booze. The guilt only made me want to drink more.

'Surprised to see you on the beer,' he said. 'I thought vodka was your tipple of choice these days.'

He'd probably heard this from my mother but I glanced at the glass of yellow meltwater on the table and felt another blast of shame.

Then his expression changed. It was a face I'd never seen on him before, and it took me a moment to recognise it as fear.

'You're not going to believe this,' he said.

'What?'

'I've forgotten my teeth.'

'What?'

Now he was laughing, with a croak and a wheeze that were heartbreaking for their submission. 'That's a first. I've never done that in thirty years.'

'I'll drive back and fetch them. You stay here and drink your wine.'

'You shan't. What'll I do sitting here for half an hour? There'll be something I can have.'

I looked at the menu. 'They might have soup.'

'What's the point in soup? Chilli prawn linguine. That'll do.'

I knew he'd be furious if I forced the issue. So we sat there as he gallantly gummed the pasta and piled the untouched prawns onto his side plate, and the sight of a heap of cooling crustaceans had never been so desolate. Eventually the food was cleared away and we sat staring at a couple of ducks on the canal outside. Watching animals always made him sentimental.

'I don't half miss her, you know,' he said.

'I know you do.'

A tear streaked the flank of his face. 'We did it all together. And she knew so much. Before she lost her way.'

His other eye on the world had gone. Four years now. All their arguments about whether or not she was still fit to drive had been in vain, because ultimately he was never one to stop a loved one doing what they wanted to do. The car had been found backwards in a ditch, wheels still turning, her face bruised and a trickle of blood down her forehead.

'Let's talk about something else,' he said. 'How are all your mates from up there doing? Is that Drake kid still stuck in his computers?'

'Sure is. And doing very well with them.'

He lowered his voice. 'Was he one of the ones?'

I nodded. 'Yeah. But he doesn't like to talk about it. I'm the only person he's told, I think.'

'Poor old lad,' he muttered. 'Good luck to him.'

'I'm seeing him next weekend, actually. We go out around this time every year for his birthday.'

'Look out, London!' he said, cheered by the prospect of fun, even if it wasn't his own. His fingers grasped inside the glass of sparkling water he'd been poured, withdrew the slice of lemon and tossed it onto the tablecloth. 'Why do they always put lemon in the water? If I wanted to taste lemon, I'd order lemonade.'

As I helped him out of the car when we got back to the home, I put my nose to the top of his head. This weak old man smelled the same now as he had when he was still a strong old man. The same as he might have when he was a young father, and a boy, and a baby for all I knew. He'd watched as the modern world encircled him, laughing at it when he could, fighting it when he couldn't. The rising waters were at his throat now, but there was no way he wasn't going out on his own terms.

'Look at that poor sod,' he said, pointing. There was a bus shelter near the front door under which an old man in an overcoat had been left like an unattended bag. 'It's not even a real bus stop. They have it so if anybody feels like they want to get away they can go and sit there. The receptionist buzzes them out, then watches through the window to make sure they don't walk off. After a while, someone comes and tells them the bus is delayed and asks them if they want a nice cup of tea. By the time they come back in, they've forgotten they ever wanted to leave.' He clutched the seat belt as he prepared to peel it away from himself. 'Listen. You needn't worry about me. I shan't be in any more pain. And if there's anything after this, there'll be plenty of folks to keep me company.'

'You're not on the way out yet,' I said. 'Come on. Maybe that nurse will be there and you can talk to her about her boyfriend.'

I took his weight and we approached the door of the place that had no right to contain him. 'Shame there isn't a piano,' he said. 'They'd all love to hear you. Music is the one thing that can still talk to a lot of them.'

'Maybe I'll bring an electric one next time. That reminds me, I've made you a CD.' I reached into my coat pocket and handed it to him. 'Put that on when you get in. There's some good stuff on there.'

'No more of that modern rubbish, I hope. That Charlie Parker does my head in.'

'I wouldn't dream of it after last time.' I tried to smile but he could see I was welling up. 'That's a nice hydrangea,' I said, gesturing at a pot plant by the door.

'Is it buggery,' he breathed. 'It's a fucking geranium.' He looked at me. 'Don't come in.'

'No, all right.'

'And leave quickly. That was what you always used to say when I dropped you off, remember?'

I nodded, though I had forgotten. 'I'll be back up this way in a couple of months. June. There's a party at Luke's farm. I could come and see you on the way there.'

'Come after. I want to see the hangover.' He went to shake my hand, which I retracted, reacting inwardly to a dire warning my mother had made to do with skin contact and

MRSA. His arm fell to his side. 'Get on, then,' he said. 'You'll set me off.'

'Okay,' I said, not moving.

His arm rose up again and fell over me and I buried my face in his shoulder.

As I got back to the car my hand went automatically to my pocket for his Victoria crown, which I still carried with me at all times. Then, knowing he'd be watching from the window, I drove off to find a nearby spot where I could pull the car over for a proper weep.

22

He was still on my mind the following Friday as I got ready to go out and meet Simon. Tradition dictated that we started early, so I'd taken the afternoon off, and Katharine was at home too having just observed a nightshift at the hospital. It was unheard of for students her age to work nights, but she would be dropping out for a year when the baby came so she'd begged for the experience of watching some. She'd reached the rather feverish conclusion that cramming in as much as she could now was the best way to mitigate the effects of her future absence. When I thought back to what I had been doing at her age, I felt hopelessly inadequate.

What I was doing now wasn't much better. I'd been working as a freelance translator for the last few years, occasionally finding interesting work for the Foreign or Home Offices, but more often accepting soul-sapping commissions translating instruction manuals or specialist trade publications. Katharine was showing me up already, and she wasn't yet twenty-one. I told myself that doctors probably had that effect on people a lot, even when they were only trainees.

Our flat was being made ready for new life. A cot and a baby buggy, eagerly passed on by Luke, sat prematurely ready in the spare room, which would in time be redecorated in some gender-neutral colour. We still had six months to go but the thing had started to loom. Not that you'd have thought so from the energy the Pocket Rocket continued to pour into her studies. She returned upbeat no matter what she'd seen, and in spite of the fact that she was suffering from an extreme form of morning sickness which had turned the hospital into an olfactory minefield.

'How was the night?' I said, and, distracted by how pleased I was to see her, went in for a hug.

'Fine,' she said. She reciprocated the embrace but kept her face angled away.

'Sorry,' I said, remembering. 'Too much?'

'A bit.' She stepped back and retched softly into her fist. 'Shit. Just let me get some air. Sorry.'

She was being heroic at trying not to mention it, but I knew because she'd let it slip eventually that the smell that most turned her stomach during the protracted sickness phase was the smell of me. The base odour of Max Denyer. The problem was particularly acute in the car, but it happened in the flat too, and no amount of washing on my part could prevent it. I felt conscious of every seeping pore.

'Anything horrendous happen this time?' I said, as she opened the window.

'Nothing too bad. One awful drunk who'd put his face through a plate-glass window, then got furious with how long it was taking us to sew it back together. He just sat there, ranting *I've had it up to HERE with the NHS, I really have.*'

I smiled. 'Charming.'

'I'm not saying he owes us undying gratitude, but I sometimes wish there were more patients like your grandpa who just want to laugh and make knob gags.'

I was grateful for her affection for him. It was one of many ways in which she understood what mattered to me and went out of her way to embrace it. The feeling made me want to stay in with her, cook her a meal and sit at a sensible distance drinking a bottle of wine for both of us. But she hadn't forgotten my appointment.

'So,' she said. 'The big night out. I can't *believe* you're all turning thirty. How did I end up living on the geriatric ward? Just you and Simon?'

'As always,' I lied.

'Doesn't my brother ever get a look-in?'

'This is just a thing we do. It's not personal.'

Time and habit had done their normalising business and it now felt as if the age gap between me and Katharine had been accepted by our families. Either that or the pregnancy had showed them we were serious. We could probably have gone public earlier than we did but we'd both ended up enjoying the secrecy.

We'd lied to so many people during those early stages that we'd made a formal promise that we would never lie to each other. But I did lie to her, around this time every year.

These evenings do not happen. History looks away. It's the least it can do under the circumstances. What memories I have of them will always make me uneasy. We undergo this once a year, because it's been deemed necessary to do so, then set about forgetting it as much as we can. The absurdity has become palpable – we both know that we have become accustomed to something that cannot continue. Even Simon knows. These are the dying days. They have to be.

There's a formula in place, designed to limit the damage. Every year I follow it unquestioningly, trusting Simon's word that this is what we have to do, just as I trust his word as to the situation with the videotapes. I don't know what accommodation they have come to. Whether the tapes were given back, or destroyed, or something else. I'm not sure I want to know. He assures me it's been resolved. Which reminds me that I only had his word to go on that it was a threat in the first place.

We'd arranged to meet in a pub at the back of King's Cross called the Gilded Cage. Simon appeared at the window wearing black jeans, an Iron Maiden T-shirt and a black hoodie, pointing apologetically at the Blackberry stuck to his ear. His hair had been cut so short he almost looked bald. He paced around outside, pulling on a roll-up as he drilled something into whoever he was talking to, which I guessed was one of his employees.

Here he is. Simon '06: lean and calm. No longer trying to strike out from under his strangeness, but lashed to it stoically, even strategically – crafting it into something lethal and productive. When he paused to let the other person speak he pointed through the window at my pint on the table, gave a theatrical nod and pointed to himself. I went to the bar.

'Sorry,' he said when he came in. 'We're launching this thing in less than two months and there are still bugs in three of the levels.' As usual it took time to bring his attention under control. Eyes ticking up and around. Staring at the midweek drinkers with the kind of insolence that can start trouble. Eventually, he relaxed. Though he wouldn't be relaxing properly until the evening was over. 'Well, fuck, here we are,' he said. 'I can't believe it's that time again.'

'We could always stop,' I said.

'One day,' he said. 'Soon.'

It felt important to catch the third member of our group as he hit town. To monitor his arrival just as we did his departure. Equally important was establishing a base level of drunkenness well before any interaction took place. When he arrived we'd take him on to one of the famous Soho drinking holes, the venue usually selected by Simon, and presented for Crimble's delectation along with the most checkered aspects of its history. The Coach. The French. The Pillars. Crimble loved any literary or artistic associations, the seedier the better, and would always pretend to be scandalised by the big city and apprehensive of what debauchery our own evening held in store. Never mind that we'd been doing this for so long now that there could be no doubt as to how it would go: everybody played along. Simon and I exaggerated our worldliness while Crimble understated his own. He played the benefactor from out of town, while we played the treated boys. This was the story he was here to believe in.

He'd drink a pint or two if we were in a pub, or if the location was more upmarket we might 'persuade' him to try a cocktail, preferably one which he could claim never to have drunk before. My role would kick in properly when we got to Ronnie Scott's, since as the musician of the group I'd have selected the act we were there to hear. Crimble would be unfailingly complimentary of my choice, and bang on endlessly about what a privilege it was to be guided by someone who *really knows his onions*.

As the evening went on, either Simon would continue to go along with the pretence that we were discerning gentlemen about town, or he wouldn't. There was rarely an in-between. If he did, the mood would be happy enough until the inevitable late surge of bitterness after Crimble had gone. If he didn't, we were in for more of a ride, but this would also give Crimble an opportunity to step in and *deal with the difficult boy*, which might even have been his preferred outcome.

Hard to say who, if anyone, enjoyed all this. The meetings functioned like a safety valve on some ancient reactor brimming with toxic waste. The machine had to be scrapped, but nobody was qualified to take the job on.

We were on our third pint by the time Simon saw him coming. The hunched stork posture. The squint into the distance. Edgy advancement of certified non-Londoner.

'Target acquired. Hello, what's this? A new parka. In *yellow,* no less.'

This too was traditional: bolstering our disrespect with mockery as we tracked his approach. He'd always wear outdoor wear to town. Rainproof coat. Hiking shoes. Implying he'd rather be up a mountain. Declaring his difference.

'Well, boys, another salubrious establishment, I see,' he said, raising an expansive hand from the doorway.

'We thought you'd like this one,' said Simon. 'It's famous. Damien Hirst was sick just over there in the late nineties.' He headed to the bar to avoid a physical greeting.

'Welcome to the smoke,' I said, shaking his hand. The usual bachelor smell, soured today with beery breath. Apparently we weren't the only ones in need of Dutch courage.

Simon returned with a pint of bitter for Crimble, who raised it in a silent toast as his free hand wandered out to pat Simon's shoulder. 'What a treat.'

Onstage, instruments gleamed in their stands. The high shine of the piano would have satisfied Weapons Davis himself. We sat in a line, faces lit red by the table lamps, angling in towards one another for this, the initial awkward phase. The club's bench seating was a significant reason why we always went there. They meant that after the precursory small talk had taken place there was no need for face-to-face interaction until the interval, by which time at least two of us would be steaming drunk.

I kept thinking of Holly. This was the last place I'd seen her. We'd come here five years previously, just before we dropped out of contact for good. Even though it was long after there'd been anything between us I remembered sitting beside her at one of these tables, the red lamps casting us in their seediness and sophistication, imagining powerful energy passing between our thighs. She'd taken her leave of me quite formally in the end. *Let's not keep in touch*, she'd said, closing the door on me and returning to the main room of her life, which I had never seen.

Simon called over our waiter and ordered two gin martinis.

'Am I having one of those?' said Crimble. 'Won't I get completely sozzled?'

'They're both for me,' said Simon. 'It can be hard to get their attention later. And I don't know what you want, do I?'

'Oh,' said Crimble. 'Well, maybe I'll have one anyway.'

'Do you mind me ordering two?' said Simon.

'Of course not. You must have what you like.'

'Great.' Simon turned back to the waiter. 'Can you open a bottle of the Pauillac as well? Get it breathing.'

Rather than take offence, Crimble decided to be delighted by Simon's command of the situation. 'You're so grand now! Not that I thought that wouldn't happen. It's just electrifying to see it in action. When I think back to how quiet you were before. But also how focused. We all knew you'd do something magnificent. And you have.'

Simon waved away the compliment. 'It's not very complicated, what I do. It's just storytelling. In another form.'

'He's a genius,' I said. 'We all know that. You should see the way the girls in his office look at him. And half the boys.'

'Really?' said Crimble. 'Well, I can't say I'm surprised. Is there anyone significant on the scene?' Nervous warmth of his grin. Grateful for any scrap in return.

'I try to avoid dating people from work,' said Simon. 'It's not very professional. But there is something sexy about a certain kind of geek. They're … imaginative, if you know what I mean.'

'Stop! You'll embarrass this old man.'

'He's being modest,' I said. 'They can't keep their hands off him.'

Premeditated torture. So ingrained a routine we no longer planned it in advance or dwelled on it afterwards. Simon did have the odd relationship, and odd they were, but rarely with anyone from work, and never in the way we painted it for Crimble. This was done to keep him in his place, and set him tussling with his own imagination.

'You should give gaming a try,' said Simon. 'You'd love all the narrative possibilities.'

'I think I'm too old and set in my ways,' said Crimble. 'I'm a traditionalist. I never did see the point of those multiple-choice books you all loved. What were they called? Choose Your Own Adventure?'

'The ones we liked were called Fighting Fantasy,' I said.

Simon lost a mouthful of his first martini as the laugh burst out of him.

Crimble smiled, truffling for the joke, desperate to be in on it. 'What?'

'Sorry. I've never thought of that before.'

'What?'

'The idea that you would let anyone *choose their own adventure* is of course totally ridiculous.' He took out his Blackberry. 'Excuse me. I have to make a call before it starts.' He put a hand on my shoulder to pull himself up. 'Maxy, order me a rare fillet steak if they come.'

'And like that, he was gone,' said Crimble, looking wistfully after Simon as he marched out to the lobby. 'Do you think he'd rather I stopped coming to see you both? I hate to think of myself as an obligation. He seems very jumpy today.'

'He's hard to pin down at the moment,' I said. 'Big release coming up.'

'How is he in general?'

'I think he's on better form than he's been in years, if I'm honest.'

'Is it true about him and the girls in the office?'

I smiled. 'And the boys.'

He sipped from the glass of water next to his warming martini. 'Is there anyone significant? I hate to think of him spreading himself too thinly.'

No, I thought. *You're not getting any relief out of me.* 'One or two, maybe. It's hard to keep track.'

I asked the usual questions of him, not that there was any need – his life hadn't changed in twenty-five years. The only variations were in the faces he saw each day, the play he put on in March, the mountain he climbed at Easter. He'd aged, though. His beard was nearly all white now and his appearance was more unkempt with every passing year. We'd heard mounting rumours of the dilapidation of the school – of a sorry place, with falling attendances, somehow clinging on in spite of the horror of the Weathers-Davis scandal. I had the impression that it had mellowed even more since the reunion, partly because of changing social attitudes, and partly because Tony Sutton's replacement was accountable to the parents and governing body in ways that neither Sutton nor his father had ever been.

'I've moved house, of course,' said Crimble.

'Really?'

'I've taken the static home at the top of the walled garden.'

'Sutton Senior's house?'

'The very same. It needed a bit of sprucing up, but it's very peaceful inside those high walls.'

'Christ, that was a sinister place. Do you remember sending us up there to crap in the snow when I first arrived? When the pipes had burst?'

'You what?' he said, laughing. 'I don't believe it. We'd never have made the boys do that.'

'You fucking did.'

'Well, it's a good story, anyway.'

'It's true.'

He shrugged. I tried to keep my cool. Luckily the waiter arrived to take our food order.

'Anyway, tell me about you,' he said, with a serious expression that made me think I was in for one of the employment lectures I'd been receiving from my father. 'Are you still playing?'

'Not much, these days. I was never going to make a career of it. I wasn't good enough.'

'You play beautifully,' he said. 'Always did. But there's something relaxing about a hobby. One often gets far more out of being a true *amateur*, in the original, loving sense of the word. And don't forget, Art Tatum said there's no such thing as a wrong note.'

There it was. His skill. That way he had of understanding how we wanted to be seen. Even now, pushing thirty, there was pleasure to be derived from his recognition.

'Yeah, well, Art Tatum's wrong notes were a lot better than mine.'

When Simon returned he saw to his second martini, ordered a beer and sent for the wine. Crimble watched him with apprehension before speaking. 'Your generation and your phones. It's amazing. You're permanently affixed.'

'You're right,' said Simon. 'And I hate it. As soon as this game is finished I'm going to take off for the summer and leave mine behind. Get off the grid completely.'

This was news to me. 'Where will you go?' I said.

'I thought I might just drive around Europe with a fishing rod and see what happens.'

The band came on. Simon ate a few mouthfuls of steak then set down his cutlery, listening with cursory, almost angry attention. He looked trapped. There was always a danger of it going this way. It hadn't happened for a few years, but tonight, as he piled more and more drinks onto Crimble's tab, he became openly disrespectful of all of it, sighing aloud at the indulgences of the band. He had a point. I hadn't chosen well. The music was anodyne. White jazz. All technique and no feeling.

Before we packed him off in his taxi to St Pancras to catch the last train, Crimble made a last-ditch attempt to prolong things. 'I don't feel tired at all. Shall we go on somewhere? I could always find myself a room for the night.'

Simon's fingers were already at play twirling up a fag. 'I'm done. And you need to get your train. Thanks for a very pleasant evening.'

'Can I give either of you a lift in my taxi?'

'I've got my bike,' I said.

'And I've got to collect my stuff from the office,' said Simon. 'Thanks again. Safe journey.'

Simon hailed him a cab. We embraced his bony frame in turn, disinhibited now by booze.

'It's always so good to see you both,' he said, leaning forward from the back seat.

'Mind how you go.' Simon slammed the door and gave the roof of the cab two brisk pats. As I watched it rumble off, it occurred to me that Simon was now probably the age Crimble had been when they first met. 'Right,' he said. 'For the love of fuck, let's get another drink.'

Down the Soho rabbit hole. Good and bad people having their good and bad times. As usual, we vowed that it would never happen again. As usual, we laughed a lot as the world flooded back in. You could be in the most public, populous place, but Crimble's company was a force field. When you got shot of him it was like gratefully slipping into a more capacious dimension.

'What did you tell Katharine we were doing tonight?' said Simon, when his nerves had begun to smooth out.

'What I always tell her: our special date for your birthday.'

'Thanks. It's not that I mind her knowing, particularly. But I can't face it all getting back to Luke.'

'I know.'

He took out his tobacco pouch and started rolling one for each of us. I fiddled with his lighter, sparking it and running my finger through the flame.

'What do you think would have happened if we hadn't burned those letters?' he said.

This got my attention. He'd never said anything like it before. 'I guess it would have depended on how far you'd wanted to go.'

'I still don't know. It would have ended his career at the very least. That felt like a big deal to me at the time. And we don't know anything about his past. What might have happened to him to make him the way he is.'

'Shouldn't his career be ended?' I said. 'Regardless of that?'

'Who am I to destroy someone's career? Especially someone who was that kind to me.'

'That's a matter of opinion.'

'Shut up – that's not the point I'm making. A career is a big, grown-up thing. Who is some kid to tamper with it?' He popped his cigarette between his lips as if settling on a conclusion. 'Society is on the side of the man with the career, not the boy with the mouth.'

'But didn't you want to see justice done?' I said, holding up the lighter. 'You never got your day in court.'

'I didn't want it. That's why I burned the letters in the first place. Tell me this: what's the difference between justice and retribution?'

I thought. 'Retribution is the form that justice takes, I guess. There is no justice without retribution.'

'Well, I don't think he deserves that. Though I do wonder if it wouldn't be more humane to put him out of his misery.'

23

DRIVING THE ŠKODA out of town, I stole glances at Katharine, who was trying against the odds to get comfortable. She could fuss with the heating all she wanted, but her problems derived from the unfurling nugget within, from jelly which had firmed insistently to cartilage and bone.

It was June, five months into the pregnancy. The worst of the sickness was past, but as usual, her body's response to being in a confined space with me was to remind her how comprehensively it had been taken from her. Her mounting fury with the machinery was making me edgy.

'Just tell me whether you want to be cooler or warmer and I'll fix it,' I said.

She flung herself at the seat back. I suppressed patronising concern for her precious cargo. 'The entire problem is that there is no *right* in this situation. Right doesn't exist. It's all wrong.'

I reached for the CDs, thinking to stick on the same compilation I'd burned for my grandfather.

'No,' she said. 'No music.'

The road ripped by. I saw hazards everywhere. The curl of a blown-out tyre. An eviscerated fox.

'Maybe you shouldn't have come,' I said.

'Why should I stay at home to feel like shit and miss the whole thing? And if you went alone, there's no telling what state you'd be in when you got back.'

'It's not as mad as all that.'

'Are you joking? They're demented. It's only a matter of time.' She leaned sideways, opened her window and faced the rushing air. 'Ah, that's better.'

I held my tongue for a moment, then couldn't help myself. 'If this is the effect of a short car journey, are you sure you want to get on a plane to Italy when you're even further along?'

She closed her eyes. 'Do you really want to do this now?'

The bickering rolled on. It gave us a structure. I thought again about that beloved old man in his airless prison. It was going to be difficult to get away with honouring the promise I'd made to pay him a visit on the way back. I wanted to bust him out of there right now and take him to the farm with us. Not that I was certain he'd have enjoyed it. He would surely feel at home among the cobbled yards, thatched roofs and slumped outbuildings. He'd fall, as we all had, for the outrageous beauty of the water meadow with its mangled fences and weeping willows. He might even relish the farm's signature brand of choreographed depravity to begin with, but not when he saw where it led.

I tried to angle myself away from Katharine, conscious of my morning breath, of the coffee I'd drunk on an empty stomach. 'Only a matter of time before what?' I asked.

'Before something breaks.'

'You're being melodramatic.'

'Am I?' She spun in her seat and turned her stare on full-beam. 'I want you to remember this moment. Because something bad will happen there sooner or later. And when it does, we are going to revisit the time, in this sensible family car, that as we passed Oxford services, you told me that I was being *melodramatic*.'

'That will be nice for us.' I exhaled, trying to relax into my angle.

'Sorry,' she said. 'The air's helping. Now if I can just fix this damn seat. God, it stinks in here.'

'Any joy?' I said, as the seat performed its contortions.

'Not for months.' She mellowed a little, pleased with her own quip. 'I might be exaggerating a bit. I felt a lot better this morning.'

'So little Blue Stripe is finally settling in. That's something.'

'We're going to have to stop calling it that sooner or later.'

It was still known as the farm, though it had long ceased to be one. It was many other things. Vice den. Centre of operations. Declaration of intent. The intent being that Luke and Ish and their business partners would behave exactly how they liked in pursuit of their goals, and let nobody get in their way. They had gone there to plot their domination like a band recording a seminal album, but instead of a chateau or an island they'd chosen a wrecked pig farm outside Banbury. It was a blend of the sacred and the profane, the serious and the resolutely silly. One outbuilding stacked to the rafters with shrink-wrapped Internet routers ready for dispatch, another laid out with a giant Scalextric track, booby-trapped with explosives.

The partners and their families all lived elsewhere, which freed up the farm for what really mattered. During the week, this was aggressive salesmanship. At weekends, it was entertainment. Luke and Ish hired anyone in whom they detected the blend of hunger and recklessness that had got them this far. It felt like a conscious programme of diversification, though it would have been indelicate to point out that the people running the show had all met at one private school or another.

They specialised in corruption: encouraging nice local boys to cheat on their girlfriends; encouraging nice local girls to *take this pill, right now.* Whatever their background, the minions all ended up falling in the end for the false equivalence that was presented to them between being interesting and being showily unpleasant. Employees lived rent-free on the farm for as long as they could bear it, and were paid handsomely if they sold well, though nobody ever got shares.

The weekends would begin with a semblance of decorum. There would be exhibition food, some extravagant cut of meat cooked on a spit or in a wheelbarrow. Cases of good wine. A centrepiece cocktail. Several of the partners had kids, so there might be a children's entertainer and a bouncy castle. As things deteriorated, the boundaries would blur. Someone would decide to heckle the entertainer or dive naked over the inflatable battlements. There was a constant sense that control was about to be lost, and an anxiety that if it was, there would be nobody there to fix it. There was also a constant sense that things *must* get out of control, because if they didn't it would mean that they were abiding by the rules, settling into the vanilla.

We parked in the usual field and headed for the barn, where music was already pounding. A group of kids played among the frames of a stack of broken sash windows nearby. The panes clung precariously to the rotten frames, some smashed into shards, some dangling intact from the pulp of the wood.

Katharine's eyes widened at the sight, then she looked at me and shrugged. 'Not our problem. Don't want to be getting all *melodramatic*.'

'Hello, Auntie!' hollered a boy of six, drawing back his arm to chuck a glass-shattering brick.

'Gus. That looks fun.'

'Jesus, is that Luke's kid?' I said. 'He's huge. When did that happen?'

'They grow up.'

A flatbed truck was backed up to the main gates, from which pieces of a circular dark-wood bar were being unloaded. To one side I saw stencilled mirrors and Victorian light fittings. Supervising the process was Luke Price.

Luke '06: laughter lines just beginning to form around those soulful blue eyes. Dirty, straw-coloured hair. His checked shirt hanging well, half tucked artfully into battered blue jeans. The gentleman farmer with the business brain. It was always a slight surprise how warm he was in person. The residual energy of his company left you with an impression of spikiness that was instantly dissolved by the real thing.

'What fresh hell is this?' I said.

'You don't recognise it? I guess you'd have to be four foot tall and pleading for Quavers. It's the Graven Image. The innards of it, anyway. I heard it was closing down so I bought all the fittings.'

'No!'

'Never going to have a problem getting served at this bar again.' He gave Katharine a kiss and patted her bump. 'You're in the blue room. I thought the en suite might be welcome since I hear that gestating a human being can put quite a squeeze on the old bladder.'

'We're honoured,' she said, flinging his hand away.

'You sure are. It's the only bedroom with a lock. Which I strongly suggest you use if you don't want unwanted visitors later on.'

'Can't we just stay with you?' said Katharine.

'And miss out on all the fun? You'll be fine. Just lock the door.' He hugged me. 'Simon coming, do you know?'

'No idea,' I said.

'I won't hold out hope. Right. Shall we go and watch some interviews?'

'Ish on a recruitment drive?' said Katharine.

'He's been at it an hour,' said Luke. 'We better go and see how he's getting on. I promised I wouldn't leave them alone with him for too long.'

We crossed from the main yard to a smaller one enclosed by stables with green-painted doors. Rusting farm machinery lay strewn on the cobbles. I could hear Ish's voice from within as we approached.

'It doesn't sound like he's killed anyone yet,' said Luke.

We looked through the stable's half-open door. Inside, Ish stood at a church lectern that rose into spread eagle's wings. He wore a red jacket with brass buttons, and military trousers with a scarlet stripe down the leg. He was gesticulating with a riding crop as he read aloud from a series of questions. In front of him, three nervous-looking young people sat in a row at a trestle table. An enamel feeding trough in the corner of the stable held bottles of vodka and tequila heaped with ice. On the trestle table sat a large metal tray onto which lines of powder had been carved, divided into two sections by a length of red ribbon. There was a lingering smell of horse-piss and hay.

'Now then, Mr Stephens,' said Ish. 'You've had a rocky start, but there's still time to atone for your sins. My question for you is this: Who used the system of land ownership known as *feudalism*? Was it the Anglo-Saxons, the Normans, the Romans or the Vikings?'

Stephens was a fleshy kid in his early twenties. There was dread on his face and his mouth was chewing itself compulsively at the right-hand side. His pupils were dilated to the point of blackening his gaze.

'This one's had *a lot* of E for error,' said Ish, glancing at us.

'What's the subject matter today?' I asked.

'Excellent question, Max. What we have here is a set of sample questions from the soon-to-be-launched *Life in the United Kingdom* test, which is a requirement for anyone seeking naturalisation as a British citizen, pursuant to the Nationality, Immigration and Asylum Act of 2002. And I must tell you that this young man is not performing well. I'll have to hurry you, Mr Stephens.'

'Normans?' managed Stephens.

Ish swished his crop onto the lectern. 'I thought we were losing you there. C for correct. Off you go then. Chop-chop.'

Stephens took his medicine and looked relieved. His foot jigged under the table.

'Miss Shah, are you with us?' A compact, composed Asian girl with a gold nose stud gave a curt nod. 'Which group of refugees settled in England before 1720? Was it the Bretons, the Welsh, the Huguenots or the Germans?'

She smiled. 'Huguenots.'

Ish turned to us, gesticulating with his crop. 'She is untouchable, this one! The only one she's stumbled on so far is the exact number of local authorities in London, which I defy anyone to know the right answer to. Go on then, C for correct. You're going to clean us out of the good stuff if you're not careful.'

Ish '06: a forbidding presence. People always think him stunning in photographs, only to be terrified of him in real life. The photos never quite communicate the tenor of his energy, which is challenging and insolent and dares you to say something he doesn't like.

'Absolutely right, Miss Green. The first Union flag was indeed created in 1606. Back to you then, Mr Stephens. My Lord, it comes around quickly, doesn't it? Would you like another shot to steady your nerves? There. Good. In which year did the Habeas Corpus Act become law? A very apt question since you're losing control of your body. Was it 1679, 1689, 1699 or 1709? Oh dear. I fear Mr Stephens may be struggling. Three, two, one. It's 1679, of course. We're back again, Mr Stephens. It's E for error time. Come along now.'

Stephens stared at the tray, steeled himself and did Ish's bidding. He sat back in his chair, eyelids half closed. I'd seen sights like this here before. They always left me feeling nauseous.

'Okay, he's out.' Luke unbolted the stable door, stepped inside and knelt by the table. 'No more for this one.' He helped the kid to his feet, put an arm around his waist and walked him to the exit.

Stephens grabbed at Luke's hand. 'Did I pass? I'm not leaving if I didn't pass.'

'You passed,' said Luke. 'Come and look at the fish pond.'

As we left I could just hear the start of Ish's next question. 'Okay, quick-fire elimination time. Answers to be given in less than five seconds. Question one: How do you spell the word *Leicestershire*?'

Spring term. Hockey. Ingrained odours of mud, grass and sweat. Ish and I stand in the boot hut wearily contemplating the cubbyholes.

David West kicks open the door, stick in hand. 'Look lively, boys! Day's not going to get any better than this. *Beano*, ten Rothmans and a Lucozade please, mate,' he adds, pulling his boots from their berth. He doesn't look in his direction but I know the remark is directed at Ish. I've noticed this before: how a few of the older boys are constantly adding comments like this in a quick, nasty mutter whenever he's around. Farmers Weekly *in yet, chief? Didn't get my* Razzle *this month, my friend, what's going on there?* I will look back and realise there is something about the way they speak that hints at learned behaviour, that its origin is adult.

Usually there would be accomplices with West to laugh at the joke, but today he is alone. Which might embolden me if thought I was being clever. In fact the question I ask is an innocent one, since I am genuinely puzzled. 'Why do you always say stuff like that to him? I don't get it.'

West sits pushing shin guards down his socks, pulsing with excitement at the prospect of an afternoon on the field. 'Don't know what you mean.'

'I mean, I know his dad's a newsagent. But what's the joke?'

One tight-laced boot hits the floor. 'Not the sharpest knife in the drawer, are we, Denyer?'

'Your dad's a farmer, isn't he? Couldn't we do the same by talking about silage and cow shit?' Ish stands waiting for the moment to be over but I notice that this has made him smile. '*Oo-aar, mornin', Farmer West. Got any o' that lovely manoor on yur trailer this mornin'?*'

West is in my face immediately. 'Shut the fuck up, you little shit.'

'Why?'

'It's not because his dad's a newsagent, is it? It's because his dad's a Paki.' Breathing heavily, embarrassed enough not to look at Ish, playing his shame as disgust.

'Oh.' I turn away, trying to stay cool, though the word and its ugliness have shocked me as he intended. Turning was a mistake. West shoves me forwards and my upper lip hits the side of a shelf as I go down.

I'm still on the floor tasting blood when the next bit happens so I only hear the noise. But it's enough. And Ish will be able to tell me later, when he has got over his justified, but momentarily hurtful fury at me for intervening on his behalf, exactly how he grabbed the boot from the shelf and swung it sideways into David West's cheek.

The three of us are called in separately by Tony Sutton to give accounts of the incident. I don't know what is said to the other two, but I will remember one of Sutton's lines to me on the subject, spoken with no trace of a stutter.

'I mean, West was only speaking the truth,' he says. 'He was describing rather than insulting.'

In the yard, strings of festoon lighting had been switched on and a mechanical spit turned a golden, grinning pig over a fire. Katharine and Luke stood by a trestle table making up hot dogs for his kids. She was endearingly attentive around her nephews, auditioning herself as a mother.

A wiry, dishevelled figure was bent over tending to the pig. As I approached I saw Josh, the younger of Luke's sons, run off with his hot dog and trip towards the mound of burning coals under the spit. The bent-over man's arm shot sideways to catch him. The intervention was frightening, and the boy started to cry. But the man had anticipated the reaction and the arm-barrier curled into an affectionate hug as the face of the boy's uncle turned angrily in the direction of his brother.

'Keep an eye on him, can't you?' said Ali.

'What?' said Luke.

'He nearly face-planted into the fire.'

'Mate, he's fine. Have a drink.'

Ali shook his head. 'You're too fucking casual.'

They settled into a friendlier conversation. The three of them in a line together: a full spectrum dose of the Price family. Luke, confident, mercurial, glowing with the self-evident fact that he had supplanted Ali in almost every way, ready to be magnanimous about that should the need arise. Ali, older, careworn, the lines on his face somehow commanding pity rather than respect, his hard-wired sense of duty intact even in this buccaneering environment where responsibility was a boring weakness. Katharine, the baby sister, given licence by her brothers to occupy a more carefree space, her customary vitality a little dimmed by the squatter in her belly. Ingredients of Roger and Selina in all three. His searching stare in Ali. Her amused detachment in Luke. Aspects of both in Katharine depending on her mood. All of them subject to many of the same experiences, with crucial differences and vastly divergent outcomes.

'I'll catch up with you later,' Ali announced, taking out his phone and wandering off. 'Stuff to do.'

'What stuff?' said Luke. He was smoking a thin cigar and browsing a bag of golf clubs. 'Does anyone know about this job he's supposed to have?'

'Nothing at all,' said Katharine.

Since Ali's return from Iraq it had become a staple of Price family conversation to wonder aloud if he was all right, then change the subject before anyone gave thought to the answer. He had lately found work with a private security firm, but nobody knew the details.

'I think we've lost him,' said Luke. 'He's like a ghost since he left the army.'

'He likes structure,' said Katharine. 'He just needs to find a new one, that's all.'

'What do you think he saw out there?' I said.

Luke sniffed. 'He had a bad time taking Basra. That's all I know.'

'Do you think he killed anyone?'

Katharine gave me a look. 'Typically direct Max question there. He probably wouldn't tell us if he had.'

'He did kill a dog,' said Luke.

'Yeah?'

'He said there were a lot of them around the camp. Strays. They kept stepping on landmines. So he killed it for its own good, or something. Although when I pushed him on it he said it was actually because the dog wouldn't stop barking and he thought everyone could do with a good night's sleep.' Luke teed up a golf ball near the wall overlooking the water meadow, and selected a club from the bag. 'He's out, you know.'

'Who is?'

'Eric Graham "Weapons" Weathers-Davis. In society and free to get back to nurturing the younger generation.'

'Shit,' I said. 'That's come around quickly. Is that what's spinning Ali out?'

'Who knows? He won't go there. Shuts it down the second you bring it up. But I've made sure he knows that I'd do anything for him. I mean it. I'd find that fucker in a chat room and get him talking. I'd entrap him if necessary. All Ali has to do is ask.'

Katharine looked away. She hated this subject. She'd been a pupil at the school while the Weathers-Davis story was playing out, and I had the sense that the scandal had poisoned the atmosphere for her there even before she became aware of any rumours about her brother's possible involvement.

'You'd help Ali more by having a proper conversation, or getting him to a therapist,' she said.

'Yeah? And how are your efforts going on that front?' said Luke. 'This is something I can actually do. I've got people ready to track him. I know the name of the street he lives on, the lot. If he so much as sniffs at anything dodgy online, we'll send him straight back to his cell.' Jets of smoke shot from his nose as he tossed the cigar.

'We need to get Ali talking, not obsessing about revenge,' said Katharine. 'If it even happened, which we don't know for sure.'

Luke limbered up with his club, widening his legs into a driving stance. 'Did either of you read the court transcripts? Because I did. You know he used to tell the victims that what they were doing couldn't be wrong because God was sanctioning it?'

'We all know he was a bastard.'

'I don't think you do know, Max. Not really. He used to get them to suck him off in his classroom when people were walking around outside, to make it as risky as possible. Turned on by the fear as well as the humiliation. Do you think it's right that someone like that is back in society? That he only went down for nine years?'

'We don't know what's happened to him in prison. He could be a different person now.'

'I love you, Max. But you've always been fucking naive.' He dropped into a George W. Bush accent. 'Now watch this drive.'

We lie staring down the long attic room in the stable block, sights trained on the paper commandos of the targets. If we weren't so nervous, our minds might be filled with war stories and cartoon Germans. Instead we are grappling with two kinds of alarm: we are in charge of loaded air rifles, and Weapons Davis is prowling behind us.

'Get your grouping in order. Price minor, that is a mess.' He sighs. 'If only your brother hadn't left us. Now there was a boy who knew how it was done. He'd have the centre of that target drilled with holes by now and be kneeling with his gun broken waiting for everybody else to finish. I bet that boy is Captain of Rifles at his new school already. Are you even related? Has none of it rubbed off on you? Who will be my new best shot?'

The soft feel of the pellets in the tin. I thumb one in, close the rifle and lie trying to tame its wavering barrel. My morning-load of fried bread fried egg fried bacon sits uneasily.

'Max Denyer.' He drops to a crouch. His voice murmurs in my ear. 'Is it you? Remember to exhale as you squeeze the trigger. Relax.' He lies down on his stomach on my left-hand side, gazing down the length of the rifle. His cheek sandpapers against mine. Coffee breath. Stale sweat.

'You should be able to concentrate whatever the distraction,' he says. His arm reaches over my shoulder and I feel something cold push into my right temple and realise that it is the barrel of his air pistol.

Breathe out and squeeze. Get it over with, get him away. But the stock falls as I shoot and I know the sighting pin has dropped too low.

'Useless.' He springs to his feet, spreads his legs and fires a pellet over my head into the centre of my target. 'Aiming is all about control.'

The sun went down. A serious fire was lit in the yard. The assault on the pig got properly under way and a DJ set up on the wall. There were suddenly a lot more guests, few of whom I recognised. Before I knew it we were at the business end of the party.

Luke wasn't flashy about drugs, showboating his consumption like those around him, but he usually had something in his pocket. He was good at it. Planned ahead. Whenever you thought it had all run out he'd have kept something back. You'd be there, about to cash in and go to bed, and he'd hold aloft a pristine wrap or a tight pack of pills, and you'd want to either hug him or kill him for ensuring that your lease on the world away had been renewed.

Him there beside me. Babble by firelight, leaning on a log. Awareness coming and going that Katharine had gone to bed angry, though I couldn't remember why. The present asserting itself in waves, until the present was all there was. Was it that night when there was a bet as to who could hold the electric fence for longest without spilling their drink? Won by nobody in the end, of course. It's an impossibility. However much you think you can hold on, the elemental forces in play override everything at the moment of truth.

Luke leaning in, smelling of woodsmoke and beer. His hand on my forearm, sticky with something spilt. 'I wasn't going to ask you in front of the wife, of course. But how's Holly? You ever see her?'

Sudden surge of memory that Katharine had left angry because she'd seen the direction the evening was headed and didn't want me tagging along. Very much time to get my head down and be off early in the morning. But you had to front up to bailing out. If I didn't tell him I was retiring, Luke would only come and find me.

I tried to stand. 'I'm turning in.'

Luke put on his finest Alec Guinness voice. 'If you go to bed now, I shall become more powerful than you can possibly imagine.' His firm hand gripped my shoulder, forcing me down.

I was losing sight of the things that mattered. And they did matter, very much. But here he was, still talking, going in and out of film quotes and hiding important things in the conversation for me to find later.

'What about Simon? You see him, don't you?'

Keeping it together, barely. 'He's been very busy. I saw him on his birthday.'

'I wish he'd come tonight. He told me he might, but I knew better than to believe him. It's amazing how little you can know about one of your oldest friends.'

Nodding. Lolling. 'He's a mystery wrapped up in an enigma wrapped up in a hoodie. I think he's all right, though.'

'I know he's all right. I miss him, that's all.' Bonfire light. Strangers. Luke's voice there. His face if I turned. 'This is probably bonkers, but have you ever thought maybe Weapons Davis got to him too?'

Sweating. Blinking. 'Fuck, I don't know. It's possible, I suppose. We'd know, wouldn't we? He'd have told us.'

'I don't know. He lives his whole life in a sort of grey area.'

'True.'

'Not like you. You know exactly what you're after.'

Turning. 'What's that supposed to mean?'

Luke guzzling from some bottle. 'Nothing sinister. You just always seemed to know what you wanted. Going after Katharine like that. Delighted to have you in the family, of course. You know that, right?'

Blinking. 'Sure. At least, I thought I did.'

The night finished as they tended to, with a twin rush of excitement and guilt at the rising of the sun.

The dawn creep to the bedroom, the treacherous morning light, the jackhammer heart next to the shamingly serene mother-to-be.

We were up and out before nine. Katharine had been kept awake most of the night, she said, by a couple screwing in the adjacent bathroom and by several other strangers who'd clattered in looking for a bed, since while I was still up she'd been unable to lock the bedroom door.

We picked our way through a corridor of coddled bodies. Some were still walking around outside. A dozing couple shivered in a sleeping bag beside the smouldering bonfire. One diehard sat on a log, ruminatively wiping his finger inside a long-spent baggie.

As we trod between the misted-up cars I looked out over the meadow and saw Ali, standing under the broad canopy of an oak tree teaching his nephew Gus to fire a longbow at a target. Arrows thunked into the rope. Ali's calm voice floated through the mist as he corrected Gus's aim. There was something anachronistic about the sight: gentlemen warriors, duels at dawn.

We barely spoke on the journey back. I was so focused on working up a plan of atonement against the constraints of my fractalised mind that I didn't remember my promise to visit my grandfather until we were parked outside our flat. An abrupt feeling of desolation on that score led as much as anything else to my capitulation.

'Fine,' I said. 'Italy. Let's go. What's the worst that could happen?'

When Katharine was settled in a bath I took out my phone to ring the care home and promise my grandfather I would visit him the following weekend, and saw that I'd missed three calls from my mother. When I rang back it took her several goes to get me to understand.

'It's happened,' she said.

'What has?'

'He went this morning.'

'Went where?'

'He's gone.'

24

I WILL BE surprised to be told later in life that I looked like I had a plan during my twenties. As far as I'm concerned the decade is one accident after another. My mind will dutifully cobble the memories into sequence later on, but none of it happens by design. I flail around making bad decisions, blundering back on myself only to strike out in equally wrong directions, leaving a trail as random and irrelevant as a set of animal droppings.

I am left in no doubt by my parents of the urgency with which I need to find a stable job after university. They could support me if they wanted to but it's made clear that there will be no handouts until I've found a path beyond playing jazz standards on bad pianos. When my lack of initiative becomes ever more apparent, my father suggests that I might consolidate my language skills with a stint at the Madrid office of his company. Perhaps out of residual guilt at having lied my way through the time I was already meant to have spent there, I accept, as if that wasted year with Holly could simply be rerun with a better outcome.

I take lodgings in a hostel near the Puerta del Sol, and spend my days compiling sales data into spreadsheets. It's clear nobody has any use for these documents. There is a sense that someone has scrabbled around to find something to meet my father's requirements. The feeling of being the boss's spoilt son parachuted in from overseas is even more humiliating than the work.

My hostel is home to four middle-aged Spanish bachelors and me. My bedroom has a door which is too short for its frame. The gaps at the top and bottom admit sour fumes from the Ducados smoked constantly in the common room outside. At night, after my compadres have finally stubbed out their cigarettes and stopped arguing, I am kept awake by the scratching of death-watch beetles in the woodwork.

Simon and I speak every week. He comes to see me and we take a road trip to Andalusia. 'This is where you should be,' he says as we sit on a wall listening to flamenco guitar and drinking from cold litre bottles of beer with the Alhambra lit up behind us. After sticking the job out for a few more months I take his advice and head south, applying for a master's degree in Hispanic Studies at the University of Granada, generating some income through piano gigs in small bars. When the gigs dry up I find work as an English tutor, and continue to do this after my course has finished, falling in with groups of young people who drift through the city as part of their own studies abroad. Swedes, Danes, Germans. Rarely the English. I discover that you can just pitch up somewhere and make a life, and time will pass. The realisation is both exhilarating and melancholy.

In 2001 I return to London, and take the first of several jobs which I deem not to be worthy of me, scowling my way through the day, doing the bare minimum, insulating myself from my surroundings with conspicuous headphones. Among many other things I miss the sight of the second plane hitting the Twin Towers, which those around me are watching in horror on live television. Years later I will discover that one of my bosses at the time used to say of me: *Max is brilliant at something – he just doesn't know what it is yet.*

Thus I end up in a situation where the only serious coalescence of friends in my life derives from a school I left at the age of thirteen. This is not at all true of the others, which bothers me at times. Either way, the fact is that little in our lives will ever be as vivid as the place where we first met. The only possible exception is Ali, who goes to a war zone. Which if we're honest he probably does to quell it or match it or, who knows, even to remind himself of it.

We can go for months without mentioning it. But even when we don't, it is there, underpinning our association. Evenings in. Evenings out. The grandiosity of the twenties. Our big story playing out. We will glamorise it all in retrospect when our lives have become more pedestrian, but in truth the places we go aren't chosen because we're part of some scene. They're just where we end up.

Somewhere along the way, it becomes accepted that Eric Weathers-Davis did get to Ali, but that he doesn't want to talk about it. This understanding isn't reached in one torrential moment but establishes itself in bursts of late-night speculation that are rarely referred to during daylight hours. During one such conversation, Luke asks the rest of us whether we think it's true, and what, if anything, ought to be done about it. In the absence of formal disclosure it's hard to propose anything beyond vigilance. Occasionally, when Simon isn't around, I suggest that Weapons Davis might not have been the only perpetrator, but there is always a brake that prevents me from going further. Keeping Simon's secret has become how I can be exceptional to him.

The past is accommodated. The banner we march under no longer feels as gaudy and terrible as once it did. Those emotions of 1997 – the rage, the guilt, the wishing people dead – come to seem melodramatic in retrospect, especially when Crimble starts leaking back into my life as the years pass.

Then, as the events of our early twenties begin to settle, they too become open to doubt. How much of what Simon told me then was reliable? To what extent was he out to shock me? And did I seriously think of going to the police and telling his story on my behalf?

Luke and Ali throw a New Year's Eve party at their parents' London flat to see in 2003. In a few months Ali will go to war, though he doesn't know it yet. Roger and Selina are in Italy, and their sons have managed to get clearance not to celebrate with them and their friends. Simon dislikes large gatherings, but assures me he will pitch up at some point. Luke and Ali are busy with other people, so I end up sitting in a corner with two bottles of wine and Katharine Price, and we don't get up for hours.

I've encountered her at regular intervals over the last few years thanks to the Italian holidays that Simon, Ish and I have been on with Luke's family. She is seventeen, and four months into the sixth form. She has been allowed to attend the party so long as her brothers keep a close eye on her – a responsibility which both Ali and Luke seem relieved to relinquish to me. Her sharpness is delightful. She makes me laugh. There's an illicit thrill to the conversation.

I receive new information about the dynamics of the Price family. Katharine tells me about the complicated relationship she has with her mother, who, in her account at least, doted on Ali and Luke while being relentlessly hard on her over everything from her appearance to what she wants to do for a living. Selina, she claims, is one of the main reasons why she wants to be a doctor. Partly because it's unladylike in her mother's eyes, but mainly because it requires an intellectual rigour that Selina pretends to but of which, says Katharine, she is incapable.

'Careful with that one,' says Luke, finding us together.

I feel embarrassed and seedy. 'Don't worry,' I say. 'She hasn't had that much.'

Luke and Katharine erupt into laughter. 'I mean, careful,' says Luke, 'because she will drink you under the table.'

Simon rolls in just before 2 a.m. with a nasty gash on his arm, which he says he sustained climbing a chain-link fence to watch the fireworks from the roof of a warehouse in Rotherhithe.

'Well, well,' he says, seeing the way Katharine and I are sitting together.

For the next year and a half it is only friendship. We email each other, and meet for coffee. We never talk about the age gap, because it has no bearing on our interaction. She isn't interested in me for my wisdom or experience, perhaps because I have so little of either. I think if I were honest I'd say that she cleaves to me because I offer myself to her completely. I may not be much, but I am hers. And she enjoys the fact that her mother is suspicious of me.

In the summer of 2004, when Katharine has been accepted into medical school, Luke and Ish and I take Simon up on his invitation to what he promises will be 'a good night out'. It turns out to be a psytrance rave in a derelict jobcentre somewhere behind Elephant and Castle. Luke brings Katharine along. We have to remind ourselves how little we know one another in their eyes. The rave doesn't start until after 1 a.m. so there's a good deal of preamble. Simon has somehow picked up the idea that what the New Age hippies on the door want for payment is seeds, so we walk in brandishing packets with pictures of nasturtiums and delphiniums on that he bought from a garden centre that afternoon. They take one look at us and demand thirty quid each, then pocket the seeds as well.

Glow-sticks and saucer-eyed ravers. Stink of sweat and dope in the cavernous black space. We spend some time watching longhairs thrashing in the bone-throb of the music, then retire to a set of offices at the back of the building where convivial groups are sharing booze and openly consuming their powders and pills. It's in one of these offices, under the influence of the speed bombs Luke has been feeding us to keep us eager, that Katharine and I kiss for the first time. The others don't see us, but they are close by. Secrecy breeds urgency. When we come clean about it later it will make good fuel for anecdotes, since by then the idea that we might be the sort of people who attend an illicit rave will seem hilariously incongruous.

We do not rush headlong into one another. There is no sense of doomed passion. Instead, a calm realisation comes to pass. We tell Simon first, who says he's known all along, and then Luke, who claims to be delighted but says that he can't guarantee the same will be true of Ali. When Ali finds out, he is endearingly thrilled. This is towards the end of Katharine's first year at medical school, in 2005.

Just occasionally, it comes out. The twist of cruelty. The probing of my intentions. Luke's late-night mutterings at the farm party will by no means be the first time it has happened. Hints of a prevailing attitude within the Price family towards me, which refuses to overlook the age gap, as they all do so carefully in person. Which holds that I somehow zeroed in on Katharine, the cradle-snatching arriviste hitching his ride.

And then in 2006 that worry becomes redundant, because Katharine buys a pregnancy test and along comes Blue Stripe, and now I need to support a student who is also an expectant mother. It would be a serious predicament indeed if her family wasn't so well off.

Meanwhile, Luke and Ish are taking wing. There are earlier abortive ideas, but the one that makes them properly rich is breathtaking in its simplicity. Share of the credit for it goes to both of them, since although the opportunity arrives fully formed, it takes two perspectives to see it clearly.

Ish first demonstrates his entrepreneurial spirit at public school, where he sets about working out what his fellow inmates most want and working out how he can supply it for a profit. Snobbery is alive and well at places like his, and Ish still gets it in the neck sometimes for his father's profession. By the time he is fifteen he has a ready answer for them.

'As my father so wisely says,' he declaims, 'if he had his time again and could be anything he wanted, he would still own a chain of newsagents. You're dealing with an imperishable, fixed-price commodity that people of every social class want, and you get to send any unsold stock back the next day. The margins are fantastic.'

Ish puts his father's lessons into practice, somehow managing to come back at the beginning of every new term with fresh wares to shift. It's unlikely that Mr Jafari sanctions the move outright, but who knows? Perhaps Ish has persuaded him of the money to be made. Either way, squirrelled away among the rest of his trunked-up paraphernalia, Ish unfailingly arrives in possession of an abundant cache of cigarettes and pornography. The former he sells at an outrageous price, the latter he leases. Hardly imperishable, but it makes it through a term, just about.

When Ish runs into Luke again at university in 1994, he has grander plans. And Luke has the cash to get them started. Perhaps foreseeing how the Internet will do away with his father's trusty business model, Ish impresses on Luke just how ubiquitous networking is about to become. He has found his commodity. Everyone is going to need this equipment, from massive corporations down to the tiniest sole trader. And one company in particular is going to clean up, since it's the one that makes the best kit.

'What's the distribution price?' says Luke. 'And what currency do they sell in?'

Setting up outside London brings down their overheads and gives them space to indulge their most childish whims. By the time they acquire the Banbury farm they have graduated from being single-line distributors of Internet routers to direct competitors of the company that makes them. They acquire their stock through unsanctioned channels then use fluctuations in the dollar price to undersell the official suppliers, and nothing can be done to stop them. All they have to do is sit tight when the price isn't right and sell when it is. There's a frontier mentality, but unlike other tech businesses, this one isn't out to change the world. It is run by people who've got this far by being lucky and bold, and reason that all they have to do to succeed is stay that way.

Flare-ups with Simon from time to time. Upswells of bitterness.

'Shall I tell you what you've got?' he says, after I've asked him too many times on a night out if he's okay. 'You've got a saviour complex. But you don't need to save me. I'm doing very well saving myself.'

Or, in a drunken spat towards the end of Luke's wedding in 2001: 'It's interesting, this story you tell about yourself – that you got away with it because you were so nobly outspoken and looked after. What if he just found you annoying, or didn't have the hots for you?'

Or, in a rare moment of candour, at the end of a very late night: 'It's all about scale. The size of it all. The sight of adult genitals. This man who wasn't your dad, with his huge fingers, his bush of pubic hair. You'll never really understand.'

Or, another time, when I think we're talking about something else: 'Yeah, well – you were lucky enough to discover sex for yourself.'

I spend much time dutifully trying to comprehend the enormity of that statement. To reflect on my leisurely introduction to pornography via a school friend's borrowed VHS tape. On the pleasure I used to take in sleeping with Holly, or the partners I've had since. On the extent to which I've taken for granted the discovery of all the ways another body is fun. And then he will toss out a phrase that instantly renders defunct all my respectful self-flagellation. They are remarks only he could make, like: 'Twelve years old probably was a bit young to be taught how to give a good blow job, but who knows?'

Male friendships which talk honestly about sex are rare. And you might think it would be an area especially to be avoided in our case. But it isn't. We tell each other plenty, without bravado or insecurity. When Katharine comes along, I share my joy at how uncomplicated sex with her is, because it isn't a form of healing for her as it was for Holly. Simon is similarly open with me, and I don't get the sense that he has any great hang-ups about the act, whenever it happens. His liaisons often end the moment the man or woman in question starts seeking explanations for his sexual topography, but he seems content to have even got that far. For him, it seems, it's enough of an achievement to have defanged sex, to have rendered it usable.

Occasionally I look online at a forum set up for former pupils of the school on the hill. They call themselves *Survivors*. The make-up is fascinating – a four-dimensional snapshot of many generations. Some share competitively horrific anecdotes about Weapons Davis and the sadists who preceded him. But mainly the chat drips with nostalgia for fun had, lessons learned, characters formed. I learn the names of stars of the scene I never knew. Psychotic drunks. Vicious matrons. Sutton Senior, it seems, was sadistic in ways we can only imagine. Always I am on the lookout for anything that might, even glancingly, refer to Crimble. I find only warm thoughts and feelings. *Thank God for Crimble and Wags* is the near-constant refrain. Weapons Davis was one bad apple, but he can't detract from the nurturing experience enjoyed by the majority.

Occasionally someone posts about how scary it felt. Ventures the opinion that the cruelty could not be said to have been normal. At times these posts refer directly to Weapons Davis and his crimes. At which point, always, they weigh in, the tally-ho defenders and never-did-me-any-harmers, who freely admit that they were beaten shitless but say in the same breath how great it was when we scrumped those apples / rode on that tractor / played the wide game in the field. A lot of the staunchest defenders seem to live in former colonies. Hong Kong. Canada. Australia. I picture them as florid men wearing fiercely knotted ties, getting weepy over old team photographs. Some directly question the allegations of sexual abuse. Claim it has all been distorted by fragile, modern sensibilities, or even made up outright. Occasionally I engage with them, to see how far they will go to defend the place. Their faith is as blind as ever. It's clear that their memories are the scaffolding of their lives. That to risk shaking it even slightly could be catastrophic.

Simon is becoming a cult figure within a certain community. It doesn't seem to surprise him. At times you can tell he is putting on a display of his success, and who can blame him?

If I had taken control of my destiny so definitively I might want to let people know as well. Just as he revealed his weaknesses to me in his Acton flat, now he periodically shows us all how strong he has become. But there is always the other Simon, too. The one who disappears in the middle of conversations. The one who micromanages the level of intimacy in his relationships, and shuts them down when they go to a place he doesn't like.

One of the first big parties at the farm, not long after Luke and Ish have acquired it. A febrile atmosphere. Clashing notes of bombast. Simon, having recently overseen his first major game launch, is feeling uncharacteristically showy.

The moment goes straight into folk memory, as he well intends. Most of those present see it as Simon's mad KLF moment, the announcement of his arrival, his declaration of indifference to material things. I am the only one who understands what it really means. The way he stands behind the bonfire, crowd whooping, withdraws the wad of fifty-pound notes from his pocket, and tosses them one by one into the flames.

There are gasps of disgust. Then a different mood catches. By the end, people are vying to thrust their hands into the fire, if only to acquire a half-burnt relic, documentary evidence that they were down with this anarchic mob.

How about that, boy?

His eyes finding mine across the fire, across the years.

25

THE DAY OF the funeral was unseasonably wet, and no one present knew how to reach the current churchwarden to ask him to turn on the heating. His predecessor was no longer feeling the cold.

Perhaps in part because of this practical distraction, the event felt joyless. Straining to summon the dead man in the old familiar church with his boxed body on trestles by the altar. It was the first time I'd ever struggled to picture him. *When you're dead, you're finished,* he'd said to me in this very building. His final word on the subject, booming in my head as the hymns struggled on.

I turned to look back down the aisle to get a better sense of who'd turned up and nearly shattered with affection when I saw the solitary figure in the back pew, checking his Blackberry through dark glasses. However he'd found out, he understood what this meant to me, and knew how much I would cherish that understanding.

'Simon's here,' I whispered to Katharine.

'Good for him,' she said, and I knew then that it was she who'd told him.

'I thought he'd gone on his fishing odyssey.'

'He must have decided to delay it,' she said. I gave her arm a squeeze.

I will follow your example, I thought, as they carried him out. It was consoling to realise that thanks to his incantatory stories I already knew how the death of a loved one can impart a determination to live more gratefully and generously. And who better to live for than this? Even today when I think of him I feel a yearning so powerful that it embarrasses me, because he's been dead for so long that I should by now have invested myself safely in other people. But when the love is that loud, it leaves a deafening silence.

Cremation then wake at a hotel restaurant he'd have hated. My parents doing the rounds. Katharine, tenderly suspending all her justified gripes, waiting around to drive us home while Simon and I got more and more inappropriately drunk. *What he would have wanted*, of course.

Here, I thought, is a true friend, as we downed pint after pint of funereal Guinness, supplementing them with whisky as the afternoon progressed. It never occurred to me to think how Simon might be feeling to be back in the area, only a few miles from good old Crimble.

'*And they came to the place which God had told him of; and Abraham built an altar there, and laid the wood in order, and bound Isaac his son, and laid him on the altar upon the wood. And Abraham stretched forth his hand, and took the knife to slay his son.*'

Crimble always wears a suit for his Sunday address. Those of us who are choristers stand up at the front in white and red, voices glowing in the sunlight. If it's as pretty as this it must be meant to be.

'This is a house of worship,' he says, one morning. 'But it isn't the only place you can pray. You can do it wherever you like.'

As Crimble speaks, Weapons Davis is scanning the room intently at floor level, so we are far more conscious of any specks on our shoes than of the words emanating from the pulpit. But I listen. And in those moments when the place gets on top of me, I do pray. To the fluorescent dial of my father's old wristwatch. To my grandfather, or his Victoria crown. *There are no atheists on turbulent airplanes*, as somebody wrote. Add to that the waiting rooms of infant A&E wards and the dormitories of boarding preparatory schools.

A month after my grandfather's funeral, my parents and I gathered by the chalk pond to scatter his ashes where he'd requested. It couldn't wait: someone had finally bought the house and we had to get this done before the sale was completed. Somehow the time constraint made the obligation feel inconvenient. And it was wet again. But even if he hadn't requested it, where else would we have chosen but the ash tree?

My mother wanted to get it over with quickly but I wanted to talk about him before we upended the pot. The contents were gravelly in places, and typically I managed to piss her off by recounting something I'd remembered to the effect that foreign objects like hip replacements and dentures don't burn, but have to be sieved out of the ashes by crematorium staff.

'Do you have to?' she said. 'Today?'

No use pointing out that he was the person who'd told me this in the first place. To cement her declaration that I'd ruined the moment, she marched off to her car as soon as it was done, and my father followed. I stayed to watch the ash settle and flurry, the material finding its place in the world. Then the rain set in and thumped it all to sludge.

Before I left, I took the Victoria crown from my pocket and lodged it in a high crease of the ash tree, where it would join the hips he'd banked there over the years. I knew by now that he'd kept no matching coin when I went to the school. It was just something he'd made up that afternoon to make me feel better. But a few years beforehand, I'd seen one at a flea market somewhere and bought it, not really knowing why until now. His went in the tree and mine stayed in my pocket, and that way the conversation could continue.

When I got home I opened my laptop, hoping for some good news about a translating job I was after, and found instead an email from someone called Rebecca Brady, the subject line of which read *News*. The name wasn't familiar, so I nearly didn't open it. And then I did.

I sat in the cafe we'd agreed, waiting for the person I now understood to be Becky Lynch, the first line of her email resounding in my head.

I'm sorry to be contacting you out of the blue but I wanted to let you know the sad news that my brother Neil died last year.

Admirable clarity.

I know you'd been in touch.

Hardly. Three, maybe four years before? An exchange of emails. Promises to meet up. We never had.

The funeral was small and private but now that the first anniversary is coming up, we're thinking of holding a memorial service.

I'd looked him up afterwards on Friends Reunited, and found a version of the man Neil Lynch became. I noted the enthusiasms he'd offered to define himself. Thailand. Diving. Cocktails. White-shirted, red-faced friends. A bad photo of him in black tie getting ready to go out in some hotel room. Life's random flares, now loaded with disproportionate significance.

Hi Max, it's Neil from all those years ago. How are you?? I think of you sometimes and wonder how you're getting on. Did you survive it all? Did you make it through? Are you in touch with any of the others? I saw Luke Price and Ish Jafari in some list of dot-com entrepreneurs! Would be great to meet up sometime for a drink if you're around. Let me know! All the best, NL.

We'd vowed to stay in touch. I couldn't remember why I'd told myself I was too busy to meet him. No doubt I had given myself a compelling excuse.

How do we ever relax enough for Weapons Davis to teach us anything about the siege engines, battering rams and trebuchets he loves so much? The answer is that for most of us by now his rage has become a parody of itself, so we just let it play out.

But when he flies, though. Oh wow.

The toxic jolt to the heart, the dose of liquid fear that accompanies his raised voice. Sometimes it is as if he is geeing himself up. Sometimes it sounds like he is letting loose a babble of competing voices from within.

Well, ALL RIGHT.

And so it BEGINS.

Wrapping up. Last lesson on a Saturday morning. High spirits. Probably Chicken à la King for lunch.

'That's enough for today,' he says. 'I wish you all a pleasant weekend. Denyer and Drake, be sure to let us all know next week if you have any more paranormal adventures this evening.' He pauses to let the laughter play out, then mutters a follow-up gag for himself. 'Ha. Denyer and Drake. Sounds like a regional solicitor's. Splendid.'

It doesn't occur to us then, of course. It will be eight years later, lying together under a bed in an Acton flat, drunk and high, when the stupefying possibility strikes us that this might have been the man who waited in the passage under the Upper Gallery, to lick the face of the boy who crawled through in the dark.

'Neil Lynch,' he adds. 'Stay behind. The rest of you, get out of my sight.'

*

I stood up when she arrived and wondered whether to shake her hand but she came in for a hug. Because the information was new to me I had expected her to be in the grip of the grief, but the event was already eleven months in the past. And there was something else commanding her attention – a baby, sweetly zonked out in a pushchair.

'I found out I was pregnant the week after Neil's funeral,' she explained. 'And at the time it had a kind of logic, you know? You're so on the lookout for signs. I've had moments of thinking I wouldn't get through it, but this person has given me plenty to focus on.' She tugged back the blanket as if to make sure the child was still there. 'It was only recently, when we'd got through the birth and started remembering the rest of the world, that it occurred to me that there might be people we hadn't told. I had his laptop, so I started going through it.'

'I don't think anyone from school knows,' I said. 'I'd have heard from someone.'

She took a sip of tea. 'We sort of kept it quiet. It's a terrible thing to admit, but I think my parents were ashamed. Because he took his own life.'

There had been doubt to begin with, because all they knew was that there had been an accident on the railway, and that he'd been drinking. It was only when they saw the CCTV footage from the little station near where he lived that all uncertainty had expired. He'd known exactly when the big cross-country expresses would blast through. The ones that wouldn't stop. The ones that wouldn't even let out their two-tone alert yell. The driver had said at the inquest that the figure on the track had turned away as the train approached, walking off with a rucksack on his back *as if he was setting out for a walk*.

'He was always good at disappearing,' she said. 'You remember him running away from school?'

I nodded. 'Everyone mobilised to go and look for him. I'm so sorry. I can't begin to imagine—'

She cut me off with a nod. 'In a way, the hardest thing is knowing that there was all this stuff going on in his head and we had no idea about it. People can be very good at keeping secrets.'

'They sure can.'

'I knew something was wrong. You couldn't not. He was so angry. These terrible rages would come and take him over. And when we were still going on holiday as a family, we'd go away to these lovely places and he wouldn't notice them. He'd just take endless pictures of rubbish, or dead animals, or graveyards. He couldn't … explain himself. Then, finally, he told us. A few years after that evil piece of shit – I hate saying his name – was convicted. He told us it had happened to him too. Systematically. Over a long period. So now we knew. But the damage had been done. It had unhinged him completely. I think that may have been why he started sending out emails to people from school. You weren't the only one.'

'Didn't he think of reporting it?'

'We all wanted him to. But he wouldn't do it.'

'We never even met up, after he emailed me,' I said. 'I feel terrible about that.'

'It might not have gone well. He was very unpredictable.'

The baby's face wrinkled with displeasure and she uttered a few warm-up whinges. Becky slid the buggy back and forth to try to resettle her.

'Why wouldn't he go to the police?'

'Two reasons, I think. One, he didn't see the point. Weathers-Davis had been convicted, so why bother? Two, he didn't like the attention he was getting as it was. There's this weird thing that goes on, when it's out there. Even when it's only a few friends and family. People vie with each other over who can be most helpful. Who can know more about how awful it is.'

'Competitive empathy.'

'Yeah. He hated that. I stopped talking to him about it because I knew how much it bugged him. People in the family who didn't even know him that well were going around talking about how much they felt for him, how much he'd suffered, all that. Which made things worse, in his eyes. Even when they're not talking about it you can feel people using it to define you. He resented being pitied.'

'I remember that about him.'

She admitted defeat and lifted the crying baby. I felt a flash of apprehension at where Katharine and I would be in a few months' time. I found myself noticing Becky's toned bicep and the confidence with which she handled the child and thought of the way she'd taken control of us both on a swing two decades before. I shook away a twinge of the old lust, or whatever it had been.

She stuck the tip of her little finger into the baby's mouth to pacify it, and rocked it gently as she talked. 'I watched the CCTV. I thought I wanted to. You just see this grainy black-and-white image of him, alone in the night, on an empty platform. You can see his head nodding up and down as he talks to himself. He walks around. Pacing, like a commuter on the phone to someone. Except he isn't talking to anybody but himself. Then he just pulls his rucksack on, and walks out of shot.' She was crying now. 'All that talking. Nobody listening. And now he's become one of those people who other people are embarrassed to talk about. They stumble every time his name comes up in conversation. They don't know what to say to us. And what is there to say? It will never go away. It will be so hard to find ways to remember him happily. We'll always be thinking back to this party or that holiday and thinking, *Was he happy then? Was he ever happy at all?* I was his twin. We shared a womb. I was meant to be closer to him than anyone else in the world. And I was there. I was right there with him at school, when it was all going on. Our parents were in Cyprus. And I never knew anything about it. I think I was even embarrassed by him sometimes. Isn't that terrible? And the worst thing is that he lost it so badly towards the end that he began to rewrite the whole history of our time there. To say things that I just knew weren't true. Weird conspiracy stuff. Like, that there was a whole lot of them, in it together, working as a team. He even said that it wasn't just Weapons Davis who abused him. That the person he went to for comfort did it too. The one he trusted. You wouldn't believe me if I told you the name. I think Neil was just in such a bad place that he'd lost all touch with reality.'

I was nodding as if I was in control though it was mainly because I couldn't think of anything else to do, and the salt and pepper on the plastic tablecloth were swimming before my eyes.

'I think you'd better tell me the name,' I said.

The words victory and surrender imply specific moments in time, but off the battleground and the sports field, many are not single occurrences. Any fool can weather one storm. Victory can take the form of a slow burn of resistance, of refusing to break. Nor is surrender necessarily a single moment of capitulation. Surrender can take decades.

26

'You hate it, don't you?' said Katharine, from an armchair in the bay window of our bedroom. I stood at the foot of the bed, wretchedly contemplating a gaping holdall.

'Hate what?'

'Packing.' She took a sip from the steaming mug of raspberry-leaf tea which was set with terrifying stability on her bowling-ball bump. She had declared this facility to be the only advantage of the pregnancy's current phase.

'What do you mean?' I said.

'It throws you into a foul mood every single time. I've noticed.'

'I don't mind packing. I'm good at it.'

'You agonise over it. Even for something fun like an Italian holiday. Look at you. You're stalled, standing there. I've read all about it. Classic trait of the boarding-school survivor, apparently.'

'Is that what they're calling us now?' I said. 'Well, it doesn't apply to me. I was a short-term inmate compared to others, and I'm the most seasoned traveller I know.'

She sipped the tea and grimaced. 'You hate it.'

She was right, of course. The sight of an open suitcase had made me bloom with dread since the age of ten. I would see one, mouth open, and picture it arrived in some bleak destination, bulging with contents which would make me sad. Unpacking was even worse. I hadn't thought she'd noticed, but she was a perceptive one, the Pocket Rocket. And she, of course, was a *survivor* too.

But packing wasn't the only source of my desolation. My conversation with Becky, the full import of which I hadn't yet been able to pass on to Katharine, was still playing out in my head. I wondered if it would ever stop.

Other stuff, too: the smell of fresh paint from the room next door, the knowledge that this thing was coming for us whether we wanted it or not. That we were bringing another person into the world who might be as unprepared for what it had in store as poor Neil. Not to mention the shaming fact that Katharine, who had far more skin in the game, was facing the future with no fear at all, and still managing to find sympathy for me.

'Snap out of it,' she said. 'Just stick in some T-shirts and pants and be done with it. Or I'll sit here grilling you about your career until you do.'

'That's a low blow.' I yanked open a drawer and began flinging stuff into the bag.

On her way out of the room, she hugged me from behind. My skin tingled with delight at feeling the taut drum of Blue Stripe at the base of my spine.

'I'm sorry,' she said. 'It's shit, what's happened. But you really don't need to feel guilty just because you didn't meet up with him. How could you have known?'

'I don't. It's just depressing how hard it is to do the right thing. Move, someone gets hurt. Don't move, someone gets hurt.'

'Pack and let's get out of here. I know things will feel better. It's a very good place for that kind of recovery.'

'Okay.'

'And when you've finished packing, come and admire how well I've cleaned out the fridge,' she said as she left.

'I've admired it,' I called.

'Come and admire it to my face.'

She left me staring at the pile of clothing on the bed. Did I need trainers? There'd probably be fucking tennis, wouldn't there? Another chance to be humiliated by how charmingly accommodating of lesser talents Luke and Ali were on the court. What else? Swimming trunks that didn't make me look too fat. And you never knew who else might turn up. I'd tried calling Simon after my meeting with Becky and heard a recorded message saying he'd be away from his phone until September. So I'd dashed off an email to him in the vague hope that he might at least be checking in at Internet cafes on his grand tour. I'd told him that I was going to Italy with Katharine's family, and given him the dates. Then, knowing he'd be furious if I didn't, I'd told him about Neil Lynch. The latter part of the conversation with Becky could wait.

I packed some clothes. Then I opened the drawer of my bedside table and reached to the back where, tucked inside an old notebook, was a ziplock freezer bag containing the three letters from Crimble that I'd taken from Simon's flat nine years before. I slid them into a side pocket of my holdall and buckled it shut, then went off to the kitchen to admire Katharine's fridge.

The house stood at the top of a densely wooded valley in the foothills of the Apennine mountains. Roger and Selina went there to recover from every trial and celebrate every triumph. When enough time had passed since their last visit they would yearn for it ostentatiously, rhapsodising about the food, the sunsets or the bright clang of goat bells in the surrounding hills. Parties had been held there for each of their fiftieth and sixtieth birthdays. They had tried and failed to host Luke's wedding there, and since it looked less and less likely that Ali would get married, there was no doubt that should I ever propose to their daughter, the event would happen here. The various stone dwellings they had done up over the decades would provide perfect accommodation for significant guests. The ceremony might even give them a reason to renovate the chapel, thus far only used as a picturesque subject for Selina's paintings.

It was their fortress. Not literally – a fortress would have been vulgar. They liked saying that it wasn't grand, like the southern Tuscan houses beloved of other English families. That they lived with more modesty because their house had been the mere bakery of a hillside hamlet. Always careful to sidestep the fact that they owned the rest of the hamlet as well. They'd bought it during the 1980s, in a move that was simultaneously depicted as wildly impulsive and cannily foresighted. More tourists were arriving, but the area was still relatively untroubled by outsiders. They were fond of saying that they'd fallen for it *before anybody else*, which presumably didn't include anybody Italian. They'd sweep down to the nearby village in a convoy of hire cars headed by the vintage Land Rover they kept there permanently, taking up residence at the bar, prattling in loud English and bad Italian, calling themselves locals. The tall CB aerial on the UK-plated vehicle might as well have been a Union flag. I don't know what they imagined happened in the village when they weren't there.

You could try as hard as you liked not to fall for the place but it would get you in the end. I liked it best in the autumn, when you could come in from a foggy walk in the chestnut forests, light a fire and eat pasta loaded with fresh porcini. In the summer its charms were more overt. Fireflies would ignite under the boughs of the trees after the sun set. During thunderstorms the sky would sometimes be coloured red from dust kicked up in the Sahara, leading to what was known locally as *blood rain*.

There was no pool, but no need for one since their demise included a derelict mill on a river with a deep, still pond. You reached it by walking down a vertiginous forest path from the bottom of the garden. There were steps made of embedded wooden posts but it was impossible not to slip on the loose soil, and it was so secluded by vegetation that you might wonder whether the path led anywhere at all. The mill had been carefully updated to ensure that externally it still resembled a beautiful wreck, but behind a locked door inside they'd fitted a kitchen and bathroom for the lavish picnic lunches they loved holding there. It encapsulated the wider ethos: engineered at great expense to look tastefully shabby, while sustaining a lifestyle that was anything but.

We parked our hire car outside the hamlet's entrance, which was as far as motor vehicles could advance. The journey had trashed Katharine's mood, and not just because she'd had to spend three hours in a hot car with me. The flight to Genoa had been uncomfortable, and made worse by an inconsiderate passenger who'd insisted on putting his seat back, further constricting her and her bump. I'd offered to swap with her but she'd insisted on staying where she was, muttering darkly about how *shamelessness ought to be tested*. I'd said nothing to the man during the flight, only to confront him at baggage reclaim, which to Katharine's mind was worse than not saying anything at all.

She walked through the archway into the cloistered calm beyond. I watched three swallows fussing on a phone wire, then got out our luggage and followed. I could worry less about her well-being now, because the place would go to work on her. And during the two days on which we'd overlap with Roger and Selina, Katharine would be under their jurisdiction, which tended to mean they got it in the neck more than me.

Beneath the arch I glanced up to see a couple of bats scuffling in their nook. In the square, mountain water trickled through old stone laundry troughs. The front door was open and I heard Katharine calling within.

I left our bags by the front door and followed her through to the sitting room. Roughly plastered walls hung with tapestries. Big, old furniture. Bright fabrics meticulously sourced by Selina on trips to India and Sri Lanka. A set of doors opened onto a terrace from which steps descended to the garden, where we found Luke working at a rickety table among the fruit trees.

'Thank fuck you're here,' he said, racing up to greet us, tanned and powerful. 'I'm desperate for an excuse to start drinking.' He wore only a frayed pair of blue shorts and smelled of sweat and cigarettes.

'Where's everyone else?' said Katharine.

'Swimming. I said I'd wait up here for you to arrive. Negroni?'

Katharine went upstairs to lie down. Luke put together a tray with an ice bucket, olives, bottles and glasses and we returned to his table in the garden. Sharp, dry rosemary in the air. Sweetness of ripening plums behind. From the river below I could hear hollering kids and the murmuring of adults. Luke made the drinks while I stood relaxing into the texture of the valley. I noted with approval how seriously he was taking the measurements, the huge ice cubes he'd brought, the fat orange he was slicing.

'Get that inside you,' he said, passing me the glass, light catching the bright red liquid within.

'I have to hand it to this place. It never lets you down,' I said, feeling the journey receding.

He smiled. 'Actually there's been a spot of trouble in paradise.'

'Pray tell.'

'Some local kids had a party down at the mill and roughed it up a bit.'

'It's a ruin, isn't it? How roughed up can it be?'

'It's a ruin with facilities. It has to feel run-down, but also have a well-stocked fridge and good cooking utensils. Very important distinction.'

'So what did they do?'

He sighed. 'Nothing much. Not really. All they did was get hammered. They chucked the pot plants into the mill-pond, and broke into the kitchen looking for booze. Only the sort of thing we'd have done in our day. From the way she's talking about it, you'd think the place had been torn down. She keeps using the word *defiled*.'

'Oh dear.'

He speared a plump green olive with a cocktail stick. 'Well, okay, there were one or two nasty elements. Some unpleasant graffiti. And the thing that's got her really upset is that they left a couple of syringes lying around, one of which was found by Gus and Josh. It's got her in quite a state. What they don't understand is that when they aren't here, people treat the village as part of the landscape, like they always have. That pond is the best place for miles around to swim. Why should they stop just because someone has tarted it up with pot plants? Hello, things have gone quiet. They must be on their way back up. Enjoy the peace while you can. Anyway, it's fine. The only real problem is what it's doing to Ali.'

'Ali's here?'

Luke struck a match on the underside of the table and lit a cigarette, nodding as he exhaled. 'I really don't think spending time with my mother is good for him. She has this accelerating effect on anything he might be worrying about. Because she won't stop banging on about it, she's got him thinking there's some issue with security. I keep finding him at night patrolling the perimeter, checking the windows and doors. It's ridiculous. Frankly the sooner Mum and Dad piss off, the better. Then we can calm him down a bit.'

'It's that bad?'

'The mill wasn't the only thing. He managed to get into some ruckus with a couple of young guys on motorbikes down the road. Said they were driving too fast, started screaming at them about how there were kids around, that kind of thing. Then later the same night someone came up here and keyed the side of the Land Rover. It's got his paranoia firing like mad. Refill?'

'I've got something messed up to tell you,' I said. 'Neil Lynch is dead.'

'Fuck off.'

'True.'

'How?' said Luke.

'Let me guess,' said a voice behind us, and I turned to see Ali standing at the garden gate, laden with baskets and towels, still soaking from the swim.

The rest of the group streamed into the garden. Luke's wife Esther carried picnic things on one arm and Josh on the other, all of which she handed to Luke. Then came Gus, tanned and barefooted. He held a serious-looking spear gun on which was impaled a green-and-gold fish.

'You didn't!' said Luke.

'We did,' said Ali. 'Trout. Pretty good one, too.' He eased the fish off the spear and held it out for the group.

'Amazing!' Luke hugged his sons, both of whom seemed numbed by their success. Josh was still naked after his swim, pulling idly at his foreskin as if it were chewing gum.

'These boys are so clever,' said Selina. 'Ali gave them a few pointers, but they caught that fish totally by themselves. They're natural-born killers!' She wore a white panama hat and a pale blue cotton dress patched with wet by the swimming costume beneath. 'Max. You've made good time. You must have driven like a maniac.' She kissed me on both cheeks, still smelling of perfume in spite of the river water she'd been immersed in.

'Well done you!' said Roger, bringing up the rear in a white linen shirt and pink swimming trunks. 'Luke's already dosing you up, I see. Where's Kathy?'

'She wanted a rest after the journey,' I said.

'I'll go and see her,' said Selina. 'I need my fix of baby-bump. Luke, I think we should bake the trout, don't you? We must do it before the boys go to bed so they can enjoy their spoils.'

'On it,' said Luke. He pointed at his brother's leg. 'You're bleeding.'

Ali wiped it with his hand. 'It's nothing. Just got spiked by a bit of terracotta at the bottom of the pond. We can clear the rest of it tomorrow.'

'Sorry to hear about all that,' I said.

'Don't!' said Selina, throwing up her hands as she set off for the house. 'It's too awful.'

On the terrace I watched as Ali and Luke cooked the fish. Ali built a meticulous fire in the wood oven, crouching to tend to the blaze as it caught. Luke operated with more flair but equal efficiency. Cigarette in mouth, third negroni in progress, he gutted the trout and tossed its innards to a stray kitten lured by the smell. He slashed the skin and dressed the fish with thyme, rosemary and wedges of a freshly picked, knobbly lemon. It was a pleasure to watch them together. Only when I'd started coming here on holiday with the family had I learned that at home Ali and Luke had nicknames for each other. I heard these now – quick nudges of assurance and fondness.

'How's my fire, Big Al?'

'Don't you want some oil on that, Lucky?'

Luke wrapped the fish in tinfoil and laid it at the front of the oven, then asked me what else I thought we should cook. My grandfather's enthusiasms were never more useful than when I needed to curry favour in someone else's kitchen. I left them laying the table and started putting together a green salad, some meat ragù and a few antipasti: bruschetta, fried courgette flowers and some translucent slices of lardo on cornbread. Luke and Ali came in to help. We were now drinking very cold white wine. Piano jazz trickled through from the sitting-room hi-fi.

'Tell us, then,' said Ali.

'What?' I said.

'What exactly did you hear from Becky?'

As clearly as I could, I told them that Neil had taken his own life, that he had been mentally unwell, and that Becky believed he had been a victim of Eric Weathers-Davis. Luke prompted me for details, drinking steadily, punctuating my account with expletives. Ali listened, barely touching his wine.

'Poor fucker,' said Luke, when I'd finished.

'Yeah. Sorry.'

'For what?' said Ali.

'Bringing the bad news, I guess.'

'Shit.' Luke got to his feet abruptly.

'What?' I said.

'The *fish*,' he said, running outside with an oven glove.

'I've been meaning to say,' said Ali, 'I was sorry to hear about your grandfather.'

'Thanks.'

Luke was calling from outside. 'It's fine! It looks great, actually. Where are those useless children?'

'Boys!' Ali was up and shouting. 'Trout-time. Come and get it!'

I went to look in the sitting room, where Roger and Selina were reading, and Katharine and Esther were chatting on the sofa. Ali was upstairs, calling and getting no answer. On a whim, I opened the cellar door and descended the steps. I heard conspiratorial voices from within.

'Come and eat!' Luke was calling, from outside. 'Why won't they come?'

I descended the steps into the first cellar room, which was full of junk: crockery, garden machinery, old furniture. In the second room, I found the two boys huddled around something on the floor. I told them their dinner was ready. They looked up startled by my arrival from what they'd found in a wall alcove, wrapped in an oily rag: a pistol and a crumbling paper box of ammunition.

A breathless Gus sought Uncle Ali's superior knowledge. Would it fire? Has it ever killed anyone? Could we shoot rabbits with it?

'Only if you didn't mind them being inedible,' said Ali, turning the pistol, which he had identified as a Beretta, over in his hands.

'What's indelible?'

'Inedible, darling,' said Esther. 'It means you can't eat it.'

'A direct hit on a rabbit with this might blow it to bits,' said Ali. 'If we could even get it firing.'

Roger was thrilled by the find, and couldn't believe it had been sitting in his own cellar all this time. Which led inevitably to a lecture.

Having toiled in anonymity for years at various universities, Roger had published his first book of popular history in the late nineties, and it had done well, leading more or less directly to his being asked to curate the Imperial War Museum exhibition at which I'd played with Holly. Two further books charting the decline of British influence had followed, and a television series. The sunset of empire had treated him well.

'I would bet,' he said, standing over us as the find was appraised, 'that this gun was hidden here during the 1940s by a fugitive soldier.'

'Really?' said Luke. 'It's that old?'

'I think so, though there's probably no way of finding out for sure. As you know, there were hordes of POWs hiding out up here in the latter stages.' He turned to Gus and Josh, knowing that the rest of us had heard what he was about to say many times. 'Picture it, boys. Escaped prisoners. Hiding out up here. Many of them British. Nazis would come up on hunting trips, trying to flush them out. And there's a village, two or three away in the next valley, where a young priest did a very brave thing. He knew there were German soldiers on their way so he rang the church bell to warn anyone hiding in the area to escape. Lots did. The priest saved their lives. But not his own. He would probably have been a dead man anyway, but to make matters worse, when the soldiers arrived they also found him to be in possession of a radio, which implied to them that he'd been in communication with other partisans in the area. The Nazis shot him dead there and then against the wall. You can still see the bullet holes. You should take the boys up there this week, Luke. They'd love it.'

Esther decided that her sons had heard enough, and shepherded them off.

'Isn't it amazing?' Roger went on. 'I've always said that what I loved about this place was the feeling of living in history. Who knew we were sitting on treasure like this?'

'Hear that, Max?' said Ali. 'It's not always the best idea to blow the whistle. Sometimes you end up with your brains splattered against the wall of your own church.'

*

Selina took a sip of her drink and winced. 'Golly. That's a rather forthright G and T. Did Luke make it? Please could someone else put some tonic in it?'

We sat round the candlelit terrace table eating the antipasti. Ali's blast of candour had shocked me, but I was buoyed now by the praise for my food.

'Man, that's delicious,' said Esther, eating the lardo. 'That is exactly the sort of thing that could thwart my intention to go fully veggie this year.'

'Bloody veggies, going round eating the food that our food needs to eat,' said Luke.

'Katharine, you must have a bigger helping than that,' said Selina, when the pasta came out.

'No room.' She smiled at me. 'No offence.'

'Darling, you can't under-eat now,' said Selina. 'It isn't fair.'

The conversation moved back to the attack on her precious mill.

'I don't know why they would hate us so much,' she said. 'It's not like we're being disrespectful to the area. I went to a lot of trouble to make sure that the plants I chose were absolutely in keeping with local tradition.'

'They don't hate us,' said Luke. 'They just wanted to get drunk and trash the place. We all know what that feels like.'

'Speak for yourself,' said Selina. 'Anyway, I'm feeling better about it tonight, because I don't think it was actually Italians who did it. It must have been those Albanian boys up the mountain working on the new housing development. I can't believe it's taken me this long to work it out.'

'Christ,' said Katharine.

'I'm certain of it,' said Selina. 'Alistair, are you going to try to fire that gun? I think you should. Let off a few rounds. Tell them we're armed.'

'You can't be serious,' said Katharine.

'I know you all think I'm being paranoid, or racist, or whatever it is,' said Selina. 'But the fact is that sometimes a place turns against you, and there's very little you can do about it.'

After dinner, at their request, I sat at the upright in the sitting room and bashed out some Cole Porter, reflecting on how much washing-up I'd managed to avoid over the years thanks to the piano.

27

ROGER AND SELINA were flying out the following afternoon, and over breakfast they invited everyone to have lunch with them at a beach restaurant on the way to the airport.

'Not in a million years,' said Katharine. 'I wouldn't get back in the car at this point if you told me I was fully dilated. Max will go.'

'What are you going to do instead?' said Selina.

'Float in the millpond. Poach in it. For hours.'

'Is that wise?'

'What do you mean?'

'Won't it be too cold for the baby? And you must be very careful going down those steps in your condition.'

'I'll stay with her,' said Ali, halfway down the stairs with his mother's suitcase. 'It will give me a chance to finish clearing up down there.'

'You're a sweet boy,' said Selina.

'He's a paid mercenary in his early thirties,' said Katharine.

I followed her to our room in search of a reprieve.

'Don't stay,' she said. 'I'll be terrible company. Have a nice boozy lunch and I'll be in a better mood when you get back. Jesus, it never ceases to amaze me, what this thing has in store for my body. My tits feel like a shelf of hot pebbles.' One of her regular reports from a world beyond my comprehension.

Esther decided to stay behind too, having put in her shift of solo parenting the previous afternoon. This left me and Luke and his boys in the Land Rover, and Roger and Selina in their hire car. It felt counterintuitive to have spent all that time getting up to the mountains only to descend again the next day, but I liked the place where they were going – a restaurant overlooking a channel along which the sea surged unpredictably. There was no beach, but a set of metal stairs had been bolted into the rock, which you could descend into deep, choppy water.

'Don't worry,' said Luke on the way. 'I'll try not to let my mother terrorise you too much.'

Hours later I sat alone with Selina at the lunch table while Roger and Luke took the kids off to swim. I could see Roger at the steps, lowering Josh into the swell, where Luke trod water with arms outstretched to receive him. The light was unbearably bright. It would have been sweltering under the awning where we were sitting but the restaurant had installed water fans that sprayed diners constantly with fine, cold mist. I'd drunk too much, and was in the process of further dehydrating myself with coffee.

'Silly girl,' said Selina. 'She'd have been fine. Probably cooler here than it is up at the pond.'

'Well, I expect she's enjoying some much needed time by herself,' I said.

That expression, *well spoken*. The implication it carries that we are something uttered. Here I was, uttering myself now. I could hear my voice going up the register, vowels lengthening, consonants thickening. Something in her brisk manner had told the changeling he would do well to upscale.

Selina rearranged a few items on the table until the layout met her requirements. 'It's funny, isn't it, Max: we've known each other a long time now.'

'I suppose we have.'

'Eighteen years, by my count. Sports Day, 1988. Katharine was there in a pushchair.'

'Wow.'

'And yet. I don't feel that I know you very well at all.'

'What would you like to know?'

Thin smile. Adjustment of gold chain at her neck. 'Nothing specific. I just think it's interesting. I mean, normally when you meet a boy at ten, and have contact with him on and off again for years afterwards, holidaying with him and so forth, then you might think one would have a handle on his motivation. But I genuinely have no idea what makes you tick. Any of the other friends of the boys, I think I could make a stab at assessing their take on the world, even that dark horse, Simon Drake. But with you I am stumped. Have you always been fond of Katharine? Were you biding your time until it was socially acceptable to make your move?'

A dish containing the remains of the spaghetti alle vongole we'd had for lunch sat between us. I swiped my fork through the food and brought a clam and some sauce to my mouth, sensing Selina's disdain at my lack of self-control. I chewed the instantly regretted mouthful, assuming what felt like the right expression to indicate that I was giving deep thought to her line of enquiry.

'Is that why you've been such a friend to my sons these last years?' she went on. 'I mean, since that night we found you playing the piano at the museum. I wouldn't hold it against you if you had. I don't see any reason to get prudish about things like this. They say that if you grow up with a member of the opposite sex from a very early age – less than three, I think – that romantic love is an impossibility. The bond can only be platonic. But after that, I gather anything's possible. I knew a man once who married his own goddaughter. He'd been present at her christening. That probably is pushing it a bit, but still, it takes all sorts. The point is that you have our blessing. We're glad that this has happened, and we feel certain you'll make a go of it.'

'Pleased to hear it,' I said.

'You can see why we had our doubts though, can't you? The way you seemed to have so little in your life other than us. I'm just speaking frankly, as a mother-in-law should, assuming I'm allowed to call myself that since we don't seem to be going near a church any time soon. And as a mother. Do you understand?'

'I think so.'

'So tell me. As a concerned mother. Because I think you might have information about this. How do you think my son Alistair is at the moment?'

I looked up. 'Ali?'

'I do worry that we've lost him. I don't know how, or to what. But he's gone to a place that I don't understand. And I want him back.'

'I'm not sure what to say about that.'

'You know he barely talks to us these days?'

'I didn't know that.'

'It's incredible that we got him along on this holiday.'

'Well, I don't see him as often as I see Luke.'

Her steepled fingers flew apart as if a little bomb had gone off between them. 'Luke is a different proposition altogether, with his plucky children and his willing wife and his monstrous business. He's making a fortune, of course, but at what cost to himself? But Luke I am not worried about. Never have been. He's always been fine. Even when he was getting into all that trouble at school.'

'He certainly did,' I said, trying to steer the conversation to more comfortable terrain. 'Right back to when we were up on the hill. They *hated* him, some of those teachers.' I glanced towards the water, where Josh was being thrown into the air to delighted squealing.

'With good reason. I don't know anyone better at annoying people when he wants to. He's a master. But this is precisely the point. Where did it go wrong for Alistair? I do have a theory, as it happens.'

I shifted in my seat. 'Really?'

'There was a housemaster at school who just took against him. Starved him of opportunity. Passed him over for things. It came as a dreadful shock for him because when he'd been with you all at the prep he'd been so used to being top of the tree. Head boy. Best shot on the range. He had it all. But all his confidence went later on.'

'Confidence isn't everything.'

'It absolutely is, you know. They have such a profound effect on the young men in their care, these teachers. It makes me more thankful than ever that you all had such a good start with Tony. It was so friendly, that place. Like a family.'

'There were downsides, of course,' I said.

'Oh?'

'I mean, what with the systemic abuse. The violence. All the physical and emotional damage we may never fully know about.'

The frankness surprised her, but she recovered quickly. 'Well, of course. All that was horrible for Tony. It quite broke him, I think. He had no idea any of it was going on.'

'You think?'

Her mouth flatlined. 'I'm certain.'

'A lot of us didn't know either. But quite a few did.'

'It's too awful. Truly. If the parents had had an inkling at the time. But one never can. Still, it's all come out in the wash.'

I fished the lemon out of my water and drank. No sense holding back now. 'I really think that perhaps you should talk to Ali about that side of things sometime.'

Her face changed as if something distasteful had happened. This was as far as I could go. I assumed it would be enough to spark something in her. The parental mind leaping to the worst, and in this case, correct, conclusion. It was the best I could do. But as usual the situation was worse than I'd imagined.

'My dear boy – do you believe I don't know that Alistair was involved in all that?'

'Oh.'

'We talked it over long ago, and he agreed with me that no good could possibly come out of airing it in public. It's not as if he needs the money, and I know several excellent therapists I could put him in touch with if he wanted.'

'I see.' I held my tongue. Literally. I clenched its tip in my teeth, hoping to draw blood.

She swept spilled sugar from a half-torn paper cylinder on the table and discarded it with flickering fingers. 'Do you think I'm cold, Max? A remote parent? Itching to pack my children away as soon as the occasion presented itself?'

'I think I know you better than that.'

'Please, don't hold back,' she said. 'Especially under the circumstances. You're going to be the father of my third grandchild.'

Right. Let's go. Not only was Ali a victim. He was one of the most viciously affected. I think it has defined his life. Blunted his ambition. Devastated his capacity for emotional connection. Before we even get on to whatever happened to him at public school or in the army. I find you and your husband repugnant, not for allowing it to happen but for ignoring its effects. And as soon as I am able, I am going to take your daughter away from this system and find somewhere with light and air where we can raise a child who will be mystified by the world's hypocrisies and never flinch from speaking out against them. And that child will be a stranger to you.

'I'm being absolutely truthful,' I said. 'I think Ali's problems stem from himself more than anywhere else. Though I'm sure the army didn't help.'

'Good boy. I think we might have a grappa, don't you?' She motioned for a waiter and ordered. 'Since we're being so candid ... do you think that part of the problem for Ali is that he might be gay? That he is conflicted because there were elements to it all that ... perhaps he enjoyed?'

'Those boys are so intrepid,' said Roger, returning to the table, breathless and wet. 'You wouldn't catch me jumping off those rocks. What are you two talking about?'

'I was just asking Max if he thought maybe Ali might be gay.'

'Do you think that Ali might be gay?' said Roger.

'Why would you ask me that?' I said, staring at a drowned mouse of hair in the small of his back.

'It might be the kind of thing that Katharine would know.'

'Is Simon Drake gay?' said Selina.

It was an attack on two fronts. I had nothing.

'Don't misunderstand,' said Roger, sitting and towelling off his reddening shoulders. 'This isn't about prejudice. I've known plenty of splendid gay chaps. Honourable. *Noble.*' He gazed into the distance, remembering in wonder.

'I was explaining to Max that we wondered if maybe the business with that horrible Weathers-Davis man had ... confused him.'

'Horrible,' Roger agreed. 'Saw plenty of it myself, of course. Boy on boy, mainly, which is a different thing altogether, but still. These people who get all outraged now about caning and so forth. It's just guilt. What did they think was going on? Were they simply looking the other way?' He motioned to a waiter and scribbled a request for the bill. 'The trouble is, people seem to have got it into their heads that the point of school is to be *happy*. When I really don't think that has much to do with it. Whatever else it may have been, you must admit it was some adventure, that place. Not always fun, but never dull. You'd be lucky to find anywhere like it now.'

'It's striking, isn't it,' I said, 'how much attitudes have changed. You'd notice it a lot if you saw some of the parenting manuals that Katharine and I have been reading.'

'Manuals,' said Selina. 'I mean, really.'

'I know,' I said. 'Awful. But they can be quite insightful. I was reading one the other day that said something I found interesting. It said that most children know that their parents love them. But what they don't always know is that their parents *like* them.'

'Where's that blasted bill?' said Roger. 'We're going to miss this flight if we're not careful.'

Luke drove the Land Rover back up the mountain at speed, as if getting rid of his parents had taken a brake off him. The kids were wiped out in the back.

'I think your mother thinks I'm some sort of Ripley character,' I said.

He glanced in the rear-view mirror to make sure both boys were asleep, wound the window fully down and lit a cigarette. 'Don't pay too much attention to her. She loves being provocative.'

'So that's where you get it from.'

'I think you get the wrong end of the stick about what people say about you sometimes. I suppose that, what with all those holidays you came on, we've all wondered at one time or another why our family was worth so much of your time. And I get it now. But it took a while for me to understand that maybe you just like being part of a big family like ours because yours … isn't like that.'

'Hasn't it occurred to you that I just liked your company, then fell in love with your sister?'

He smiled. 'Anyway, Mother didn't terrorise you too much.'

'I can handle her these days. And she was mainly asking me about Ali.'

'Yeah?' He ashed out of the window and looked sideways at the view of a teetering clifftop village.

'She says she's known about Weathers-Davis and him for years.'

'That's news to me. But it's no fucking surprise.' I waited for his irritation to clear. 'I get that he doesn't want to talk about it. But I wish he could relax, especially when the kids are around. He's always got to be curating some magical experience for them, building a smokehouse or catching langoustines or something. I just want him to think about himself for a change.'

'Maybe that's precisely what he doesn't want to do,' I said.

I had assumed that those who'd stayed behind would be relaxed after their childfree day. But the atmosphere of the house felt clenched from the moment we got back and saw the gun on the kitchen table, cleaned, oiled and apparently ready for use.

'Please can we not leave this thing lying around where the kids can find it?' shouted Luke.

'I wasn't going to,' said Ali, coming in from the terrace wearing sweaty running gear. 'I found a video on how to field-strip it. It's a beautiful thing, don't you think?' He picked it up. It was black and stubby with a metal ring at the base of the butt. 'I reckon Dad's wrong, though. I think it's from later than the 1940s. And I don't think it's been used much.'

I found Katharine lying on our bed with a book, and asked her how the day had been. She said that she and Esther had had lunch on the terrace together but had hardly seen Ali. He'd taken our hire car off to buy replacement plants and pots for the millpond and whatever he'd needed to clean up the pistol.

'And then he fired it,' she said, lifting her T-shirt to cool her domelike belly.

'Really?'

'When we were up here this afternoon. He was down in the garden. Scared us shitless. He might at least have warned us.'

After midnight I woke with a powerful thirst. I pictured the bottles of chilled mineral water in the kitchen, pulled on some shorts and went downstairs. I stood bathing in the cold of the fridge, letting the water chug down my throat until my head ached. I browsed the paper packages on the shelf until I found some ham and folded a few slices into my mouth, then drank some more. On my way back I noticed a light on in the sitting room and saw the terrace door standing open. I found Ali outside with his back to me, wearing pyjama bottoms.

'Someone's here,' he said. 'I saw headlights coming up the hill. They stopped at the car park.'

I was about to tell him he was being paranoid when his head turned sharply and he stepped away from the house. I saw a shape move from one rooftop to another.

'Front door's bolted,' whispered Ali. 'So they're coming over the top.'

Closer movement now. The scuffle of soles on roof tiles.

'*Chi c'è?*' shouted Ali. '*So chi sei, figlio di puttana!*'

More movement, even closer. Then from the shadows came a contemptuous laugh and a low, mocking voice.

'Aren't those statements contradictory? If you know who I am, why ask me who's there?'

The figure sprang down into the light and a bearded Simon Drake stood with his arms outstretched and a broad smile on his face.

'Motherfucker,' said Ali.

'How can you be that easy to sneak up on? Don't they teach you anything in the army these days?'

'Bastard,' said Ali, submitting to Simon's fierce embrace. 'Son of a bitch.'

28

THE VEHICLE ALI had spotted coming up the hillside was the van in which Simon had been sleeping for nearly two months, having set out the day after my grandfather's funeral. He'd driven half the length of France, stopping to fish wherever the mood took him, but never finding the right place. Finally he'd chanced on a lake somewhere in the Limousin which felt right, and parked up beside it. Confused locals had told him repeatedly that they knew the lake to contain no fish, situated as it was near the site of a uranium mine whose land had yet to be remediated. He'd fished the dead lake for three days straight, feeling content for the first time in ages. Eventually he realised that he might need a new activity, so he'd bought a leather sketchbook and some pencils. He showed me the book. It was filled with meticulous architectural drawings. Cathedrals, roofscapes, village squares. Since then he'd gone from town to town, eating outside, sketching the buildings. The pictures were stunning.

'I didn't know you could do this,' I said, looking at them the following morning.

'Neither did I,' he said, then added under his breath, 'How have you been getting on here without me?'

'I'm pleased to see you, if that's what you mean.'

'Aren't those boys amazing?' said Simon. 'They look like the kids in a Patek Philippe advert. *You never actually OWN your neuroses. You merely look after them for the next generation.*'

'Stop it,' I said, erupting with relief.

With Simon here, the group felt more complete and content. Perhaps it was a matter of diluting the Price family. Perhaps it just took a day for the influence of Roger and Selina to recede.

I hadn't seen Simon and Luke together in a while. At the river, I remembered how much of their interaction was punctuated by laughter. I envied them their long-running jokes and unburdened friendship. Katharine had brought her camera and took close-up portraits of everyone as they lazed by the water. I still have prints of them somewhere. Luke with his surfer hair and insolent eyes. Simon looking thin and bohemian with his scraggy artist's beard. Few good photos of him ever, since cameras made him so edgy. Esther borrowed Simon's book and did some sketches of her own – impressionistic drawings of the boys at play, of Luke basking on a rock, of Katharine floating in the water.

Ali worked throughout, diving for broken terracotta, scrubbing away graffiti, unpacking and planting the fresh pots he'd bought the day before. The kitchen was up and running again thanks to him, and Luke made a barbecue lunch.

'This corn on the cob is sick,' said Gus, wiping his mouth with the towel he was wrapped in.

'And that's a good thing, apparently,' said Esther.

'Your dad was never a fan, funnily enough,' I said.

There followed a light-hearted recap of Luke's feud with Eric Weathers-Davis that didn't turn dark in spite of the recent news about Neil. Laughing at it was still the best retort we had. I watched Ali as we talked. Saw him smile at some of the references, never letting up from his work.

'I don't know why we bothered going to Iraq in search of Weapons of Mass Destruction,' he said eventually. 'We had plenty to be looking for back home.'

This prompted a conversation about the London anti-war march in 2003 – who'd been there, what they'd seen. Reminiscences of the speeches given by Jesse Jackson and Harold Pinter. I expected this to be almost as uneasy a topic for Ali as school, but he surprised us all when he said that he'd been there too.

'You went on the march?' said Katharine. 'I don't believe it.'

'Of course I went on the march,' he said, on his knees, easing the root ball of a plant to bed it in potted compost. 'I went on an anti-war march, and then I went to war. Because however much I didn't believe in the war, I still wanted to be a soldier.'

We were back at the house preparing for dinner when Katharine realised she'd left her camera by the river, and asked if I would go and fetch it.

'Are you worrying it's going to get nicked?' I said. 'Careful, or you'll turn into your mother.'

'It might rain. Do you mind?'

I descended through humid orchard scrub hearing the noise of the house recede. Bugs tickled my face and arms. Fireflies sparked in tangled fruit cages. As I slipped down the earthen steps, the rush of the river intensified. Maybe I'd have a solitary swim for my trouble.

Then I became aware of a warm glow through the trees and saw Ali, sitting cross-legged in front of the mill, surrounded by citronella candles in terracotta dishes. The air was thick with their fragrance. I felt embarrassed for intruding, and nearly turned to go. He'd surely find the camera himself and bring it up. But once it was clear he hadn't noticed me, I couldn't help but keep watching.

He muttered something like a prayer. Twice he put his head in his hands as if he were washing it. Then his hands dropped to his lap and brought up the gun. He thumbed a round into the magazine and palmed it into the butt. He cocked the pistol with a quick sliding motion and set it back down.

Shout? No.

He lifted the gun in his right hand and rested it against his forehead, pointing skywards. Then with his left, as if two sides of himself were in conflict, he dragged the gun down his face, rotated it sideways and opened his mouth to receive the barrel.

I threw myself forwards, crashing into view on the path, and shouting in genuine pain as I skinned my leg on a fallen tree. 'Fucking hell. Fuck, fuck, fuck. Ouch.' I went on for as long as I could, so he'd think I hadn't seen him, and to give him time to put the gun away, which he must have done, because I never saw it again.

He was on his feet. 'Max! Are you all right?'

I started. 'Ah! You scared the shit out of me. I didn't think anyone was still down here. It's basically impossible to come down this path without falling over, isn't it?'

It was a cooler evening, so we ate inside. I said nothing and consumed little. A tiredness which felt like it had been building for years was weighing on me, compressing the tissue of my brain. Luke, Simon, Katharine and Esther ate and drank heartily. Thick veal steaks. Giant, wickered bottles of red. Ali, too – now mystifyingly cheerful since his return. Drinking. Cracking jokes. Allowing jokes to be cracked about him.

'Who wants a raspberry?' said Esther, holding up a bowl.

Simon shook his head. 'Can't be doing with soft fruit. Makes me retch. Too close to putrefaction.'

'Has anyone noticed,' said Luke, pulling the cork from a third giant wine bottle, 'how sexualised the confectionery advertising was in our childhood?'

'Go on,' said Simon.

'I've been thinking about it. I reckon it says something very worrying about the culture of our era.'

Esther laughed. 'You think too much.'

'*Made to make your mouth water. Bet you can't put one in your mouth without chewing it.* It was all filthy.'

'*Taste the rainbow of fruit flavours,*' said Esther.

'*The mint with the hole,*' said Simon.

'I'm sorry,' I said, 'but I can't let this pass. I've got to say something.'

'Max is right,' said Simon. 'Why would you want to *chew* it? That one's not sexy at all.'

'Say something about what?' said Luke.

'You were in danger down there,' I said, staring at Ali.

Ali stared back. 'We're doing this, are we?'

'You were going to hurt yourself. Admit it.'

He set down his glass. 'I don't know.'

'What is this?' said Luke.

'He had that gun. He put it in his mouth. I'm sorry. I think they should know. Because we all love you, Ali. I think they should know.'

'What's he talking about?' said Luke.

'Down at the mill. He loaded the gun and put it in his mouth.'

'Is it true?' said Katharine.

Ali spoke calmly. 'You want to talk about it? Okay. Was I going to kill myself? No. If I were going to, would it be tempting to do it at her sacred place, to show her how you really *defile* something? Maybe. I wouldn't have done it, even without Max's heroic intervention. I've come closer than that. It's an experiment I do from time to time. Which, weird as it may sound, leaves me feeling better. Because it's good to know that there's a part of me that wants to stay.'

Simon slowly chewed a mouthful of bread and cheese. I thought Katharine might cry.

'You wouldn't do that to us,' she said. 'I don't want to believe that.'

'To you?' said Ali. 'Do it to you?'

'Okay. Stop.' Luke had stood up. 'Everybody stop.'

And so we took delivery of Ali's long-overdue dispatches from the front line. The gory details of extra gym lessons and weight training. How he and his body were divided from one another. His sexuality tethered forever. The way the secrecy was yoked to masculinity and responsibility. The fear drilled into him from the start of how quickly the world would end if he *told*. Because there was nothing worse in the world than that. And nothing more unthinkable than letting the world know he was gay, which was a *contemptible thing to be*. Then, the second phase: the reliving of it all in a foreign desert amid charred bodies in burned-out cars and severed limbs littering the streets.

Anger and sorrow snaked their way around the room. Esther cried. Katharine sat beside Ali and didn't let go of his arm as he spoke. Luke listened with seething concentration. Only Simon seemed detached from it all. If the others hadn't been so fixated on Ali, his bearing would have stared them in the face. But that wasn't where they were looking.

'Okay,' said Ali, much later. 'I think we can stop now.'

'I know I don't understand it,' said Katharine. 'But why didn't you say something?'

He shrugged. 'Power. The power of *it's my word against yours*. The power of *I have nothing to lose and you have everything to lose*. It seems ridiculous now, but it wasn't back then.'

'I hope you feel better,' said Simon.

'I don't know yet,' said Ali. 'But there are some things I'll never feel better about. Can you believe I even drafted a letter in *support* of Weathers-Davis when it all came out? I never sent it, but that gives you an idea of how far gone I was. When I could have been helping myself, and people like Neil. And, Max, I owe you an apology. Do you remember asking me? In the pub, after Luke's finals? You were right. It wouldn't have been too late to help him then. We could have done it together. Joined up with the others. Built a case. Got him locked up for longer. But that's something I'm going to have to live with.'

'No,' I said. 'It isn't.' I didn't look up from the table.

'What do you mean?' said Luke.

'With Neil. It wasn't just him. It wasn't just Weathers-Davis.'

Steps receding in the darkness. His, then mine, thundering behind. Bats swooping in and out of the arch. The urgent whisper of their wings.

'Wait,' I said. The footsteps continued. 'Please.'

Simon stopped and turned. He stood patiently, almost to attention, his resolve undented. I started to bluster something and was cut off by his raised hand.

'I know,' he said. 'You had to tell them. Thank you for not telling them about me.'

'We should talk about this.'

'No,' said Simon. 'No more chat. I'll be all right. But I'll probably just push off, okay? You can tell them it's Simon being weird again.'

'Whatever you want.'

He looked at me. 'Are you sure that's what Becky said?'

'Yes,' I said. 'I'm sorry.'

'You have *really* got to stop saying that.' He put a hand on my shoulder. 'You can tell them about me if you want. You should, probably. But I don't want to be there when you do.'

I went to hug him but he stepped away with something verging on a shudder.

I waited under the arch for the van's engine to start and watched the red dots of his tail lights receding down the valley until they'd disappeared from sight.

29

THE LATE SHIFT. Just me and Lucky. Everybody else retired to sleep, or otherwise absorbed. All eyes had been on Ali as he went to bed, and he'd laughed and told us to calm down. Now Luke sat alone under a pool of light thrown by the lamp in the sitting room, a pink throw rumpled on the sofa beneath him. He had a tin ashtray on his chest and a bottle of whisky and some ice on a table. Dylan crooned softly from the turntable, steel guitar whining.

Lay, lady, lay

Lay across my big brass bed.

'Glasses are on the side there,' said Luke. I dealt myself in and sat down. 'He must be feeling better. He didn't think to lock a single door.'

'Ha.' Cold gulp of smoky fire. Exhale the fumes. The careful fadedness of the room. Tall lamps dotted about but none on the walls or ceiling, so you didn't see the damp and the cracks. Luke slid a credit card and a fold of paper out of his shirt pocket and delivered a corner of white powder to his nostril. He offered it to me and I shook my head. 'Did you get that here?'

'Brought it with me. If you just stick it in a sealed envelope you can walk through customs with it right there in your pocket. Especially if you've got a wife and kids in tow.

You'd be amazed at the psychological barrier presented by a sealed letter addressed to somebody else. They might pick it up and examine it, but basic social niceties make them totally blind to the idea of tearing it open.' He pinched at his nose while sharply inhaling, clearing the dregs. 'Crimble. I never worshipped him like you all did. Never even liked him. But I didn't see this coming.'

'You don't know the half of it,' I said. 'Give me a minute.'

I took the creaking stairs quickly and crossed the dark-boarded landing to our room. Grassy smells and cicada noise through the open window. Fan frantically spinning. Endearing little snores. Beautiful hump of suffering incubator beneath the sheet.

I pulled open the unpacked holdall and felt for slippery, freezer-bag plastic. Almost sprinted back downstairs, aware that to think about the impulse too much would be to annihilate it.

I said nothing while Luke read. The record had come to its end, little ticks of needle in the endless groove.

'How long have you known?' he said.

'Nine years. He told me just after the reunion.'

'After his sign. Jesus, I can't believe I'm so stupid. He sent up an actual *flag*.'

'I know how you feel,' I said. 'Get this. I even thought about going to the police myself and saying Crimble had done it to me, because Simon wouldn't.'

'Why didn't you?'

'Lost my nerve. Thought it wasn't my story to tell.'

Proud of my intel. Showing it off. It was the closest I'd felt to Luke in ages. When he next had a corner, I had one too. The night accelerated, the words tumbled out.

Very late now. He poured me another. 'Enjoy this. We're almost down to the limoncello.' We lay back, staring. 'It would have worked, you know.'

'What?'

'Your plan to flush him out. I can't believe you've kept it to yourself all this time. You're a good friend. God, it makes you furious, doesn't it?'

'It does.'

'Crighton, up there still. Carrying on. I don't know, actually. Is he still there?'

'He's still there.' Deep breath. No stopping now. 'We saw him only a few months ago.'

'You fucking what?'

An angry phase then. Camaraderie shattered. Fun while it lasted.

'You kept seeing him? You drank? Broke bread? It's one thing Simon doing it, but you? He did it to Neil and he did it to Simon too. And you don't think he's still doing it now? Bullshit.'

'It was what Simon wanted. You've read the letters. He's been under Crimble's control for years. I don't think we'll ever know just how much.'

Making a display of my intimacy with Simon. Letting it run. *Get a load of this. Get a load of what you fucking missed.*

Sometime after 4 a.m., I gave in, and we hugged with narcotic sincerity.

'I need to think about all this,' he said. 'Don't worry, I'll go to bed soon – otherwise I'll run into the fucking kids.'

'What about those?' I said, pointing at the letters.

'Let me hold onto them. I'd like to read them again. I won't leave them lying around.'

I left him alone with limoncello and letters, more Dylan on the turntable, apparently lost in the faded tapestries on the walls.

The dawn creep to the bedroom, the treacherous morning light, the jackhammer heart next to the shamingly serene mother-to-be.

In the morning we found a note from Esther on the kitchen table which said that she and Luke had taken the kids off first thing to a water park. Katharine stuck to Ali all morning. After lunch they fell asleep beside each other on loungers in the orchard. Simon's disappearance was so in keeping with his usual behaviour that nobody thought to question it. It wasn't until Esther returned alone with the boys at sundown that we discovered that Luke had flown back to London.

'He'll be back tomorrow night,' she said. 'He got a panicky call from Ish this morning to say that Cisco are filing a lawsuit against them. Trying to get them shut down. It happens from time to time. He had to go back straight away to some crisis meeting with their solicitors.'

'Were you there?' I said. 'When he took the call.'

'No, he told me about it. Why?'

'No reason.'

30

HE DID WELL to keep the fury constant. Most people's late-night resolutions would not have survived the hangover he must have had, or the fact that he hadn't been to bed. Others would definitely have bottled it in the time it took to get hold of a flight and be dropped at the airport, leaving his wife and kids behind. Not Luke. He was up and running from daybreak. He got started as soon as he hit the ground. He got his best people on it.

They waited until the new term had started. I'm not sure why. I expect Crimble had been unreachable up some mountain, squeezing the last drop out of his summer. Either way, thanks to the number of witnesses, the story passed into legend quicker than any before it, disseminated and analysed for clues.

Crimble is crossing the gravel on his way to breakfast. He sees the police car parked outside the front door. Some say he asks a boy nearby if he knows why the car is there.

Half an hour later, he is overseeing the dining room from the masters' table when Tony Sutton's successor enters and tells him that the police are waiting in his private-side and need to speak to him. He replies that he'll be there directly, and the headmaster leaves.

The breakfasting pupils watch him gather his bag and walk across the room. But he does not walk in the direction of the door. Instead he goes to the big windows in their curly stone frames, pushes one open and climbs out onto the North Lawn.

Oho. A fine prank in progress. Just the sort of unpredictability for which he is adored. But the children are left wanting. Nothing more comes of it. He just walks away across the grass with his satchel slung over his shoulder.

The sensationalist version that did the rounds had him found by a group of boys on their way to a rugby match. Police reports dispute this. The place was in lockdown. A search was on. Whatever the circumstances of his discovery, it's difficult not to imagine those tracksuited legs swaying in the wind, the tree bearing its dangling man. *An expertly tied knot*, it says in the inquest report. He knew what he was doing there.

It was seized on by some that he must already have had the rope in his bag when the police arrived. This was said to be a telling detail, confirming his guilt in the eyes of the mob. It was assumed that he had been waiting for this to happen. That he'd lived under its weight for years. Which cemented the views both of those who were ready to declare him guilty, and those in the other camp who contended that while he had never actively participated, he had known, but failed to act.

Only a handful of us knew that he had been labouring under no such weight, and that the only reason he had the rope ready was that as soon as the police had informed Luke of their decision to take Crimble in for questioning, weeks after we'd got back from Italy, Luke had phoned him personally to let him know what was coming, and get one or two other things off his chest.

None of this came out until much later, by which time verdicts had been reached, definitive accounts made. And nobody thought to connect any of it to an incident that took place in a flat in Great Yarmouth just before Christmas the same year, wherein a frail ex-convict known locally as Eric Davis was cable-tied to a chair and had boiling water poured over his head in a methodical and brutal session of torture lasting an entire night. In spite of the victim's criminal record it was reported in the local press that the perpetrators had been thieves in search of money. That they'd kept asking him, over and over again, to give up the location of something he swore he didn't have. That they hadn't taken no for an answer, even when he could no longer utter the word.

FOUR

The Victoria Crown

31

I HAD JUST turned onto Katharine's street when I fell down the hole. It was square, over six feet deep and covered with planks that gave way the moment I stepped on them. A stage trapdoor wouldn't have done the job any better.

I plunged, regaining enough forward momentum that my right leg, in mid-stride, struck the lip of the pavement. My ribcage slammed into the same edge on its way down. My right ear tore on one of the splintered planks. Then I landed.

It must have looked as if I had dropped out of existence, though I doubt anyone was watching. If they were, you'd hope they might have come to help as I swore and flailed trying to get out, which I did for some time.

When I had finally extricated myself, I stood for a moment looking back into the hole, as if having so catastrophically intervened in my day it might have more to offer, another dose of malevolence, a follow-up jibe. I cursed the hole, and whoever had dug it. The universe gave no reply. It had delivered its insult and now it was looking the other way.

It was a bright, windy day. The leaves of London plane trees clattered to the pavement around me like rolls of parchment. This was in October 2015, on the morning of my son's ninth birthday.

*

My incredulity faded as the accident's implications hit home. I'd been told to get there by nine thirty if I wanted to see him, and now it was after ten. Katharine would be sympathetic but not surprised. I was a past master at meeting her low expectations.

My ripped jeans were sticking to my leg. My right ear felt unfamiliar. The chest pain had started to sing, and it was only getting started. I hurried on, picturing the tragic scene that would play out when his stepfather's car sped past and I caught a glimpse of his bed-head hair, or his unwitting face creased in a yawn. I was already finding ways to blame it on her. If she didn't live in such a flashy area, people might concentrate more on watching where they were going.

I didn't ring the bell. Instead I used my emergency key and marched straight through to announce myself in her always-surprisingly-enormous kitchen.

'I've just fallen down a fucking hole.'

She looked up from her newspaper at the table. 'Oh, the one down the road?' Cosily domestic morning smells. Lingered-over coffee. Ghost of toast.

'Yes, the one down the road! Why is it there?'

'Fibre-optic cabling. They're doing the whole street.'

'Why can't they cover these things properly? I think I've cracked a rib. Possibly several.'

She noted her place in the article and stood up. I tried to stay calm, remembering who else might be in the house.

No. The energy was wrong. Heartbreaking absence of background noise. No magic scamper of feet on stairs.

'It's Saturday,' she said, in response to my hangdog expression.

'So?'

'He has tennis club.'

'On his birthday?'

She shrugged. 'He likes it. I did warn you.'

'How much did I miss him by?'

'Over half an hour. You'd have missed him even without your hole. Come on, let's take a look at you.' She steered me towards one of the sofas at the garden end of the kitchen. I inhaled a deep draught of her neckline. Slight flutter. Not a problem. Neither of us was under the illusion that we should be together.

'Are you wheezing?' she said. 'Is your breathing shallow?'

'No.'

'Does it hurt when you cough?'

I coughed. 'Yes! Fuck.'

'You've probably just bruised your intercostal muscles. But the leg might need a stitch. Let me look at it.'

'Ow!' I shouted as she eased up the fabric. 'Stop catching it on the wounds.'

'I might have to cut these off you.'

'These are my best jeans.'

'Say your farewells. They're coming off.'

'Now?'

'Oh for goodness' sake. There's nothing under there I haven't seen before.' She opened a drawer, took out a pair of kitchen scissors and began chopping up my trouser leg.

She checked me over, declared that I could get away without stitches, and dabbed iodine on the worst of the wedges hacked into my shin. As she worked, I took in a photo on the wall of Katharine and Fraser and my beautiful boy holidaying somewhere expensive. I smiled at the sight of him looking so happy and she joined me in fond appraisal, as parents do regardless of where they stand with each other.

'I can't believe he's nine,' I said.

'He left you something.'

She brought over a Lego construction from the kitchen counter. I handled it reverently, its status instantly promoted above that of a normal worldly object. It was an old set of my own, modified by him: two castle walls folded together, affixed with the wheels of a siege engine and decked out with wings and spoilers. The knight-pilot wore a black helmet and sat at a bank of computers on battlements which were now a streamlined cockpit.

'I love it,' I said. 'But I won't take it with me in case he wants to keep working on it.' I detached the knight as a souvenir.

'Do you want to borrow a pair of Fraser's trousers?'

'Only if they aren't dad-jeans.'

She went upstairs, leaving me to enjoy charming pictures drawn by my son, pinned to a corkboard. I noticed a separate, ribboned-off area titled *Things I Am Glad About*, under which each member of this happy family had pinned their original, optimistic thoughts.

I stood up, removed my shredded jeans and walked over in my boxers to Fraser's floor-to-ceiling wine cooler. I opened the door and browsed the bays of serious bottles kept at cellar temperature inside. I withdrew and returned several before alighting on a Château Palmer, something I'd always wanted to try.

As I stowed the bottle and the Lego man in my satchel, my phone buzzed from within. *Still good for 11 am departure?* read the message. I replied in the affirmative. The wine was safely hidden by the time Katharine returned and handed me a pair of frighteningly blue Levi's.

'Thanks,' I said, putting them on. 'I might try to catch him tomorrow if that's okay.'

'Of course,' she said. 'Whenever. You know that.'

I kissed her goodbye. 'Better go. I've got a date with Simon.'

She looked at me with pity. 'Do you have a present for him, at least?'

'I'll bring it tomorrow, okay?'

'You'll need a corkscrew,' she shouted, just before the front door slammed.

I set out for the meeting point, trying not to limp.

Katharine was well on her way to qualifying as an anaesthetist. She saw people come and go from existence on a regular basis. Very much a grown-up, while I trod water somewhere at least a decade behind my thirty-nine years of age. Incredible to think there'd been a time when anybody had been scandalised by the age difference between us.

We didn't separate until a year after the birth, each new challenge of which had brought my deficiencies into sharper focus. Perhaps I should have just come out and told them the lie they all seemed to want me to tell: that I had been one of the victims too. I knew they'd all thought it at one point or another. If I'd said that I had, nobody would have doubted me for a second. The sympathy might have been beneficial. Who knows, it might even have reduced the speed with which I was hustled out of Katharine's life by Roger and Selina when the split was made public. But I doubt it. They reached their conclusions about me long before then.

That I should even have contemplated saying something like that was depressing enough, highlighting as it did the fact that unlike so many others, I had no grand reason for my fuck-ups. Which made them seem like much bigger fuck-ups than anyone else's.

But Katharine and I were fine. We affected a consensus that our affair was nothing but a bump in our respective journeys, which had never been destined to run together – a bump that merely happened to resound, thanks to the glorious boy we now had to show for ourselves. It wasn't actually a consensus, since the idea originated entirely from her, but she'd never asked for my opinion and I'm not sure what it would have been if she had.

Besides, there was now the question of Fraser, a pragmatic, softly spoken Scot who was patient and caring, even with me, and whose lawyer's income far better enabled Katharine to pursue the life she wanted than mine ever could have. I couldn't bring myself to dislike him. By any measure, he was perfect for her. They'd got married the previous year in a ravishing ceremony at the Italian house, with my son bearing the rings. A stepsibling would probably come along soon, and that would be fine too. It was all fine, fine, fine.

We'd talked about sharing custody equally but had come down on the side of stability, so I saw my boy every other weekend. It wasn't enough, but at least the time we had was undiluted. Katharine would brief me on his well-being as she disembarked from the car and dumped whatever kit he needed for his stay. I would listen as best I could in spite of the obliterating explosion of excitement I always felt at the sight of him.

'He's got something called *molluscum contagiosum*,' she'd said, one recent Friday afternoon. 'You've got to put cream on it.'

I'd hated myself at bathtime for being so unnerved by the way he bent over, tail in the air, waiting for me to administer the cream. Almost as much as I'd hated Fraser the instant predator, with his long game and his canny angle of attack. And then of course I'd made the mistake of looking it up, and discovered that *molluscum contagiosum* can sometimes be sexually transmitted, and become enraged that they would even think to put those two words beside an ailment that most commonly afflicts children aged between one and eleven.

I knew better than to give voice to thoughts like this when they occurred.

*

I waited at the agreed corner for the smooth approach of Simon's black Mercedes. He pulled up and I opened the passenger door.

'Jesus,' he said. 'What happened to you?'

'I didn't think it was that obvious,' I said, climbing into the showroom-fresh car. 'What's this?'

In the back seat beside his overnight bag was a large, wrapped present.

'That's for my godson. It is today, isn't it? What did you get him?'

'I'm still working on that.'

'How is he?'

'I don't know. I missed him.'

'Oops. Katharine okay with that?'

'I think she was almost expecting it.'

'Never mind. You can make it up to him.'

'You look like shit too, of course,' I said, as he pulled into traffic. 'How do you do it?'

The joke about him ageing badly was long established. Distinguished grey flashes at the temples. Features tightly knit. Torso, too. Much time spent with the nutritionist and the yoga teacher.

'The money helps,' he said.

I didn't realise until it had fallen away again how much my investment in Katharine's life had caused me to lose. I'd resolved to enjoy the ensuing statelessness but found it impossible to do so. New roots were required.

I'd ended up in a basement flat on a street of terraced houses in south-east London. I live there still. My upstairs neighbours in ascending order are a seventy-two-year-old retired plumber called Arthur and a forty-something West African couple called Rita and Eddie who run a record label. They leave boxes of unwanted vinyl out in the street for passers-by. Thanks to them I have become quite the aficionado of the music of Mali and Gambia. I make ends meet by writing bilingual travel pieces for in-flight magazines, which enables me to escape when I need to and be at home for my son when he comes.

From the moment I moved in, I made sure that the flat was homely and that my boy's bedroom was immaculate. When he stayed over I would always make sure I'd brushed my teeth and shaved before I went in to kiss him goodnight, in case my breath stank or my bristles irritated his skin. Later I would watch him, stocking up on his smell. Reflecting on the journey that parents must take, from disbelief that their actions should have kindled another being to acceptance that the being in question is not their property.

Stand over a slumbering child and contemplate the miracle of blood and bone and consciousness, and if you tickle their palm their tiny fingers might well curl around yours. But that doesn't necessarily mean anything. It's just what they do in their sleep.

'When are you going to tell me where we're going?' I said. I'd picked up some clues from the route we were taking, but not enough.

'Do you really want to spoil the surprise?' said Simon.

'Absolutely. Yes.'

'Okay, well – I'm taking you to the theatre.'

'You made me miss my son's birthday so we could take in a show? I'm not a tourist.'

'It's not in London, you idiot. You're going to love it.'

'Tell me then.'

'You're no fun,' he said. 'Fine. Ever heard of Revenant Arts?'

'No.'

'It's an immersive theatre company. They do these, sort of, guerrilla productions in atmospheric buildings. They did *One Flew Over the Cuckoo's Nest* in a derelict asylum on the south coast last year, and *Turn of the Screw* in some famously haunted house the year before that. Guess where they're doing it this year.'

I stared out of the window. 'Ah.'

'I don't know what the play is yet. They don't tell you until you get there. But wouldn't it be incredible if it was *Murder in the Cathedral*? I bought tickets for the matinee so we can go on for dinner afterwards. I've got a feeling being back there might make us want to blow off steam.'

'Sounds great,' I said.

'What's the matter?'

'Nothing.'

He sighed. 'I didn't know you were going to miss out on seeing him, did I? All right, how about this? We can just skip dinner if you like, and I'll run you straight back. You can catch him at the end of the day. Okay?'

'It's not that,' I said. 'I just wonder whether it isn't time to leave that place alone.' I also wondered about the wisdom of us going back there to watch a theatre company profiting from its singular atmosphere. How could they ever top our memories? They could lay on whatever spectacle they liked and it would ping off us like peas off a tank.

'Don't you at least want to see what it's like? Especially if it's falling down.'

'I guess.'

'Oh, come on. Anyway, it's not just because I can't stay away. It's research. We've got a plan to make *Monsters 5* a mobile game. When you have it installed on your phone, you'll be able to play it everywhere you go, just like we used to. Creatures hiding in plain sight, all over the world. It's called augmented reality. I thought that since the first version of the game began there, I might hide a really nasty one somewhere on the grounds.'

'I guess you could have a mad, bloodthirsty knight, like in the play.'

'*Who will rid me of this troublesome priest?* Ha. Funny to think that Luke was put out when I got the part of Thomas. He was perfect casting for someone committing a murder because of something he'd overheard.'

I knew what state the place was in, because I'd been there. Two years after the school had finally closed down, I'd been in the area and had pointed my car up the hill on a whim. A man in hi-vis had turned me away at the head of the avenue, which had only made me more determined. This was during what I now thought of as the 'wandering' phase of the post-Katharine period, during which anyone telling me not to do anything would light me up with defiant purpose.

I'd parked in the village and walked up through the woods. The house had looked all but derelict. Scaffolding wrapped around the church spire. Open wounds where the render had slaked off. Ground-floor windows all boarded up. I'd prised one open and climbed into the Lower Gallery. Upstairs, the iron skeletons of the dormitory beds lay bare, their mattresses piled in heaps. In the dining room, the scholarship boards had been taken down and stacked at one end against a wall. All those glorious names, gathering dust on the floor. I'd taken careful aim at one and split it with my foot.

I told myself at the time that my behaviour was only an extension of my grandfather's mantra to 'speak up'. That you could speak up with actions as much as with words, just as I had been telling myself that I was living for him in deformed versions of his old pronouncements. *Nothing like an enlivening whisky at breakfast. A strong afternoon lager always hits the spot.*

Hearing my words in his voice, telling myself that my indulgences were ones he'd surely sanction. Almost, but never quite, able to believe myself.

Other highlights from that vagrant, lost time:

A disastrous trip to Liverpool, where Holly was now living, having taken up a full-time position with the orchestra. I'd shown up drunk at her house and it had taken her some time to get me to leave. The sight of framed wedding photographs and floors carpeted with toys had done little to put me off.

A solitary weekend when I'd run amok on the Survivors forum, spitting venom at anyone who suggested that Crimble's death had been a tragedy. That it was born only of his guilt for having known what was happening and done nothing to stop it. I'd found their tribalism perfectly intact. They'd just carried on fouling the page with infantile joy at being spooned extract of malt and getting a good thrashing from someone who *never did them any harm.*

The dinner I'd arranged with Wagstaff. He'd tried to stay jovial, but I could see that the manner in which the school had ended had broken his heart. Towards the end of the meal, he'd become emotional. Flushed face all desperate and sad.

'I just can't get over it,' he said. 'He could have talked to me any time. I would have helped him.'

'We all feel that way. It's nobody's fault.'

'You don't understand. He was my friend. We did everything together.'

The penny dropped. 'You're not talking about Neil.'

'No,' he'd said. 'I'm talking about *Ian*.'

I'd been back again too, in a manner of speaking: putting the school's name into a search engine one day, I'd come across recent footage taken by one of the urban explorers for whom the building had become an object of fascination. The camera shot had smoothly ascended to show an aerial view of the young guy operating the drone, standing with his radio-controlled handset near the balustrade just like Simon on the day I'd first met him. I'd watched the video countless times. The square of lawn shrinking down to the centre of a rapidly expanding landscape. The fields and woods dropping into place as the camera shot up, away from the building's noble geometry and into the comfort of the broader context.

Everyone else, out there in the world. While there was I, apparently the only one of us still unable to get beyond himself. And I might justifiably have asked myself the question of why Simon in particular had ended up functioning so magnificently in spite of his past, while I could not. But the truth was that I had no idea what might be festering inside him. From the moment I heard about Crimble's death I had assumed that some reckoning with Simon was due in the future. That at some point he would find out I had taken the letters, and shown them to Luke. And that when he did, it would terminate our friendship. But the reckoning had never come. When it had transpired that the letters would no longer be needed as evidence in a trial, Luke had returned them to me, and never mentioned them again. I had no reason to think Simon would ever know they hadn't gone up in flames with all the others.

There must have been a time when he was angry with Luke. Possibly with me too. But we'd never seen it. On the surface he'd accepted the outcome as if it had always been where things were headed. Only the occasional action or remark betrayed the ongoing instability within.

He'd shown me the video one night at his house without telling me in advance. Just cued it up on his computer and sent it to the big plasma screen on his wall. I'd been expecting a movie, but here instead was his youthful face. The film was shot in unforgiving close-up, but you could still make out the familiar backdrop of Crimble's old room outside Trafalgar.

Old audio, poorly recorded. Metallic echo to the voices from the past.

Do you ever think about what you want to be when you grow up?

Pause. Suppressed laugh. Unbroken voice.

Sometimes. But I don't know . . .

Don't know what?

I don't know what kind of person I'm going to be then. So I might want something very different from what I want now.

So what do you want to be now?

I don't know. Something that makes money. So I can look after Mum.

Winter light on his pale skin. Fatigue on his face when in repose. I'd forgotten the freckly charm of his features at this age. Was he twelve? Thirteen?

Who's your best friend?

Crimble's voice all warmth and comfort.

I don't know.

Apart from me, I mean.

His bashful smile filling the screen.

What does best friend mean?

Good question. Maybe the person you'd tell anything to?

Like what?

I don't know. Secrets. Things you're afraid of.

Max is my friend.

Of course he is. Good old Max. Soft clearing of the throat. *What do you think your friends think of you?*

I don't know. I hope they like me.

Do you ever wonder what they might say about you behind your back?

Simon's hesitant young face. Super 8 resolution. Shot wobbling as the cameraman adjusts his position.

Do you ever talk to God?

Sometimes. To ask for things.

Simon sniffing, scratching the end of his nose.

Like what?

I don't know. A new fishing rod.

Smiling at his own predictability.

How do you think you've changed over the last year?

I've got better at programming, I think.

You're a genius at that stuff. If I had to guess what you were going to do with your life I'd say it would probably have something to do with computers.

I do like them.

What is it you like about them?

Serious look. Shifting on the bed. Long pause.

I like that when you program them correctly, they do exactly what you want them to. And if they don't, there's always a reason why.

Noises off. Young voices. Laughter. Doors banging. The sonic detritus of a long-forgotten afternoon. One school day like countless others, suddenly plucked from the past. Where had I been? How close?

Apprehension in the young face. Eyes widening, looking to the adult behind the camera for reassurance.

It's all right. Soothing, familiar voice. *Nobody's coming. Carry on.*

The young face smiling back into the lens.

Low-slung in the passenger seat of his sleek machine. Crimble's house, freshly painted, leaping out at me from the line of cottages. Simon didn't seem to notice it.

The car pulled up the hill and approached the pair of bulls' heads crowning the pillars. I could picture what was coming with total clarity. Wagstaff's old lodge. The plunge down the tracking trees, avenue and past opening up before us. The familiar, cold soak. The sense of possibility draining away, of being stripped of my will, becoming subordinate to rules I didn't comprehend.

'Stop,' I said.

He brought the car to a halt in the middle of the road. 'What's the matter?'

'I'm not coming.'

'Okay,' he said. 'I understand. If I was in your shoes, I'd want to get back and see him too. Tell you what – why don't you take my present, and say it's from you? I don't mind at all.'

'No need,' I said. 'But thank you.' I leaned forward and kissed him on the cheek. 'Listen. Why don't we both go? We can give him our presents together, then find something else to do.'

He shook his head with a smile, staring ahead at the barcode shadows thrown down on the avenue by the trees. I got out of the car and started walking back down the hill.

32

SIX MILES TO my destination. But it was a good day for walking. For taking in some cool draughts of nature, free of the signal junk of the city. My injuries hurt to begin with, but eased off as I settled into a rhythm. Old country. Farming country. Riding country. Rolling country. Countryside laid out with such order that its beauty feels like a product of consensus, because surely nothing could look this good out of mere practicality.

And birds and trees and flowers without a name / All sighed when lawless law's enclosure came.

A grand pile in every village round here, at one time. Many still there. Many gone. My heaven and my hell had once been two such households, and for all I knew they were both alike in dignity, though it seemed unlikely given their respective atmospheres. Each mentioned in the Domesday Book. Each with its grand history, interleaved with that of the country. Each subject to the privations and accelerations of the post-war world. Each saved through repurpose. Better than a demolition job I suppose, if you were looking at it from the building's point of view. Which would of course be a complete waste of time.

Coming up from the base of the valley my breathing got shallower, but I didn't slow down. I was keen to get onto home ground. I had the idea it would give me sustenance. Sure enough, when I saw the park I felt myself starting to relax. The oaks and ashes were all where they were supposed to be, leaves aflame. The hall spread imperiously before its domain, windows glinting in the sun. I entered by the lower gate, off the lane, picturing all the centuries of journeys it had seen, including the one I'd made on the morning of my interview when we passed my grandfather trimming hedgerows and he dropped me a peach through the sunroof.

A fence had been built around the icehouse. I climbed over it and stepped inside. The footholds were all where I remembered them. I felt sideways across the wall until I found the indented place where the spare key was kept. I palmed it and stowed it in my pocket before climbing back out.

The Hall gardens were strictly divided now according to the size of each flat owner's portion, fanning out from the centre in segments. As I trudged up the big field, a man paused from forking his bonfire to observe me from his slice of the pie.

'Good afternoon,' he offered, with deep suspicion.

'Lovely day,' I said.

Let him offer to help me if he dare.

The house had changed hands only once since he died, but nine years was enough: there would be change. Today, for the first time, I felt able to face it. It wouldn't be easy. From the moment I arrived I saw prissy clean-ups, ignorant abolitions. Earth had been moved, angular flower beds established. Some of the gnarliest, most sacred trees had gone. Others had been affixed with ominous-looking tags suggestive of condemnation. No doubt the courtyard had been stripped of its wheelbarrows and pianos.

At least the orchard gate was still there. I took the key out of my pocket and pushed it into the lock, knowing how to open the door without it making a sound. I not only knew the man who'd made it, I had probably used it more than anyone now living. I walked down the short avenue of fruit trees that led to the workshop and chalk pond, making no effort to be discreet as I crossed in view of the house. If they saw me, it would be over. No way you could see me in your garden and not be alarmed. Not unless you were tolerant to the point of self-sabotage. With my ripped ear, my limp and Fraser's jeans, I looked like a destitute executive about two weeks into his definitive breakdown.

No cars. They were out. Relax. I sat with my back to the slope of the sprawling ash tree at the top of the pond and took out the bottle. I removed the foil, found a stick of the right size and strength and pushed in the cork. He would not have approved of my treatment of the wine. To my knowledge, he'd never drunk anything as good as this, and if I was going to toast him with it, the thing ought to be done properly.

It was the right kind of day to be drinking to him. The right kind of weather, too: cold but alive. His dogs would have been batting around the tree as he sat here on his bench, sending steaming breath through its roots to flush out the scent of quarry. Today the only things breathing here were me and the wine. I made an offering to the tree. Only a drop. The wastage would infuriate him. I lifted the bottle and took a swig, savouring the blood and iron. When I was settled into the flavour, I rolled a smoke.

Nearly thirty years since I was sent out on that ladder and dropped through the ice. Was it as serious as I remembered? At the time I had thought I sensed a level of relief that betrayed how close the call had been. As I sat by the water now it seemed laughable to think there had been serious danger. No ice here today, only sunshine and falling leaves. Close by, the hoarse coo of a wood pigeon, forever impossible to hear without remembering my grandfather's interpretation of their song.

'Hear it?' he'd say. '*My shoes, Betty. They're my shoes.*' So that was what I heard.

I drank more wine and smoked another. The pile of wrinkled cigarette ends grew on a roof slate I'd found wedged into the turf. Ash was teased by the wind and taken away, in a miniature re-enactment of what happened to his remains on the day we scattered them here.

Here. The new owners.

Swish of gravel as the car drew up. Slam of doors. Two kids cannoned out and were immediately at play. Back from their Saturday-afternoon excursion.

He'd have loved this: the laughter of children in the garden he grew. Fresh blood. The old place in good hands.

Withdrawal was the best course of action. I'd paid my respects. No need to alarm these good people unduly. On the other hand I wasn't even halfway down the bottle, and I was curious to meet them.

The kids' voices had been at full pitch, but now I was conscious of a reduction in the sound, a dispersal. Two voices in cackle-concert had diminished to one, and it was counting aloud.

Quick breaths of someone approaching at speed: a girl with a hiding place in mind. Face still lit with the glee of the chase as she caught sight of the breakdown executive with the bottle of wine.

She came to a halt but the thrill of the hunt won out over surprise. Rather than question what I was doing in her garden she only put a finger to her lips as she kept her gaze beyond me, on the spot she had chosen. I made a sloppy zipping motion across my face and looked away to put her at ease. *My lips are sealed.*

She darted for the holly bush. I could have suggested ten better hiding places but this wasn't the time. The counting had stopped and the game was on. After a suspiciously short time that hinted that somebody had been looking through his fingers as he counted, a boy came into view who could only be her twin.

'Afternoon,' I said.

'Hello.'

'Are you looking for someone?'

'My sister,' he said, looking at me with far more suspicion than she had. The right amount of suspicion.

'Well, I haven't seen anybody. She must have gone the other way round the pond.'

The boy walked off looking puzzled. His sister re-emerged from the holly with an irritated expression on her face, as if I had missed the point of the game. She had a suitably elfin face for a wood sprite.

'Are you twins?' I said. She nodded. 'That's good. That means you'll always have someone to travel with.'

They were beautiful children. Something golden about their skin. Open faces, confident and uncluttered.

'Hey! You're supposed to be hiding,' said the returning boy, who had doubtless been glancing back over his shoulder as he retreated.

'Do the two of you like living here?' I said.

'I like the garden,' said the girl. 'We didn't have one where we lived before.'

'Have you been down to the icehouse in the park?'

'We're not allowed in the park,' said the boy. 'The Hall people don't like it.'

'They've always been a stuck-up lot,' I said. 'But you know, there's magic right here on your doorstep.'

'What magic?'

'Why don't you both sit down and I'll show you a trick?'

They looked uncertainly at each other, then back in the direction of the house. There were trees in the way, but I could still hear the sound of their parents talking as they unloaded the car.

I took another swig from the bottle, then reached into my satchel and took out the heavy, old coin. 'Have a look at this.'

The children sat as requested. They had consented to be entertained. I would never have been so trusting at their age. I thought of that film, *Whistle Down the Wind*, where the kids find a murderer in their barn and think he's Jesus, so they don't tell any of the grown-ups he's there and bring him food. It had terrified me when I was young. I'd wanted to scream at the kids in the movie to run, get away, make as much noise as you can, not hide the fucker.

'Have you ever seen a coin like this?' They shook their heads. 'It was minted in 1844, when Queen Victoria was still a young woman. Have you heard of Queen Victoria? It's not important. What's important is what this coin can do. It has magical properties.'

I picked up the slate and tipped the cigarette-ends away. I wiped it with my sleeve and sat it on my knees. I was conscious of my shaky fingers, of the blood on my ear, of the smell of wine and smoke I must be giving off.

'Watch carefully,' I said. 'I'm just going to place the coin on the slate, like this.' I put both hands down, then lifted up my right hand to reveal the coin beneath it. I raised both hands, showed them the coin again in my right palm, then slammed both palms down hard. 'Where's the coin?'

The girl slapped the back of my right hand. As she did, I sent a ripple up my right arm, across my shoulders and down to my left hand, as if to suggest that some power conferred by her had sent the coin travelling through my flesh and down the other side of my body. I lifted my left hand, revealing Victoria's battered young profile. The girl smiled. She wanted to believe.

Her brother was unimpressed. 'You just threw that from one hand to the other. I saw it flash across the middle.'

'Is that right?' I said.

'And I heard it scratching across the slate.'

'Very well. It looks as if we're going to need to pull out something more special to impress the likes of you.' I tossed the slate into the grass and got to my feet. I wanted this to be an athletic spring of intent but the booze had caused me momentarily to forget my injuries. My ribcage yelped. The girl was staring at my ear in a way that suggested it had started to bleed again. I took several steps back from the tree. 'Watch carefully.' I raised my right hand so they could see the coin. I pulled the hand back and threw.

'Where is it? I didn't see it go.' The girl had spun round while her more suspicious brother watched me intently.

'I'm going to stay right here so you can see exactly how magical this is. Both of you, go round to the other side of the tree. You'll have to lift your arms high over your heads. But you'll find that almost exactly halfway round, at about the height of your hand, is a knothole in the tree a bit like a pocket. I want someone to put their hand inside. If you can't reach, one of you will have to give the other a leg up.

'You see,' I continued, as they scrabbled to find what I was describing, 'this tree is a time machine. You just have to know how to operate it. And luckily for you there's nobody in the world who's better at operating it than me. When I threw that coin, it flew back in time, over a hundred and seventy years, to the year it was minted, when this huge tree was just a sapling. It lodged in one of the tree's young branches and was gathered up. And ever since, it's been inside waiting for you to come along and take it out. Have you found the pocket? Good. Now, reach inside and see what you find.'

It was him, not her, of course. He didn't trust me so he had to do it himself. There was every chance this wouldn't work, but I didn't let that show on my face. But then I could tell from the boy's widening eyes and the way he turned to his sister that there was no need to worry, because my ancestor was here and he was never going to let me down.

The coin the boy held as he allowed himself to fall back down the trunk of the ash tree was blackened by age and the elements but was incontrovertibly an 1844 Victoria crown.

'Let me clean it up for you,' I said, taking it quickly and wiping it in the folds of my jacket, swapping it for the one I'd brought with me. 'You can keep that,' I said. 'So long as you share it. And make sure you look after it. That coin has travelled through time.'

While they were distracted, I took the little Lego knight from my satchel and placed him in the high nook of the tree where the coin had been. It felt like the right thing to do. I was just bending down to pick up the bottle, feeling pretty pleased with myself, when, as it tends to, the world moved on.

'Do you mind telling me what the hell you think you're doing?'

So it was the mother. At least now I could stop wondering which parent was going to come and tell me to clear off.

Bold, tiger-stripe sunset. The sky tuning up like an orchestra. One of those evenings when the weather puts you in your place. I had explained myself to the kids' mother as best I could and set off down the park, fingering the coin in my pocket. If I hurried, I might still make a train that would get me to town in time to give it to my boy before he went to bed.

How had his birthday gone? I wondered. He was one year off the age I'd been when I lay alone on that first night listening to the groans of frozen pipes as snow fell outside.

They didn't happen often now, but when he was five and six there'd been a spate of nightmares. They'd worried me at the time, though I saw now that they were the healthy assertion of primal fears. He'd be so lost in them that the only thing for it was to remove him from the bedroom, to show him that the world outside still existed. I'd hoist him out of bed, buttocks clenching with fear in my palm. Feel his sweat cooling on my neck as his body relaxed and I could talk him back to reality. Sometimes there'd be a late resurgence of the fear when we returned, because the dream was still there waiting for him, and we'd have to walk away again until the bed had become fully detoxified.

Liking them is one thing, but nobody told me that you actually fall in love. The smell of him on a hot day: scalp, sun lotion, traces of food. Butter from his breakfast toast. Cereal sweetness soaked on skin. His hair tickling my chin. Restless squirm of him there. Fingers idly tracing the shape of my own as I read him a story. His head on my booming ribcage. Feeling the vibrations of my own voice resound. The tap of his heartbeat against the palm of my hand. Gather a pinch of forearm to know it's safe from the world. See him looking at his hands, his fingers, the fragments of his nails, and it all feels so familiar, and I realise how much time I must have spent looking at my own hands as a child. How much time we all must spend. The pure bell of his voice. Those moments which feel like they're made of thin glass. That day he heard me on the phone using Spanish for work and said *Why are you speaking a different colour?* Feeling from the first moment the texture of my life changing, my boy becoming the shape of my love. The way he used to say, *I love my daddy in the whole wide world.* Katharine kept correcting him on it, but I longed for him to keep saying it. I knew from the moment I laid eyes on him that he was here to teach me, not the other way round.

Acknowledgements

HEARTFELT THANKS TO:

Clare Alexander, for being the wisest, hardest-working agent imaginable;

Nick Skidmore, for editing with such insight and care;

Dan Franklin, Katherine Fry and Michal Shavit, for indispensable support and advice;

Nick Armstrong, Christo Daniels, Louise East, Evan Fallenberg, Henry Hitchings, Dan Light and David Merritt, for perceptive reading of early drafts;

Nick Duffell, Matthew East, Robert Montagu and Alex Renton, for kind assistance and fruitful discussion;

Alan Warner, for friendship and counsel;

Hybrid, a.k.a. Charlotte and Mike Truman, for providing the soundtrack to so much of my writing life, and for a lovely compliment;

Professor Dai Fan and the Sun Yat-sen Writers' Residency, for some crucial time and space;

Rose Grimond, for everything.